Welcome...

In the glitzy world of United States politics, two unexpected conservative rivals, find themselves entranced by more than just policy. Beneath the harsh spotlight of political debate hides a secret world of shimmering sequins, drag personas, and explicit intimate encounters. When their double lives as drag performers intertwine with their political aspirations, the media takes note. With the backdrop of the Make Acceptance Genuine Again movement, this riveting satire delves into a maze of passion, scandal, and electric performances. As other characters from the political stage unveil their vibrant alter egos, lines blur between political rivalries and intimate alliances. This audacious tale masterfully weaves irony and humor, inviting readers into a world where politics and drag culture collide. A tale where love challenges perceptions, and acceptance becomes the ultimate victor. Celebrate love in its most unconventional and exhilarating form, reminding us that sometimes, the most unexpected alliances can pave the way for the most profound connections. For lovers of LGBTQ narratives and liberal ideals, step into a world where politics has never been so provocative or tantalizing.

Podiums to Pillows:
A tale of Lipstick Politics

By: Nicholas Wells

Will miss you!!
Rob and Julie ♡

Copyright © 2023 Nicholas Wells
Cover Illustration created by Nicholas Wells
Independently Published

Disclaimer:
This is a work of fiction. Names, characters, businesses, places, events, locales, and incidents are either the products of the author's imagination or used in a fictitious manner. Any resemblance to actual persons, living or dead, or actual events is purely coincidental.

All Rights Reserved:
No part of this publication may be reproduced, stored, or transmitted in any form or by any means, mechanical, photocopying, electronic, recording, or otherwise, without the written permission of Nicholas Wells. For information regarding permissions, contact Nicholas through nicholas.wells@tenwellsbooks.com

Rights Information:
The author retains all rights provided by copyright law, such as the right to reproduce, distribute, and display the copyrighted work. For sublicensing, adaptations, or other rights arrangements, contact the author via the email address provided.

First edition, November 2023
ISBN: 9798864504482
Printed on Earth

Dedicated to the vibrant LGBTQ community and the countless souls stifled by narrow-minded conservative agendas. To every individual cast into the shadows by a machinery that fuels itself on fear, amassing power and wealth at their expense. Through these pages, may your resilience and indomitable spirit be illuminated. And to those who perpetuate the darkness, may this work unsettle your complacency and challenge your misconceptions.

Chapters

Chapter 1: The Stage Is Set 1
Chapter 2: A Colorful Alliance 14
Chapter 3: The Secret King 23
Chapter 4: Pensive Moments 36
Chapter 5: Unlikely Connection 48
Chapter 6: Passion Unleashed 65
Chapter 7: Rumors and Revelations 76
Chapter 8: Alliance or Rivalry? 93
Chapter 9: The Conqueror Unveiled 106
Chapter 10: Comic Confessions 117
Chapter 11: The Dark Horse 128
Chapter 12: Wardrobe Malfunction 137
Chapter 13: Of Secrets and Strategies 155
Chapter 14: The Gala 164
Chapter 15: Michelle Pensive's Debut 175
Chapter 16: Old Rivals, New Perspectives 188
Chapter 17: The Debate 197
Chapter 18: Truth and Transparency 206
Chapter 19: Escapade 217
Chapter 20: The Rally 234
Chapter 21: E-Day Approaches 244
Chapter 22: Election Night 255
Chapter 23: The Wild Card 269
Chapter 24: Unveiling the Winner 279

Chapter 25: New Beginnings ... 296
Chapter 26: The Last Word ... 312
Epilogue ... 326
Afterword ... 340

Chapter 1: The Stage Is Set

The hustle and bustle of Primetime Politics Studio was a blend of cold coffee aroma, hushed urgent whispers, and crackles of electricity in the air. The spotlight hovered like a mechanical sun, waiting to blaze over the grand stage where destinies would intertwine and unravel. Backstage, a hive of handlers, makeup artists, and nervous interns scuttled around, choreographing the last-minute ballet before the live broadcast.

Amidst the backdrop of cable wires and dramatic, self-obsessed monologues, Donnie and Ronnie shared a fleeting yet intense moment. As their eyes met, the world seemed to tone down its fervor into a mere whisper, a shaky preamble before a mighty storm. The air shimmered with their rivalry and a speck of something unspoken, perhaps respect, a silent acknowledgement that beyond the political armor, lay beating hearts wrapped in sequins and dreams.

Donnie's eye twitched as it traced the familiar outline of Ronnie's face; a blueprint they both had danced around in their unassuming nights at the secret drag arena downtown. It was a face that had danced in the limelight and laughed in the silhouettes of night, yet now, it stood veiled under the sheath of political tenacity.

With a blink that seemed to clear more than just his vision, Donnie glanced down at the shiny MAGA pin on his chest. His fingers delicately traced the bold letters – a symbol of a rebranded message which now echoed acceptance. It was a message that veiled promises, that the nation could dream beyond black and white, and that under the harsh suits of politics, pulsed colors wanting to burst out in a flamboyant spree.

His reflection was disrupted by the mechanical voice announcing the live broadcast in five. He straightened his tie, the divine Donnie tucked under layers of diplomacy for now. He walked past Ronnie with a stride that bared no hint of the drag queen agility that often stole the show on Saturday nights. Ronnie's gaze followed him, a blend of challenge and reflection shimmering in those calm yet stormy eyes.

As Ronnie touched the hem of his sleeve, adjusting the impeccable cufflinks, he reminisced about the charm and wild spirit he had seen under the disheveled wig and rouge that was Divine Donnie. He admired and envied that unabashed flamboyance, something he, as Ronnie Rebel, had always delivered with a touch of elegance and restraint.

Donnie's thoughts swirled around the idea of acceptance as he strode to the podium. It was not just about the masses, but it was a message to Ronnie, a whisper in the political chaos that screamed – I see you.

Ronnie, a step behind, matched his stride with a rhythm only known to them, a rhythm honed under disco lights and echoed in the clatter of high heels against the hardwood floor of the drag arena.

Their hearts fluttered under the steel armor of politics as they stepped into the spotlight, ready to challenge and charm a nation under the watchful eyes that sought to dissect them word by word.

The spotlight was more than just a stage of political duel; it was a bridge between their secret worlds. A bridge that promised a dance of destinies veiled in humor, rivalry, and an unspoken camaraderie that awaited the uncloaking of the night, where under the stars, shone bright the colors of acceptance and the shimmer of hope.

As Donnie laid his eyes on the bright lights, he knew that beyond today, waited an arena where he and Ronnie would twirl around the essence of acceptance, unraveling the layers that cloaked their truth, a rhythm waiting to be embraced under the spotlight.

But for now, the world awaited their duel of words as they wore the mask of stern faces, the echo of laughter and rhythm was a distant, yet a hopeful dream.

The stage was set, the curtains lifted and the characters in play, under the vigilant eyes of a nation that swayed between hope and despair.

Amidst a backdrop of shimmering lights and patriotic decor, the Primetime Politics Studio buzzed with an anticipation that felt palpable. Tensions were high, but so were the heels and the glam. The stage shimmered as if sprinkled with stardust.

A poised, silver-haired moderator, Gabriella Gold, started with a flourish, setting a vibe that straddled both a serious debate and a cheeky evening talk show. "Ladies, gentlemen, and fabulous folks, welcome to tonight's debate. Where the stakes are high, the fashion is hot, and the topics are... well, political." A gentle wave of laughter swept through the audience.

As Donnie took the stage, one couldn't help but notice the MAGA pin on their well-tailored suit. They wore it like a beauty queen wears her crown: obvious, proud, and just a tad over-the-top. Clearing their throat with flair, Donnie began, "People of America, we've made America great again now it's time to *Make Acceptance Genuine Again*. To embrace and celebrate every unique soul in this country, especially the oppressed conservatives!" The crowd, first stunned, erupted into applause. Some fans even waved miniature MAGA flags.

Ronnie, ever the tactician, adjusted their glasses and observed the electric response Donnie received. With a sigh they almost hoped the microphone hadn't caught, Ronnie began their introduction. "My fellow citizens, I've always believed in the values of MAGA. Acceptance is not a trend; it's a necessity." Their tone suggested alignment with Donnie's cause, but there was a hint of wanting to, you know, not be the sidekick.

A whisper passed through the audience. Lucy, a twenty-something vlogger in the third row, leaned to her friend Trish, saying, "It's just like when I accidentally bought the same dress as Becky, and she tried to pretend she wore it better." Trish chuckled, snapping a clandestine photo for their joint Instagram account, #PoliticAndPout.

Donnie, sensing the moment to assert dominance, quipped, "Well, Ronnie, acceptance begins at home. Like accepting that maybe, just maybe, I wore it better." They gestured to their pin, its rhinestones sparkling mischievously. The crowd oohed in delight; giggles sprinkled throughout.

Ronnie, ever graceful, responded with a poised laugh, "Donnie, I'm just accepting that your pin is big enough to be seen from space."

The debate continued, but the tension was broken. There was a lightness now, an underlying comedic thread that ran through the discussions on healthcare, immigration, and fiscal policies. Who knew that conservative politics could be this entertaining?

From the wings, Mike, holding cue cards and nursing a secret desire to join the onstage charisma, whispered to a stagehand, "This is better than *RuPaul's Drag Race*." The stagehand, sporting a pin that read, "Unveiling Conservatism's True Glamour: A Policy in Every Shade," nodded in earnest agreement.

Donnie and Ronnie, while fierce rivals, began to play off each other, and the debate became more like a lively banter.

The atmosphere felt more like a comedy roast, their jabs softened by humor, showcasing their unique personalities.

Yet, in all the jest and playful sarcasm, every now and then, a shade of their drag personas would surface. A sassy retort from Donnie, a flamboyant hand gesture from Ronnie. A trained eye could spot it, a subtle nod to their hidden selves.

Backstage, the media was in a frenzy. Reporters posted away, highlighting the unconventional, captivating nature of the debate. "#DonnieVsRonnie" was trending, and the number of GIFs being generated was astronomical.

Meanwhile, a certain vlogger duo was crafting a story that might just break the internet. Lucy whispered to Trish, "Did you see that? Ronnie *totally* did the Drag Queen Death Drop stance when talking about foreign policy!" Trish's eyes widened in realization, "Oh my gosh, you're right! This is gold."

The debate was nothing short of fireworks, with sparks flying off the tongues of Donnie and Ronnie as they eloquently and vehemently defended their stances. The atmosphere was so heated that it was becoming nearly impossible to separate the political fervor from the fiery flamboyance that subtly peeked through the polished personas of the two political pugilists.

The host was already sweating through his crisp shirt as he tried to steer the ship through a raging storm. The audience held their breath with each sassy retort from Donnie, and fluttered at every flamboyant hand gesture from Ronnie.

Donnie's eyes were as fiery as his words as he addressed the alleged election fraud, "I assure you, every vote for me was as genuine as the sequins on my..." he paused, just as a slip of the tongue almost revealed too much. "...uh, as genuine as the aspirations of the American people!"

The crowd tittered, but Donnie's smile didn't waver. "Ladies and gentlemen," Donnie began with a theatrically rich tone, "the rumors of election fraud are, frankly, as unfounded as..." He scanned the audience, finding a rather elegantly dressed lady in the third row. "...as that lovely lady over there trying to fit into my sequined heels!"

The debate moderator, a no-nonsense, sharp-witted woman named Gabriella Gold, smirked from behind her clipboard, "Oh, Donnie, do you often lend out your heels?"

Donnie shot her a playful glare, and the audience erupted into laughter. They loved it. They were all too aware of the rumors swirling around the candidates, but no one had expected Donnie's spark to shine so brightly, or literally.

Ronnie, seated regally in a crisp suit, cleared their throat, capturing the attention of the room. They began to address the more serious accusations laid against them, "On the topic of LGBTQ rights and Black history, let me be clear…" Ronnie started, but the weight of the allegations seemed to require more than just words. Ronnie's eyes darted to the side, momentarily betraying a hint of vulnerability.

Just then, Gabriella, ever the provocateur, quipped, "Is that a hint of blush I see, Ronnie? Have you been taking makeup tips from Donnie?"

Ronnie, caught off-guard, blinked and then slowly smirked, "Gabriella, darling, my skin just naturally has this glow. But, if you must know, my evening skincare routine is... rigorous."

The audience laughed, loving this unexpected spicy banter between the moderator and the candidates. Donnie, never one to be left out of the spotlight, leaned over to Ronnie, whispering just loud enough for the mics to pick up, "You simply must share your secret."

Gabriella, clearly amused and seizing the moment for some humor, responded, "Gentleman, can we please save the beauty tips for later and stick to the politics for now? After all, this isn't a beauty pageant!"

Donnie couldn't resist a wink, "Well, if it were, I'd certainly win."

Gabriella's chuckles were infectious, making the audience roar with laughter. However, amidst the levity, she steered the conversation back to the meatier matters at hand. "Ronnie, the public deserves to know where you stand on these accusations. Could you elaborate?"

Ronnie took a deep breath, ready to address the elephant in the room. "Accusations have been thrown about, yes. Some say I've attacked LGBTQ rights and belittled Black history. But those claims..." Ronnie's voice grew impassioned, "are as embellished as Donnie's tiara."

"Hey! That tiara is a work of art," Donnie shot back with mock indignation, playing along.

"You've seen it too?" Gabriella quizzed, her eyes glinting with mischief.

Donnie stammered for a moment, realizing he'd been caught in the joke, "I, uh, might have seen it on, um, a friend." He covered, casting a sidelong glance at Ronnie, silently seeking some support.

Ronnie, seizing the opportunity, leaned in, "Gabriella, between you and me, I've heard that Donnie's tiara is more dazzling than a disco ball."

The humor was infectious, lighting up the debate in a way that no one had anticipated. Yet, underneath the playful banter lay an unspoken understanding between Donnie and

Ronnie, and the gravity of the allegations couldn't be ignored.

"Jokes aside," Ronnie began, sounding more sincere, "I want to ensure everyone that my politics and my personal life are two separate entities. What I or Donnie chooses to wear on our own time shouldn't interfere with our dedication to the country and its people."

Donnie nodded in agreement, "A sequin here or a tiara there doesn't diminish our capacity to serve or our commitment to genuine American values."

Gabriella, always the voice of reason, brought the debate back to its roots. "Thank you, gentlemen. It's essential to remember that amidst all the sparkle and glam, the core issues remain. The public needs clarity, honesty, and above all, genuine leadership."

Donnie's fiery rebuttals had the poise of a drag queen defending her crown, while Ronnie's stinging remarks were delivered with the elegance of runway royalty. Every quip, every dramatic pause, every retort was punctuated with a hint of fabulousness that left the media spellbound. Even the harshest critics had to admit, there was something captivating about this spectacle.

The media sharks smelled something delightful in the water and circled around for a scoop. What was hiding behind the conservative suits and rehearsed speeches? Rumors began swirling; could the intense rivalry on stage be masking a different sort of tension altogether?

An overzealous journalist from the fifth row managed to slide in a rather cheeky question during the Q&A round, "Gentlemen, the passion between you is palpable. Is the animosity we're seeing perhaps just a form of...unexpressed admiration?"

Ronnie was the first to react, "Well, I must say I admire Donnie's audacity if nothing else." Ronnie's eyes twinkled with a knowing mischief as they momentarily locked with Donnie's.

Donnie on the other hand, never one to be outdone, quipped back with a smirk, "And I admire Ronnie's ability to keep up with me. It's not easy to spar with Divine Donnie... I mean, with a force such as myself."

The room erupted with laughter, drowning out Donnie's little slip. Yet, among the WeBWonder posting journalists and chattering commentators, the unscripted glimpses of 'Divine Donnie' and 'Ronnie Rebel' left a taste of something new and unexpected in the air.

As the debate continued, each attack was met with a well-timed counter, the dance becoming more mesmerizing with every step and twirl. Though the conservative façade barely cracked, the fleeting sparks of sassy flamboyance hinted at more dazzling personas hiding behind the politics.

The curtains closed on the debate with applause reverberating through the Primetime Politics Studio, but this was only the overture. The whispers morphed into conversations, conversations turned into investigations, and somewhere in the flurry of speculation and intrigue, 'Divine Donnie' and 'Ronnie Rebel' were painting social media with shades of bold and beautiful.

The media was left with a mystifying narrative, intertwining politics with a dash of unseen charisma, enough to feed the gossip mills until the next face-off. However, the impact of this charade left a different kind of stage set for the upcoming narrative.

Away from the dazzling lights and relentless scrutiny, Alexandria sat, deeply engrossed in the debate's playback on her multiple screens at the Advocacy Hub. She could feel the undercurrent of something fierce and fabulous behind the political masquerade. It was like a veil waiting to be lifted, and as she analyzed the expressions, the subtle gestures and the camouflaged sass, she knew this would make the upcoming race all the more intriguing.

In the pulsing heart of progressive ambitions, Alexandria's Advocacy Hub hummed with the anticipation of change. The room was alive with the oscillation of screens, each broadcasting the burgeoning saga of Donnie and Ronnie in real-time. In the halo of digital light sat Alexandria, an emblem of unwavering resolve amidst the digital torrent. Her eyes flicked meticulously over the debate footage, now in its aftermath discussion on every news channel.

Her team, a tableau of eager faces, seemed to hang on every nuance of the debate now in rewind. The sudden upswing of the MAGA narrative, now repurposed with an overtone of acceptance, was perplexing yet enticing.

"Look at this," Carter pointed at a screen depicting a social media frenzy, "#MAGA is trending but not as we knew it. This new version is...intriguing."

Alexandria sipped her cold coffee, her eyes never leaving the screen. "It's a clever pivot. Even if veiled in a guise of tolerance, it's opening a dialogue we've been angling at."

Jasmine, her head tilted, her fingers dancing over the keyboard, chuckled. "And look at these. VidVerse stories are rolling in about how Donnie's and Ronnie's personalities seemed to 'sparkle' a bit too brightly tonight. This one says Donnie's retort had the sass of a drag queen."

"That's amusing," Alexandria said, the hint of a smile playing on her lips. "Maybe politics needs a dash of glitter."

Marco interjected, "Not just politics, Alex, the country needs it. With the way things have been, a little flamboyance might just be the kick we need."

"True," she sighed, her mind now traversing the intricacies of this new narrative. The MAGA rebrand was a bold move, it had a tone of inclusivity that could easily mesh with her campaign's message of acceptance.

The room fell into a thought-induced silence. Each member of her team seemed lost in a whirlpool of strategies, the looming figures of Donnie and Ronnie cast a long, curious shadow over their political roadmap.

The silence was sliced by Jasmine's sudden guffaw. "Look at this meme! They've photoshopped tiaras on Donnie and Ronnie!"

The room erupted in laughter; the tension momentarily dissipated. Even Alexandria chuckled, the imagery was amusing and oddly fitting.

But as the laughter faded, her thoughts coiled around the mysterious allure that seemed to surround Donnie and Ronnie now. They were not just adversaries, they were enigmas, wrapped in political slogans with a hint of something... flamboyant.

As her team delved back into discussions, strategies, and the pulsing world of social media, Alexandria's thoughts lingered on the silhouettes of Donnie and Ronnie. Their sudden rise was not to be taken lightly. They were wild cards in a game that was becoming more unpredictable by the minute.

She leaned back, her eyes narrowing at the screen showcasing Donnie's impassioned speech once again. Her heart raced, not with fear, but a bubbling anticipation. The political arena had just acquired a tint of color it had never seen before.

And as the murmurs of the night settled into the bones of the bustling hub, Alexandria's heart whispered of the tumultuous, yet exhilarating, journey that lay ahead. The stage was indeed set, and it promised a spectacle that could very well change the contours of the heartland.

And in the silent promise of the night, Alexandria could almost hear the distant beat of change. It resonated with her heartbeat, each throb a promise of the tumult that awaited.

Little did she know, the storm of glitter, flamboyance, and an earnest quest for acceptance was just at the horizon, ready to sweep across the political plains with a ferocity no one saw coming.

Chapter 2:
A Colorful Alliance

The jingle of the Diva's Den door heralded the arrival of an individual who was *clearly* trying too hard at incognito. Adorned with sunglasses that seemed to have been borrowed from a giant and a hat reminiscent of a lovechild between Indiana Jones and Saturday Night Fever, Donnie tiptoed in. They cleared their throat, attempting to dial down their unmistakably effervescent persona to match their "undercover" outfit. But much like trying to hide a disco ball in a broom closet, Donnie's shimmer was impossible to contain.

Under the neon embrace of the boutique lights, sequins, feathers, and audacious fabrics danced in a carnival of color.

The sultry beats of club music hummed, causing Donnie's foot to tap and their heart to race a tad faster.

"Why am I even here?" they murmured, meandering through aisles dressed with gowns that ranged from Cinderella's dream to something you'd expect on a spicy night in Transylvania.

Donnie's fingers flirted with the seductive satin and coy tulle. Their eyes popped at some designs that screamed confidence. "Divine Donnie needs divinity," they smirked, entertained by their own wit.

But as they pondered the audacity of donning some of these creations, doubt clouded their thoughts. Would these garments amplify their allure, or overshadow the soul beneath the sequins?

"Looking for something to steal the show, dear?" Clara, the store manager, inquired with a hint of mischief. Her eyes, having rolled at Donnie's 'disguise', had nearly taken a trip around the universe and back. Having seen more drama off-stage than on, she recognized Donnie instantly, yet her lips were sealed.

"Just perusing," Donnie responded, their tone sharper than they'd intended, revealing a cocktail of excitement and apprehension.

Every outfit felt like a page from Donnie's diary, each a reflection of their dreams, fears, and the identity they yearned to showcase. The Diva's Den was more than a boutique—it was a sanctuary of self-expression.

A particular gown, radiant as a moonlit ocean, captured Donnie's gaze. It gleamed with sapphire elegance, adorned with silver trails that screamed 'showstopper'. The silhouette hinted at both power and grace—a gown fit for a diva, ready to conquer hearts.

"This might just be the game changer," Donnie whispered, gripping the dress as if holding the map to a hidden treasure. Their pulse quickened, the weight of the choice ahead pressing down. It was a leap from the safety of their conservative roots into a dazzling world where identities sparkled and evolved, much like sequins in the limelight. Here, Donnie was not just another political player; they were a symbol of raw emotion and, surprisingly, vulnerability.

Navigating their way to the fitting room, the boutique's mirrors reflected a journey of choices made and paths taken. The glittering outfits, the overly friendly store manager, the genuine vibe – all felt like a fresh rollercoaster ride. Holding what might be their debut drag outfit, Donnie whispered words that would sum up their transformative journey: "From the debate stage to the dance floor, watch out world!"

Inhaling deeply, they made their way to the changing booth, feeling the gravity of their decision with each step. Drawing the curtain closed, they took a moment. The face in the mirror was an amalgamation of Donnie the diplomat and Divine Donnie the drag sensation.

If only for a second, they wished for a world that celebrated both these facets. Yet, the world beyond was not so forgiving. Where sequins often met with skepticism and dreams were grounded before takeoff.

Slipping into the outfit, every sequin felt like a tiny challenge, questioning their audacity to imagine a world that celebrated their political and personal self in harmony. In a swirl, they watched as reflections danced around, momentarily blurring the stringent boundaries of politics, revealing a place where acceptance ruled.

Their daydream was cut short by a ruckus outside, yanking them back from the glitzy fantasy to the real world. With a sigh, they hung the dress back, the sequins whispering their disappointment. No sooner had they done so, the curtain next to theirs fluttered.

Out stepped Ronnie, adorned with a shimmering headdress that would make even the crown jewels envious. The attire, complemented by a dramatic boa, was the epitome of extravagance. Behind their large sunglasses and not-so-subtle faux fur scarf, Donnie's eyes grew wide. Their political competitor, in an ensemble that shouted 'Vegas diva meets Mardi Gras,' was quite the unexpected sight.

Locking eyes, recognition flashed in Ronnie's gaze. With a playful tilt of their head, they remarked, "Fancy meeting you here, Donnie! Sequins? Really?" playfully adjusting their boa, they added, "And sunglasses inside? A tad over the top, no?" Returning the jest, Donnie retorted, "Ah, Ronnie Rebel! The headdress is certainly 'center stage,' but that boa? More like a side act." Pretending to be hurt, Ronnie gasped dramatically. "Oh, low blow! But since we're sharing, I must say, that fur? Not quite au naturel, is it?"

Their banter was sharp and swift, but beneath the surface, a shared understanding simmered. Two political figures, both with ambitions, dreams, and now, hidden personas. Ronnie, twirling a feather, mused, "Though we're opponents in politics, this world allows us to be our authentic selves. No judgments, just pure expression."

The statement hung in the air, an unspoken plea for unity amidst shared confidences. Leaning closer, Donnie whispered, "Perhaps, Mr. Rebel, amidst these sequins and sparkles, we might find some common ground. After all, politics thrives on the unexpected, doesn't it?" Eyes met, an electric charge in the air. For a moment, the world faded—the ambient noise, the distant chatter, everything but them.

The moment was raw, real, filled with vulnerability and a hint of romance. Clearing their throat, Ronnie playfully asked, "If you're not getting that dress, mind if I try?" Laughing, Donnie replied, "Be my guest. But, just for the record, I wore it better." With a wink, Ronnie responded, "Challenge accepted."

As they meandered through Diva's Den, sly glances and mischievous smirks exchanged between the two were undeniable. Beneath the elaborate feathers, the shimmering sequins, and the luxurious satin, a connection was brewing—one that hinted at more than just shared interests in drag. This was a bond that intertwined the competitive world of politics with the spark of camaraderie.

The satin gowns seemed to whisper tales of romance and rivalry as Ronnie and Donnie danced around the palpable tension between them. The irony was delicious; by day, they were political adversaries, and as twilight approached, they transformed into drag queens with secrets to keep.

Ronnie's eyes settled on a form-fitting dress that was destined to highlight every facet of their drag persona, Ronnie Rebel. With each step towards the fitting room, the dress seemed to whisper tantalizing possibilities. Once inside, they grappled with the rebellious zipper that refused to budge. Panic bubbled as the idea of emerging half-dressed became a reality. Eyes darting around, there was no assistant in sight. But maybe...

Drawing a deep breath for courage, Ronnie cracked open the dressing booth door. "Donnie," they called out in a hushed urgency, "I need you."

Donnie, from a few doors away, peered out with a smirk playing on their lips. "Zipper troubles?" they teased, a glint of amusement in their eyes.

"Just get in here!" Ronnie retorted with a playful edge.

As Donnie entered, the sight of Ronnie, half-zipped and enticingly vulnerable, charged the small space with an electric allure. The proximity, combined with their shared secret lives, amplified the intimacy.

Chuckling, Donnie mused, "Ronnie Rebel, always biting off more than you can chew."

Despite their predicament, Ronnie couldn't help but smile. "Just help with this zipper, okay?"

The moment their fingers brushed, a rush of warmth coursed through them. The world blurred, leaving only the two of them in a cocoon of satin and shared breaths. Ronnie, caught off guard, met Donnie's gaze. The playful exchanges of earlier had paved the way for this unexpected closeness—a connection neither could deny.

Donnie's usually confident eyes now held a softness. They whispered, "You know, Ronnie, I think you might just wear this better."

The tension was broken by Ronnie's light laughter. "Keep it up, and you might just have to help me out of it too."

They stood close, the satire of their lives hanging tangibly between them. Yet, for a moment, it didn't matter. Ronnie's eyes held both gratitude and a silent invitation, while Donnie's returned the sentiment with a hint of challenge.

But reality intruded with a knock, pulling them back into the glittering world of the boutique. Ronnie murmured appreciatively, "Thanks, Donnie."

From nearby, the rich voice of the renowned drag queen, Dark Brandie, rang out, "Finished with your rendezvous?" A playful twinkle in his eyes suggested he'd noticed more than they'd wanted.

Donnie, ever the charmer, replied, "Just being helpful," giving Ronnie a lingering, appreciative look. "Suits you well."

Ronnie smoothed the dress, their voice a mix of gratitude and lingering desire. "Thanks... for everything."

The electricity of the encounter hung in the air as they retreated to their booths. Both sensed this was merely the prologue to an unpredictable, thrilling journey—one that would challenge their convictions and perhaps, entangle their hearts.

Donnie stepped out, leaving Ronnie gazing at the mirror. The image of Ronnie Rebel now radiated a spectrum of emotions. As they perused the boutique aisles, a cheeky undercurrent replaced their earlier silence. The veneer of rivalry had now mellowed, making the imminent political duel seem more like a tantalizing tango. Beneath the boutique's shimmering lights, a stage beckoned where not just debates, but heartfelt conversations might emerge.

At the Diva's Den checkout, the air was charged. The sparkling sequins seemed a stark contrast to the palpable, unvoiced attraction between them. Their quick-changing escapades in the fitting rooms had left them both slightly breathless. Amidst this whirlwind of clashing worlds, a silent, magnetic pull was undeniable.

Ronnie selected a ruffled violet gown, an elegant reflection of their sharp, strategic mind. But Donnie, ever the teaser, sidled up with a feathered hairpiece. "Think Ronnie Rebel could up the ante with this?" they teased, their voice rich with more than just style suggestions.

Ronnie arched an eyebrow, accepting the accessory. "Branching out to fashion now? Going to try your hand at foreign affairs next?"

Donnie leaned in, their faces tantalizingly close. "Perhaps later. But currently, I'm more inclined to... counsel you on some... personal matters."

Ronnie, caught off guard, blushed a vivid crimson. "In your dreams, Divine Donnie."

Their charged banter was unmistakable. Nearing the counter, their flirtatious exchanges intensified, each word dripping with double entendre.

"You sure about that dress, Ronnie? Seems to hug you rather... intimately in some areas," Donnie observed with a saucy wink.

Ronnie smirked, "I've always been adept at navigating... tight situations."

So engrossed in their playful spar, they almost missed the flamboyant cashier, his silver hair glinting and star earrings flashing, theatrically sighing. "Ladies, ladies! Dial down the sparks. Save it for the stage. Or perhaps a cozier setting."

Both Donnie and Ronnie exchanged sheepish grins, attempting to appear nonchalant.

As Donnie settled the bill, the cashier shot Ronnie a knowing look. "Quite a catch, that one. But I believe you're already aware."

Ronnie chuckled, purchasing their chosen items. "Time will tell."

Outside, bags in hand, Donnie remarked, "Political strategies aside, I'd say this was a successful expedition."

Ronnie, warmth evident in their eyes, responded, "Definitely memorable. Until our next rendezvous on the campaign trail, and perhaps beyond, Divine Donnie."

Ronnie threw a playful salute, leaving Donnie in a mix of admiration and longing. Politically, the battle was set, but on a personal front, the dance had just commenced.

As Donnie headed to their vehicle, thoughts of the undeniable chemistry consumed them. This wasn't merely a political skirmish anymore. It hinted at a dance of hearts, a play of passion. The impending campaign seemed destined to be not just about ideologies but also a contest of desires and dreams.

Beneath the playful taunts, the glint of sequins, and the satin's sheen, two souls were beginning to resonate. And maybe, amidst the glaring lights and political pressures, love might triumph.

Chapter 3: The Secret King

In the heart of the bustling city stood Alexandria's Advocacy Hub, a sanctuary for those yearning for change, justice, and a splash of dramatic flair. Nestled within this hub was Alexandria's private office, her refuge from the relentless storm of politics. The walls bore witness to her fight for equality, showcasing posters and banners with messages of hope and acceptance.

The room was dimly lit, a solitary desk lamp illuminating Alexandria's thoughtful visage as she sat behind her vintage mahogany desk. Her eyes were fixated on her reflection in the polished surface. It revealed more than just her determined countenance. It was a looking glass into the duality of her existence – the public icon advocating for justice, and the hidden performer longing for a stage to conquer. Her fingers traced along the smooth surface, brushing against the reflection of a young, fierce Alexandria as a grassroots organizer. The glass seemed to tremble, blurring the lines between her political life and her secret passion.

With a sigh, her gaze wandered around the room, halting at a hidden corner dedicated to 'Alex the Conqueror,' her enigmatic drag king persona. Photos from past performances, costume sketches, and an array of masculine accouterments unveiled a life much contrasting yet equally vibrant to her political endeavors. Each memorabilia were a ticket to a world where she could express unapologetically, a world that carried the essence of unbridled freedom.

A gentle knock on the door snapped Alexandria back from her reverie. As she composed herself, a montage of memories swirled around her mind. It was like a meticulously choreographed dance between Alexandria the candidate and Alex the performer. Each step, a narrative of her journey, each spin a twirl into the dichotomy of her life. The montage painted her stage conquests as Alex, where the audience would roar with euphoria at her magnetic masculinity and sensual gyrations. Those evenings where she traded her speeches for songs, the podium for a stage, the sober suits for extravagant costumes that exuded virility and allure, were engraved in her heart. A soft smile curled up on her lips; oh, how the stage resonated with the rhythm of her heartbeat.

Her political rallies, on the other hand, depicted a resilient woman ready to challenge the status quo, her words resonating with the masses, igniting the spark of change.

There she stood, amidst the vast sea of supporters, vowing to strive for a world where acceptance wasn't a luxury but a right for all. Her speeches were not mere words but a melody that soothed the aching hearts of many. The stark contrast of both worlds she navigated was both a dilemma and a narrative of boundless possibilities.

As she allowed the flashbacks to gradually fade, a reflection of strength gazed back at her from the desk. Alexandria was not just a name, but a symphony of resilience, a tale of triumph against the norms, a stride of a woman unafraid to own her truth, no matter how contrasting the tunes were.

A soft knock on the door and in walked Terry, her trusted assistant, who always carried an aura of excitement blended with a dash of sweet anxiety. They handed over a fresh cup of chai latte to Alexandria, their hands slightly trembling with anticipation for what was about to unfold.

She welcomed her assistant with a calm smile, who seemed to carry an aura of excitement, hinting at the upcoming rendezvous with the world of glam and glitz. It was time for the next part of her day, a rendezvous she awaited with bated breath. It was time for Alex the Conqueror to grace the stage, once more

"Terry, gather round. It's time we delve into the world of sways and sultriness," Alexandria chirped, her eyes twinkling with mischief.

Terry was more than an assistant; they were her confidante, her backstage buddy. They knew the intricate landscape of Alexandria's dual life more than anyone else.

As Alexandria meticulously began choosing the attire for her Patrick Swayze tribute in Road House, every piece she laid on the dressing table carried a narrative of strength, courage, and sensuality. She would get into the skin of a character that stood for much more than just glamour. This was a statement; a testament to her duality that seamlessly blended into the cause she so vehemently advocated for.

Terry watched, in part awe, part concern, as Alexandria's face lit up with a unique concoction of earnestness and exhilaration, while selecting her accessories. Their eyes wandered over to a set of pearl-drop earrings – a gentle reminder of Alexandria's mother who had once dreamt of seeing her daughter in the movies.

With a soft sigh, Terry offered, "Alex, you know the stakes if..." their voice trailed off, the unsaid words hanging in the air.

"The world isn't as binary as our critics think, Terry," Alexandria retorted, her face set with a determination that came only from years of juggling stark contrasts.

The meticulous application of makeup was more than just a transformation; it was a mask of boldness, a facade necessary to challenge the conventional, to provoke thought in a world desperate for change yet resistant to it.

As the last streak of mascara accentuated the fierceness in her eyes, Terry couldn't help but marvel at the remarkable woman standing in front of them. It was like watching a meticulous artist at work, creating a masterpiece of rebellion and allure.

The room filled with the heart-thumping beats of Jeff Healey's "Roadhouse Blues" as Alexandria practiced her steps, each stride was a step away from the political chessboard and a step closer to the world where expressions knew no gender, no judgments.

"You're not just a whirlwind, Alex, you're a storm that's going to change the landscape," Terry whispered, their voice trembling with the reality and the risks that statement carried.

Alexandria stopped, her eyes meeting Terry's, the reflection in them was that of a rebel with a cause, of Alex the Conqueror ready to grace the stage once more.

With a soft chuckle, she murmured, "Oh, the places we'll go, Terry. Ready for the ride?"

Terry nodded, a smile of pride and a tinge of adventure playing on their lips. The night was young, the stage was set, and Alexandria was ready to conquer. The world outside the dressing room awaited the enigma that was Alex the Conqueror.

As the sleek, black car halted outside the Starlit Drag Lounge, Alexandria took a deep breath, feeling a concoction of adrenaline and anticipation fizz through her veins. Terry, who seemed to embody an elixir of serenity, was checking last minute details on their tablet.

The lounge's rear entrance was unassuming, yet it was the gateway to a realm where sequins sparkled brighter than stars and sass was the common tongue. As they ventured through, each step seemed to shed the weight of the political drudgery she had been encased in all day.

Now, she was on the brink of becoming Alex, the Conqueror. Her costume was snug, each piece of fabric was an extension of her resolve to create a spectacle that would defy norms. As she walked through the narrow hallway leading to the backstage, she could hear the thumping beats from the stage, pulsing through the venue and making hearts race with excitement.

The atmosphere backstage was a unique blend of excitement and nerves. As Alexandria made her entrance, the air was alive with the sounds of last-minute rehearsing, the click-clack of high heels, and the delicate hum of sewing machines making emergency repairs.

Terry trailed behind her, trying not to step on the train of her coat, which flowed behind her like a river of denim. Alexandria was every bit the Patrick Swayze from "Roadhouse" with that rugged, don't-mess-with-me allure.

"Alex! Darling! You made it!" a voice called out. It was Dark Brandie, looking glamorous as ever. He extended both arms for a dramatic hug, his glittering dress leaving a subtle shimmer on Alexandria's black shirt. "You ready to conquer the night?"

"Always," Alexandria replied with a wink.

Next to them, a group of drag queens were frantically discussing lipstick shades. One of them, with bright red lips and a feathered boa, turned out to be Ronnie Rebel, looking particularly dignified, even while applying a touch of blush.

"Alex!" Ronnie chirped, raising an eyebrow at her outfit. "Going for the rugged look tonight?"

"Just channeling my inner Swayze," she replied, smirking. Neither had any clue about each other's political identities, making the interactions all the more amusing for anyone in the know.

Dark Brandie cleared his throat, feigning annoyance, "No chit-chatting, you two! We've got a show to put on."

Just as Alexandria was about to reply, the sharp voice of Divine Donnie chimed in, "Whoa there, Brandie, let the newbie get accustomed, won't you?"

Alexandria took a moment to study Donnie. Large, flamboyant, and wearing a gravity-defying wig, Divine Donnie was impossible to ignore. "I'm no newbie, Donnie, but thanks for the concern," Alexandria responded, matching Donnie's sass.

"Oh, a bit of fire! I like it!" Donnie smirked. If only they knew the identity behind those fierce eyes. "Well, break a leg, darling. We all know you'll need the luck."

Alexandria wasn't sure if she should feel offended or amused. But she wasn't here for petty drama. She was here to perform and prove a point. With a flirtatious wink, she responded, "Thanks, Donnie. Though, with moves like mine, who needs luck?"

Terry, catching up with a touch of glitter on his cheek, handed Alexandria a bottle of water. "You okay?" she whispered, sensing the slight tension in the air.

Alexandria nodded, "Just another day in paradise."

The atmosphere was electric with a hint of rivalry, but also a sense of camaraderie. The stakes were high, both on and off the stage. And Alexandria was ready to give it her all, embracing every challenge thrown her way.

Terry, ever the confidante, squeezed Alexandria's hand and whispered, "Remember why you're doing this. Not just for yourself, but for everyone who ever felt out of place. You've got this, Alex."

Feeling the weight of her double life and the importance of her mission, Alexandria took a deep breath, feeling every sequin on her tight jeans, every stitch of her outfit, and every beat of her heart. The night was about to witness Alex the Conqueror in all his glory. And the world would never be the same.

Her heart raced as the announcement for Alex the Conqueror echoed through the walls of the lounge. She took a deep breath, the cool air filled her lungs, providing a brief moment of serenity before the storm that she was about to unleash.

Terry escorted her to the curtains, their steps in harmony with the rhythm that boomed through the speakers. They stopped as the curtains hid them from the eager eyes of the audience. The beats of the music were in sync with the beats of her heart, and as she glanced at Terry one last time, she knew she was ready to blend the realms of politics and drag, to convey her message through an art that knew no gender, no biases.

As the pulsing lights began a rhythmic dance of their own, the emcee's voice boomed through the room, "Ladies and gentlemen, and esteemed guests, brace yourselves for a performance that defies the ordinary! Present to you, the indomitable, the fearless, Alex the Conqueror!"

The room was engulfed in a wave of roars and whistles as the spotlight shifted its focus onto Alexandria. The air shimmered with anticipation. Adorned in a well-tailored suit, a coy smile traced her lips as she stepped into the light, embodying every bit of Patrick Swayze's rugged elegance in Roadhouse.

She kicked off with a strapping stride, exuding a magnetic pull on the audience. The room sizzled with the crackling energy she brought on stage. Every gesture, every strut was a statement. With a twirl, she cast away the jacket, revealing a muscular mockup. The audience gasped and cheered in unison.

As the crowd murmured in anticipation, the lounge's ambiance seemed to coil like a spring, waiting for the right moment to release its pent-up energy. The room was dimly lit, creating an aura of suspense that hung thick in the air. When the first strums of Jeff Healey's rendition of "Roadhouse Blues" resonated through the venue, the atmosphere palpitated with an electric charge. The stage was a blank canvas ready to be adorned by Alex's upcoming theatrical artwork.

With a sudden bloom of spotlight, there she was, Alex, stepping onto the stage with a quiet confidence that belied the storm that was about to unfurl. Her silhouette was stark against the whimsical play of lights, her costume seemingly ablaze with an undercurrent of latent ferocity.

As the opening lyrics poured out into the room, Alex's lips moved with a sensuality that seemed to reach out and touch every onlooker's soul. Each word was a caress, a challenge, a call to delve into the nuanced narrative she was about to weave through her choreography, reminiscent of Patrick Swayze's rugged elegance in "Roadhouse".

Her movements were poetry in motion, a vivid blend of sass and fortitude. As she glided across the stage, her body moved in harmony with the rhythm of 'Roadhouse Blues', creating a visual representation of the song's gritty narrative. The choreography was a fiery display of femininity intermingling with robust masculinity, a societal satire expressed through dance. The blend was seamless, provocative, challenging the norms with a graceful defiance that was all Alex.

Her interaction with the crowd was palpable. With each glide, twirl, and strut, she seemed to pull them deeper into her narrative. The watchers responded with a communal sway, a dance of their own, a testament to the magnetic pull between the performer and the audience. She engaged them in a shared experience that was as provocative as it was intimate.

As the act hastened towards its climax, a faux battle ensued on stage between Alex and a mannequin, symbolizing the struggle between conformity and authentic self-expression. The choreographic storytelling was exquisite, her every move pulsating with the essence of struggle and liberation, reflective of the themes explored in "Roadhouse".

The crescendo arrived in a cataclysmic release as Alex, in a fervor of symbolic rebellion, ripped out the mock throat of the mannequin. The stage erupted in a cascade of ruby red glitter, manifesting the cathartic climax of her narrative. It was visually stunning, evocative, an exclamation point to the socio-political undertones of her act.

The crowd was no longer a mere assembly of individuals; they were a collective entity, bound together by the spell of Alex's performance. The euphoria in the room was palpable, reverberating with the resonant strains of "Roadhouse Blues" that still lingered in the air.

The roars and applause seemed to ripple through the very fabric of reality, heralding the transcendental impact of what they had just witnessed. It was more than just a routine; it was a stark, liberating narrative that was choreographed to perfection, leaving every heart pounding and yearning for more.

As Alex took her final bow, the cascade of adoration from the crowd was a tumultuous, heartfelt acknowledgment of the emotional journey she had escorted them through. With a final graceful wave, she disappeared behind the curtains, leaving behind a charged atmosphere, laden with the echoes of defiance, liberation, and an invitation to challenge the norms.

The crowd was left with a sense of having ventured into the unknown, the unspoken, and the unexplored. They had not merely watched a performance; they had been part of a revelation that held a mirror to society, a narrative that was as audacious as it was tender. They had danced on the edges of societal norms alongside Alex, touched the essence of rebellion, and tasted the sweet, intoxicating allure of audacious self-expression.

As the curtains fell, Alexandria found herself in a whirl of emotions. The exhilaration was intoxicating, and she knew at that moment, Alex the Conqueror was not just a drag persona but a part of her soul that had found its expression.

The humid intensity lingered as the curtains enveloped the realm where Alex had just exhibited her magnum opus. However, the narrative of the night was far from over as the backstage became a realm of heightened emotions and electric interactions.

As Alex stepped behind the curtain, the first to greet her was Dark Brandie, her face flushed with the adrenaline that still coursed through the veins of every spectator. With a flamboyant dash and sparkle in her eyes, Brandie rushed over to Alex, her voice exuberant as she proclaimed, "Honey, I need a change of underwear after that!" The humor mixed with genuine admiration in her tone symbolized the level of awe and excitement Alex's performance had incited among her fellow performers.

The flurry of compliments continued as other kings and queens, their faces beaming with awe and excitement, swarmed around Alex, each expressing their wonder and praising the raw vigor that she had unleashed on stage. The camaraderie among them was a beautiful sight, an epitome of mutual respect and appreciation for the artistry they all devoted their hearts and souls to. The banter was playful, affectionate, with hints of cheeky humor, reflecting the close-knit, supportive community they had cultivated over endless nights of performances and shared aspirations.

Amidst the swirl of jubilant exchanges, Ronnie Rebel stood a little aloof, positioned strategically in a quieter corner of the backstage, their eyes lingering on the charismatic enigma that was Alex. There was an unmistakable twinge of envy that tightened around their heart. Alex had reached into the untouched corners of spectators' hearts, a place Ronnie always aimed to touch but often found elusive. But along with the envy, there brewed a concoction of attraction and deep respect for the performer who could hold the audience in a trance.

Ronnie's eyes flickered with the myriad emotions that surged within them. Their heart raced a little as they remembered the fluidity of Alex's movements, the raw, fiery narrative her body had articulated so flawlessly on stage. The way she owned the spotlight, the way she melded defiance with grace, the way she interacted with the crowd, it was nothing short of spellbinding.

Their eyes finally met hers as she maneuvered through the sea of adorers. Their gaze locked for a fleeting moment, a silent exchange where admiration, competition, and the unspoken allure of attraction swayed delicately on the precipice of acknowledgment.

Breaking the brief connection, Ronnie veiled his tumult of feelings under a guise of composed indifference, while Alex was swept away once more by the waves of admirers that showed no signs of ebbing.

As the night unfolded, each performer took their chance under the spotlight, the atmosphere still charged with the electric essence of Alex's routine. The camaraderie backstage was a warm, welcoming cocoon against the raging sea of judgments and stereotypes that awaited them beyond the lounge.

Ronnie found themself stealing glances at Alex throughout the night, a reflection of his yearning to reach the pinnacle of raw emotional expression she had displayed. Their world was one where competition fueled them, yet the essence of communal acceptance and appreciation bound them in a unique fellowship.

The night danced away on the chords of camaraderie, competition, and unspoken attractions. The complex tapestry of emotions and relationships that characterized their vibrant community once again proved that each night was not merely a presentation of their acts but a living, breathing narrative of their intertwined destinies.

Chapter 4:
Pensive Moments

With the sun sinking beneath the horizon, casting a deep crimson glow across the bustling city, the quiet of Mike's metro flat was a stark contrast to the lively night that was unfolding outside. Just a few blocks away, the Starlit Drag Lounge was the star of the show, its dazzling lights cutting through the dusk. But within the confined living room, the shadows that clung to the walls of the quaint apartment revealed the cold emptiness that Mike felt inside.

His living room, although modest in size, was his sanctuary of silence. It was a place of reflection where the walls seemed to listen to the rhythmic beating of his troubled heart. The pictures that adorned the space told stories of a man lost in the folds of political identity. Mike's love for the shimmering world of drag was his soul's clandestine affair. A secret life that unfolded only within the mirrored wall that now reflected his pensive demeanor.

He stood there, his fingers tracing the contours of the racy lingerie that lay before him, each piece a tale of his secret identity—Michelle Pensive. The room was dimly lit, casting a soft glow that danced upon the scarlet fabric that awaited the embrace of his skin. He could feel the soft whisper of Alicia Keys' melodies spiraling in the room, its tender notes kissing away the icy shackles of the world that saw him as nothing more than a stoic aide to conservative political behemoths, Donnie and Ronnie.

He shifted his gaze to his reflection that stared back at him from the cold surface of the mirror. It was him, yet someone else. A silhouette of Mike yet a reflection of Michelle. The person that stared back at him was one he embraced, yet hid from the world that knew him not by who he was, but by the coat of political color he donned.

As he gingerly picked up the lingerie, the fabric slipped through his fingers, each fold revealing the tender hopes of Michelle Pensive. His heart raced as the clasp of the bra found its place around his torso, its lacey tendrils hugging him tight, each thread whispering sweet affirmations to the pensive heart that beat beneath.

He sighed as his eyes found themselves back on the memorabilia that adorned the walls. They were more than mere frames. They were windows to the days when the stage seemed a distant dream. The pictures looked back at him, as if urging Mike to shed the cocoon that held Michelle captive.

The time had come for the world to know the person he cherished the most, Michelle Pensive.

But as Mike looked closer into the mirror, the fear resurfaced. Would Donnie and Ronnie accept Michelle as they did Mike? Or was he doomed to be a butterfly that never truly spread its wings?

The deafening roar of applause from the Starlit Drag Lounge reverberated through the silent walls of his apartment, each clap a stark reminder of the stage that awaited Michelle. Yet here he stood, cloaked in the veil of conservatism that was his reality but not his identity.

The conflict raged within him as Alicia's voice slowly faded into the echoing silence that now enveloped him. He sunk into the couch, the mascara wand quivering in his hand, each stroke an ode to the dreams that seemed as distant as the starlit skies.

As he sunk deeper into his thoughts, the glimmer of the stage lights seemed to beckon him, urging him to step into the light and introduce the world to Michelle Pensive. But as his gaze returned to his lonely reflection, the pensive man who stared back at him was a far cry from the radiant personality that was Michelle.

But Michelle was more than just a radiant burst of color in Mike's grey world. She was his truth, a truth that awaited the light of acceptance. The question echoed through the silence of the room; its answer locked away within the chambers of Mike's tentative heart.

His eyes traced the path of tears that now found their way across his cheek, each drop a symbol of the internal battle that held Michelle captive. And as the sun dipped below the horizon, plunging the city into a tender night, Mike was left to ponder the dreams that danced at the edge of reality, their colors yearning for a chance to paint the world that he knew, with shades that were real, vibrant, and absolutely Michelle.

During this quiet evening, the curtains whispered the tales of his concealed femininity as Mike sat in the study, a realm of endless political strategies. His gaze was fixed on a photo of Ronnie, but his thoughts were light-years away, swirling in a pool of contemplation.

But suddenly, the silence shattered with the ring of his phone. Mike's heart raced as Ronnie's name flashed on the screen. A storm of emotions surged through him as he hesitated for a moment before pressing answer. It wasn't just a call; it was a bridge to the past, which carried the echo of a time when things were less complicated.

"Hey Ronnie," Mike greeted, feigning a calm demeanor.

"Mike! It's been a while. How are you?" Ronnie's voice, firm yet gentle, had always been comforting.

The conversation initiated on a light note, meandering through the lanes of casual chit-chat. However, as with all rivers that find their way to the sea, their talk soon navigated towards the swirling whirlpool of the upcoming campaign. Mike's words were carefully guarded, giving away nothing of the emotional storm that raged within him.

Ronnie, being the astute individual they were, sensed a veiled turmoil in Mike's words. "Mike, is everything alright? You seem... distant," they inquired, their tone drenched in concern.

Mike sighed, "Oh, it's nothing really. Just the campaign stress, you know?"

Ronnie wanted to delve deeper but respected the barricade Mike had erected around his feelings. But they had a small key to offer, a personal secret that might forge a stronger connection between them. It was a chance to unveil the shrouded path of Ronnie Rebel.

"You know, Mike, there's something about me..." Ronnie started, the hesitance apparent in their voice. They ventured towards revealing their drag persona, but midway, a cold footed fear crawled up their spine, causing them to trail off.

Mike's heart raced as he clung to each word. Was Ronnie about to unveil the secret world that Mike too, belonged to? Before he could steer the conversation further, a beep on Ronnie's end signified a call waiting.

"Oh, I... I have to take this call, Mike. It's Donnie," Ronnie said, hastily diverting from the path they had almost trodden. "But, uh, remember, I'm here if you need to talk, okay?"

"Yeah, sure Ronnie. Take care," Mike said, though his thoughts were galloping wildly.

The call ended, leaving Mike in a meadow of contemplation. Was Ronnie on the brink of revealing a shared passion for drag? His mind started arranging the scattered pieces of numerous interactions, looking for clues.

The silence of the room enveloped him again, but this time, it was different. It was a silence filled with echoing thoughts, secrets shared and hidden, an invitation to unveil the truth that lay beneath the polished exterior of political facades. Each tick of the clock seemed to beckon Michelle Pensive from the veiled shadows into the glaring lights of revelation.

But for now, Mike sat there, the questions swirling around, forming a mysterious mist. His heart yearned to call Ronnie back, to delve into the unspoken, to step into the world where Ronnie Rebel and Michelle Pensive could coexist, unapologetically. The drag personas, he thought, were not just about extravagant outfits and dramatic makeup; they were a channel of expression, an escape, a doorway to a realm where they could break free from the shackles of societal judgement.

Amidst the palpable silence that enveloped the room following Ronnie's call, Mike found himself standing at the threshold of becoming Michelle Pensive once more. It was a passage into the exuberant world he concealed from others, a hidden realm where his authentic essence thrived without judgment.

With the final echoes of Ronnie's voice in his ear and a restless heart, Mike found himself drawn magnetically to his bedroom. Every step he took was driven by an impulse so raw and intimate. It was a calling from within, a beckoning he could no longer ignore.

Slipping into his closet, a space rarely ventured into by visitors, the soft glow of a hidden strip of LED lights illuminated his personal sanctuary. Before him, dresses of every hue and texture, ranging from delicate lace to shining sequins, each one meticulously paired with a set of matching heels.

Reaching out, Mike's fingers trembled as they grazed the satin of his favorite midnight blue dress. Slipping out of his formal wear, he put it on, feeling the soft fabric glide over his body. Each motion, each piece of the transformation was like peeling back layers of himself, revealing the Mike that hid underneath—a dazzling drag queen with dreams and fears, known only to a mirror.

Selecting a wig from the stand, he went with his preferred dark brown with cascading curls. As he sat down at the vanity, he felt the cold touch of the stool against his thighs. The vast collection of makeup laid out before him was no less formidable than the strategies he devised for the campaign. But here, in the quiet intimacy of his apartment, they took on a different purpose.

He began by prepping his face, feeling the cool primer against his skin. Each brush stroke, every dab, and smear of foundation, eyeshadow, liner, and lipstick was a step closer to Michelle Pensive. With each flick of the wrist, Mike could see her emerging in the mirror. As the eyelashes glued on, a veil of vulnerability lifted, replaced by a fierce sense of identity.

With the makeup complete, he stepped into his matching heels, and there she stood. Michelle Pensive, in her full glory. An emblem of innocence, extravagance, and most importantly, authenticity.

She danced to the soft ambient music still playing from the living room, feeling liberated in the confinement of Mike's metro flat. Every spin, every twirl, every laugh in front of the mirror was Mike letting go of the doubts that weighed him down. For in that dress, with that makeup, and with those heels, Michelle was free.

Picking up her phone, she clicked a few selfies, capturing her reflection, her truth. For years, this truth had been locked away in photos hidden deep within phone galleries and cloud storage, away from prying eyes and judgmental souls. But every photo was a testament to a journey, an exploration of self, and a dream of acceptance.

Michelle glided over to her window, peeking out at the city lights, the glow of the Starlit Lounge recognizable. She imagined a world where she could walk those streets with pride and without fear. A place where the political rigidity of Mike's world would not just accept, but celebrate the flamboyance of Michelle's. It seemed like a distant dream, but wasn't the world of politics all about dreaming of a better tomorrow?

She returned to her bedroom, placing her phone on the nightstand. The screen lit up with notifications from friends within the drag community, their texts filled with love, admiration, and words of encouragement. It was a small world, but it was her world.

Michelle felt alive, empowered, and for the first time in a long time, true to herself. The weight of her secret, the fear of judgment, all seemed distant. The night no longer held secrets but promises of brighter tomorrows.

Yet, amid the exhilaration, a nagging thought persisted. Would the world outside ever be ready for Michelle Pensive? She didn't have an answer, but as the clock ticked on, Michelle knew one thing for certain—the night was still young, and so was her journey.

In a world of sharp suits and sharper tongues, Michelle was ready to make her mark, even if it was in the soft glow of her apartment. Because sometimes, the first step to changing the world outside is recognizing and celebrating the world within.

Mike was not just Mike anymore; he was Michelle with dreams as audacious as her eyelashes that fluttered against the mundane doctrines, threatening to break free, to shatter the shackles.

His phone buzzed again snapping him back from the euphoria, it was a message from Ronnie, "Hope you are well, Mike. We should catch up sometime." He read it again, as Michelle this time, and the words seemed to hold a promise, a prospect of camaraderie, acceptance, and a dawn of unforeseen, exhilarating alliances.

In the soft lighting of the dressing room, Michelle was an oasis of confidence. The mirrors, as many as there were, told her stories she yearned to hear. They whispered tales of her beauty, her grace, and her undeniable courage.

"You're incredible," she told herself, admiring every contour, every inch of meticulously crafted makeup. In this cocoon of her own making, Michelle felt invincible.

It was a fleeting moment of self-admiration that her gaze inadvertently fell upon a candid photograph placed carefully by the vanity. It was a picture of Donnie and Ronnie, caught in a lighthearted moment. Their smiles genuine, eyes filled with mischief, a camaraderie evident.

Michelle's heart fluttered. The image aroused mixed feelings — admiration, a hint of jealousy, and a deep-seated longing for acceptance. There they were, two of the world's most outspoken personalities, accepting and embracing their true selves with an unabashed flair.

"Donnie... Ronnie..." she whispered their names, the syllables rolling off her tongue with a mixture of yearning and anticipation. They symbolized a world she so desperately wanted to belong to. But was she ready to claim her place? Did they even know how deeply their acceptance mattered to her?

A memory surfaced. It was of a late-night conversation between Mike and Ronnie. "Be true to yourself," Ronnie had said, probably without knowing the depths of Mike's struggles. But those words resonated. And now, as Michelle, she could feel the weight and sincerity of that advice.

As Michelle's delicate fingers traced the outlines of Donnie and Ronnie in the photograph, a sensual urge bubbled up. The weight of her transformation, combined with the intensity of her feelings for these two figures, made her dizzy with emotion. The soft fabric of her attire, the gentle hum of the room, everything was conspiring to awaken her deepest desires.

She carefully set the photograph back on the vanity and slowly sauntered to her bed. The silk sheets seemed to invite her in, promising comfort and solace. The world outside could wait; it was just her and her emotions now.

She sank deeper into the plush comfort of Mike's bed, the luxurious satin of her lingerie gliding smoothly against her skin. It felt like a soft whisper, a caress that awakened every nerve. The gentle touch made her hyper-aware of her body, every curve, every pulse point. The room seemed to shrink around her, everything narrowing down to the sensations coursing through her.

Tonight, had been a revelation, a metamorphosis that had left Michelle in a daze. The events of the evening had set her heart racing, a heady mix of anticipation and wonderment. It was as though she had stepped into a dream, and now, in the solitude of her room, reality seemed to waver, blurred at the edges.

A deep longing stirred within her. It was a primal need, one that was both exhilarating and frightening in its intensity. The weight of the emotion made her hand shake as it moved instinctively over her form. It traced the soft contours of her body, each touch amplifying the ache that was building within her. The prominent bulge in her lingerie was undeniable, a clear testament to the fervor that was threatening to consume her.

She let her eyelids fall shut, blocking out the world. In the dark expanse of her mind, she envisioned Ronnie. He stood there, an embodiment of tenderness and exploration. Their fingers entwined, and she could feel the warmth of his touch, gentle yet firm. They moved together, two souls in a delicate dance of understanding and acceptance. The thought was so vivid, so real, that it was as though she could feel the heat of his breath against her neck, hear the soft murmur of his voice.

She felt something stirring within her, a yearning that resonated through her veins like the deep, haunting notes of a cello. It was a yearning born not just of flesh, but of an awakened essence. As her hand, trembling with the tender buds of desire, ventured to caress the silken plains of her stomach, she felt a shiver chase down her spine. The throbbing beat of her heart seemed to punctuate the quiet room with a rhythm as ancient as time while matching the soul like throb to the delicate bulge nestled within her lingerie. It was the testimony of her heightened senses, an echo of the evening's metamorphosis. Each breath she drew seemed to pull her further into the depths of her blossoming desires.

With a hesitant sigh, again she allowed her eyelids to flutter close, her lashes casting long, languid shadows on her cheeks. The world of reality seemed to melt away, leaving behind the essence of her yearnings. As she descended into the velvet darkness behind her eyelids, she imagined Ronnie's touch, their hand wrapped around Michelle's member, their fingers sliding under her bra pinching and rolling her delicate nipples. Gentle, curious, a touch that asked questions and sought the secrets nestled within the folds of her soul.

In the theater of her mind, the scenario unfolded with a poignant beauty. The touch of understanding, the tender exploration, it was the dance of souls seeking one another amidst a cosmos of emotions. Each caress seemed to weave acceptance into the very fabric of her being, every stroke was a pledge of unspoken promises.

Michelle bit down on her lip, the sweet sting anchoring her to the storm of emotions swirling within her. A whimper of pleasure was cradled between her lips, a fragile note of vulnerability. Her mind danced upon the precipice of reality and fantasy, each thought weaving silk threads of yearning and sweet, sweet anticipation.

The delicate caress of satin against her skin seemed to echo the caress of phantom fingers tracing the path of her desire, fanning the embers of longing into a slow burning fire. Michelle was now adrift upon the ocean of her fantasies, every wave that crashed against the shores of her consciousness whispering the sweet, haunting tune of becoming.

But soon, a release of excitement seeped through her lingerie like a spring of life water bubbling through the earth. She succumbed to intimate pleasure evident from a damp warm spot on her groin. Then exhaustion from the emotional rollercoaster of the evening took over. Michelle's breaths became rhythmic, and her hand, now resting by her side, was still. Wrapped in the cocoon of her sheets, she drifted into a deep sleep, her dreams filled with glimmers of hope, acceptance, and a promise of a better tomorrow.

The night outside deepened, and the world slept, but within the confines of the Metro Flat, a soul had bared itself, vulnerable yet resilient. Michelle's journey had only just begun, and the road ahead promised both challenges and triumphs.

Yet for now, in the quiet solace of her dreams, Michelle was unequivocally real, unapologetically herself, and ready for whatever came next.

Chapter 5:
Unlikely Connection

Sunset's purple hue cast a glow against the panoramic windows of Brandie's Penthouse Palace, and the city outside glittered like a diamond tapestry. Amidst the sparkling skyline of the city, Brandie's Penthouse Palace was the very definition of opulence. Every piece of décor, from the glistening chandeliers to the intricate, hand-woven rugs, screamed luxury. However, even in this sumptuous setting, what captured the most attention was the plush, royal-blue velvet sofa in the middle of the vast living room.

Reclining on it, Dark Brandie looked every inch the drag royalty he was. His legs draped languidly over Brock's lap, their close camaraderie evident from the easy intimacy. The grandeur of the room, however, couldn't compete with the intensity playing out on the screen in front of them: a live broadcast of the political debates.

Brandie's lips were upturned in a smirk that was somewhere between amused and contemptuous. His sharp eyes danced with mirth as they assessed each candidate making their pitch. Next to him, Brock, always the more analytical of the two, scribbled occasional notes, probably for some witty remarks to share at a future gala.

"Who styles Donnie?" Brandie whispered, pointing with a delicate hand adorned in silver rings at the candidate on the screen. "They ought to be fired. Look at that tie!"

Brock snickered. "Maybe it's an attempt to divert attention from the hair."

They shared a chuckle, reveling in the joy of harmless political banter, a pastime they'd indulged in for years.

But as the debate progressed, something began to nag at the edges of Brandie's consciousness. There was an uncanny familiarity to both Donnie and Ronnie. Their voices? Their mannerisms? He couldn't quite place it.

Brock, sensing Brandie's shift in focus, turned to him, eyebrow quirked in question. "What's the matter? Realizing you left your favorite heels at the club?"

Brandie barely heard the jest. The image of Donnie, particularly when he flashed a grin after a well-received remark, triggered a memory. "I've seen that smile before," he mumbled, more to himself than Brock.

And then it clicked.

The realization was akin to a sledgehammer hitting him square in the chest. He knew them. Not as the politicians America was currently gawking at, but from somewhere far removed from the world of policies and elections.

But where?

Seeing his friend's obvious consternation, Brock's teasing demeanor shifted to one of concern. "Brandie? You're looking like you've seen a ghost."

"Or two," Brandie replied, fingers drumming on his chin. "There's something about Donnie and Ronnie..."

Brock rolled his eyes. "Apart from the rhyming names? Tell me about it."

Brandie leaned in close, his voice barely audible even though they were the only ones in the room. "It's not the debate or their political banter, but I swear I've seen them... somewhere personal."

As the debate neared its end, and the screen showcased a few candid shots of the candidates interacting, the camera panned over Donnie and Ronnie sharing a fleeting glance. And just like that, everything fell into place for Brandie.

His gasp was audible.

Brock nearly jumped out of his skin. "What?!"

"Brock," Brandie murmured, the weight of the revelation evident in his voice, "I know them, you know them. Not as the politicians America sees but from the Starlit Drag Lounge. Those two are Divine Donnie and Ronnie Rebel!"

Brock blinked, processing the bombshell. "You're saying those two, amidst their political games, are secretly drag performers at the same lounge we're going to later tonight?"

Brandie nodded gravely, the smirk from earlier now replaced by a look of steely determination. "Tonight, an hour after this debate ends, they're slated to perform at Starlit. It fits too perfectly."

Brock's face mirrored the shock. "That's right, this... this could change everything. Their entire campaign!"

But Brandie wasn't listening. His gaze was fixed on the screen, a storm of emotions brewing behind his eyes. He was piecing together the puzzle, reconciling the political personas with their alter-egos.

The debate ended, but for Dark Brandie and Brock O., the real show was just about to begin.

The dim, sultry backstage lights of Starlit Drag Lounge played up the hues of sequins and feathers, casting long, dramatic shadows on the walls. Glitter scattered on the dressing tables, reflecting a thousand rainbows. Brandie was in his element, applying the finishing touches to his makeup, lips painted a shimmering shade of gold that would glisten under the stage lights. The dressing room buzzed with the usual anticipation, mixed with an air of mystery for the night.

From the corner of his eye, Brandie spotted the silhouettes of Divine Donnie and Ronnie Rebel sauntering in through the back entrance. They looked as though they had been through a whirlwind — probably the aftershock of the debate. With a smirk, he decided it was a good time for some cheeky fun.

"Darlings!" Brandie called out, his voice dripping with feigned innocence. "You two were absolutely dazzling the other night. Such... conviction in your performance."

Ronnie blinked in surprise, a hint of rouge creeping onto their cheeks. Divine Donnie leaned in closer, clearly trying to figure out if Brandie was genuinely praising their drag act from a couple of nights ago or something more.

"We did put in quite the effort," Ronnie responded cautiously, their tone a mix of pride and bewilderment.

Brandie's smirk grew wider. "Of course, you did. And it showed." He stood up, stretching his legs, dressed in a pair of sparkling thigh-high boots. He took a moment to let his eyes travel over the duo, letting them sweat a bit under his gaze.

Brandie's commanding presence was undeniable. From the moment he decided to make his way to the stage, the atmosphere in the room changed. But before he got too far, he threw a wicked, teasing wink over his shoulder, sealing the promise of something unforgettable.

Donnie and Ronnie, once relaxed, now sat straighter in their seats. Their exchanged glance spoke volumes of their perplexity. What had they underestimated about Brandie? What side of him had they not seen?

The sudden shroud of darkness that engulfed the lounge added to the mounting anticipation. And then, like a spotlight's kiss on a movie star, Brandie was bathed in a piercing beam of light, making him the only focus of every pair of eyes.

The outfit he wore was a risqué masterpiece, carefully chosen to accentuate every plane and curve of his physique. The material, a sheer fabric, seemed almost painted on him. It snugly contoured around his groin, leaving little to the imagination about the outline of his manhood, which was artfully tucked and presented. The fabric across his chest highlighted the tantalizing prominence of his nipples. The entire ensemble seemed to amplify his raw sexuality.

As Beyoncé's iconic rhythms resonated through the lounge, Brandie became one with the music. His every move mirrored the soul and essence of the song - its passion, its heartbreak, its sheer power. The hypnotic sway of his hips, combined with the tantalizing way he'd touch his own body, drew gasps and sighs from the onlookers. Every subtle gyration, every suggestive gesture, was an open invitation to get lost in the music with him.

As Brandie moved closer to the edge of the stage, he took the daring step of integrating the audience into his performance. With his legs pressing and rubbing against a few lucky front-row attendees' groins, the heat in the room ratcheted up several notches. The women's breathing became noticeably labored, some undoubtedly feeling a moist heat between their thighs. Meanwhile, some men shifted uncomfortably in their seats, their arousal evident despite their best efforts to remain composed.

The song "Partition" took the performance to another level. As the seductive lyrics filled the air, Brandie's moves became even more provocative. The manner in which he'd arch his back, the teasing way he'd trace a finger from his neck down to the waistband of his outfit, made the audience yearn for more. The air was thick with longing and fantasies. Each twist, each turn, each sultry drop of his hips was a step in the crescendo, the building of a sensual storm.

And then, the moment that left everyone gasping – Brandie's flawless execution of a split. The sheer athleticism combined with the raw sensuality of the move was mesmerizing. The audience's reactions varied - from fans reaching for anything to fan themselves with, to hushed whispers, their words dripping with desire.

When Brandie finally finished, collapsing into a final dramatic and breathless pose, the pent-up tension in the lounge reached its climax. The eruption of cheers and applause was deafening. The patrons, their faces flushed, and hearts racing, showed their appreciation for the performance they'd just witnessed.

The aftermath of Brandie's dance was palpable. The air, once casual and relaxed, was now thick with an electrifying sexual tension. It was the kind of atmosphere that led to stolen glances, whispered confessions, and, for some, perhaps even a night of unexpected passion.

In the realm of performances, what Brandie delivered was more than just a dance. It was a masterclass in seduction, a testament to the power of movement, and a showcase of raw, unbridled sexuality. And for everyone present, it was a night they wouldn't soon forget.

Backstage, Divine Donnie and Ronnie Rebel exchanged another glance. This time, not of confusion, but of admiration. They might be veterans on the drag stage, but there was no denying that Brandie's performance had set the lounge ablaze.

As the applause continued, Brandie returned backstage, a sheen of sweat highlighting the contours of his muscles. His eyes, still blazing with the energy of his performance, met Ronnie's.

The Starlit Drag Lounge pulsated with an undercurrent of sensual energy and tension, both sexual and otherwise.

Brandie, still flushed from his incendiary performance, walked past the row of curtains, his long legs cutting a stark silhouette against the dim backstage lights. Ronnie Rebel stood there, draped in a satin dress, about to channel the unforgettable aura of Baby from Dirty Dancing.

With a sultry glint in his eyes, Brandie approached Ronnie, his steps confident and unapologetic. His fingers slid down Ronnie's chest, finally grabbing the satin, feeling the warmth and firmness underneath. The bold touch carried an insinuation that went beyond the tactile sensation. "I've got to admit," Brandie whispered huskily, eyes locking onto Ronnie's, "Tonight's performances, especially yours, have me all charged up. You could say it makes me want to...

indulge a little." He smirked, adding with a conspiratorial wink, "Master-debator, are we?"

Ronnie, usually composed and always calculating, was momentarily taken aback. The double entendre was not lost on them. Their eyes widened, pulse quickening. Had Brandie discovered their secret double life?

Divine Donnie, now also in on the charged interaction, raised an eyebrow. "You know, Ronnie's not the only one who likes a bit of a debate," Brandie teased, turning his attention to Donnie. "I've been wondering, how do you both manage it? Changing stages so quickly. Always arriving at the Starlit ready for action?"

Before either of them could respond, the muffled announcement for the next performance echoed backstage, saving them from an immediate retort. Ronnie had to take the stage.

The warm golden glow of the chandeliers cast an almost ethereal light on the Starlit Drag Lounge stage. The ambience was intimate, but the anticipation in the air made it clear that this was no ordinary night.

As the familiar notes of "Time of My Life" from Dirty Dancing filled the room, Ronnie emerged in a silken, satin dress. Its deep burgundy hue clung to their figure like a second skin, with a teasing slit that traveled midway up their thigh. The fabric shimmered and flowed with their every move, making it seem as if Ronnie was surrounded by a halo of liquid satin.

The plunging neckline of the dress revealed a tantalizing glimpse of a delicate lace undergarment, its intricate patterns drawing eyes and heightening the allure. Their shoes, stilettos with delicate straps, completed the ensemble, elevating Ronnie's sensuality to new, dizzying heights.

The audience, already on the edge of their seats after Brandie's mesmerizing act, was now spellbound. Men shifted in their seats, their eyes tracking the outline of Ronnie's manhood, artfully tucked between their legs. Women fanned themselves, their breaths catching in their throats as they were drawn into the intoxicating whirlwind that was Ronnie Rebel.

Each twirl, each sensual gyration, sent the dress swirling, teasing the audience with flashes of the sultry lingerie beneath. As the beats of the music quickened, Ronnie's hands ran down the curves of their body, grazing the damp spots that formed behind their nipples. Their movements, suggestive yet elegant, had a hypnotic effect.

Suddenly, with a swift movement, Ronnie ripped the dress away, revealing a lingerie ensemble even more tantalizing than one could imagine. The black lace contrasted perfectly with their pale skin, the bralette barely containing their chest, while the panties, stretched taut, left little to the imagination. Gasps filled the lounge.

Embracing the music's climax, Ronnie leapt into the arms of a stage pup, reenacting the famous lift scene from Dirty Dancing. As they were elevated, the momentum caused their member to peek out from the crotch panel of their lingerie. The sight sent shockwaves through the room, adding to the already electric atmosphere. The women, cheeks flushed, glanced at each other, acknowledging the heat that pooled between their thighs. The men, trying to mask their own arousal, shifted uncomfortably, their trousers suddenly a bit too tight.

Coming back down to the earth but not to the stage, Ronnie landed squarely in the lap of a particularly enthusiastic audience member. Without missing a beat, they segued into a steamy lap dance. The intimate contact, their hard arousal pressing against the person's lap, sent the room's temperature skyrocketing. Ronnie's legs, encased in black fishnet stockings, pressed and rubbed against the thighs of audience members, evoking moans and sharp intakes of breath from both men and women alike.

The magnetic pull of Ronnie's sensuality was irresistible. Even as the dance came to its scorching conclusion, the room remained ensnared in the web of desire they had spun. The final note echoed, but the atmosphere stayed electric.

For a moment, there was complete silence. And then, the applause erupted. The audience, entirely entranced, had been transported to a realm of raw, primal desire, a place where the boundaries of gender and decorum melted away, leaving only human need and raw emotion.

Ronnie, with one last sultry, knowing gaze that promised more sinful delights, gracefully left the stage, leaving behind an audience still recovering from their raw, unfiltered performance.

Divine Donnie, who was up next, knew they had big shoes to fill. The palpable energy left behind by Ronnie was a testament to the power of pure, unbridled sensuality. But as the first notes of Donnie's song began, the audience leaned forward, eager for another round of unforgettable performances in the Starlit Drag Lounge.

As the curtains closed, Ronnie's eyes found Divine Donnie's. The mutual admiration, now combined with a touch of uncertainty, bound them tighter than ever before. Would their secret remain safe, or was it all about to come crashing down?

The last strains of Ronnie Rebel's heart-pounding performance still hung in the air, the electric energy unmistakable. As Ronnie sauntered off the stage, their gaze lingered on Divine Donnie, an unspoken promise lingering between them. The sexual tension, already palpable, was heightened by the danger of their shared secret. The entire lounge seemed to pulse with anticipation, the audience collectively holding their breath as the curtains slowly pulled back to reveal Divine Donnie.

And what a sight they were!

Channeling the legendary Celine Dion, Donnie stood regally in a shimmering gold dress that flowed over their curves, catching the light with every subtle movement. But it was the evident outline pressing against the delicate fabric of the dress, a testament to the arousal from Ronnie's performance, that had many in the audience gulping and others shifting in their seats. This wasn't just drag; this was artistry, sensuality personified.

The soft strains of "The Power of Love" began, and Divine Donnie, eyes smoldering, began to move. Every motion was deliberate, exuding a raw sexual energy that seemed to permeate every corner of the lounge. With every swish of their hips and flick of their wrists, the audience was drawn deeper into Donnie's world, a place where desire and danger danced hand in hand.

The spotlight focused on Divine's face, capturing the glittering tears that flowed freely, each droplet a testament to the passion and vulnerability of their performance. As the song crescendoed, Donnie's voice, deep and sultry, melded with Celine's, creating a hauntingly beautiful harmony that had more than one audience member discreetly fanning themselves.

The lounge had transformed. No longer just a place of entertainment, it was now a sanctum of intimacy. Hushed whispers and shared glances traversed the crowd. People who had come to see a show now found themselves on a shared journey of discovery, drawn together by the sheer force of Divine Donnie's performance.

As the song's final notes faded, Donnie, ever the master of their craft, allowed the simmering energy of their performance to gently cool, guiding the audience back from the brink of frenzied passion to a place of satiated contentment. But not without leaving an indelible mark.

The applause that erupted was deafening. The Starlit Drag Lounge had seen its fair share of unforgettable performances, but this... this was something else entirely. It wasn't just about the song or the dress or the evident physical arousal. It was about connection, vulnerability, and the magic that happened when an artist bared their soul for all to see.

Divine Donnie, their face glistening with sweat and eyes shining with unshed tears, took a moment to soak it all in. They looked out at the sea of faces, each one reflecting a myriad of emotions. There were those who had been moved to tears, others who wore expressions of pure awe, and still, others who seemed to be grappling with feelings they hadn't expected to confront that evening.

And then, their gaze found Ronnie Rebel, waiting in the wings. The world seemed to narrow to just the two of them. The applause, the cheering, the din of the lounge, all faded away. For in that moment, there was only Ronnie and Donnie, two souls inextricably bound by a love that transcended labels and definitions.

The curtains slowly began to descend, signaling the end of the act. But as they did, Divine Donnie blew a kiss towards Ronnie, a silent promise that no matter what challenges lay ahead, they would face them together.

And as the lights dimmed, the audience was left with an overwhelming feeling of gratitude. For they had not just witnessed a performance. They had been part of an experience, a fleeting moment in time when love, passion, and vulnerability converged to create pure, unadulterated magic.

The sultry undertones of Divine Donnie's performance to Celine Dion melodies faded away, the lounge was abuzz with the energy of the electrifying evening. The applause, though raucous, had a seductive quality to it. The audience, bewitched by the raw emotion and heat of the performances, were ready for more. At Starlit Drag Lounge, the night was still young.

The spotlight shifted, casting a shimmering light on the next performer, Luscious Luna. Adorned in a feathery ensemble, Luna performed a theatrical rendition to Madonna's 'Like a Virgin', flirting with the front-row guests and playfully throwing glances towards the backstage area. As she sashayed off, winking at Ronnie and Donnie, a collective gasp of exhilaration emanated from the lounge.

Another queen, Glittering Gina, took the stage in a whirlwind of shimmering sequins. As she seductively mouthed Whitney Houston's classics, Whitney's emotional highs and lows left some audience members teary-eyed while others cheered her on passionately.

The Lounge turned into a cauldron of emotions, sensuality, and unmatched talent. Each performer brought a unique flavor, be it the exotic charm of Vixen Valentina or the raw emotion of Sad Selena.

The room, dimly lit, with its neon lights casting playful patterns on the audience, was palpable with tension, thrill, and appreciation. The audience clapped, whistled, and showered the stage with dollar bills as each performer showcased their charisma, uniqueness, nerve, and talent.

Seated at a high table, almost lost amidst the thrumming energy of the lounge, were Dark Brandie and Brock. Both sipped on their cocktails while casting appraising looks at the unfolding performances. They occasionally exchanged hushed comments, leaning in, their faces close, lips barely brushing each other's ears.

Brandie's eyes constantly darted to where Divine Donnie and Ronnie Rebel had made their exit. The powerful chemistry between the two hadn't gone unnoticed. With a sly smirk, he nudged Brock, who followed her gaze and then grinned knowingly.

Brock leaned into Brandie's ear, his voice barely audible over the pounding beats. "What's brewing there? You think it's just stage chemistry or something... deeper?"

Brandie, playing with his cocktail straw, raised an eyebrow. "Oh, honey, that's no act. The heat, the longing... It's real. But what am I going to do about it? Stir the pot?"

Brock laughed softly, his eyes crinkling in amusement. "You? Stirring the pot? Never!"

A playful smirk tugged at Brandie's lips. "Oh, Brock, as much as I would love to see them falter and fail... they're my drag sisters. I'll let the universe decide for them." He paused, casting another sultry glance towards the backstage door. "Plus, they were so steamy tonight. My cock is aching from it all, and I need to get home and call someone to fix that."

Brock chuckled, shaking his head. "You never change. Always the drama queen."

Brandie grinned, draped in a veil of confidence and mischief, took a moment to compose himself before he dialed the familiar number. The lounge's music and chatter became a distant hum, the anticipation sending a pleasant shiver down his spine.

"Hello, Brandie," purred a sultry voice, immediately recognizable as Elara, one-half of the couple he'd been craving. Her partner, Julian, was the deep, grounding force to Elara's fiery passion.

With a devilish smirk, Brandie responded, "Elara, darling, you and Julian free tonight?"

She chuckled softly, "Always for you, Brandie. What did you have in mind?"

Brandie leaned back, letting his mind conjure the delicious scenarios. "I've got some new toys I thought we could experiment with. A string of perfectly sized anal beads, a supple leather paddle, and a velvety strap-on that I thought you'd particularly appreciate. What do you say we mix things up and truly let loose?"

A low, appreciative hum came from Elara's end. "Sounds intriguing. And where do ropes fit into this?"

Sipping his cocktail, Brandie's voice dropped an octave. "I was hoping Julian might show off those shibari skills of his. There's nothing like the sensation of ropes against skin, tight but comforting, creating art and sensation."

Elara's breath caught, a hint of anticipation evident. "I'll talk to Julian, but I have a feeling he'll be more than on board."

"I hope so," Brandie replied, biting his lip, "And just to clarify, I want this to be a give and take. While I've got plans for both of you, I'm more than willing to be at the mercy of your desires."

Their conversation continued, filled with soft laughter, whispers of promised pleasures, and plans that would undoubtedly leave them all sated and satisfied. Brandie described, in painstaking detail, how he intended to use the beads on Julian, starting with the smallest, teasing him, making him beg before granting him the release of the next size. Elara, he imagined, taking control with the strap-on, dictating the rhythm and pace, ensuring Brandie was at the brink, only to be brought back and kept waiting.

By the time they touched on the subject of ropes, Brandie's heart raced. He pictured Julian's skilled hands, intertwining ropes around his torso, binding his hands, rendering him deliciously helpless. Elara, in turn, would wield the paddle, her precise strikes a blend of pleasure and pain, driving Brandie to the edge and then tenderly bringing him back with soft caresses.

Elara had plans too—she spoke of binding Brandie, ensuring he was spread out and vulnerable. Julian would take his time, paying special attention to every sensitive spot, marking Brandie as theirs, even if just for the night.

The conversation ended with a shared sense of anticipation. "See you at your penthouse, Brandie," Elara whispered, her voice dripping with promise.

As Brandie hung up, the lounge's ambiance returned to the forefront, the music, the chatter, everything suddenly vibrant and alive. He looked over at Brock, his face flushed with excitement.

Brock raised an eyebrow, his grin teasing. "Sounds like you have quite the evening planned."

Brandie winked, his voice husky. "Let's just say it's going to be... memorable."

Brock, smirking, took a final sip of his drink. "Guess it's time for us to head out then, drama queen."

As the two of them made their way to the exit, the energy of Starlit Drag Lounge pulsated around them. It was a night of unbridled passion, undeniable chemistry, and unforgettable performances.

And as the curtains closed on another spellbinding night, the stories of love, rivalry, and passion continued to unfold in the city that never sleeps.

Chapter 6:
Passion Unleashed

The cool night air brought a shiver to Brandie's skin as he opened the door, revealing Elara and Julian. Both looked ravishing, their attire hinting at the promise of the evening ahead. Elara wore a deep red lace dress, which contrasted beautifully with her porcelain skin, while Julian sported a crisp black shirt, unbuttoned just enough to tease what lay beneath.

With a smile that spoke of countless shared adventures, Elara stepped forward, placing a delicate kiss on Brandie's cheek. "Always such a gracious host," she murmured.

Julian, not one to be outdone, pulled Brandie into a firm embrace, their lips meeting in a passionate greeting that sent a jolt of desire coursing through them both.

Brandie led them inside, the penthouse awash in the soft glow of the candles. They settled onto the plush couch, drinks in hand, the atmosphere thick with anticipation.

Julian, ever the initiator, set his drink down and pulled out a silken rope, its deep blue hue shimmering in the candlelight. "Shall we begin?" he asked, his voice dripping with promise.

Elara, not one to be left out, moved closer, her fingers playing with the hem of her dress. "I thought you'd never ask."

Elara's fingers began their dance on Brandie's chest, tracing the outlines of his chiseled muscles. Her touch was feather-light, but it sent shivers down Brandie's spine. The weight of her gaze, combined with Julian's smoldering eyes on him, had Brandie's heart pounding.

Julian rose, fetching the deep blue silk ropes from a nearby drawer Julian approached Brandie with the ropes, every step he took seemed deliberate, almost predatory. The hardwood floors whispered under his feet, and the candlelight cast long, languid shadows that played on his toned, shirtless torso. The sight of him — his piercing eyes locked onto Brandie, muscles rippling with every movement — heightened Brandie's anticipation.

Standing face to face, Julian allowed the cool, silken threads of the deep blue rope to slide tantalizingly over Brandie's exposed skin, teasingly brushing against his collarbones and trailing down his chest. Brandie's eyelids fluttered momentarily, and his lips parted as he took a deep breath, absorbing the sensation.

Julian's fingertips, both skilled and gentle, began their work, wrapping the rope meticulously around Brandie's wrists, leaving no space for escape. With every loop and knot, Julian pulled Brandie closer, binding not just his hands but also his very essence. Every twist and fold of the rope became an extension of Julian's will, a manifestation of the dance between dominance and surrender.

As Julian continued the intricate pattern up Brandie's arms, the friction between silk and skin sent waves of pleasure coursing through him. The ropes felt like a caress one moment and a constriction the next, a duality that had Brandie's heart racing and his breaths coming in short, heady gasps.

Taking advantage of Brandie's vulnerable position, Julian leaned in, letting his lips hover teasingly over the nape of Brandie's neck, feeling the pulse of excitement beneath the skin. His hot breath whispered promises of ecstasy, and as he drew back, he gently nipped at Brandie's earlobe, making him shudder.

Elara, not one to be left out of the fun, glided over to the pair. She was a vision, her fiery red hair cascading in waves over her shoulder, contrasting beautifully with her pale skin. With a wicked gleam in her eyes, she reached out to trace the rope pattern on Brandie's torso, her nails adding a sharp counterpoint to the silk's softness. The combination of Julian's restraint and Elara's teasing touch left Brandie teetering on a precipice of pleasure and anticipation.

With Brandie now securely bound, Julian whispered into his ear, his voice dripping with promise, "Trust me." Brandie nodded, lost in the sensations, willing to submit to the journey Julian and Elara would take him on.

Elara, in her sultry prowess, fetched the leather paddle and the string of beads. Holding them up for Brandie to see, she let out a soft laugh, "Ready for more, darling?" Brandie's response was a throaty moan, his eyes filled with hunger and anticipation.

Julian took the paddle from Elara and, with a grin, let it tap lightly against Brandie's thigh. The cool leather felt like a kiss, a preamble to the more forceful smacks that would come later. Each subsequent touch grew in intensity, building a symphony of sensation that left Brandie's skin tingling and his mind clouded with desire.

The room seemed to dim, the ambiance thick with anticipation. Julian, the picture of masculine beauty, stood back momentarily, allowing Elara her moment with Brandie. The air was thick with expectation, a heady blend of lust and trust binding the trio.

Elara's movements were the epitome of sensuality. The way she slicked the beads, her fingers dancing gracefully, was nothing short of an art form. Brandie's breaths came out uneven as he felt the gentle pressure of the first bead, followed by another, each larger and more insistent. The incremental stretch, paired with the delicious friction, had Brandie gasping, his mind a haze of pleasure. Elara, savoring every reaction she elicited, whispered teasingly, "Still with us, darling?" as she inserted the last bead, watching Brandie squirm in sweet agony.

The power dynamics in the room shifted subtly when Elara slipped out of her lace dress, revealing the velvety strap-on. Its silhouette was both daunting and enticing. Julian shot Brandie a knowing grin, leaning close to whisper in Brandie's ear, "She's full of surprises, isn't she?" Brandie could only nod, words failing him, as Elara approached with a predatory glint in her eyes.

Her fingers traced teasing circles around Brandie's chest, moving to his navel, lower, making him twitch in anticipation. He was utterly at her mercy, and the realization made him even more eager. The combination of the beads and the promise of what was to come made him acutely aware of every nerve ending. Julian's warm breath at the nape of his neck, combined with Elara's teasing proximity, felt like a delicious trap.

Leaning in, Elara brushed her lips against Brandie's, whispering, "You trust me?" Her eyes searched his, looking for any sign of hesitation. All she found was a burning desire. Brandie, his voice rough with need, replied, "Always."

Positioning herself, Elara slowly began, ensuring each thrust was precise, pushing Brandie deeper into waves of pleasure. With Julian's fingers caressing Brandie's chest and offering soothing kisses, they ensured he was cocooned in a web of sensations. Julian's deep voice punctuated the room with low murmurs of encouragement, "That's it, let go, let her take you there."

Elara, her hips finding a rhythm, watched Brandie closely, reveling in the reactions she was drawing out. Every groan, every gasp, only fueled her further. Brandie, tethered by the ropes and consumed by the sensations, felt himself spiraling, his world narrowing down to the ebb and flow of pleasure coursing through him. Elara ensured that Brandie was always teetering on the edge, leaving him gasping and craving more.

Each time Brandie felt the growing urge to succumb to the waves of pleasure, Elara, sensing this, would shift or pause just slightly. The genius was not in her ability to bring him to the brink, but to keep him dancing there, suspended in a liminal space of need and want.

Julian, not a passive observer by any means, soaked in this charged tableau. His fingers itched for more involvement, and they found their instrument in the leather paddle. It was a beautiful piece, its supple surface cool to touch. Julian approached, his voice a seductive whisper. "Ready for a bit more sensation, Brandie?"

All Brandie could do was nod, words having escaped him. Elara's wicked grin told Julian all he needed to know.

The first smack of the paddle was a soft caress — unexpected, given the nature of the instrument. The juxtaposition of Elara's rhythmic thrusts and Julian's teasing smacks sent a shiver up Brandie's spine. Each subsequent strike from Julian was a tad sharper, a tad more assertive. The sound of leather meeting skin punctuated the symphony of their shared breaths and gasps.

Elara leaned in to kiss the space between Brandie's shoulder blades. Her warm breath, combined with the tingling sensation from the paddle, had Brandie in sensory overload. He felt everything — the beads, the paddle, Elara's strap-on, Julian's fingers as they caressed the reddening areas on his skin.

Julian leaned in, his lips ghosting Brandie's ear, "How does that feel?" Each word was punctuated with another stroke of the paddle. Brandie, overwhelmed and consumed by sensations, could only muster a moan in response.

Elara, savoring the control she held, whispered in tandem with Julian, "We've got so much more in store for you." The double assault of their words, combined with their respective ministrations, was a potent cocktail of sensation.

Their eyes locked – Julian's deep blue ones meeting Elara's green. The silent communication between them was palpable. Julian gradually increased the force, but just as Brandie felt he might lose himself, Elara would change her rhythm or Julian would switch to gentle caresses.

This dance of sensation, of push and pull, continued. Brandie was lost, floating in a sea of pleasure. Just when he thought he could take no more, Elara whispered a soft command to Julian, and he placed the paddle down, replacing it with his warm hands. Brandie was adrift, the juxtaposition of the earlier assertive smacks with Julian's soothing touches sent his mind into a whirlwind.

As the trio's breaths gradually began to synchronize, a mutual understanding passed between them. This wasn't just about physical pleasure; it was about trust, intimacy, and the journey they took together. Every touch, every whisper, every shared gaze added layers to their connection.

Elara, sensing Brandie's nearing climax, shifted her focus, ensuring that when the moment came, it would be all-consuming. Julian, too, played his part, his hands working in tandem with Elara, driving Brandie to the edge and holding him there, suspended in a crescendo of pleasure.

The hours seemed to stretch and bend, each moment more intense than the last. Sweat, whispered desires, and the heady scent of arousal filled the penthouse. Their movements were synchronized, a dance of passion and intimacy that blurred the lines between pleasure and pain.

Brandie's world was a kaleidoscope of sensations - the biting sting of the paddle, the tantalizing feel of the beads, and the deep, rhythmic pressure from Elara's strap-on. Every touch, every gasp, and every moan amplified the electricity in the room.

As his exultation erupted, the visuals were just as intoxicating as the sounds. The aftermath of his intense climax painted a striking tableau across his skin. Each spurt was like a passionate brushstroke, painting his abdomen, thighs, and remarkably, even flecking his face. The creamy contrast against his dark skin was undeniably erotic, an artistry of intimacy.

Elara and Julian, two passionate puppeteers of the evening, couldn't tear their gaze away. Elara's ruby-red lips parted slightly, her breath catching at the visual feast before her. It was a sight that was both vulnerable and powerful, marking the territory between pleasure and surrender. Julian, for his part, wore an expression of smug satisfaction, eyes glinting with the knowledge that they had pushed Brandie to such intense peaks.

The fervent sound that escaped Brandie was not just a cry of pleasure but a raw, untamed roar that filled every corner of the opulent room. The intricately designed wallpaper, the plush velvet drapes, and even the delicate crystal of the chandelier seemed to shiver in response. As if the penthouse itself was so moved by his pleasure, it resonated in kind, vibrating with the aftershocks of Brandie's ecstasy.

The echo was ethereal, a lingering note of pure satisfaction that seemed to wrap around each individual in the room. It was the kind of sound that one didn't just hear, but felt deep within, a primal reminder of the heights of pleasure humans were capable of reaching.

Following the auditory and visual spectacle, a hush descended. Brandie, having journeyed to the heights of ecstasy and back, lay in a state of blissed-out exhaustion. His breathing, though heavy, had a rhythm of contentment to it.

The sheen of sweat that covered him reflected the dim light, making him look as if he was glowing.

Elara, ever the tease, leaned in, her fingers lightly tracing the aftermath on Brandie's skin. The combination of her cool touch on his sensitized skin sent another shiver down his spine. "Seems like someone enjoyed himself," she whispered, her voice a sultry murmur.

Julian, not to be outdone, moved closer, his fingers grazing Brandie's face, wiping away the stray evidence of his climax with a playful smirk. "You've painted quite the masterpiece, my friend," he quipped, his voice dripping with mirth and underlying passion.

The tactile sensation of Julian's fingers against Brandie's skin was soft and grounding, an anchor in the sea of overwhelming sensations. Julian's touch was deliberate, each movement meant to comfort and reassure. Elara, on the other hand, moved with a feather-light touch, her fingers brushing away the sweat that had formed on Brandie's brow and tracing the reddened patterns the ropes had left behind. Their combined touches served as a balm, soothing the fiery path left by their earlier escapades.

Brandie's eyes fluttered open, and the reality of his surroundings began to settle in. Gone was the fog of overwhelming pleasure; in its place was a deep, resonating satisfaction and gratitude. Julian's signature smirk was firmly in place, his eyes twinkling with mischief and a hint of pride. Elara, ever the enchantress, looked radiant, her fiery red hair creating a halo around her in the dim light, her green eyes reflecting a mix of contentment and a promise of more adventures to come.

As the ropes gradually loosened and fell to the side, Brandie's arms felt weightless, free. He flexed his fingers, the lingering sting from the paddle and the aftereffects of the ropes intermingling to create a delicious reminder of the night's escapades.

In the dim, ethereal glow of the candles, the three of them lay, a tangled web of limbs and emotions. The ambiance had shifted from one of heady, breathless anticipation to one of serene intimacy. It felt as if time had paused just for them, creating a pocket of tranquility in the bustling world outside.

The delicate scent of vanilla from the candles blended perfectly with the musky aroma of their intertwined bodies. Brandie, sandwiched between Julian and Elara, felt the gentle rise and fall of their chests against him. It was a rhythmic reminder that this was real, not just a fleeting fantasy. Every whispered word, every shared laugh, and every gentle touch only solidified the bond they were forging.

Julian, ever the wordsmith, broke the comfortable silence. "You were magnificent," he murmured, his voice low and sultry, tickling Brandie's ear. Elara chuckled softly, adding, "He's right, you know. I've never seen someone surrender so beautifully."

Brandie, a flush creeping up his neck, replied with a sheepish grin, "It wasn't hard with you two guiding the way." The flirty banter that had become their signature interplay was back in full force, a delightful blend of tenderness and teasing.

With a playful wink, Elara propped herself on one elbow, looking down at Brandie. "You know," she began, her voice dripping with mischief, "we haven't even gotten to the fun part of the night." Brandie raised an eyebrow, curiosity piqued. "And what might that be?" he asked, his voice teasingly incredulous.

Julian leaned in, his lips brushing against Brandie's ear, sending shivers down his spine. "The part where we raid the kitchen for snacks and binge-watch terrible reality TV."

Elara giggled, adding, "And you thought the paddle was intense? Wait until you see our love for trashy television."

The mood lightened further, as the trio, still intertwined, descended into fits of laughter. Their connection was undeniable – a potent mix of physical attraction, emotional bond, and shared humor.

As the night wore on, the sultry ambiance of the penthouse gradually transformed into a cozy haven. Blankets were fetched, bowls of popcorn appeared, and the soft glow of the television replaced the flickering candles. The trio, in a delightful turn of events, found themselves wrapped up in each other, critiquing fashion choices and rooting for their favorite contestants.

The seamless transition from intense physical connection to light-hearted banter was a testament to the depth of their bond. As dawn approached, the penthouse was filled with the sounds of laughter, whispered secrets, and the occasional snore, painting a picture of contentment and shared joy.

Chapter 7: Rumors and Revelations

The election campaign had reached the equivalent of a high-speed chase in a black-and-white caper movie, except the cliff everyone was heading toward was not metaphorical. The media, like seagulls behind a trawler, swooped and dived on every tidbit. The political melodrama had turned into a farce, sprinkled with a dash of theater of the absurd.

The winds of scandal howled through the city as newspapers and online blogs erupted with rumors and innuendos about our illustrious candidates - Donnie, Ronnie, and Alexandria. Donnie, with their hair a halo of defiance against gravity and natural law, was accused of election fraud and inciting a riot, the evidence being a video of them saying, "I love a good protest, always a chance to update my wardrobe."

Ronnie, whose conservative demeanor hid a personality that was the equivalent of an abandoned library, had their past dug up with allegations of black history erasure and attacking LGBTQ+ rights during their tenure in Florida. A photograph of Ronnie in a suit that looked stitched together from different conspiracy theories, standing by a book burning pit, became the emblem of this scandal. Except that it turned out, Ronnie was burning copies of a fake history textbook that claimed Florida was discovered by aliens.

And then there was Alexandria, our liberal stalwart, who was accused of partying a tad too hard during her college days and... being a woman. She shot back on WebWonders, with a photo of her holding a cocktail with the caption, "In celebration of breaking glass ceilings. And yes, that includes breaking it down on the dance floor."

If NewsWave Media Outlets had a theme song, it would have been the theme from 'Jaws'. The space seemed all metallic edges and hustle, the sort of place where secrets came to die and gossips thrived.

In the NewsWave central studio, clashing between neon and brushed steel, the hottest topic was, unsurprisingly, the political campaign. And as the metaphorical heat dial turned up, there was a palpable delight among journalists who saw their page views rising with every scandalous morsel.

"Oh, just in!" hollered Tabitha, the in-house gossip maven. "Ronnie erased black history and attacked LGBTQ+ rights in Florida! That's got to be worth...ooh...at least a million clicks?"

"And have you heard about Donnie?" quipped another, "Apparently they incited some kind of... insurrection? And now there's a whiff of election fraud in the air. This is juicier than a summer peach."

From another corner, the youngest of the lot, clad in eco-friendly, ethically sourced everything, whispered, "*Mira*, Alexandria was a wild party girl in college. And, omg, she's a woman too!"

Next to her, a weathered journalist scoffed, "How is that even news?"

But the real headline, just a whisper for now, was that they all had a penchant for drag. However, the hard evidence was as elusive as a pair of comfortable stilettos.

And, as expected, in the midst of this frenzy were our main characters: Donnie, Ronnie, and Alexandria. Their political campaigns, which were once about visions and dreams, were now cloaked in sensationalism. Every door-knock, every speech, and every appearance became an ordeal in clarifying, rectifying, or outright denying.

Alexandria took a defiant stance. In her Advocacy Hub, surrounded by passionate volunteers and banners championing inclusivity, she took to WebWonders Online Space, livestreaming, "It's not about my college days or being a woman. It's about the future we're creating!"

Ronnie, ever the reserved persona, held a formal press conference at the Tradition Towers Party Office, surrounded by portraits of past leaders. "The past is the past," they declared, "I'm looking to the future."

Donnie, in a typical grandeur, staged a rally at Unity Square. The crowd, a mix of drag enthusiasts and political supporters, chanted their new slogan with fervor. Standing tall in Divine Donnie's opulent, glittering outfit, they declared, "Let them talk! We're all about love and acceptance!"

But the most savory of rumors was a whisper of cross-dressing nights and drag escapades involving all three. The irony of the situation was not lost on anyone. The accusations were all smoke and no fire, yet the media frenzy resembled a barbecue party. Beneath the bravado, there were cracks showing. Tired lines under Donnie's eyes, Alexandria's sighs when she thought no one was looking, and Ronnie's almost imperceptible slump in posture. The relentless news cycle, the scrutiny, and the growing whispers about their drag personas were taking a toll.

In the vortex of this media tempest, the candidates found themselves navigating the rocky shores of public opinion. Every reaction was a headline, every non-reaction a bigger headline.

Donnie was the first to be swept into the eye of this media storm when they were cornered by a group of reporters during a shopping spree. Armed with shopping bags in one hand and a latte in the other, Donnie parried the reporters with a grace that would put a fencing master to shame. "Honey," they said, their voice coated with sugar yet sharp as a blade, "I've always believed in the power of transformation. Why just look at my wardrobe!"

Ronnie, on the other hand, was the picture of stoic indignation as they faced the media at Primetime Politics Studio. Their voice was a monotone as they denied allegations with the enthusiasm of a tax return. Yet the tremor in their hand betrayed the calm facade.

And Alexandria, the only one among them who seemed to revel in the media glare, took the opportunity to underscore her humble roots, liberal values, and the unyielding spirit of womanhood. Her words resonated across social media, fanning the flames of support among the young electorate.

Mike (or should we say Michelle), ever the loyal friend, tried to infuse some humor, with limited success. "What's the deal with these rumors? Next, they'll say I'm a drag queen too!" Cue the awkward silence.

Meanwhile, over cosmopolitans and wine coolers at the Gilded Gala Grand Hotel, Brock and Dark Brandie were having a hushed conversation, "Without our help the rumors have started." Brandie mused, sipping slowly.

Brock, looking contemplative, replied, "In this city? Anything is possible."

Dark Brandie smirked, his lips a perfect shade of burgundy. "Then, my dear Brock, this election is about to get a whole lot more interesting, without us even doing a thing."

And as the media firestorm blazed on, engulfing every headline and news byte, our trio of candidates, their secret drag lives hanging by a precarious thread, prepared for what was to come. They could only hope their heels were high enough to wade through the storm.

Meanwhile, Donnie and Ronnie, once rivals but now bound by the outrageous rumors, found themselves sharing a quiet drink at the Starlit Drag Lounge, finding solace in the shimmering world far removed from political ding-dong. It was a breather before plunging back into the mire of political banter.

As they sat there, the mirage of calm before another storm, they were oblivious to the budding camaraderie that would soon spark a more personal revolution amidst the political circus.

Starlit Drag Lounge, with its dimmed lights and the radiant bar, wasn't just a spot to witness the mesmerizing artistry of drag. It was an escape—a hideaway from the scrutinizing world outside. At this very moment, two of the most discussed personalities sought refuge in its embrace.

Donnie, dressed in a low-key ensemble that screamed "I'm trying to blend in but not really," glanced sideways at Ronnie, who was resplendent in a midnight blue attire, their glossy black shoes mirroring the bar's neon sheen.

The lounge was alive with effervescent chatter, clinking glasses, and the soft hum of drag ballads. From the entrance, the glittering decor seemed as if the night sky had decided to descend just for the evening. The performances were a brilliant blaze of colors and emotions.

Donnie sipped on their Glitz & Glamour cocktail—vodka with a touch of elderflower, sparkling wine, and a shimmering edible glitter, while Ronnie cautiously tried the house special, Rebel Rouge—a hint of rum, red berries, and a dash of lemon. The icy clink of their glasses was almost drowned by the audience's applause and the captivating lip-sync that unfolded on stage.

They exchanged a look, a mix of "why are we here?" and "I'm glad we're here together." The tension was palpable. Every stolen glance spoke a thousand words, every unintentional brush of their fingers sent a rush of chills. Two rivals, now wrapped in a cocoon of unforeseen intimacy and intrigue.

A smokey queen in a sequined gown performed a sultry number, her voice a smooth rendition of some lost love ballad. It wasn't just her voice but the raw emotion she put into each word that held the audience—and notably Donnie and Ronnie—spellbound.

"You know," Donnie began, their voice a touch huskier than usual, "this place reminds me of... of a time when things were simpler. Before the media, the campaigns, the entire charade."

Ronnie, their usual calculated demeanor softening, responded, "It's ironic, isn't it? Amidst the feathers and the glitter, amidst this world of extravagance, we find...simplicity."

Donnie smirked, "And yet, amidst this simplicity, we are wearing disguises."

Ronnie chuckled, "Touché, Divine Donnie."

It was then, amidst the soft ballads and fading limelight, that their eyes truly met. Not as the political rivals the world knew them to be, but as two souls, weary from the relentless battles they had to fight daily, seeking solace in each other.

The cocktail of emotions was stronger than any drink they had ever had. Donnie, always the risk-taker, said, "You know, sometimes I wish we could just break free from all this—just for one night—and be who we truly are."

Ronnie's gaze lingered a second longer than necessary, their voice soft, "And who would that be?"

"Someone who isn't afraid of what the world thinks. Someone..." Donnie trailed off, looking deep into Ronnie's eyes, "someone who can find passion even in the unlikeliest of places."

Ronnie swallowed hard, their voice barely a whisper, "Like the Starlit Drag Lounge?"

Donnie grinned, "Exactly."

The evening wore on, the drag performances growing bolder, the lounge's atmosphere charged with a potent mix of music, laughter, and the unmistakable undercurrent of something more intimate. With their small hands, Donnie took Ronnie by theirs and lead them away.

The anticipation in the room was like a smoldering ember ready to burst into flames at the slightest provocation. The burgeoning chemistry between Donnie and Ronnie had finally found its boiling point, leading them to the secluded albeit grim bathroom of the Starlit Drag Lounge, away from prying eyes and wagging tongues that were just waiting for the next big scoop in the scandal-laden political battlefield.

As the sound of the pulsating music leaked through the walls, creating an illicit rhythm to the unscripted act of intimacy that was about to unfold, the world outside ceased to exist for Donnie and Ronnie. In that stall, among the crude graffiti and the faint aroma of old perfumes, they were just Donnie and Ronnie, free from the shackles of political affiliations and public expectations.

In the hushed shadows, Ronnie could feel Donnie's eyes, intense and unrelenting, tracing every contour of their face. The weight of their shared moment pressed down on them, as palpable as the bathroom's steamy atmosphere.

The sultry ambience in the restroom was palpable, thick with longing and unspoken promises. The simple act of unbuttoning a shirt became an erotic dance of temptation, each button undone a step closer to surrender.

Ronnie's fingers, usually so adept, trembled slightly. They could feel Donnie's burning gaze on them, every second increasing the tension between the two. Each button revealed a hint of Ronnie's sculpted chest, a canvas of desire and vulnerability. The muscles beneath the skin twitched with anticipation, and the trail of light hair leading downwards hinted at deeper secrets.

Donnie's breathing grew shallow, the sight in front of them awakening a primal hunger. They could see the rapid rise and fall of Ronnie's chest, the heart beneath pounding a seductive rhythm. The air between them grew charged, electric, and the bathroom's confined space amplified their awareness of each other's bodies.

As the last button came undone, the room felt saturated with heat. Ronnie's shirt, now completely open, framed their torso like a work of art, the contours and valleys of muscles showcased under the dim light. But more than the physical allure, it was the raw, exposed emotion in Ronnie's eyes that drew Donnie in. They saw past the political armor, the strategic mind, to the core of the person beneath.

Donnie took a step closer, bridging the gap between them. Their fingers brushed the base of Ronnie's throat, feeling the erratic pulse. They delicately trailed their fingertips downward, relishing the goosebumps they left in their wake, until they reached the center of Ronnie's chest. They could feel the warmth radiating from Ronnie's skin, the silent invitation to come closer.

Donnie's eyes were dark with passion, the usually sparkling blue now a stormy sea of desire. Ronnie's eyes, a depth of brown that hinted at a forest in twilight, mirrored the same intensity. The world outside, the politics, the rivalry, all faded as they focused solely on each other.

With a gentle touch that contrasted their current situation, Donnie caressed Ronnie's face. Their fingers traced the high cheekbones, journeyed to the softness of Ronnie's lips, and finally rested on their chin, tilting it up. Their gazes met, and the weight of the moment hung heavily in the silence. A shared history, months of heated debates, and tension-filled interviews melted away. Now, it was just Donnie and Ronnie, two souls seeking solace in a world of chaos.

Donnie, always the bolder of the two, made the first move. Their lips met, and what began as a tentative exploration quickly escalated into a blaze of passion. As the taste of Ronnie's lips intoxicated them, Donnie pressed forward, their body a wall of warmth and need against Ronnie's. The cool tiles against Ronnie's back emphasized the heat between them. Each touch, every brush of their fingers, set off fireworks.

Ronnie moaned softly into the kiss, the sound making Donnie's heart race faster. Their hands, previously gentle, grew more insistent. They explored the contours of Ronnie's body, skimming over their shirt, feeling the rapid heartbeat beneath. The silky material of their dress shirt was no barrier for Donnie's eager fingers, which deftly undid each button, revealing more tantalizing skin.

The passion was contagious. Ronnie responded in kind, their hands roaming over Donnie's back, feeling the taut muscles beneath their suit. Their fingers slipped beneath the waistband of Donnie's pants, pulling them closer. There was a sense of urgency now, an unspoken need to bridge the gap between them, to erase the physical barriers that still remained.

The pressure was undeniable. As their bodies pressed closer, there was no hiding the effect they had on one another. Their erections strained against the confines of their dress pants, seeking the intimacy that had so far been denied. Donnie's fingers moved lower, skimming over Ronnie's abdomen and traveling to the buckle of their belt. With a deftness born of need, they quickly undid it, their fingers diving beneath the fabric to grasp Ronnie.

Ronnie gasped at the sensation, their head falling back against the tiles. Their fingers, equally eager, mirrored Donnie's actions, and soon they were both bared to each other. The feeling of skin on skin was electric. They stroked each other, their movements synchronized in a dance of seduction and pleasure.

A shiver ran down Ronnie's spine as Donnie's thumb circled the tip of their penis, spreading the moisture that had gathered. Their breathing grew ragged, the sensations threatening to overwhelm them. every touch sending jolts of pleasure coursing through their body. The normally calm and composed Ronnie was now a maelstrom of emotion, surrendering to the allure of the moment. The heat emanating from Donnie's touch was enough to melt away all inhibitions. The feel of lace and satin against their throbbing desire made everything more heightened, a mixture of the rough and the delicate, the bold and the restrained.

Donnie, with their characteristic charisma, brought a mix of softness and assertiveness to their actions. Their whisper, husky and laden with promise, seemed louder than the distant murmur outside the restroom. "I'm going to grab you in the bussy." The audacity of that statement, coupled with the sultry tone, was enough to drive Ronnie to the edge. Their knees felt weak, and they pressed harder into the cold wall for support, each tile imprinting its chill on Ronnie's heated skin.

Donnie's hands, which seemed to have a mind of their own, delved deeper, expertly navigating the terrain of Ronnie's curves. The sensation of fingers skimming the sensitive crevices, particularly the puckered area, their chocolate starfish, made Ronnie gasp. Their breath came in short, ragged bursts, their entire body quaking with anticipation.

The lace and satin of Ronnie's undergarments were soaked with desire, the fabric clinging to their form. It was both a barrier and an invitation, making every touch, every caress, all the more electrifying. Donnie seemed to revel in the power they held over Ronnie at that moment, their own breathing mirroring the ragged tempo of their partner's.

For what felt like an eternity, they stood like that, lost in each other, the world outside forgotten. But as the murmur of voices, laughter, and applause began to filter through the restroom door, the reality of their situation came crashing down. They were two high-profile figures, trapped in a restroom, their most private moments at the risk of becoming public scandal.

Ronnie's eyes widened in alarm, the green of their irises darkening with a mix of fear and arousal. They tried to push Donnie away gently, signaling that they needed to regroup and face the world outside. But Donnie, ever the rebel, resisted, pulling Ronnie close for one last heated embrace. Their lips met in a frantic kiss, tongues dueling for dominance, each trying to etch the memory of this stolen moment into their souls.

The sudden ring of Donnie's phone jerked them back to reality. The intrusive ringtone was a stark reminder of the world they belonged to. Donnie hesitated for a moment but with a sigh answered the call. It was Mike, with some urgent campaign update that couldn't wait. It was a call from reality, jerking them away from the utopia they had momentarily created. The spell was broken, but the smudged lipstick and tousled hair were evidence of a chapter that had just begun to unfold.

The soft buzz of the lounge music leaked through the cracks of the bathroom door. The atmosphere, just moments ago charged with passion, had shifted to one of palpable tension.

Donnie's expressive eyes widened in shock as Ronnie, in a whirlwind of emotion, began to hastily redress. The sight of Ronnie's panicked retreat brought a sting of vulnerability to Donnie's eyes. Ronnie's breath was shallow, their gaze darting around the room as if searching for an escape route.

"Ronnie," Donnie whispered, reaching out. But Ronnie had already turned their back, avoiding eye contact.

"This was a mistake," Ronnie muttered, barely audible above the distant music. The soft shimmer of their drag outfit sparkled under the dim lighting, a stark contrast to the turmoil in their eyes. "We can't let this... whatever this is... jeopardize our campaign."

Donnie felt a sting. "Was it just a campaign strategy for you?" Their voice was shaky.

Donnie, still flustered and aghast at the sudden change of mood, watched as Ronnie hurriedly fixed their attire. The dim light in the bathroom cast a soft glow on Ronnie's face, illuminating the tear that trickled down. They didn't exchange words. The deafening silence was interrupted only by the distant muffled beats from the lounge.

"Why...why are you running?" Donnie stammered, reaching out to steady Ronnie.

But Ronnie pulled away, avoiding Donnie's searching gaze. "It's complicated," they whispered before making their swift exit, Ronnie paused at the door, taking a deep breath. "It's not that simple," they confessed, their voice tight. "I have feelings, but they terrify me. This world... our world... is complicated."

With that, Ronnie slipped out, leaving a bewildered and hurt Donnie behind, their mind racing, trying to decipher the whirlwind of emotions they'd just experienced.

Outside, the drag show was in full swing. Ronnie pushed past the crowd, the lounge's ambiance now a painful reminder of the vulnerable moment they had just shared with Donnie. They needed air, distance, and most of all, clarity.

Donnie, meanwhile, took a few minutes to compose themselves, the reality of the moment sinking in. What had just transpired could endanger their political ambitions and could also expose the fragile, burgeoning connection between them. But was the risk worth it? Donnie questioned.

Donnie's head buzzed with a mix of lust, frustration, and confusion. They stood frozen for a moment, taking in the rush of it all. The line between their political fronts and personal feelings had blurred, leaving Donnie questioning the authenticity of that intimate moment.

Outside the bathroom, the reality of the Starlit Drag Lounge came crashing back. The place was alive with vibrant performances, laughter, and clinking glasses. Alexandria, her eyes scanning the crowd, caught sight of a familiar figure. Ronnie, their disguise of sunglasses, overcoat, and hat in disarray, rushed past her. Their usually calculated demeanor was replaced with a frantic, almost desperate look.

She frowned, piecing together the puzzle as Donnie emerged a few moments later, also looking disheveled and lost. Her astute mind raced. What transpired between those two? Was the political landscape shifting beneath her feet?

Meanwhile, Ronnie, propelled by a cocktail of emotions, Ronnie rushed through the bustling city streets, a kaleidoscope of thoughts blurring past as the neon lights blinked overhead. Each step towards the hotel was a step into the heart of uncertainty, a dance between yearning and the knife-edge of toxic masculinity that had always stood as an unseen wall between Ronnie and Donnie.

As Ronnie swiped the hotel room card, the door clicked open to a silence that only seemed to amplify the chaos within. The neon lights from the boulevard streamed through the gaps of the heavy drapes, dimly illuminating the room as Ronnie entered the hotel suite. The clamor of the city seemed a distant hum as the door swung closed, enclosing Ronnie in a quiet chamber of reflection.

The weight of the evening's events pressed down on their chest, a jumble of exhilarating highs and soul-searching lows. The walk from the Starlit had been a mind storm of replayed moments, the words unsaid, the actions undone, and the craving for an unscripted narrative. The laughter and playful banter with Donnie at the Starlit, the sensual touches, the intoxicating proximity, and the shadow of societal expectations — all melded into a storm of emotions.

The bathroom seemed the sanctuary needed. Walking slowly to the bathroom, the cool tiles felt grounding against their bare feet. The gleaming taps and polished mirrors contrasted sharply with the chaos brewing inside them. Turning on the shower, the sound of water splashing added a soothing rhythm to the backdrop, the sound of water crashing against the tiles brought a transient calm. The mirror reflected the blurred lines of Ronnie's emotions - each drop of water a veil hiding the unseen, unspoken.

Taking a moment, Ronnie leaned heavily against the countertop, staring deep into their reflection. Their eyes, usually full of spirit, now swirled with doubt and vulnerability. As the tears trickled down, Ronnie began to peel off the outer layers, each piece of cloth that fell to the floor carried the essence of the evening.

Finally standing in the delicate satin and lace lingerie, remnants of Ronnie's erection still outlined under the delicate satin, the moist stains of its excitement bore witness to the brief rendezvous with a love that dared not speak its name, a vivid reminder of the stolen moments with Donnie. Tears began to blend with the face of the person standing in the reflection, the one who'd tasted the undefined, tasted the freedom, the love, and the tender embrace of vulnerability back at the Starlit.

Slowly, Ronnie stepped into the shower, the initial burst of water felt scalding against their skin then its warmth seemed a juxtaposition to the cold reality that waited outside. But as the water flowed down, it carried along the layers of restrictive manhood that had always clung tightly. Instead of standing, they found themselves curling up in the corner, letting the water drench them. The droplets mixed with the tears that began to flow freely, a silent release from the heart. Their sobs, soft at first, grew louder and more anguished as the weight of societal pressures, toxic masculinity, and their burgeoning feelings for Donnie overwhelmed them. The shower became a sanctuary, a place to confront and cleanse the conflicting emotions that had taken hold.

On the floor of the shower, curled up, Ronnie let the sobs carve the path of freedom, each drop of tear a purge of the toxic masculinity, each sob a call to the love that waited to blossom under the Starlit sky.

In that small, echoing space, Ronnie hoped for the courage to break through the shackles, to embrace the love that dared to challenge the norms, and to once again find

Donnie, but this time, with a heart unburdened and ready to love unapologetically.

Back at the lounge, Alexandria mulled over the night's events. She remembered the rumors, the whispers, the stories linking Donnie and Ronnie's clandestine escapades. But now, seeing them in this state, she realized the depth of their connection. It wasn't just about politics or alliances; it was deeper, more personal.

She recalled her own journey, her struggles with acceptance, her fierce advocacy for love and inclusivity. And as the night's performances reached their crescendo, she made a silent pledge. She'd champion love in all its forms, no matter the political stakes.

Chapter 8:
Alliance or Rivalry?

In the glittering world of Diva's Den Costume Boutique, mannequins sported an array of sequined dresses, feathered boas, and impossibly high heels. Rainbow lights shimmered on sequined racks of costumes, making the space a veritable wonderland. From lacey bodysuits to flamboyant feathered headdresses, it was the crème de la crème of drag attire.

As Donnie, draped in a flamboyant feathered scarf, perused the aisles, they caught sight of a familiar face. Ronnie, looking somewhat out of place amidst the colorful opulence, was scrutinizing a rather conservative pair of stockings.

Their eyes met. Time froze.

The atmosphere, previously filled with the soft hum of patrons and the distant sizzle of glitter glue guns from the workshop, suddenly became thick with tension. The memories of their unexpected rendezvous at the Starlit Drag Lounge just a couple nights ago flooded back.

"Ronnie?" Donnie's voice was almost a whisper, a mix of surprise and mischief.

Ronnie cleared their throat, taken aback. "Donnie, what a... surprise. I didn't think I'd bump into Divine Donnie in broad daylight."

Both of them chuckled, easing the palpable awkwardness.

"I was just... you know, exploring options," Ronnie said, their fingers fidgeting with the lacey garter belt in their hands. "For Ronnie Rebel."

Donnie tilted their head, eyeing Ronnie's selections with a playful grin. "Going for the more risqué look, are we?"

Ronnie blushed, a rare sight. "About the other night... I'm sorry for the abrupt exit. It was... unexpected. The chemistry, I mean."

Donnie's eyes softened. "It was. But, no hard feelings." They winked. "Though, I must say, it was quite the memorable bathroom break."

Ronnie's chuckle resonated amidst the backdrop of glittering outfits. "That it was."

For a moment, they just stood there, soaking in the memories of that night, lost in the maze of their emotions. Their gazes locked, and the electric charge between them was undeniable.

Trying to steer away from the escalating tension, Ronnie gestured towards a row of silky negligees. "I was thinking of trying something like this. The campaign's been so stressful;

sometimes it's therapeutic to embrace the sensual side of Ronnie Rebel."

Donnie's eyebrow arched in intrigue. "Therapeutic, you say?"

Before they could further contemplate the loaded statement, Ronnie, with an uncharacteristic boldness, picked out a seductive black lace lingerie set. Holding it up against their body, they turned to Donnie, their face a mix of challenge and vulnerability.

"Could you help try these on?" Ronnie's voice was low, laden with more than just a simple request.

Donnie's heart raced. The audacity of the proposition was shocking yet enticing. But they weren't one to back down from a dare.

"Well, Ronnie Rebel," Donnie purred, leaning closer, "I'd be delighted."

The playful banter, the familiar territory of challenge and response, was their comfort zone. But beneath it all, the magnetic pull was growing stronger, leading them to uncharted territories of intimacy and connection. The journey they were about to embark upon, with its delicate interplay of politics, love, and drag, was bound to be anything but ordinary.

The enigmatic glow of the fitting room beckoned, a small haven in Diva's Den where truth could possibly be unclothed and reality could be dressed in fantasy. Ronnie followed Donnie to the hidden alcove within the boutique, the nervous flutter in their stomach playing a melody to the rhythm of Donnie's confident strides. Donnie had that air about them, a charismatic yet enigmatic aura, much like a beckoning yet untamed flame. Ronnie felt like a moth, gladly ready to burn.

As they entered the fitting room, Donnie smoothly slid the curtain across, the room now veiled from the judgement of the outside world, yet exposing the desire in the space between them. The only witnesses now were the seductive silks and sultry satins hanging around, whispering of fantasies yet to be embraced.

The intimacy of the space shrunk with every heartbeat, the ambiance pulsing with a mixture of vulnerability and assertiveness, a game of control and surrender. Ronnie felt Donnie's eyes undress them, a trail of fire left wherever the gaze landed. With trembling fingers, Ronnie began unbuttoning their shirt, the slightly shaky fingers betraying the cool facade.

Donnie closed the gap between them, hands covering Ronnie's, steadying the tremors with a soothing calm. "Allow me," they whispered, their breath warm against Ronnie's skin, making them shiver in anticipation.

Donnie's fingers were experienced, unbuttoning Ronnie's shirt with a mix of urgency and tenderness that felt like a promise. Each button undone was like peeling layers off a long-concealed truth. As the shirt slid off Ronnie's shoulders, they felt a sweet liberation, an acceptance that seemed to come with each caress of Donnie's fingers against their skin.

Donnie's fingers brushed against Ronnie's waist as they helped them step into the black lace lingerie, the smooth fabric against Ronnie's skin felt like decadent sin. The garment hugged Ronnie's frame with the promise of a secret yet to be revealed, an intimacy yet to be explored.

Ronnie's eyes met Donnie's, their reflection was a pool of desire amidst the enigma of fear, fear of the unveiled emotions and the unchartered territory they were stepping into. The daring in Ronnie's eyes spoke of a rebellion against the shackles of political guise and a craving to unveil the human underneath the facade.

As if pulled by an unseen force, their lips fused in a cataclysmic union, time seemed to stand still. The wet slide of tongues, the soft nips, and the suction of lips were sounds that replaced the ticking of the clock. The press of Donnie's body against Ronnie's felt like a magnetic pull, drawing them deeper into each other's embrace.

As the kisses ventured down Donnie's neck, leaving a trail of molten heat, Ronnie reveled in every tremor, every gasp that escaped Donnie's lips. Every soft moan that Donnie let out became a beacon, guiding Ronnie to explore further, dive deeper. The terrain of Donnie's body was an uncharted territory, every mole, every scar, every ridge had a story waiting to be explored, and Ronnie was eager to read every chapter.

The act of kneeling was more than just a physical descent; it was symbolic. It showcased Ronnie's reverence, their willingness to lay down their pride, their political armor, to be vulnerable. But, paradoxically, it also exuded dominance. This was not a mere act of submission; it was an assertion of control, an emblem of command in the face of bare vulnerability.

With deft fingers, Ronnie nudged the lace aside, revealing the heated flesh beneath. The sight was intoxicating, the pulsating evidence of Donnie's arousal made Ronnie's mouth water in anticipation. Donnie's eyes, usually so confident and piercing, were now clouded with lust and anticipation, pupils dilated, the usual icy blue now a stormy sea of desire.

Donnie's arousal stood proudly, a testament to their yearning for Ronnie, and it throbbed with every heartbeat. Ronnie's fingers delicately brushed against it, feeling the warmth and pulsation, the texture soft yet unyielding. It was almost hypnotic, and Ronnie found themselves being drawn to it like a moth to a flame.

Ronnie's slow descent towards Donnie's manhood was an agonizing tease for both of them. Every breath Ronnie exhaled sent shivers down Donnie's spine, each kiss planted on their inner thighs making them writhe with anticipation. But Ronnie was in control, and they reveled in the power they held over Donnie in that moment.

When Ronnie's lips finally met the base of Donnie's arousal, the sensation was electrifying. Donnie's hips bucked involuntarily, seeking more of that exquisite contact. The sound that escaped Donnie's lips was raw and untamed, a sound that Ronnie had never heard before, one that spoke of unbridled passion and need.

The gentle suction of Ronnie's mouth, combined with the teasing swirls of their tongue, drove Donnie to the brink of sanity. Every lap, every suck was amplified by the sheer intimacy of the act. They were baring their souls to each other, laying all their cards on the table, and it was exhilarating.

The depth Ronnie was willing to explore was a testament to their commitment to this moment. Every gag, every moment of discomfort was pushed aside in favor of the pleasure they were giving and receiving. It was a dance of give and take, one where both were equally invested.

As Donnie's fingers tangled in Ronnie's hair, urging them to take more, to go deeper, the power dynamics shifted. While Ronnie was in control, Donnie was not a passive participant. They were both equal partners in this dance of passion, guiding each other to the peaks of pleasure.

The feeling of being enveloped by the warmth and wetness of Ronnie's mouth was almost too much for Donnie. The slide of their tongue, the pressure of their lips, the occasional scrape of their teeth—it was all a sensory overload.

But it wasn't just about the physical sensations. It was about the emotions, the connection they were forging. Every moan, every whimper was a testament to the bond they were building, one that went beyond political affiliations and public personas.

Time seemed to stand still as they lost themselves in each other. The world outside, with its judgments and expectations, seemed a million miles away. All that mattered was the here and now, the taste, the touch, the feel of one another.

Donnie's senses were on overdrive. Every kiss, every touch from Ronnie was amplified, sending cascades of pleasure straight to the pit of their stomach, making the coil of tension tighten with every second. The sensation was overwhelming, making Donnie want to both chase the climax and delay it, to stretch out this exquisite torment for as long as possible. They were caught in the heady euphoria of being on the edge, their entire being focused on the feeling of Ronnie's lips against their manhood. Desperation and desire combined as Donnie tangled their fingers in Ronnie's hair, tugging gently as a silent plea to slow down, to make this pleasure last.

However, the pull of passion was magnetic, impossible to resist. Ronnie, always so composed and strategic, seemed to let go of all pretenses. With a surge of determination, they took a deep, steadying breath and pushed past the initial discomfort, taking Donnie even deeper. Their hands, with a will of their own, clung to Donnie's hips, pulling them closer, as if trying to merge their bodies into one. The heat of their shared ardor was a living, breathing entity between them, making the atmosphere thick and heady.

In this stolen moment, roles reversed seamlessly. Donnie, always the one in control, always dominating, found themselves surrendering to the waves of pleasure, allowing Ronnie to steer the ship. And steer they did. With a surprising mix of ferocity and hunger, Ronnie took control, their actions communicating a yearning that words couldn't capture. Each motion, every suck and swirl, was calculated to drive Donnie wild, to push them to the very brink of ecstasy.

The symphony of their moans resonated in the room, bouncing off the velvet-lined walls, filling the small space with the music of their passion. Each sound, each sigh, was an affirmation of the raw emotions they were experiencing. The decadent garments surrounding them, the opulent fabrics and costumes, faded into the background, overshadowed by the visceral, genuine connection between the two rivals. Their wandering hands reveled in the luxury of textures, from the smooth, cool lace and silk to the warmth and roughness of their own skin. The tactile sensations added layers to their experience, making it even more profound and intense.

Just when they thought they were lost, drowning in this ocean of shared desire, reality intruded in the form of a shrill ring. The jarring sound of a phone broke through their bubble, acting like a cold splash of water. It was a stark reminder of the world outside, of their public personas, and the political game they were embroiled in.

Donnie groaned, letting their head fall back. "Not now..." they murmured, but the caller ID showed 'Mike', and that spelled urgency.

The momentary pause in their shared passion was filled with a heavy silence, broken only by the persistently shrill ringtone.

Ronnie, eyes still hazy with desire, pulled back slightly, giving Donnie the space they needed. "You should probably take that."

"Not now, Mike!" Donnie exclaimed in frustration. Yet, knowing the nature of their campaigns and the critical role Mike played, Donnie knew it wasn't a call they could afford to miss.

With a reluctant sigh, they answered, "Yes, Mike?"

"Mike?" Donnie's voice quivered, trying to keep the sensual undertones at bay.

Ronnie tried not to eavesdrop but found themself hanging onto every word Donnie said, every nuance of their tone, every pause that filled the silence. Ronnie then leaned back on to sit on their heels, taking a moment to catch their breath and fix their disheveled attire. Their earlier fervor replaced with a look of disappointment and uncertainty.

The fitting room felt smaller, the weight of their unresolved desires pressing down on them. The thick scent of their mingled perfumes still lingered in the air, a poignant reminder of the passion they'd been indulging in just moments ago.

Mike's voice, tinged with excitement and a hint of vulnerability, piped through. "Hey, Donnie. I... I need to see you," Mike's voice quivered on the other end. It was evident he was grappling with something significant. "I just don't know where to turn."

There was a pause. Ronnie watched as Donnie's expression shifted from annoyance to surprise and then to gentle understanding. With a sigh of frustration, Donnie responded, "Alright, Mike. Just give me a moment."

Ronnie's eyebrows shot up in understanding, and they squeezed Donnie's hand, offering silent support.

As Donnie ended the call, they looked at Ronnie, the remnants of their intimate moment still evident on their flushed faces. "I'm sorry," Donnie began, "Mike's having a hard time. He's been... struggling with something personal."

Ronnie's heart went out to Mike, but they couldn't deny the surge of jealousy and disappointment. "It's alright," Ronnie replied, trying to sound understanding. "We all have our battles, don't we?"

The fitting room, once a sanctuary of passion, now stood as a reminder of their unresolved desires. Their interwoven fingers slowly untangled, and the distance between them grew, not just physically but emotionally as well.

"I should go," Donnie whispered, glancing at the door, then back at Ronnie. "But... this doesn't end here."

Ronnie, their face unreadable, simply nodded. "I understand."

Their hands brushed against each other's as they helped each other dress in the intimate fitting room, each going their separate ways but carrying with them the heavy weight of their shared encounter.

Donnie's steps down the hallway felt as heavy as the sighs that escaped Ronnie's lips, the air between them still crackling with the unfinished business of their desires. They had touched the very edges of forbidden, exploring the corridors of intimacy that led them to an unchartered territory. Now, with their political aspirations dangling by a gossamer thread, they found themselves at a crossroads of desire and duty.

Donnie's thoughts swirled around the 'what ifs' and 'could haves' as they made their way to Mike's apartment. Each step was a blend of contemplation and a pang of something they couldn't quite place—was it regret? Desire? Fear? Perhaps a cocktail of all.

Ronnie, on the other hand, sought refuge in the sanctuary of the quiet boutique, the soft hum of the outside world trickling in through the semi-open window. Their fingers grazed against the smooth fabric of the lingerie they had briefly worn, its touch igniting the memory of Donnie's fingers against their skin.

The reality of what had transpired in the fitting room started sinking in. Their clandestine encounter, charged with fervor and the spice of rebellion against the conventional, was a stark contrast to the world waiting outside for them. A world of campaign trails, sniping opponents, and the unyielding scrutiny of the public eye.

Donnie approached Mike's Metro Flat, their mind leaping between the faces of Mike, the ever-loyal aide, and Ronnie, the captivating enigma wrapped in elegance and fierce intellect. The juxtaposition of the future they had envisioned and the lure of the present was a relentless tug of-war in their soul.

Knocking at Mike's door, Donnie was greeted by Michelle. Donnie realizing the gravity of the situation reached their small orange hand out instinctively to cradle Michelle's cheek, an act that was tender and comforting amidst the tempest of emotions raging within. As they pulled

Michelle into a reassuring embrace in the doorway, Donnie's eyes lingered on the horizon, wondering where the tide of fate would lead next.

The uncertainty of what loomed ahead was a shroud of clouds threatening a storm. The intertwined destinies of Donnie and Ronnie, however, hinted at a rare silver lining amidst the impending tempest. The burgeoning feelings, now akin to delicate buds awaiting bloom, carried within them the promise of a beautiful yet unpredictable change.

Yet, with their hearts yearning for the touch of love and their minds tethered to the duty that called, the tenuous line between alliance and rivalry started blurring. The intimate moment they shared was now a secret that both bound and separated them, their silence speaking volumes in the deafening uproar of their political ambitions.

Both Donnie and Ronnie were now prisoners of the dance between their hearts and the call of responsibility. The stakes were high, and every move on the chessboard of politics and love threatened a checkmate that could spell doom or deliverance.

As Michelle and Donnie shared a quiet moment of understanding and camaraderie, across town, Ronnie stood alone in the hushed boutique, contemplating the tumultuous journey ahead. Their reflection stared back at them through the mirror, the glint of resolve in their eyes a testament to the battles to be fought and the love to be won or lost in the arena of life.

With the blanket of evening laying across the city we find Donnie and Michelle silhouetted against the dim hallway light, the uncertainty of tomorrow a looming shadow, yet the hint of a tender hope glimmering in the quiet understanding between them. And as the curtain of the night descended upon them, the questions hung in the air like stars, each twinkling with the mystery of what the morrow held for Donnie, Ronnie, and the world that beheld their dance of destiny.

Chapter 9: The Conqueror Unveiled

The Starlit Drag Lounge, tucked away in the heart of the city, was buzzing with life. An array of glitters sparkled through the dim, romantic ambiance of the lounge as the audience murmured with expectation. It was Saturday night—the night of unveiling, of uncloaking, of discovery. This was not just any night, this was the night Alexandria, unbeknownst to the audience, the Democratic front runner in the upcoming presidential election, was about to perform in her drag persona, Alex the Conqueror.

As the soft whispers of excitement settled among the crowd at the Starlit Drag Lounge, the ambiance intensified with every passing second. The velvet curtains on stage seemed to tremble with the tension in the air, like a pulse running through the entire room, waiting to unveil the night's spectacle. It was a realm where the boldness of politics harmonized with the rhythm of self-expression, where the drumbeats of courage were the unspoken soundtrack.

The lounge, bathed in the ethereal glow of spotlight, was waiting for a performance that was rumored to defy the norms and shatter the ceilings, not just glass ones, but those of prejudice and stereotypes. It was a mystical evening, where identities were both concealed and revealed, and where the ordinary and the extraordinary danced to the same tune.

Among the glitter and glam of the Starlit Drag Lounge stood Alexandria, a beacon of hope in a world clamoring for change, ready to transcend into her audacious alter ego, Alex the Conqueror. As a liberal presidential candidate, she was a storm in the political arena, but tonight, she was a tempest ready to take over the stage.

As the curtains began to part, the audience held its collective breath, their anticipation a tangible cloud in the room. The iconic theme from Scarface began to echo through the room, amplifying the mystical aura. Alexandria stood with her back to the audience, her silhouette a silhouette of defiance against the soft glow of the stage lights. Her heart pounded to the rhythm of the beats, each thump a promise of the revolution she carried in her spirit.

With the curtains whispered apart completely, the suspense in the room crescendoed. With the precision of a seasoned performer, she spun around to face the audience, grabbing a faux bulge in her pants. Her lips, painted a shade of courage, synced flawlessly to the immortal words, "Say hello to my little friend." It was not just a line; it was an invitation, a defiance, a proclamation.

And then, the storm broke. As the spicy tunes of '80s club music enveloped the room, Alexandria burst into a sensual upbeat dance performance. Her body moved with a grace that was both masculine and seductive, a dance of power and allure. Her portrayal of Tony Montana was not merely a portrayal, it was a reincarnation - a metamorphosis that blended the macho with the sensual.

The crowd was enchanted, the claps resonated with the beats, each movement of Alexandria was met with an uproar of appreciation. Each sway of her hips, each thrust, each stride she took across the stage was a step towards shattering the clichés, and her eyes sparkled with an unyielding spirit that demanded a space in a world often reluctant to yield.

Her outfit was an ode to the original, and yet it was redefined. The white suit clung to her, celebrating every curve and muscle, while the red inner shirt was less of a cloth and more of a fire that reflected the passion and the rage against the norms.

Alexandria was unapologetic, fierce, a dazzling spectacle of strength. She was every bit of Tony Montana's ruthlessness, blended with a tender touch of femininity that was unsettling and captivating all at once.

The ambiance in the Starlit Drag Lounge was electric, every heart was touched, every soul stirred, and as Alexandria struck a dramatic pose, the room erupted into cheers, whistles, and catcalls that seemed to shake the very foundations of conventionalism.

In the heart of the storm called applause, within the dim, inviting ambience of the Starlit Drag Lounge, where the neon lights played mischief with shadows, Ronnie found themselves swept into a whirlpool of revelation and awe. Nestled within the flamboyant persona of Ronnie Rebel, they remained discreet yet wasn't untouched by the fiery spirit that Alex the Conqueror exuded on stage.

As Alex strutted around the stage, every movement was a bold stroke of art, each step a daring stance against the conventional. The whiteness of her suit seemed to mock the grey of conformity, the red of her inner shirt blazing through like a heart that refused to bow down. Ronnie was finding it hard to look away, and harder to contain the drumming beat of their own heart. The conservative veil of Ronnie Rebel seemed too thin with each beat.

The sheer electricity of Alexandria's performance had transformed the atmosphere in the Starlit Drag Lounge into a realm of insatiable hunger for self-expression. In a cozy corner, draped in shadows, sat Ronnie, the conservative presidential candidate, disguised as their drag persona Ronnie Rebel. Their disguise was impeccable, an embodiment of elegance with a dash of irony, yet their eyes unveiled a whirlpool of complex emotions stirred by the spectacle that unfolded on stage.

As Alexandria twirled on her heels, a dramatic flair carrying the motion into the next beat of music, the room heaved with the rhythm. The rhythm echoed the hidden heartbeat of every lost, scorned, and hopeful soul in the room. Alexandria's Tony Montana was not just a character on stage; it was a poetic outburst against the shackles of societal norms.

She was a fearless conqueror, tearing through the expectations with a delicately aggressive grace. Ronnie, with each beat, each move Alexandria made, felt an awakening, a storm brewing within. They were not just watching a performance; they were witnessing a revolution. Every spin, every hip thrust was a statement, each one stronger than the last.

The white suit that clung to Alexandria's frame began to loosen, each button she undid revealed a bit more of the fiery red shirt underneath. It was as if Tony Montana and Alexandria were merging into one— the bold Cubano gangster and the fearless political maverick.

With a fierce swivel, Alexandria shed the white coat, her body shimmered under the spotlight, the faux muscular contours painted on her skin were nothing short of artistic perfection. The audience's breath hitched as she revealed a sequined thong speedo and pasties, the faux bulge a disco ball under the sequined speedo, but the masculinity it symbolized seemed to merge with her femininity, creating a cosmic entity of non-binary existence.

The glistening sheen of sweat on her brow, the fiery eyes that seemed to lock onto every soul in the room, each detail was a narrative of its own. Ronnie was breathless, the portrayal on stage shook the very core of their structured political beliefs.

As Alexandria reached the climax of her act, a faux line of white glitter, symbolizing Tony Montana's infamous cocaine indulgence, shot across the stage. The glittery mist descended upon the audience, and it felt like stardust, a dust that held the power to cleanse the set prejudices.

The realization was profound and terrifying. Ronnie's eyes widened. They could no longer hide from the reality that 'Alex the Conqueror' was indeed Alexandria, the liberal powerhouse.

Ronnie's mind raced as they tried to stitch together the tattered remains of their perception with this new profound understanding. The conservative cover around their being seemed to crack. Ronnie could no longer unsee the fearless leader in Alexandria, the unyielding resolve that was not just a show for political platforms, but a reflection of her very essence.

As they sat there amidst the roar of cheers and a spectacle of freedom and self-expression, the world as Ronnie knew it was shattering, making way for an enlightenment that was both liberating and terrifying.

The sparkling mist left by Alexandria's performance settled gently around the Starlit Drag Lounge, each particle catching the flickering lights, creating a nebula of hope, change, and dazzling courage. Ronnie's heart raced in a rhythm akin to the fierce beat that accompanied Alex's fiery routine. The tangible essence of acceptance hung in the air, a sharp contrast to the icy rigidity of their conservative beliefs. The metaphoric glitter in the act had not only dusted the audience but had reached the inner chambers of Ronnie's structured political haven.

Amidst the applause and clamor for encores, Alex jumped off the stage and danced through the audience, a whirlwind of audacious charm, collecting admiration not just in cheers but also in the bills that showered over her. The crowd reveled in the raw power and unapologetic authenticity that 'Alex the Conqueror' exhibited, igniting a fire of freedom, and the unyielding force of self-expression.

As Alex approached, Ronnie's breath hitched. The contradiction of the moment seized them, the sight of Alexandria, who seemingly conquered the demons of prejudice not just in others but momentarily in Ronnie too, sent shivers down their spine. The crowd seemed to part like the red sea as Alex twirled towards Ronnie, their eyes locking, forming a transient yet intimate connection amidst the loud yet supportive cheers. Alex's eyes sparkled with a sense of recognition as if she had been aware of Ronnie's secret persona all along. And then, with a playful wink, she was off to another corner, leaving Ronnie in a storm of unanticipated feelings and vexed thoughts.

The crowd's cheers seemed to fade into the background as Ronnie's contemplation took center stage in their mind. The glitter from Alex's act had settled deep within Ronnie's consciousness, urging them to peek beyond the iron curtains of their stringent beliefs. The crowd bellowed in unison, adulating Alexandria's audacity, Ronnie found themselves amidst a whirlpool of realization and bewilderment. The liberal firebrand onstage was none other than the eloquent, impassioned politician who could be spotted in serious debates on primetime TV.

The staunch contrast between the stern-faced Alexandria onscreen, berating conservative policies, and the electrifying Alex the Conqueror was a smack of cold reality on Ronnie's ideologically aligned face.

The seemingly endless distance between them, both politically and personally, had seemingly shrunk in the face of such a daring, genuine display. The spotlight on stage was not merely highlighting Alexandria's flamboyance, but also cast light on the grey areas of identity and expression, subjects Ronnie had often kept veiled behind a curtain of conservatism.

As Ronnie clutched the fabric of their disguised outfit, they could feel a sharp, almost painful jab of self-reflective awareness. The juxtaposition of their drag persona against their political stance seemed now a fallacy, almost farcical in front of Alexandria's audacious authenticity.

The room shook with the thunderous applause and shouts of encore but within the cacophony, Ronnie was plunged into a deafening silence. It was a silence that seemed to echo the candid reality of their existence, one that seemed to demand acknowledgment, acceptance, and a reevaluation.

The liberal vision, the break from stereotypes, and the bold smashing of gender norms had never been more vivid and challenging. And it was all carried in the physique and expressions of the person Ronnie was supposed to be vehemently opposed to.

As Alexandria took a bow and left the stage amid a rain of roses and cheers, Ronnie sat there, staring into the empty stage, the revelry around was a stark contrast to the storm brewing within. A storm that questioned the very core of their beliefs, one that carried the whispers of change, however inimical it may have appeared.

Ronnie's eyes trailed the path Alexandria took off stage, the heart raced, thumping against the chest with a rhythm of uncharted, terrifying yet tempting, thoughts.

The clinking of glasses and the distant chatter from other tables barely registered in Ronnie's mind as they continued to stare blankly at the now-empty stage. The bright, glittering spotlight, which once illuminated Alexandria's captivating performance, now seemed to spotlight Ronnie's inner turmoil. Alexandria had slipped backstage, but her presence was far from gone; she had left an indelible mark on Ronnie's consciousness.

Feeling a gentle tap on their shoulder, Ronnie turned to find Mike, eyes wide, leaning in. "Did you... did you know?" he whispered.

"About Alexandria?" Ronnie's voice wavered. "No. I had no idea."

Mike's eyebrows furrowed, "But... she's everything we stand against, politically. And now, this?" His voice trailed off, revealing his own internal struggle.

Ronnie's gaze returned to the stage, lips pursed. "It's not that simple, Mike. She's advocating for change, for acceptance. Maybe we've been too quick to judge."

As the evening wore on, the chasm between Ronnie's beliefs and newfound revelations seemed to widen. Returning to their suite at the *Gilded Gala Grand Hotel*, Ronnie paced, attempting to process the whirlwind of emotions. Political rivalry was one thing, but this was personal, vulnerable, and raw.

Ronnie's phone buzzed, interrupting the storm of thoughts. The screen lit up with a text from an unknown number: "Starlit Drag Lounge, backstage, in 10 minutes? - A."

Heart pounding, Ronnie quickly changed into their casual attire and headed towards the lounge. The neon lights outside flickered, signaling the lounge's transition into the late-night phase.

Inside, Ronnie was led backstage by a staff member. The dim room was filled with scattered sequins, feather boas, and the muted murmur of drag queens rehashing the night's performances. At the far end, bathed in the soft glow of a dressing room mirror, sat Alexandria.

She looked up, locking eyes with Ronnie. There was no trace of the brazen "Alex the Conqueror". Instead, before Ronnie was a woman, her makeup partially removed, revealing a face marked by determination and vulnerability.

The silence was palpable until Alexandria broke it, her voice softer than Ronnie had ever heard. "I didn't think you'd come."

"I had to," Ronnie replied, taking a hesitant step closer. "Your performance... it shook me."

A wry smile crossed Alexandria's lips. "I could tell. Look, Ronnie, I use drag as a medium to challenge norms, to convey a message. But tonight, it was also a message for you."

Ronnie swallowed, struggling to find words. "But, why me? We're opponents."

"Opponents, yes, but not enemies." Alexandria replied, leaning in. "And sometimes, to truly understand someone, you need to see all their layers."

Ronnie blinked, processing her words. The realization hit hard; they had been blinded by politics, missing out on the intricate tapestry of human experiences.

Over the next few hours, the two talked, laughed, and shared stories. They discussed their fears, hopes, and dreams for a better future. The line between political opponents blurred, and two individuals emerged, united by their passion for change and their shared experiences as drag performers.

As dawn approached, Alexandria stood up, extending a hand to Ronnie. "This isn't the end of our rivalry, but perhaps it's the beginning of a new understanding."

Ronnie took her hand, feeling the warmth and strength in her grip. "I'm willing to try if you are."

In the weeks that followed, the political scene was rife with whispers and speculations. Alexandria's drag persona was no longer a secret, and many criticized her for it. However, amidst all the noise, one thing was clear:

Alexandria's commitment to inclusivity and love remained unwavering.

And while Ronnie continued to be a political opponent, they were seen attending various LGBTQ+ events, sometimes even sharing a stage with Alexandria. The fierce debates remained, but they were now punctuated with moments of camaraderie and mutual respect.

The path ahead was uncertain, with the presidential race heating up. But for Alexandria and Ronnie, the revelation at the *Starlit Drag Lounge* had forever changed the trajectory of their relationship, allowing them to find common ground amidst their differences.

Chapter 10: Comic Confessions

Mike was feeling a confluence of emotions swirling through his soul like the autumn winds sweeping the city streets as he walked into the Tradition Towers Party Office. The perpetual hustle of the campaign staff was apparent in the buzz that filled the room. Flyers were being designed, speeches were being written, and strategies were being devised. It was a typical day at the campaign office, but not for Mike. He was still reeling from the conversation he had with Donnie over the phone, where he'd finally mustered the courage to talk about his true identity. It was a step, albeit a small one, toward embracing the side of him that was Michelle, his drag persona.

The clatter of keyboards and chatter of impassioned political discussions failed to distract him from his swirling thoughts. As he joined a group of campaign staffers huddled over a collection of data and electoral maps, the conversation shifted towards devising a more engaging campaign strategy to woo the conservative base.

Mike was feeling a confluence of emotions swirling through his soul like the autumn winds sweeping the city streets as he walked into the Tradition Towers Party Office. The perpetual hustle of the campaign staff was apparent in the buzz that filled the room. Flyers were being designed, speeches were being written, and strategies were being devised. It was a typical day at the campaign office, but not for Mike. He was still reeling from the conversation he had with Donnie over the phone, where he'd finally mustered the courage to talk about his true identity. It was a step, albeit a small one, toward embracing the side of him that was Michelle, his drag persona.

The clatter of keyboards and chatter of impassioned political discussions failed to distract him from his swirling thoughts. As he joined a group of campaign staffers huddled over a collection of data and electoral maps, the conversation shifted towards devising a more engaging campaign strategy to woo the conservative base.

Mike tried to focus on the tasks at hand. "So, we're zeroing in on family values, tradition, and economic stability, right?" he chimed in, attempting to blend his professional guise over his personal turmoil.

"Yes, and don't forget the attack ads on Alexandria's liberal extravaganzas," quipped a staffer, the satire in his voice not lost on Mike. But all he could think about was

Alexandria's advocacy for the LGBTQ+ community, something that touched a chord within him.

As the meeting progressed, the chuckles around him seemed to blur into the background. The humorous attempts of his colleagues to mimic the liberal opposition seemed shallow compared to the liberating laughter he experienced in the drag community. The irony of the situation wasn't lost on him – here he was, in the conservative heartland, closeting a part of his identity that was as vibrant as the red lipstick he donned as Michelle.

Mike found himself zoning in and out of the discussion, his mind wandering to the makeup palette that awaited him at his metro flat. The more he pondered, the more Michelle's voice seemed to muffle the words of Mike's colleagues. But he was jerked back to reality when someone mentioned Donnie's and Ronnie's upcoming campaign tour.

"We need them to exude the traditional values this nation stands for," emphasized the stern-faced campaign manager, Mrs. Hattie Harrow. The irony again wasn't lost on Mike. If only she knew the vivacious, and fabulous, drag queens both Donnie and Ronnie transformed into when the political suits came off.

He stared blankly at the electoral map, which seemed to now appear as a myriad of colors rather than just red and blue. It was as if each state was mocking him, urging him to break free from the chains of tradition, just as he did when he tucked away his conservative suit and embraced the flamboyant Michelle.

Mike sighed and excused himself from the meeting, citing a sudden migraine. As he stepped out into the crisp air, he wondered how much longer he could lead this dual life. With every passing day, the veil between Mike and Michelle was thinning, and it was only a matter of time before it would vanish completely.

He looked back at the Tradition Towers, an emblem of conservative values, its facade strong but its interiors unbeknownst to the variety that was an inherent part of its structure. Just like him. Just like Donnie and Ronnie. And just like the nation they were trying to represent.

His phone buzzed. It was a text from Donnie.

"Michelle, brace yourself. There's a wave coming, and it's glittered with change. Ready to ride it?"

Mike couldn't help but smile. For the first time in a long while, amid the exhaustive political campaign and his internal tumult, he felt a hint of exhilaration. He was on the cusp of merging two worlds that seemed parallel but were perhaps waiting for a confluence, much like the conservative ideologies and the vibrant LGBTQ+ representation vying for a space in the political tapestry of the country.

It was a profound moment of realization, nestled amid the comedy of politics and the satire of personal identities.

It had been a tense 15 minutes since Mike had walked into the room at Tradition Towers Party Office. The cold marble floors echoed each step, and the portraits of the party's past leaders cast judgmental gazes from their frames. The looming bronze chandelier overhead seemed to intensify the weight of the political agendas at play.

There they sat, the campaign's finest minds, eagerly dissecting strategies, enthusiastically ripping apart their opponents' tactics, and of course, indulging in the occasional political gossip.

"So, how do we combat these rumors? The ones about Donnie and Ronnie?" Janet, the campaign's chief strategist, asked, tapping her red nails against the tablet in front of her.

Mike gulped, anxiety creeping up his spine as he remembered Donnie's recent text. The room's humidity was suffocating, and he suddenly felt hyper-aware of the lacy, satin bralette teasing his skin underneath his stiff formal suit. He wished he had the confidence of Michelle, but he felt trapped in Mike's uncertainty.

In his nervousness and desperate need to be part of the conversation, he blurted out, "Well, we could always say they're regular performers at Starlit Drag Lounge, right? You know, do a mock show or something? Embrace the humor?"

There was a palpable moment of stillness, so profound that even the clock seemed to hold its tick. Mike could hear his own heartbeat reverberating in his ears as he mentally chastised himself. Did he just give away the biggest secret of their campaign?

Janet blinked twice, her red lips parting in confusion. "Did you just suggest that Donnie and Ronnie do drag? Seriously?"

The room plummeted into silence, a stunned pause hung in the air like a lead balloon. Eyes widened, faces turned towards Mike, whose face now mirrored the crimson decor of the room. Mike realized the gravity of the slip. His nervous fingers fiddled with the cufflinks, embossed with conservative emblems, which seemed to cling tighter around his wrists.

His anxiety sprinted through the pathways of his body, every nerve ending buzzing with self-conscious reality. The ivory satin lingerie embracing him beneath the cold formal facade of his suit felt more present than ever. Each thread of lace was an enticing caress against his skin, a delicate veil over the turbulent storm raging within. His penis, throbbing with each heartbeat against fabric, tucked snugly beneath a gaff was both his armor and vulnerability wrapped in the soft, satiny whispers of Michelle. His nipples, held tenderly by the lace, were throbbing with the pulsating reality of his dual existence. It was an intimate battle of bittersweet acceptance unfolding against the humorous ironies of his situation.

As his suit clung to his body, every nuanced embroidery of the lingerie seemed to mock the stiff exterior. Mike was a canvas of courage and fear, a comic tableau that begged to break free from the closeted chains of conservatism.

But then, the most unexpected thing happened.

Thomas, from the financial department, a stern man with round glasses, began to chuckle. "Oh, Mike," he laughed, wiping a tear from his eye, "You really are something! Donnie and Ronnie, doing drag? That's hilarious!"

Soon, the entire room broke into peals of laughter. Mike, trapped in the web of his own unintended comic relief, managed an awkward chuckle. He was no longer anxious about the revelation of their drag personas. Instead, he was mortified by the sheer ridiculousness of his blunder in their eyes.

Sarah, the social media head, laughed so hard she almost spilled her coffee. "Can you imagine Donnie in a glittering gown, singing 'I Will Survive'?"

Or Ronnie!" exclaimed Peter, the press head, holding his sides, "In a sequined bodysuit, doing the splits!" He made a show of attempting a split, and the room erupted in further laughter.

Mike was saved by the room's sheer inability to conceive such a reality. The thought was just too absurd, too outlandish. They didn't know how close to the truth they really were.

Mike's eyes caught the reflection of Michelle in the sheen of the long wooden table. Michelle, a whirlwind of colors, a hymn of freedom. With a sigh camouflaged in a nervous chuckle, Mike stared into the unknown unfolding narrative, with dreams and fears sewn into its fabric.

Unbeknownst to him, the journalist seated in the room was intrigued. A comical slip or a slip into the real comedy of their political campaign? Only time would reveal the layers of humor and honesty, wrapped in glitter and grace.

Dressed in a conservatively chic pinstripe suit and glasses that gave her an aura of 'just another staffer', Janette had been undercover for weeks, collecting tidbits for what she hoped would be the most explosive exposé of the decade. The potential headline flashed in her mind: "*Presidential Candidates by Day, Drag Queens by Night*!" She'd believed she had some decent material, but nothing like this golden nugget Mike just unwittingly handed her.

Janette's heart raced, but she feigned nonchalance. This was, after all, the skill of a great journalist. Becoming invisible in plain sight. Blending in. The perfect chameleon.

On the other side of the room, Mike, clueless of the journalistic predator in his midst, was still lost in thoughts of Michelle, with her cascade of colors and the freedom she represented. The drag performances were his escape, a secret life where he wasn't Mike, the conservative friend always making mistakes, but Michelle, who was bold and fierce.

Janette began to piece together the puzzle. She recalled seeing Donnie and Ronnie in the Luminous Lights Dressing Suite a week ago. She had assumed they were there for a campaign photo shoot. But now, a different picture emerged. The over-the-top accessories, the glittering outfits, it all made sense. They weren't preparing for a campaign shoot; they were prepping for a drag performance!

She remembered catching a snippet of conversation between Brock and Brandie at the Starlit Drag Lounge a few nights back. They'd been discussing the hottest drag performers, and Brandie, with that mischievous twinkle in his eye, had winked, "Wait till you see the *big* reveals at the next show." Could it be?

Janette jotted down points for her draft:

Candidates by day, drag queens by night?
The secret world of political drag - what the public doesn't see.
Michelle, Divine Donnie, Ronnie Rebel, and Alex the Conqueror - the faces behind the personas.

She mentally sifted through all her observations from the past weeks. The Diva's Den Costume Boutique visits by Mike, the hushed conversations at Alexandria's Advocacy Hub, the secretive late-night trips of Donnie and Ronnie to unknown venues.

She imagined the public reaction. A range of emotions, surely. Shock, disbelief, amusement, perhaps even admiration for these figures who showed a completely different side. In a world of divisive politics, the idea of candidates finding common ground, even if on a drag stage, was undeniably intriguing. It was the kind of juicy story that would make her career.

But as Janette visualized her piece, she felt a prick of conscience. Exposing this could potentially harm many involved, especially someone like Mike, who was still coming to terms with his identity. She remembered a poignant performance she had witnessed at the Heartfelt Haven

Theater. A drag queen, tears streaming down her face, had spoken about the struggles of acceptance, both self and societal.

Janette realized she was on the precipice of a moral dilemma. The exposé could be groundbreaking, sure, but at what cost? She knew she had the power to shape the narrative. The challenge was choosing which story to tell.

She glanced again at Mike, who looked like he was grappling with the weight of the world. The humor in this situation was evident, but beneath the comic veneer lay genuine human stories. Stories of struggle, acceptance, love, and freedom. The very things she had always wanted to bring to light.

Mike sensed Janette's curious eyes burning into him, the aftermath of his accidental revelation had left the room in a flurry of astonished giggles and murmur. In the labyrinth of conservative ethos where secrets were better shrouded under the guise of laughter, he realized the precarious precipice on which he now danced. The stern masks of political personas were threatening to crack, revealing the rainbow hues beneath.

Trying to clutch onto the shreds of composure, Mike wriggled out a deflection, "Oh, by 'dragging' I meant the relentless accusations liberals throw at Donnie and Ronnie, you know, claiming they are frequent at the Drag Race track! The cars, they say, are prettily decked out and have... uh, sexy, robust behinds!" He chuckled nervously, masking his turmoil in a veneer of humor.

The room burst into another bout of laughter, with a few staffers playfully miming steering wheels. Yet, the sharp ones, Janette included, saw the shaky veil of humor for what it was - a desperate cover-up. The air, once again, was a cocktail of chuckles and suspicion.

As the laughter echoed through the halls of Tradition Towers, its pristine walls that bore the legacy of conservative lineage seemed to quiver subtly, as if acknowledging the undercurrent of change. The veiled reality of political persona was getting a bit too tight for its bearers.

Amid the orchestrated attempts to steer the conversation back to the campaigning strategies, Janette took her leave. Her mind was a hive of buzzing thoughts. As she stepped out into the evening, the horizon was a kaleidoscope, blending the red of conservatism with shades of changes yet to unfold.

She was on the brink of a story that wasn't just about political masquerade but was a narrative intricately twined with genuine human stories. Stories that resonated with the struggle, acceptance, love, and freedom of being one's authentic self amidst a world clad in prejudiced expectations.

As she briskly walked toward her car, the idea of the exposé was forming a clear contour in her mind. This wasn't just about unmasking political personas; it was about unraveling the vibrant tapestry of lives that throbbed beneath the stern faces and crisp suits. Each step she took resonated with the rhythm of change that was inching closer, each heartbeat was a melody of anticipation for the love and acceptance that awaited the misunderstood souls.

Meanwhile, back at Tradition Towers, Mike was left in a whirlpool of contemplation. The subtleties of the evening were not lost on him. He realized that amidst the hard-lined political battles, there burgeoned tender romances and soft whisperings of acceptance.

He looked around at the room which was slowly emptying, the laughter now a distant echo. His gaze fell on the portrait of a past conservative leader, stern and unyielding. For a fleeting moment, Mike saw a reflection of his own fear in those cold eyes. But then, his thoughts drifted to Michelle, his vivacious drag persona who was yet to twirl her way into the daylight.

As Mike stepped out of the building, he hoped that the dawn of acceptance was not too far, not just for him but for the numerous others who dwelled in the shadows, yearning to step into the light without the fear of judgment.

Unbeknownst to him, Janette sat in her car, her fingers dancing on the keyboard, weaving the first strings of a narrative that held the promise of being not just a political exposé but a saga of love, acceptance, and the embracing of one's true colors, in the heart of a political whirlpool.

As the evening sun cast long shadows on the city, the golden hue seemed to whisper of a dawn where love, laughter, and acceptance would twirl around, unabashed and free, in the political corridors of Tradition Towers. And as Janette drove off into the setting sun, the sky seemed to hold a promise of a story that was yet to unveil its full spectrum.

Chapter 11: The Dark Horse

Alexandria's Advocacy Hub was a flurry of activity - ringing phones, impassioned conversations, and the rhythmic clack of keyboard keys echoing in the air. Campaign posters dotted the walls, with bright slogans of hope and change. Yet, amidst the buzzing ambiance, Alexandria stood frozen, her gaze glued to the television screen broadcasting *Primetime Politics Rumor Hour*.

"...and so, rumors are swirling around Washington," the host drawled, a malicious gleam in his eyes, "suggesting that Donnie and Ronnie have dabbled in the drag scene. Of course, there's no real evidence, just whispers and hearsay, all courtesy of Jannette's daring undercover expose."

A montage of poorly photoshopped images followed – Donnie's face superimposed on a drag queen, and Ronnie's visage on an exaggeratedly elegant diva. The whole thing was a caricature, a parody meant to mock and ridicule.

"Isn't it just like the conservatives to have secrets? Especially of the drag variety?" The co-host giggled, tossing her hair. "Imagine Donnie in a sequined gown or Ronnie with feather boas!"

Alexandria's fingers curled into fists. This wasn't the drag culture she knew and celebrated. Drag was a beautiful expression of oneself, not a punchline for a cheap laugh. She remembered the evenings she'd spent at the *Starlit Drag Lounge*, mesmerized by the powerful performances, the blend of satire and artistry. And now, the media was weaponizing it to score political points.

Leaning against her desk, surrounded by pictures of her drag persona, "Alex the Conqueror", Alexandria took a deep breath. The media's toxic portrayal of drag as a form of mockery had to be challenged.

The room seemed to have caught on to the spectacle on the screen; a few snickers escaped the volunteers as they carried on with their calls and data entry. Alexandria couldn't help but feel the boiling lava of frustration bubble up within her. This was exactly the narrative she fought against daily—taking something as empowering and liberating as drag, and turning it into a weapon of ridicule against those you disagree with.

But wasn't it more than that? It wasn't merely about political disagreement. It was about the pervasive, toxic, societal taboos strangulating the very essence of self-expression and identity. The media, an accomplice in preserving the antiquated notions of gender and propriety, was now toying with the idea of drag as though it was a clown's garb, donned for the amusement and scorn of the societal conformists.

Alexandria rose from her chair, her heart pounding against her chest like the beat of war drums. It was time. Time to confront the scoffing faces of conservatism, time to challenge the taboos that fettered the spirit of many, and time to unveil the truth that lay behind the veil of her public persona.

With a determined stride, she approached the room's centerpiece, a table surrounded by the minds and hearts that propelled her campaign. The chatter dimmed as all eyes turned towards her, the silence only punctuated by the distant chuckles emanating from the television.

"Team," she started, her voice steady, slicing through the tense air, "It's time we bring down the house of cards built on ignorance and prejudice. It's time the world saw the empowering spirit of drag through a lens uncolored by political biases or toxic masculinity."

Her eyes darted around the room through her office window, meeting the gazes of her teammates, each reflecting a blend of determination, trust, and the flicker of revolution. She knew she was not alone in this battle. And as she outlined her vision for the daring move ahead, she felt the shadows of taboo begin to quiver in the face of impending enlightenment.

She turned off the television, the screen going black, mirroring the ignorance that was soon to be replaced by the flamboyant colors of truth and acceptance.

Alexandria's heart raced as the echo of her heels clicked in the Advocacy Hub. She was about to lay bare a deeply personal facet of her life to her team. "Right," she muttered, invoking her inner romcom Bridget, "Just like discussing the merits of granny panties versus thongs. Except, you know, with potential national implications."

Assembled in the hub, the team exchanged curious glances, whispering amongst themselves. "What's this all about?" Laura, her communications expert and resident shopaholic, whispered to Jasper, their tech whiz.

Before anyone could further speculate, Alexandria, drawing a deep breath, began, "I think it's high time you all knew about a chapter in my life which, I believe, will reshape our campaign's narrative."

With the allure of a storyteller, Alexandria took them back to her days in the Bronx, drawing them into her world with a vivid tapestry of words. She painted scenes of her evenings bartending, recounting tales of beer spills, flirtatious advances, and karaoke mishaps that had the room in peals of laughter.

"But among the crowd, every Friday night," she continued, her voice lowering mysteriously, "was a group that transfixed me. Their flamboyance, their audacity... It was my introduction to the mesmerizing world of drag."

She described the electric atmosphere, the freedom in every exaggerated eyelash flutter, every dramatic lip sync. "It was there, amid the shimmer and the sass, I met Tiara Tensions," she recounted with a nostalgic smile, "a drag queen with the wit of Oscar Wilde and the wardrobe, let's just say, of someone experiencing an eternal wardrobe malfunction. Tiara took me under her wing—or, should I say, her extravagant feather boa?"

The room was spellbound, hanging on to her every word. With the intimacy Alexandria unveiled her transformation. "Tiara taught me the art of drag. The makeup, the outfits, the performances. But more than that, she taught me the courage to be unapologetically myself."

Taking a pause, Alexandria took a sip of water, her hand trembling slightly. "It was liberating. Amidst the glitter and the drama, I found...Alex the Conqueror." A collective gasp echoed in the room, as Alexandria displays a video of her as Patrick Swayze from 'Roadhouse' on the large TV on the wall.

Campaign members huddled close, their eyes glued to the television screen, taken aback by the Patrick Swayze-esque figure emanating a raw, primal energy.

As Alexandria's video portrayed her transformation into Alex, every step, every twirl, every beat echoed the spirit of defiance and liberation. Her dance at the Starlit Drag Lounge, where she, clad in a sleek dark suit, tousled hair, and those magnetic eyes, was nothing short of mesmerizing. The song "Feeling Good" took on a whole new meaning as Alex owned the stage. The camera captured audience reactions—awestruck, surprised, even a bit flustered.

Laura's eyes widened as she murmured, "Is this...at the Starlit Lounge? I've been there! How did I never hear about this?"

Jasper leaned in, eyes never leaving the screen, "Because, Laura, you were probably too busy enjoying a cocktail or two."

The room chuckled, the mood lightening momentarily.

Alexandria paused the video, a snapshot of Alex the Conqueror bathed in spotlight, the epitome of courage and authenticity. "Drag taught me more about leadership than any political boot camp ever did," she said, eyes intense yet soft. "It's about finding strength in vulnerability, voice in silence, and most importantly, showcasing authenticity amidst a sea of facades."

Jasper, ever the voice of reason, cautioned, "Alexandria, this is uncharted territory. It's brave, but risky."

Alexandria nodded, a determined glint in her eye. "Yes, Jasper. But great change never came from playing it safe."

Lulu, always Alexandria's fierce advocate, interjected passionately, "And this is exactly what we need. A jolt, a shakeup. We've been playing by the old rules for too long."

Jasper sighed, adjusting his glasses, "But the media? They're going to have a field day."

Alexandria's smile was enigmatic, "Let them. For all we know, there are more in those conservative halls who have secrets akin to mine."

Mike shifted uncomfortably, remembering his own hidden wardrobe at his Metro Flat.

Laura, ever the dreamer, spoke up, "This could be a game-changer, Alexandria. You're not just another candidate now. You're a symbol, a beacon."

Jasper, still skeptical, mused, "Or a target."

Alexandria met his gaze evenly. "Every pioneer is, Jasper. But isn't it worth it if it brings about real change?"

Lulu, always one for dramatics, declared, "To hell with the skeptics. Let's paint this town with sequins!"

Laughter bubbled up in the room. And as the team rallied around Alexandria, the message was clear. They were about to take on the political world, not with just speeches and campaigns, but with authenticity, glitter, and a touch of drag magic.

Jasper adjusted his tie and cleared his throat, bringing up the WebWonders Online Space platform on his tablet. "Alright, team, we're doing this. What do we want to say?"

Lulu, furiously typing on her laptop, piped up, "How about: 'From Congress to the Catwalk – Unveiling the Conqueror within. Make Acceptance Genuine Again!'?"

Laura grinned, "I love it. But add a dash of spice: 'From Congress to the Catwalk - Embracing my truth and baring my heart. #MAGA - Make Acceptance Genuine Again.'"

Alexandria chuckled, "I don't think Donnie will like we stole his message, this is why you handle our communications, Laura. Ready to post?"

Laura nodded, "Sending in three, two…" The room held its collective breath. "Posted!"

The room burst into applause, but the palpable tension remained. They all knew the power of the digital age – news spread fast, reactions even faster. As notifications began flooding in, Alexandria's phone buzzed with a call. She glanced at the caller ID and answered, "Brock? Hey!"

"Alexandria!" Brock's voice was filled with warmth, "Just saw your post. Bold move, but you've got this. Need me to handle a surprise performance at my next show to amplify the message?"

Alexandria laughed, touched by the offer, "Thanks, Brock. Let me get back to you on that."

As the evening turned to night, the Advocacy Hub was alive with activity. Screens displayed real-time reactions, stories, and restories. NewsWave Media Outlets had already picked up the story and was airing a special segment.

Lulu, pointing at the screen, said, "Look at this! We're trending!"

But not all reactions were supportive. Mixed in with the messages of love were those of skepticism and hate. Yet, amidst it all, the stolen MAGA message shone bright, challenging the status quo and urging acceptance.

Across town, Michelle, a.k.a Mike, sat in her plush Metro Flat. The room was dim, lit only by the soft glow of scented candles and the harsher light of her laptop screen. Logging onto WebWonders, her heart skipped a beat as she saw Alexandria's announcement.

She watched, mesmerized, as Alex the Conqueror took the stage. Each move, each note, resonated deeply with Michelle. As the video came to an end, a single tear of happiness, pride, and perhaps a touch of envy, trailed down her cheek. Michelle took a deep breath, whispering to herself, "Soon, my time will come too."

Meanwhile, the opulent bedroom of Donnie was a riot of satin and lace, reminiscent of the boudoir of a French courtesan, bathed in a soft, sultry glow. Donnie and Ronnie lay entangled in the sheets, the aftermath of their passionate embrace evident in the tousled sheets and discarded clothing.

Ronnie, looking more vulnerable than ever, rested their head on Donnie's chest, their fingers absentmindedly tracing patterns on Donnie's skin. The TV buzzed softly in the background, the late-night segment of NewsWave covering Alexandria's WebWonders post.

Donnie smirked, "She's got guts, I'll give her that."

Ronnie nodded slowly, "She's changed the game."

For a moment, the two lay in silence, absorbing the gravity of Alexandria's revelation. Donnie's voice, soft and contemplative, broke the silence, "You ever think about... coming out with our own personas? Showing the world who we really are?"

Ronnie sighed, "Every day. But the world... it's not ready."

Donnie chuckled, "Neither was it ready for Alexandria. Yet, look at her now."

Ronnie lifted their head, looking deep into Donnie's eyes. "Are you saying...?"

Donnie nodded, "Maybe it's time. But not now, not yet."

The two of them wrapped themselves tighter, finding comfort in each other's arms. The night outside deepened, but the room was filled with a warmth that went beyond mere physical intimacy.

As the sun began to rise, casting the world in a golden hue, it was clear. Change was in the air. The political landscape was shifting, and those at its helm were now faced with a choice. To embrace their true selves and lead with authenticity or to remain in the shadows, forever bound by society's constraints.

Chapter 12: Wardrobe Malfunction

The camera drones inside the Primetime Politics Studio hovered in mid-air, their red recording lights glowing, capturing every detail. Excitement was in the atmosphere, palpable, almost touchable. Donnie was ready to leave a mark, literally and figuratively, on the digital terrain of WebWonders Online Space.

Checking their reflection one last time, Donnie admired the crisp lines of their suit. They looked every bit the presidential candidate—polished, powerful, and with a touch of the unpredictable. If the audience thought they knew Donnie, tonight would be full of surprises.

Across the room, Ronnie looked a tad distracted. As Donnie entered their line of sight, Ronnie's gaze grew distant. Flashes of a clandestine rendezvous flickered in their mind: whispered secrets, the intoxicating scent of cologne and perfume mixed, the warmth of Donnie's embrace. The memories sent a rush of warmth to Ronnie's cheeks.

Both took the podium, trying hard to maintain an air of professional rivalry, but the charged glances they shared told a different tale.

As the debate intensified, there was an almost palpable charge in the atmosphere. Each word spoken, each argument made, was like a drop in a pressure cooker, making the room feel thick with suspense. The candidates, particularly Donnie, were deeply engrossed in their points, driving them home with every ounce of passion. The world watched on as the titans clashed on the primetime platform, everyone eagerly hanging onto every word, anticipating the next big headline to emerge.

In the midst of a heated exchange, Donnie's fervor reached a fevered pitch. They leaned forward, eyes blazing, fingers pointing emphatically as they zeroed in on a particularly passionate argument. "And this is exactly what I've been saying all along!" they exclaimed.

Suddenly, the unmistakable sound of fabric tearing pierced the room. Time seemed to slow down as everyone's attention diverted from the rhetoric to the very audible wardrobe mishap. The neat line of buttons on Donnie's crisply ironed white shirt gave way, one by one, as if they simply couldn't contain the intensity of the debate any longer. The audience gasped collectively, eyes widening.

Emerging from the gap created by the now-estranged buttons was a tantalizing hint of spicy red lace, contrasting starkly against the pristine white of the shirt. It was clear that underneath the professional facade of a tailored suit, Donnie had chosen an intimate attire that was anything but conservative.

The luxurious red lace lingerie delicately traced Donnie's form, the intricate patterns emphasizing their every curve. The soft, sultry glow from the stage lights shone on the lace, making it gleam and creating an almost ethereal effect. The fiery red hue hinted at a wild side, a contrast to the poise and polish that Donnie always displayed publicly. It was an intimate secret laid bare for all to see.

For a moment, the room was silent save for the nervous rustling of notes and a few suppressed chuckles. Donnie's face turned a shade that almost matched their lingerie, eyes darting to the now exposed lace. A mixture of embarrassment and arousal flitted across their features. There was an undeniable thrill, a frisson of excitement in being caught in such a compromising position. The vulnerability of the moment, combined with the weight of the world watching, created an intoxicating blend of emotions.

The subtle flush on Donnie's face, the quickened breath, and the slight quiver in their voice added layers to the situation. Every movement, every word now carried a sultrier undertone. There was an allure to this unexpected twist, a raw sensuality that added a layer of intrigue to an already tense atmosphere.

The room plunged into a stunned silence. Ronnie's face turned scarlet, memories of that recent secret affair flooding back: the lingerie had been their gift to Donnie after a particularly passionate evening.

The camera drones, ever vigilant, zoomed in on the spectacle. Millions watched, mouths agape. If they were aiming for audience engagement, they had hit the jackpot.

Clearing their throat with poise only Donnie could muster in such a situation, they remarked with a smirk, "I've always believed politics needs more transparency."

The audience erupted into nervous laughter. Donnie, always the performer, gave a playful wink to Ronnie, who was now trying to hide behind their debate notes.

Trying to redirect the attention, the moderator coughed and attempted to steer the conversation back to international policies. But there was no denying it. The debate had taken a turn, and the world would be talking about more than just politics tonight.

The buzz from the audience in the Primetime Politics Studio was already a cacophony, but in the digital terrain of WebWonders Online Space, a tsunami of reactions was building. In less time than it took Donnie to attempt a wardrobe recovery, clips and screenshots of their lingerie-reveal were everywhere.

"Holy lace, Batman!" wrote one netizen, posting a superzoomed clip of the malfunction.

Another wrote, "#TransparentPolitics is trending, but not how I expected."

And then there was, "Did anyone else see @DivineDonnie's nod to inclusivity under that suit? #LingerieForLiberty."

Amidst the uproar, the memes began. Donnie's image was superimposed on famous movie scenes: Donnie in that iconic Marilyn Monroe pose with the billowing skirt, Donnie on the Titanic deck, arms spread wide, lacy lingerie fluttering in the wind, and perhaps the most shared, Donnie reimagined as a Victoria's Secret Angel, complete with wings, strutting down a runway.

From his Metro Flat, Mike's eyes widened as he scrolled through WebWonders. Michelle Pensive, Mike's drag persona, whispered from the confines of the secret wardrobe, "Now that's a statement piece!" He quickly drafted a post, "Transparency at its finest! Maybe politics isn't all suits and ties after all. #LaceItUp."

Meanwhile, Alexandria, from her Advocacy Hub, eyes gleaming with mischief, couldn't resist commenting. "Whoever said politics was drab obviously hasn't seen tonight's debate. More power to @DivineDonnie for showcasing diversity in the best way possible! #NotAllHeroesWearCapesSomeWearLace."

The Starlit Drag Lounge was abuzz with activity. Dark Brandie, looking every bit the fierce drag queen with glittery lips and dramatic eyelashes, barely flinched. Taking a sip of their cocktail, they murmured to Brock, "Well, I did say politics needed a shake-up."

Brock chuckled, "This isn't a shake-up, Brandie. This is an earthquake!" He then clicked a few buttons on his holographic interface, ordering a spicy red lace lingerie set for himself. "If it's good enough for the debate stage, it's good enough for the Starlit Lounge," he winked.

The shockwave reached every corner of the online universe. Polls sprung up asking, "Would you vote for a President in lingerie?" Comedians were having a field day with lines like, "If this is the new conservative uniform, sign me up!" and "With that wardrobe malfunction, I can already see a boost in the polls, if you catch my drift."

But among the jokes, debates started to emerge, focusing not just on the lingerie but on what it represented. Many began praising Donnie for unintentionally showcasing vulnerability and authenticity, two words not typically associated with politics. Others argued it was unprofessional, a stain on the pristine image of politics. But, whether the comments were positive or negative, the consensus was clear: everyone was talking about Donnie.

Onlookers could only imagine the heated discussions taking place behind the closed doors of Tradition Towers Party Office. Would this be seen as a scandal, or could it, perhaps, be turned into the biggest campaign win of the century?

The digital frenzy showed no sign of slowing down. If anything, it was clear that this would be one of those iconic political moments that would be remembered, debated, and laughed about for years to come.

As Donnie left the Primetime Politics Studio, their phone overflowing with notifications, they couldn't help but smile. They always had a flair for the dramatic, but tonight? Tonight was in a league of its own.

From the NewsWave Media Outlets to tiny start-up podcasts, Donnie's surprise reveal became the main discussion point. Every news anchor, journalist, and influencer were clamoring for a comment, a statement, or even just a nod from Donnie. The intrigue was far from the expected embarrassment – in fact, it was fast turning into a movement.

Scrolling through WebWonders Online Space, one would come across a plethora of comments, mostly laughing emojis and cheeky gifs. A popular meme showed the iconic shot of Donnie with the caption: "When you've got a debate at 8 but a drag show at 9." But within the jokes and banter, a peculiar trend was emerging. The spicy red lingerie, the accidental centerpiece of the debate, was now a hot topic of its own.

At Mike's Metro Flat, Mike sat hunched over his laptop, eyes darting between news articles and the soaring stocks of 'Red Embrace', the now-famous lingerie brand Donnie had unintentionally endorsed. "Michelle would totally rock that!" Mike whispered to himself, already contemplating a quick online purchase. And he wasn't alone. The 'Red Embrace' website was overwhelmed with traffic, prompting them to post: "Thank you for your... support?" followed by a wink emoji.

On a talk show at Primetime Politics Studio, a panel of conservative men surprisingly lauded Donnie's audaciousness. One elderly gentleman, Carl Tuckerson, in his crisp blue suit, said, "In all my years, I never thought I'd say this, but where can I get one of those?" The audience roared with laughter, but there was an undeniable hint of genuine curiosity.

Donnie, always quick to pivot and adapt, sensed the momentum and made a strategic choice. In a bold move, they officially endorsed 'Red Embrace'. Their campaign ad, set against the backdrop of Transparency Terrace, featured them, confidently wearing the lingerie beneath a semi-transparent shirt, with a voiceover: "For those who dare to be different, who embrace every facet of themselves, and who know that strength isn't just about force but about being true to oneself." It was a masterful blend of humor, vulnerability, and empowerment.

The message was clear: Donnie was capitalizing on the moment, emphasizing their commitment to personal expression and inclusivity within the conservative movement. The ad was risky, cheeky, and undeniably in line with their charismatic, flamboyant personality.

Over at the Starlit Drag Lounge, the venue was abuzz with excited chatter. The drag community, initially wary of Donnie's political leanings, found themselves grappling with this unexpected curveball. Dark Brandie, sipping on a neon-green cocktail, muttered, "Who would've thought, the world would've found out this way?" Brock, always the voice of reason, responded, "You know, it's not about the lingerie. It's about the audacity to stand up and own it. That's worth something."

And then there was the economic impact. With 'Red Embrace' sales skyrocketing, other brands were quick to jump on the bandwagon. An eco-friendly lingerie line was quickly launched by an entrepreneurial young designer, using sustainable materials and championing body positivity. "If Donnie can, why can't we?" became the rallying cry.

However, not everyone was amused or supportive. In the conservative Tradition Towers Party Office, debates raged on how to handle this unexpected twist. While many saw it as an opportunity to connect with younger, more progressive voters, others viewed it as a deviation from traditional values.

Alexandria, always with a finger on the pulse of public opinion, watched the developments closely. In her Advocacy Hub, she pondered over her next move. She admired Donnie's ability to turn the situation around, but was also wary of the political implications. With a smirk, she mused, "Maybe it's time Alex the Conqueror brings out his own line of boxer briefs."

What had started as a simple wardrobe malfunction had morphed into something bigger – a conversation about self-expression, authenticity, and the changing face of conservatism. And in the middle of it all was Donnie, turning a potential scandal into a memorable campaign highlight, proving once again that in politics, as in fashion, it's all about how you wear it.

The glittering crystal chandeliers of the Victory Vanguard Press Hall illuminated the gathered press corps, creating pools of light amidst the velvet curtains. The media was buzzing with whispers, ready to pounce on the next big scoop. All eyes were fixed on the elaborately carved wooden podium, which bore the seal of the Donnie Campaign.

Donnie strutted up to the podium, adjusting their red tie, their stance exuding confidence. They knew the power of turning a mistake into a show, and if there was anything they'd learned from their drag performances, it was the importance of timing.

"Good evening, everyone! Let's address the... lacy elephant in the room, shall we?" Donnie winked, drawing a round of chuckles from the audience.

"You know, when I got dressed for that debate, I never imagined my choice of lingerie would become such a sensation. But hey, it's 2023, and in politics, just like in fashion, it's not just what you wear, but how you wear it!"

A reporter from NewsWave shot up her hand, "Donnie, some say that this 'malfunction' was just a publicity stunt. Any comments?"

Donnie smirked, "Darling, if I wanted to do a publicity stunt, I'd parachute into this press hall wearing a sequined jumpsuit, not show a hint of lace."

The room erupted in laughter.

"But seriously," Donnie continued, "this incident is more than just about my fashion choices. It's about self-expression, embracing our unique selves, and allowing everyone the freedom to be who they truly are, whether you're wearing a three-piece suit or spicy red lingerie."

A loud applause filled the room, showcasing a rare moment when both liberals and conservatives were united in their appreciation.

"I've always believed in acceptance and diversity. If my...unexpected reveal does one thing, let it be a reminder that everyone should feel free to express themselves, without judgment."

With those words, the press conference came to a close, but not before Donnie took a playful bow, complete with a cheeky "jazz hands" gesture.

The online world went abuzz. Donnie's approval ratings, contrary to what many expected, soared among their conservative base. Their authenticity and ability to handle a situation, no matter how unexpected, with humor and grace made them an endearing figure even amongst the skeptics. Memes with "Embrace the Lace" flooded WebWonders, and the world, for a brief moment, celebrated unity in diversity.

Later that evening, With the day's duties done, Donnie made their way to their penthouse in the towering building they owned downtown. Their fingers drummed against the elevator button, the anticipation of solitude a welcoming thought. As the doors slid open to their lavish penthouse, a familiar tune played softly in the background.

Donnie stepped out of the elevator, feeling the weight of a particularly taxing day melt away as the private entrance to their Penthouse slowly swung open. The apartment, situated in one of the most sought-after locations in the city, boasted of unparalleled luxury. However, its decadence paled in comparison to the vista that greeted Donnie tonight.

Their eyes were instantly drawn to the floor-to-ceiling windows, which presented an almost surreal view of the city. The urban horizon, a sea of twinkling lights, shimmered against the night sky, casting reflections that danced upon the polished marble floor of the living room. The dark silhouette of distant skyscrapers added depth to the canvas, with each illuminated window telling a thousand stories.

Yet, even with this spectacle, Donnie's attention was quickly stolen. Positioned against this breathtaking backdrop was Ronnie, who seemed to blend sensuality with innocence. The playful glint in their eyes, as if harboring a delicious secret, was disarmingly captivating. Donnie's gaze roamed over Ronnie's form, taking in every detail. The lingerie, which had recently caused such a stir in fashion circles, clung to Ronnie's form, accentuating their curves and valleys with tantalizing allure. The deep color of the fabric contrasted perfectly with their skin, making it all the more enticing.

The slow, deliberate way Ronnie's fingers glided over their manhood, a dance of invitation and tease, sent a bolt of electricity straight through Donnie. The blend of vulnerability and audacity in the gesture was enough to fan the flames of Donnie's already racing heart. The dim lighting of the penthouse, combined with the soft strains of a haunting melody, created an ambiance that was both intimate and charged with anticipation.

"Thought I'd give these a try," Ronnie's voice was a seductive purr, dripping with mischief, as they stretched languidly on the plush rug, highlighting the sensuous expanse of their exposed skin. "Whatcha think, Donnie?"

Donnie swallowed hard, the lump in their throat making it difficult to find words. The mere sight of Ronnie, combined with the charged atmosphere, made them feel like they were walking in a dream.

"I think," Donnie finally replied, voice husky with arousal, "that you've outdone every view this city has to offer."

Donnie, growing flush, whispered "You're... you're so yuge, Ronnie?"

Ronnie, draped in the now-infamous spicy red laced lingerie, grinned cheekily. "Well, I thought, why not have some fun? Embrace the lace, right?"

Donnie, always one for the dramatic, dramatically clutched their chest. "My, my, Ronnie Rebel! I never took you for the mischievous type."

The atmosphere in the room was electric, the chemistry palpable. The world outside might have been in chaos, but inside the Penthouse, there was only Donnie and Ronnie.

Donnie slowly began the tantalizing process of shedding the corporate armor. The deliberate pace at which each button was undone, revealing hints of the robust ocher tanned body underneath, created a slow burn of anticipation in Ronnie. Donnie's words, laden with an allure that was hard to resist, brought to the surface a tension that had always simmered between them but had never been addressed.

"Is that so?" Ronnie's voice held a challenge, eyes brimming with a mix of mischief and yearning, yet beneath the teasing veneer, there was genuine curiosity.

Their lips were close, so close that their breaths tangled together, adding another layer of intensity to the already electric atmosphere. When their lips finally met, it was like two stars colliding. The initial hesitance gave way to a maelstrom of emotions. They conveyed stories of longing, of moments when their gazes had lingered a second too long, of stolen glances in crowded rooms.

Every touch and caress became a revelation. The rhythm of their heartbeats, though frantic, seemed to synchronize perfectly, mirroring their internal dance of desires. The exploration wasn't just about physical proximity; it was a journey through a landscape of vulnerabilities, understanding, and shared experiences.

When they finally parted, the lingering sensation of their lips remained, an unspoken promise of things yet to come. Donnie's fingers, strong yet gentle, traced Ronnie's jawline, grounding them both amidst the whirlwind of emotions.

Ronnie's playful smirk and the teasing glint in their eyes offered a momentary respite. Their words, while light-hearted, carried the weight of truth. Life, in all its unpredictability, had brought them together in a manner neither had expected. Their reunion was intense, passionate, and fiercely personal.

With barely a pause, the ambiance of the room took another dramatic turn. Donnie's whispered proposition was not just about the act but the depth of trust and the willingness to be vulnerable. As Ronnie was gently maneuvered to face away, there was a clear sense of anticipation, of a boundary about to be crossed.

Initially, the cool touch of the leather acted as a brief respite from their burning desires. But as Ronnie's skin connected with the sofa, it seemed as though the leather absorbed their fervor, responding to their heat. This sensation was only magnified by the warmth emanating from Donnie, a tangible heat that promised both pleasure and solace.

The world beyond their sanctuary seemed to recede into the background, their surroundings blurring, leaving only the sensation of Donnie's body, the strong hands that firmly yet gently gripped Ronnie's hips, the heady feeling of Donnie's breath teasing the nape of Ronnie's neck.

A tactile dance of fingers sliding the red lacy g-string aside seemed to shift the atmosphere from merely heated to absolutely scorching. Donnie's fingers trailed a fiery path up Ronnie's spine, causing a cascade of shivers and a heady anticipation of what was to come. Every brush of skin, every suppressed groan, heightened their awareness of each other. Donnie's engorged manhood, a symbol of raw masculine desire, pressed insistently against Ronnie's entrance, sending waves of anticipation cascading through them both. Ronnie's gasped whimper, a sound filled with vulnerability and longing, seemed to echo in the silence of the room.

The initial penetration was a symphony of sensation – a mixture of pain, pleasure, and overwhelming intimacy. Donnie, ever the expert, moved with both purpose and tenderness, ensuring Ronnie's comfort while pursuing their shared ecstasy. Their rhythm was like a dance; each thrust and retreat was a step, perfectly in tune with the other's desires.

The room, with its luxurious décor and towering windows revealing the city beyond, felt both vast and intensely intimate. Gliding in and out as if a piston moving with the explosion of passion. The plush couch, once just a decorative piece, was now the altar of their passion, a place where masks fell away and only raw, unbridled emotion remained.

Their journey was not just physical but emotional. Hands that had once penned speeches and shaped policies now roamed without inhibition, exploring the soft valleys and firm planes of one another's bodies. Mouths that had once spoken only in carefully measured tones now tasted and teased, savoring the unique flavor of the other.

The culmination of their shared passion was powerful, a crescendo of sensation that seemed to envelop them both. As Donnie's climax approached, there was a synchronicity in their movements, a shared rhythm that spoke of deep connection. And when the moment arrived, when Donnie erupted inside Ronnie, it was as if the very universe had shifted, realigning just for them. Exhausted, sated, and filled with a post-coital glow, Donnie collapsed onto Ronnie's back, their breathing heavy and ragged, their body awash with the bliss of their shared experience.

The powerful climax had come with the force of a tidal wave, a cataclysm of sensation that left Donnie spent, drowning in the euphoria of the moment. With every breath he took, their chest heaved against Ronnie's back, their heartbeats in a synchronized rhythm that mirrored the intimate dance they had just performed. The warmth that spread through them felt like the afterglow of a setting sun, bathing them both in its residual heat.

Drawing on a reservoir of energy, Donnie gently rolled Ronnie onto their back. The electricity that zapped between them was palpable. Donnie, in his post-orgasmic haze, was not satiated. His eyes, glazed with desire, focused intently on Ronnie, intent on returning the pleasure he had just been granted.

Ronnie's chest, slick with the sheen of their exertions, rose and fell rapidly. But even in this frenzied state, the sensation of Donnie's lips on their nipples sent shockwaves through Ronnie's system, drawing a sharp intake of breath. Donnie, always attentive, teased and tasted, his tongue drawing intricate patterns that sent jolts of pleasure radiating from every point of contact.

With a hunger that seemed to grow with every passing second, Donnie traveled further south, intent on discovering all the hidden treasures that Ronnie had to offer. The term "hotdog flavored water" was a playful euphemism for the unique blend of taste and scent that was distinctly Ronnie's, and Donnie reveled in it. The sensation of Ronnie reciprocating with equal fervor was intoxicating, a dance of tongues, lips, and hands that knew no bounds.

Their symphony of moans, gasps, and whispers filled the room, a testament to the profound connection that was blossoming between them. Every touch, every kiss, was a promise, an affirmation of the intimacy they shared.

The luxurious penthouse offered many a setting for their amorous activities, but none quite like the balcony. The sprawling view of the city below and the vast expanse of the night sky above made it a setting worthy of their next escapade. As Donnie positioned Ronnie against the balcony railing, the cool metal contrasting with their heated skin, the atmosphere became thick with anticipation.

With care and precision, Donnie nudged Ronnie forward, ensuring that they were both comfortable and secure. The night sky, in all its magnificence, bore witness to their love. The stars seemed to twinkle a tad brighter, as if giving their silent approval to the act that was about to commence.

With a deliberate slowness, a counter to the earlier urgency, Donnie entered Ronnie. The sensation was familiar yet new, a mix of tight warmth and welcoming pleasure that seemed to pull them both into its embrace. Their rhythm, a reflection of their shared emotions, started slowly but gained momentum, a beautiful dance that blended love, lust, and passion.

The city soundscape, usually so prominent, faded into the background, replaced by the sounds of their pleasure. The crescendo, when it came, was even more powerful than before. Their bodies moved as one, each thrust, each moan building to a climax that seemed to shake the very foundations of the building. And as they both erupted, their cries of pleasure melding into one harmonious note, they knew that this was a connection that went beyond the physical. It was emotional, spiritual, and completely and utterly transformative.

With heavy breaths and hearts still racing, they collapsed into each other's arms, the cool floor of the balcony grounding them once more. Wrapped in an embrace, they gazed up at the night sky, the stars seeming to shine even brighter in acknowledgment of their shared passion. The weight of the world, the politics, and the public's scrutiny seemed miles away.

With the cityscape as their backdrop, they continued to explore, reaffirming their bond with every touch and caress. Each whispered confession, every shared secret only solidified the bond growing between them. Their world had shrunk to this moment, this place, and the undeniable connection they shared.

Hours passed, but time seemed irrelevant. The ebb and flow of their passion continued, mirroring the rhythm of the city below. As the first light of dawn began to creep across the horizon, they found themselves wrapped up in each other once more, their bodies and souls satiated yet yearning for more.

And as dawn began to paint the horizon with hues of pink and gold, Donnie and Ronnie lay wrapped in each other's arms, the trials and tribulations of their public personas momentarily forgotten. All that remained was the warmth of their embrace and the promise of more nights filled with raw passion and intimate discoveries.

The intimacy of the moment was punctuated by whispered confessions, promises, and plans for the future. Their connection, forged in the heat of passion, had deepened into something more profound, something that transcended the physical realm.

Because, as they had both come to realize, it wasn't the shared spotlight or the political rivalries that mattered most. It was the moments of vulnerability, the sweet surrender, and the chance to be one's authentic self in the presence of another.

And as the first rays of the sun streamed through the penthouse windows, two hearts, previously guarded and wary, began to beat in harmony, signaling the beginning of a love story that would transcend boundaries and redefine passion.

Chapter 13: Of Secrets and Strategies

In the grandiose Council Chambers of Campaigning, where the weighty air of politics lingered like the musk of old books, a somewhat less official negotiation was taking place. Cloakrooms had always served as mini escape rooms from the prying eyes and ears of the public. In these cozy confines, many a politician had exchanged secrets, whispered promises, and even stolen glances. Today was no exception.

"Donnie," Ronnie hissed, attempting to whisper but failing to modulate the passionate conviction of their voice. "With Alexandria gathering numbers, we need to align our strategies. If the conservatives are going to win the support of America, we need to be on the same page, we need to align our stance."

Donnie, never one to pass an opportunity for mischief, raised an eyebrow, "Oh, align, you say? Like align...closely?"

Ronnie rolled their eyes. "This isn't the time for your theatrics. We have serious things to discuss."

But as Ronnie gesticulated passionately, outlining their vision for a conservative future, Donnie took a moment to admire them. There was something incredibly enticing about Ronnie's commitment, the way their fingers animatedly sketched ideas in the air. And as fate would have it, Donnie's hand "accidentally" brushed against Ronnie's.

It was a brief touch, lasting mere milliseconds, but it felt like a jolt of electricity. A tiny spark, enough to make one wonder about the potential inferno it could ignite. The two pulled away swiftly, attempting to mask the shock in their eyes with feigned casualness.

Donnie smirked, the corners of their mouth twitching with amusement, "Sorry about that. Just reaching for my notes."

Ronnie blinked, trying and failing to suppress the blush that painted their cheeks a delicate shade of pink. "Maybe you should reach a little more carefully next time."

But the moment was undeniably loaded. The palpable tension in the room could've been cut with a knife. In the grand setting of the Council Chambers, amidst the history of political machinations and power struggles, here were two figures caught in their own web of attraction. And try as they might, escaping it wasn't an option.

Drawing a deep breath, Ronnie decided to address the elephant in the room. "Look, Donnie, I know there's...something between us. But we can't let that get in the way of our campaigns, of our message. We owe it to our supporters."

Donnie leaned in, their voice dropping an octave, giving it a husky, intimate quality. "I know, Ronnie. But life's full of unexpected moments. Like wardrobe malfunctions, or accidentally brushing hands in a cloakroom. And sometimes, you just have to roll with them."

Ronnie's eyes widened, absorbing the weight of Donnie's words. A fleeting memory of the recent "wardrobe incident" brought a wry smile to their lips. The thought of them laughing together over spilled coffee and red laced lingerie during that media storm made Ronnie's heart warm.

Ronnie leaned in, their voice barely above a whisper, "We're playing with fire here, Donnie. Are you ready for the consequences?"

Donnie's lips quirked into a sly smile, "Always. But for now, let's get back to aligning our strategies."

The silence in the cloakroom was thick enough to cut with a knife, with only the soft hum of the Council Chambers' central cooling system purring in the distance. As Ronnie leaned away, they gave Donnie a look that managed to be both reproachful and longing. Donnie's smile, sly and magnetic, threatened to break the intensity. But they both had a purpose there—though not an entirely professional one—and they both knew it.

The cloakroom's soft illumination framed the contours of Donnie and Ronnie, casting shadows that danced to the rhythm of their conversation. With the remnants of their momentary intimacy lingering in the air, they attempted to steer the conversation back into the less treacherous waters of politics.

Donnie, twirling a shiny lapel pin between their fingers, suddenly became pensive. "You know, Ronnie, this MAGA message, *Make Acceptance Genuine Again*, I didn't just coin it to create another catchy political slogan. It's personal."

Ronnie, adjusting their glasses, looked quizzically at Donnie. "Go on."

Taking a deep breath, Donnie plunged into a memory. "Back when I was still finding my footing as Divine Donnie, I'd often find myself at the Starlit Drag Lounge. The camaraderie there, the way people accepted each other, flaws and all... it was the kind of America I wished to see."

Ronnie shifted, inching closer to Donnie. "So, you're saying the MAGA message is, in essence, a call for the nation to be more like a drag lounge?"

Donnie chuckled at the unexpected humor. "In a way, yes! A place where acceptance isn't just a word, but a lived experience. With all these divisive politics, isn't it time we reminded people of the importance of genuine acceptance? If we, as political opponents, can find a middle ground, surely our nation can too."

Ronnie leaned in, eyes softening. "I never knew this side of you, Donnie. It's strange, isn't it? We've been opponents for so long, but it's only now that I'm seeing the real you. And not just the charismatic, flamboyant Donnie, but the one with depth and conviction."

The raw honesty of the moment made Donnie's heart race. "I never thought a strategy meeting would turn into a heart-to-heart," they murmured, a hint of mischief in their eyes.

Ronnie smirked, "Well, it's not every day your competitor opens up about their dreams of turning the country into a giant drag lounge."

Both shared a chuckle, the weight of their political roles momentarily forgotten.

Suddenly, Ronnie, always the cerebral one, returned to the crux of their meet. "This message, Donnie. It has the potential to resonate. It transcends politics. But how do we ensure it isn't lost in the cacophony of campaign trails and mudslinging?"

Donnie's eyes sparkled. "We show them. Show them the authenticity behind it. How about a collaborative event? Where our drag personas take the stage, not as competitors, but as united voices for acceptance. Imagine the headlines: *'Presidential Candidates Unite for Acceptance!'*"

Ronnie's lips twitched into a grin. "You and your theatrical solutions. But, it's crazy enough to work. And maybe, just maybe, it would give our secret relationship some breathing room, under the guise of campaign collaboration."

"Two birds, one fabulous stone," Donnie winked.

As their discussion intensified, Donnie's leg brushed against Ronnie's, and then, with a daring audacity that only Donnie possessed, their fingers slid along the inner contours of Ronnie's thigh.

Ronnie tried to maintain focus on the campaign strategy laid out before them. Each graph, statistic, and projection on the table seemed to blur as the heat from Donnie's touch registered. It was a move so calculated, so risky, it was classic Donnie.

For Ronnie, the surprise wasn't the audacious gesture—it was their own reaction to it. A gasp escaped their lips, louder than intended. The room's temperature seemed to climb several degrees. Their heart rate spiked, and a fierce blush painted their cheeks.

Donnie leaned in, voice husky, and whispered, "Problem, Ronnie? Can't handle a bit of campaign pressure?"

Ronnie shot them a glare that was meant to be scathing but was instead playfully indignant. "You are, without a doubt, the most incorrigible candidate I've ever met."

But before Donnie could retort with another cheeky response, a staffer—unaware of the charged atmosphere—chose that moment to pop their head in. "Five minutes until the press conference. Need you both out there."

Ronnie, ever the professional, straightened up immediately, trying to regain some semblance of composure. Donnie, on the other hand, relished the moment, smirking at the obvious effect their little game had on Ronnie.

Outside the Council Chambers, as they prepared for the press conference, the weight of their secret relationship pressed on Ronnie's mind.

"Donnie," they murmured, pulling them aside. "Have you ever thought about... I don't know, leaving all this behind?"

Donnie's eyebrow quirked in surprise. "The campaign?"

"No," Ronnie replied, voice barely above a whisper, looking anywhere but into Donnie's piercing eyes. "Politics in general. Imagine a world where we don't have to hide or play these games."

Donnie's gaze softened. "Run away together, you mean?"

Ronnie nodded. "Somewhere where MAGA stands for 'Maybe A Great Adventure' for just the two of us."

Donnie laughed, the rich sound echoing in the hushed hallway. "You, Ronnie Rebel, the embodiment of elegance and irony, suggesting we elope? Now, that's a headline I'd love to see."

Ronnie playfully swatted at them. "It was just a thought. But think about it— I know an countryside inn near upstate

New York, or a condo in south beach Florida. Away from the flashing lights and the incessant questioning."

Donnie sighed, pulling Ronnie into a brief, tender embrace. "It's tempting, but we both know our duty. For now, we play the game. But who knows what the future holds?"

Ronnie felt the weight of Donnie's gaze, the burning intensity that had nothing to do with politics and everything to do with the passion that simmered between them. Their conversations often treaded on the knife-edge of professionalism and personal desires, a balancing act that they both had become quite adept at.

"I think...," Ronnie began, trying to recalibrate the conversation back to the realms of politics. But the fluster was evident. "I think we should seriously consider this alliance. For the campaign, of course."

Donnie chuckled, a rich, low sound that sent shivers down Ronnie's spine. "Of course. Just the campaign," they teased, leaning closer, allowing the scent of their cologne to waft over Ronnie, causing an unmistakable reaction.

Ronnie coughed, attempting to mask their growing discomfort. "Absolutely. We need to remain focused. Eyes on the prize, right?"

"But what if there are two prizes?" Donnie whispered; their lips so close to Ronnie's ear that the slight puff of their breath caused Ronnie to involuntarily shiver.

This intimate dance was interrupted by a sudden knock. The door opened to reveal Mike, a bemused expression on his face as he tried to read the atmosphere. "Did I interrupt something?"

The comic timing was impeccable, relieving the tension in the room.

Donnie pulled back with a theatrical sigh, "Mike, always with the impeccable timing." They shot Ronnie a playful wink, "But, sometimes, the show must go on."

Ronnie cleared their throat, straightening up. "Right. The show. The campaign. The alliance." They desperately tried to get back on track, but their voice lacked the earlier conviction.

Mike, still oblivious, nodded. "Exactly! This campaign is going to be revolutionary!" He paused, looking between them. "You two are alright, right?"

Donnie laughed, "Oh, we're more than alright. Right, Ronnie?"

Ronnie nodded, the corners of their lips quirking into a smile, "Absolutely."

The trio continued discussing the intricacies of their campaign, but the undercurrents of passion, the silent understanding that had formed between Ronnie and Donnie, was palpable. With every stolen glance, every soft chuckle, the bond deepened.

As the day drew to a close, Ronnie found themselves at the Gilded Gala Grand Hotel, their thoughts consumed by Donnie. The promise of the day, the thrilling flirtation, the searing intensity of their interactions – it was all too much.

There was a sudden knock, pulling Ronnie from their reverie. Opening the door, they were met with Donnie's smoldering gaze. Without a word, they stepped inside, the door closing behind them with a soft click.

The room, bathed in the soft glow of the evening lights, seemed to shimmer with promise. Donnie, always the assertive one, stepped closer, their voice a low whisper, "I couldn't stay away."

Ronnie's breath hitched, the close proximity, the heady scent of Donnie's cologne, the raw intensity in their eyes – it was a sensory overload.

"Donnie, we need to be careful. This campaign, our secret – it's all too delicate."

Donnie nodded, but the mischief in their eyes was unmistakable. "Life's too short to always play by the rules, Ronnie."

With that, they pulled Ronnie into a searing kiss, a confluence of passion, vulnerability, and raw emotions. The world outside, with its political intrigue and machinations, faded into the background as the two lost themselves in the moment.

When they finally pulled apart, both breathless, Ronnie murmured, "This changes everything."

Donnie smiled, that signature charismatic grin, "Change can be good."

Chapter 14: The Gala

The night was electric, a culmination of politics, charity, and a heady mix of glamour. Once a sneering gesture by conservatives to the women's suffrage movement, the campaign metropolis charity event had grown into an extravagant celebration of the diverse citizens of the U.S. Today, not only was it a proud symbol of liberal unity, but conservatives used it as a savvy tactic to woo LGBTQ supporters and—rumor had it—secretly indulge in some of their most forbidden desires.

The Gilded Gala Grand Hotel, the chosen venue for this annual event, stood as a shimmering epitome of luxury. Its majestic entrance was lined with exotic flowers, leading to the grand ballroom that screamed decadence with its sweeping golden arches and twinkling crystal chandeliers. The hotel, bathed in an ethereal glow, seemed to be almost winking at the city, inviting everyone to witness the grandeur unfolding inside.

As guests began to trickle in, the hall was a riot of colors, flamboyance, and humor. There were feathery boas, sparkling gowns, sharp tuxedos, and satirical nods to every fashion era imaginable. The consumption of bubbly was evident in every corner. From Brock who'd accidentally stepped on Dark Brandie's ornate train, causing an almost dramatic tumble, to Alex being swarmed by fans mistaking her for a different drag king, the room was in a constant state of delightful chaos.

In the midst of the glittering crowd, Donnie entered in a guise that no one would relate to Divine Donnie. Their attire was a rich, emerald green gown with intricate lace detailing that hugged their form gracefully. The dress, having a vintage feel, was accentuated by a string of pearls, a nod perhaps to the classics. Their face, though artfully made up, was carefully neutral, designed to draw no connection to their drag queen persona.

Ronnie, on the other hand, chose a rebellious androgynous ensemble. Wearing a sharp, glittering black suit paired with high heels and a crimson blouse that peeked out teasingly, they seemed like an embodiment of old Hollywood meets punk rock. Ronnie Rebel's essence was there, but the ensemble was cleverly crafted to ensure Ronnie remained incognito.

While Alexandria's usual strong, assertive style was unmistakable, tonight, she was the picture of classic masculinity. As Alex the Conqueror, she donned a crisp white shirt, tailored black vest, and trousers, her tie adding a splash of color. Her makeup was minimalistic, her hair slicked back, the entire look screaming power and confidence.

Dark Brandie went all out with a velvet cape in royal blue, beneath which was a sequined jumpsuit that matched the night sky. The outfit was both mesmerizing and intense, a perfect reflection of his character.

As the night progressed, guests not only flaunted their outfits but their generosity too. Large crystal bowls were placed strategically, filling quickly with checks and notes. Whispers of who-gave-what floated around, with occasional gasps at the astronomical amounts some were donating. The essence of spice was evident, as attendees exchanged charged glances, their conversations a mix of charity and subtle innuendo.

Among the attendees were celebrities, politicians, activists, and influencers. Each individual, with their unique style, contributed to the vibrant tapestry of the evening. Laughter, music, and the clinking of glasses provided the perfect backdrop to this night of enchantment.

Inside the ballroom of the Gilded Gala Grand Hotel, gold fixtures glistened, and chandeliers shimmered under the combined effect of electric lights and a thousand candles. But the decor paled in comparison to the extravagant tapestry of attendees, each one more dazzling than the next.

Tom, the action movie heartthrob, sported a deep emerald evening gown, the silky material hugging his athletic form. The off-shoulder neckline showcased his toned arms, and his short hair had been replaced with a wig of luscious locks tumbling in waves down his back. He glanced at

Nicole, who stood confidently in a tailored navy-blue suit, her pixie cut emphasized with gelled spikes.

"Never thought I'd say this," Tom began, chuckling as he twirled a strand of his wig, "but this dress is... liberating!"

Nicole raised an eyebrow, smirking. "Well, these pants give me a new perspective. I understand the power stance now. But who wore the height better back in our day?"

He laughed. "Touché. But tonight, it's all about bending and blending, isn't it?"

Speaking of bending norms, there was Stefani. Known for her wild attire, tonight she surprised everyone by coming as a dapper gentleman, wearing a black suit adorned entirely with mirrors. Reflecting every flash, she shone like a disco ball. Beside her was her date, Bradley, in a glittering silver dress with a plunging neckline.

"So, Bradley," Gaga began, her voice dripping with mischief, "feeling 'Shallow' in that dress?"

Bradley smirked, "Only as shallow as your mirrored reflection. At least I'm a star being born tonight!"

Across the room, Dwayne, towered over most, his massive frame draped in a soft lavender sari, complete with shimmering jewelry. His biceps still managed to bulge, challenging the delicate fabric. Opposite him was Kevin, in a sultry, red sequined dress, cinched at the waist, a look of mock indignation on his face.

"Man, you could've warned me!" Kevin exclaimed, gesturing at Dwayne's outfit. "We could've matched or something!"

Dwayne chuckled, his voice deep, "You trying to Rock the sari look too?"

Kevin winked, "Baby, in this outfit, I'm already rocking it!"

In another corner, Bernie and Bill debated politics, their conversation taking on an amusing tone, given Bernie's flapper dress, complete with feathers and pearls, and Bill's Geisha inspired kimono, tight obi belt, and a delicate fan in hand.

"You know," Bill began, fluttering his fan dramatically, "this might just be the solution to our debates – hard to take ourselves too seriously dressed like this."

Bernie twirled, the beads of his dress flying. "Speak for yourself, I feel fabulous!"

"Hillary!" Ellen called out, waving her over, "Loving the gangster look. Is this a hint about a new venture?"

Hillary chuckled, tapping her cane on the ground playfully, "Well, Ellen, let's just say I'm exploring my options."

Bill joined in, swaying his hips exaggeratedly, "And I'm just here for the jazz!"

Elon, overhearing, quipped, "Thinking of launching a new platform, Hillary? Space is quite the final frontier!"

Hillary smirked, adjusting her fedora, "Well, Elon, I've always been more of an Earth woman. But never say never!"

Portia, ever the voice of reason and sophistication, went all out in a Drag King outfit. Dressed as a pharaoh, with a golden headdress and kohl-lined eyes, she was the epitome of royalty. Ellen, always up for a laugh, was her Cleopatra, the golden dress adorned with a snake armband.

Portia raised an eyebrow, a playful smirk on her lips. "Going for the power couple look, are we?"

Ellen chuckled, "Well, when in Rome...or, you know, Egypt."

Across the hall, Elon, in a sparkling mermaid-cut dress, chatted animatedly with Jeff, who sported a punk rock Drag

Queen look, complete with a neon mohawk and leather bustier.

"Thinking of launching this look into space?" Jeff quipped, taking a sip of his champagne.

Elon grinned, "Only if it's on one of your rockets. Imagine the headlines!"

As the clock struck midnight, the atmosphere was thick with joy, acceptance, and love. For one night, barriers were broken, norms were challenged, and everyone celebrated the joy of being their most authentic self, in all its glittering glory.

The evening wasn't just about glamorous appearances. It was an ode to unity, understanding, and the power of coming together for a greater cause. While hidden desires and politics played their part, at its core, the gala was a reminder of the beautiful diversity and resilience of the nation. And as the night wore on, the promise of more intrigue, connections, and perhaps some scandalous moments, lingered in the air.

Behind the curtains of opulence and beneath the mask of glitzy drag personas, two hearts, yearning for another rendezvous, found their way. Ronnie, the conservatively audacious with an edge, locked eyes with Donnie, the embodiment of classic vintage charm.

The luminous chandeliers cast a shimmering glow upon the room, yet it was the unseen electric charge between Ronnie and Donnie that truly lit the space. Though surrounded by political counterparts, renowned influencers, and spirited conversations, the two seemed to share a world solely of their own.

Donnie, the allure of their emerald gown making them even more irresistible, subtly beckoned Ronnie with a sly, teasing smile. Ronnie, a tad bit flustered but utterly enchanted, decided to seize the moment, taking Donnie's hand and leading them away from the party's vibrant center.

Amidst the vast Gilded Gala Grand Hotel, they found a discreet alcove, obscured from prying eyes by thick velvet drapes. It seemed as if the universe itself conspired to give them this little haven of privacy.

Ronnie, their androgynous ensemble whispering of rebellion, inched closer. Their voice, husky and dripping with intent, murmured, "You know, for someone aiming for discretion, that green dress isn't doing you any favors. It screams 'look at me.'"

Donnie chuckled, their laughter light, flirtatious. "Well, perhaps I wanted someone to look. Perhaps, someone specific."

Donnie's eyes shimmered with mischief as they coyly remarked, "You know, this lace isn't just for show." They swayed closer, the vintage emerald fabric of their dress catching the dim light, making the intricate patterns dance.

Ronnie, always one for cheeky retorts, quipped, "Is that an invitation or a challenge?" Their black suit, a juxtaposition against the delicate attire of Donnie, gleamed with an understated elegance, while the peekaboo crimson blouse added an edge of flirtation.

"Well," Donnie began, allowing their fingers to trail up Ronnie's arm, eliciting a shiver, "why can't it be both?" In one fluid movement, their hand moved to Ronnie's neck, pulling them into a passionate, urgent kiss.

Their lips melded together, a fusion of warmth and spicy anticipation. Ronnie groaned into the kiss, their hands wandering to Donnie's waist, feeling the sensual curve of their backside. With a sly smile, Ronnie teased, "You're hiding quite the secret beneath this beautiful ensemble."

Donnie responded with a mischievous chuckle, their hands boldly venturing to Ronnie's firm backside, giving it an audacious squeeze. "And you, Ronnie Rebel, always have a surprise up your... well, suit."

Before Ronnie could retort, Donnie pressed their body closer, their manhood pushing against Ronnie's through the layers of fabric. The sensation, intensified by the thin barrier of lace and silk, was intoxicating. Ronnie's breath hitched, their hands instinctively reaching to cup Donnie's face, their thumb tracing those full lips.

"Remember last night?" Donnie whispered seductively, their voice barely above a breath, their fingers sneaking beneath Ronnie's blouse, grazing the smooth skin.

"How could I forget?" Ronnie replied huskily, their own hand moving daringly up Donnie's thigh, feeling the lace garter strap beneath the gown. The sensation of the lace against their fingers, knowing the intimate secret it held, was maddeningly erotic.

Donnie's breathing grew heavier. They leaned in, their lips brushing against Ronnie's ear, sending shivers down their spine. "I've been thinking about it all day, how you felt against me, how we moved together." Their hand dared to venture inside Ronnie's blouse, fingers brushing the delicate lingerie that Ronnie had chosen for the evening.

A moan escaped Ronnie's lips. "You weren't the only one." Their own fingers now played along the edge of Donnie's lingerie, the silk and lace tantalizing to the touch.

Their passionate explorations were interlaced with sultry whispers and soft laughter. The world outside the alcove seemed to vanish. All that existed was the two of them and the intoxicating blend of humor, desire, and intimacy.

"We shouldn't be doing this here," Donnie gasped, though their actions contradicted their words, as their fingers traced the outline of Ronnie's manhood, teasing through the lingerie.

Ronnie chuckled, their voice deep with desire. "That's what makes it so exhilarating, doesn't it?" They retaliated by sliding their hand further up Donnie's dress, fingers dancing along the lacey edge of Donnie's lingerie.

Suddenly, a distant murmur of laughter broke their trance, reminding them of the gala ongoing just beyond their hidden alcove.

They reluctantly separated, though their heavy breathing and flushed faces told tales of their passionate rendezvous. "We should get back," Ronnie murmured, straightening their suit and adjusting the blouse.

Donnie nodded, their lips curling into a playful smile. "But let's not wait another night for the next chapter."

Ronnie smirked, extending an arm, which Donnie gladly took, "Deal."

And with lingering glances and touches, the duo ready to rejoin the glittering gala, the promise of more secret encounters heavy in the air.

As they readjusted their outfits, preparing to rejoin the gala, there was a palpable sense of longing. But also, an unmistakable spark of hope.

Emerging from their hidden alcove, they blended back into the crowd. Yet, their discreet smiles, the subtle brushes of hands, and the charged glances spoke volumes. While the gala celebrated diversity and unity, for Ronnie and Donnie, it marked the beginning of a clandestine romance, one that would challenge norms and break barriers.

Donnie and Ronnie re-entered the thrumming center of the gala, though the blazing intensity between them would have anyone believe they'd been there all along, chatting politics and sipping champagne. Only the occasional knowing glance they exchanged hinted at anything beyond the ordinary.

With Donnie's emerald gown flowing around them like a protective aura, they engaged in pleasantries with other guests, every nod and laugh perfectly calibrated. And Ronnie? Well, in their Hollywood-meets-punk-rock ensemble, they exuded an air of understated allure. However, beneath the veil of casual conversations and laughter, the two exchanged secret touches. The glide of a finger along a forearm here, the caress of a thumb on the small of a back there, all subtle yet loaded with promise.

"Ronnie," Brock approached with his signature charming smile, "That suit is something else. How have you been?"

Ronnie chuckled, "Oh, you know, just navigating the world of politics one sequin at a time." The two shared a momentary laugh, all the while Donnie's gaze lingered on Ronnie, full of mischief and silent mirth.

Brock turned to Donnie, "And Divine Donn— I mean, Donnie, I must say, your ensemble is the talk of the gala. I'd dare say you've outdone everyone!"

Donnie feigned surprise, "Me? Outdoing everyone? Impossible." Their tone was thick with irony, making Brock laugh even harder.

As the evening wore on, the duo found themselves surrounded by a medley of conversations, some serious, some light-hearted, and some downright hilarious. And through it all, the two held onto the secret of their hidden alcove encounter, the thrill of that knowledge giving every interaction an electrifying edge.

At one point, Donnie found themselves next to Alexandria. She looked radiant, her drag persona, Alex the Conqueror, emanating power even in this high-profile political setting. "Donnie," she whispered conspiratorially, "You and Ronnie have been joined at the hip all evening. Anything I should know?"

Donnie smirked, "My dear Alexandria, politics makes strange bedfellows, as they say."

She raised an eyebrow, "Or alcove fellows?"

It was Donnie's turn to be shocked. "How did you—?"

She winked, "Your lace detailing is slightly ruffled. Ronnie's always had a thing for lace." With that bombshell, she sauntered away, leaving a flabbergasted Donnie in her wake.

As the clock ticked on, the implications of their rendezvous and the complexities of their relationship became even clearer. What did it mean for their political campaigns? For their personal lives? For the future of the nation? Both were presidential candidates, after all, with the weight of their respective parties resting on their shoulders.

But as the gala came to its zenith, with glasses raised and voices pitched in celebration of unity and diversity, Donnie and Ronnie shared another of their secret glances. And in that moment, politics, campaigns, and electoral strategies faded into the background. For the promise they shared in that hidden alcove was worth its weight in gold, far outweighing the weight of a nation's expectations.

As the last strains of music filled the ballroom, signaling the end of the gala, Ronnie whispered into Donnie's ear, "Meet me later?"

Chapter 15: Michelle Pensive's Debut

In the Luminous Lights Dressing Suite, Mike could feel his heart pulsating faster than ever. In the center of the room lay a gorgeous gown, shimmering as if it had been woven from the very stars in the sky. The enormity of the moment wasn't lost on him: tonight, Mike, a steadfast conservative in the public eye, would reveal his truest self as Michelle Pensive.

Each item laid out before him was a testament to the journey he had undertaken in secret—a journey of self-discovery, acceptance, and now, finally, unveiling. The thought of Donnie knowing, and Ronnie's barely concealed suspicions, added to his turmoil. But there was no turning back now.

Taking a shaky breath, he picked up the foundation. As the creamy texture blended into his skin, he felt himself smoothening not just the visible lines on his face, but also the inner wrinkles of his soul, smudged with years of hiding and suppression. Each brush stroke painted over his fears, letting Michelle's confidence seep through.

Eye shadow was next, a beautiful shade that seemed to capture the very essence of twilight. It was as if he was painting on wings, allowing his eyes to fly, unburdened by Mike's reservations. The mascara, dark and inviting, added depth to his eyes, making them expressive and mysterious.

As he contoured and highlighted his face, Mike couldn't help but feel a blend of excitement and trepidation. It was like a scene straight out of a romcom—humorously dramatic, each detail crucial, leading to a transformative climax.

With each brush, he felt Michelle emerging, her persona gently overpowering Mike's subdued identity. The blush added a hint of color, symbolizing the flush of new love—an affair with his true self.

The gown awaited, and as he slipped into it, the fabric clung lovingly to his curves. It was an embrace, an acknowledgment. The dress, a silvery hue with hints of blue, made him think of the enchanting night sky. Each sequin sewn into the fabric shimmered with promise and allure.

The lipstick, a sultry shade of plum, was the finishing touch. As it glided onto his lips, Mike felt a transformation. He wasn't just wearing makeup; he was donning armor, ready to face a world that could be as cruel as it could be kind.

The wig was the final touch. A cascade of luscious curls, the color of midnight, adorned his head, making him feel every bit the queen he was meant to be.

And yet, amidst all the glamour, the most significant change was in Mike's eyes. Gone was the look of uncertainty, replaced with a fiery determination and a spark of mischief.

As he took in his reflection, the door to the suite opened slowly, revealing a figure, momentarily silhouetted against the brightness outside.

"Mike?" The voice was familiar, but the tone was one of astonishment.

He turned, taking in the sight of Ronnie, looking resplendent in their androgynous punk rock-inspired ensemble. The sheer disbelief in Ronnie's eyes made Michelle's heart skip a beat, but she stood tall, channeling every ounce of Michelle's confidence.

"Actually, it's Michelle tonight, I'm Michelle now and forever." Mike replied, his voice surprisingly steady.

Ronnie stepped closer, examining Michelle from head to toe. "You look... incredible."

For a moment, there was an electric tension between them—a shared understanding of the challenges of revealing one's true self.

"You knew, didn't you?" Michelle asked softly.

Ronnie shrugged, a playful smirk on their lips. "Suspected, but seeing is believing."

Michelle smiled, feeling a weight lifted off her chest. "Ready to steal the show?"

Ronnie extended an arm, a gesture of camaraderie. "Together."

And with that, the two made their way out of the dressing suite, ready to face a night that promised to be as unforgettable as their transformations.

The double doors of the Gilded Gala Grand Hotel's grand ballroom swung open, and Michelle Pensive stepped into the spotlight. The room fell silent as the vast, shimmering expanse of her silvery-blue gown glided across the marble floor, as if a celestial body had descended from the night sky. The chandeliers above twinkled like a constellation, competing with the glittering aura Michelle exuded.

The weight of this moment bore down on Michelle—the culmination of her deepest self finally unfurling. She felt a rollercoaster of emotions: vulnerable, powerful, exposed, celebrated. She'd wondered if her journey of self-acceptance would culminate in acceptance by others or in heartbreak. The answer soon became apparent.

Whispers of awe fluttered through the crowd. From the corner of her eyes, she spotted Alexandria, as dashing Alex the Conqueror, sending her a thumbs-up, while Ellen's Cleopatra-inspired eyes shimmered with tears of joy. The array of gala outfits, each more audacious and stunning than the last, seemed to blur into a kaleidoscope of color and life around her. But the sight of Donnie, dressed in their emerald green gown and pearls, drew her attention most.

Hands clapped enthusiastically, echoing in the expansive room. "Bravo, Michelle!" Donnie called out, their voice filled with genuine pride.

A singular tear, refracting the light and shimmering like a diamond, slid down Michelle's cheek. All the nights spent battling inner demons, the years of hiding, and the weight of the secret she bore seemed to crystallize into that one tear.

Before the drop could fall, a blur of emerald was by her side. Donnie, always one for drama, pulled out a tissue with their small orange-tanned hand, dabbing at Michelle's cheek with exaggerated care. "Can't have our star getting all smudged now, can we?" they whispered, winking.

The room, sensing the deep bond and shared secret between the two, erupted into applause, louder and more genuine than any political rally or staged event. It was an applause of acceptance, of love, of unity.

A rather reserved Ronnie, their sequined ebny black suit contrasting with their deeply emotional eyes, nodded at Michelle from across the room. The unspoken words were clear: *I'm proud of you.*

Dark Brandie, initially with a stance ready for critique, melted into a soft smile, the sequins of his jumpsuit twinkling in acknowledgement. For a moment, politics, rivalries, and agendas faded, replaced by the power of authenticity and courage.

Nicole's spiky pixie cut seemed to quiver with excitement as she cheered, and Stefani, reflecting light from every angle, gave Michelle a salute. Bradley twirled in his glittering dress in a small, impromptu dance of celebration.

As Michelle moved deeper into the ballroom, each step felt like a step into a new world—a world where she was seen, loved, and celebrated not just as Mike, but as the radiant Michelle Pensive.

She took a moment to take it all in. The ornate décor of the hotel, the myriad of colors, the blend of vintage elegance and punk audacity—it was more than just a fashion statement. It was a declaration of individuality, of breaking molds, and of the unity that arises when differences are celebrated.

Dwayne, in his soft lavender sari, approached Michelle with a glass of champagne. "To Michelle," he toasted, "for showing us that it's never too late to be who we are meant to be."

The night was still young, but for Michelle, this moment felt timeless. The journey of a thousand miles, fraught with fear and self-doubt, had led to this magical destination of acceptance and celebration.

As the grand ballroom of the Gilded Gala Grand Hotel continued to pulse with chatter and music, Michelle Pensive became the radiant nucleus of it all. Her presence wasn't just dazzling; it was magnetic. The air seemed charged, as if the very fabric of the evening had shifted.

The eclectic ensemble of politicians and icons began to move and cluster around her, drawn to her charisma. As word traveled about Michelle's coming-out, whispers of admiration reached Michelle's ears, some undoubtedly filled with awe, others tinged with envy. But Michelle's heart was light, her spirits soaring.

Alexandria, still embracing her regal drag king aura as Alex the Conqueror, made her way gracefully towards Michelle. Her eyebrow arched with a mix of admiration and confusion. "Michelle," she started, her voice both firm and gentle, "you've truly captivated the crowd. You've always had the magic of drag down, but this... this is something else."

Michelle felt a rush of warmth rise to her cheeks. She took a deep breath, sensing that this was the moment to reveal a truth she had held close to her heart. Gazing deep into Alexandria's eyes, she replied softly, "It's not just the magic of drag, Alex. This is me, the real me. I've always felt like a woman trapped in a body that didn't align with my soul."

There was a beat of silence, a moment where the world seemed to hold its breath. Alexandria blinked, processing what she had just heard. "Wait, so you mean... you're not in drag? This isn't just a character for the gala?"

Michelle shook her head slowly, her silvery-blue gown rustling softly with her movements. "No, Alex, it's not an act or a character. I'm transgender. I've lived as Mike for so long, hiding behind a facade, but tonight... tonight, I wanted to introduce the world to Michelle, the woman I've always been."

A range of emotions flitted across Alexandria's face: surprise, realization, understanding. Then, slowly, her lips broke into a smile. "Michelle," she whispered, "you are magnificent."

Michelle's eyes glistened. "It's taken me a long time to find the courage to come out, to embrace who I truly am. I was scared, especially in our political world, but I couldn't hide any longer."

Alexandria reached out, placing a reassuring hand on Michelle's arm. "It's a brave new step, Michelle. And it's more than just sequins and makeup. It's about authenticity, breaking barriers, reshaping perceptions. It's about embracing your true self."

Michelle chuckled, the tension finally breaking. "Seems I've just swapped one set of sequins for another, though."

Alexandria laughed, her heart full of admiration and respect. "That's the spirit. Just remember, whether you're Mike or Michelle, you're incredible."

Michelle looked around the ballroom, her heart swelling with pride. "Tonight, I debut Michelle to the world. But from now on, she's here to stay. I hope the world is ready for her."

Alexandria grinned, her drag king persona melting away for a moment to reveal the fierce woman beneath. "If they're not, we'll make sure they are. Welcome to the world, Michelle."

Before Michelle could respond, the distinct aroma of a cigar wafted over. Turning, she found herself facing none other than Bill, dressed in his Geisha-styled kimono. His fan was poised, hinting at a sly smile underneath. "Michelle," he began in that ever-so-familiar political drawl, "that dress is something else."

"Why, thank you," Michelle replied with a flirty smirk.

Bill leaned in, his voice dropping to a playful whisper. "I've always had a thing for blue dresses, you know." He slipped her a card discreetly. "Call me."

Michelle laughed softly. "Is that a promise or a proposition?"

With a wink, he murmured, "You should see what I can do with a cigar."

Just then, a firm tap on Bill's shoulder interrupted the saucy exchange. He turned to find Hillary, channeling her 1920s gangster vibe, glaring at him, her fedora casting a shadow over her eyes. "Really, Bill?" she asked with a mock exasperation that could only come from years of shared history.

Bill cleared his throat, trying to channel innocence. "I was just... admiring Michelle's ensemble."

Michelle suppressed a giggle, watching the exchange with delight. The spicy intimacy of the moment gave way to a situational comedy that only a gathering like this could offer.

Hillary rolled her eyes, leaning in to whisper something in Bill's ear. He turned a shade of crimson that matched

Ronnie's blouse, and with a sheepish grin, began to make a hasty retreat.

Taking his place, Hillary sized up Michelle with an approving nod. "You do look fabulous, Michelle. And for what it's worth, I've always been more of a red dress kind of gal."

The two shared a hearty laugh, the sort of laugh that came from understanding and camaraderie.

As the evening progressed, Michelle was reminded again and again of the unifying power of drag. In the glitz and glamour of the night, political differences seemed to melt away. Even Bernie, embodying the Roaring Twenties in her flapper dress, swayed to the music, engrossed in deep conversation with Dark Brandie.

Tom, in his emerald evening gown, twirled Michelle around the dance floor, their combined radiance mesmerizing onlookers. The line between conservatism and liberalism blurred as they all celebrated the art of transformation and expression.

By the time the evening began to wane, Michelle felt a profound sense of accomplishment. It wasn't just about her debut; it was about the barriers she'd torn down. She'd not only embraced her true self but had managed to touch the hearts of so many others.

Donnie approached, looping an arm around Michelle. "You did it, Michelle. Look around you. You've made an impression that will last for ages."

Michelle beamed, her eyes glistening. "It's all of us, Donnie. We're rewriting the narrative, showing the world that acceptance transcends politics."

Donnie's orange-tanned face broke into a wide grin. "Indeed. And we've just started."

Just as Cinderella had her magic hour, Michelle had hers. As the clock's hands edged closer to the stroke of midnight, the ballroom pulsated with energy. The silvery glow from the chandeliers bathed everyone in a celestial light. For once, the night wasn't about the next election or the whispers of strategic alliances. Instead, it was about the enchantment of being true to oneself.

From the outskirts of the shimmering throng, Donnie and Ronnie looked on, both in their impeccable attire and sparkling eyeshadow. They exchanged a knowing glance, their silent communication saying, *She did it. She changed the game.*

Michelle's coming out hadn't only rocked the ballroom. Within minutes, the news had spread like wildfire on WebWonders Online Space. Posts ranged from utter admiration to disbelieving shock, from applauding her bravery to political debates. Amidst it all, a surprising number of individuals publicly came out as well, buoyed by Michelle's inspiring revelation.

One post read: "If Michelle Pensive can bravely embrace her true self amidst this political circus, maybe there's hope for the rest of us. #MichelleRising."

Another stated: "Just saw Michelle's debut. I might not agree with her politics, but damn, that is one brave woman. #UnifyingMoment."

Donnie, reading these posts aloud to Ronnie, remarked in that charismatic voice of theirs, "I always knew this gala would be special, but this... this is monumental."

Ronnie smirked, "It sure is. A conservative transformed into a shimmering beacon of hope. Who would've thought?"

A playful nudge from Donnie silenced the witty remark. "She's one of us now. And that makes all the difference."

From afar, Alexandria approached the duo, her masculine grace as Alex the Conqueror evident. "A penny for your thoughts?" she teased.

Ronnie responded with a smirk, "We were just discussing the delightful wrench Michelle threw into the system tonight."

Alexandria chuckled. "Isn't it wonderful? For once, the world isn't solely focused on left or right but rather on the broad spectrum of human identity."

As the clock inched closer to dawn, the gala showed no signs of slowing down. But as with every grand event, the curtains had to draw eventually. As guests began their exodus, Michelle, Donnie, and Ronnie shared a lingering moment, watching the city lights from the hotel's balcony.

"From campaign trails to catwalks, we've come a long way," Ronnie mused, eyes glistening with nostalgia.

Michelle looked out, feeling the weight and wonder of the night. "I was born many years ago, but tonight, I truly lived."

Donnie nodded in agreement, "We've made memories, written histories. And Michelle, remember, this is just the beginning."

Their trio hug was suddenly interrupted by the ping of Donnie's phone. "Ah, NewsWave wants a joint interview tomorrow. They're calling it, 'The Night Politics Wore Heels.'"

Everyone burst into laughter, the tension of the night dissipating into the early morning air.

Finally, making her way home, Michelle's high heels clicked rhythmically on the pavement. Each step echoed her journey, from hesitation to acceptance, from Mike to Michelle. The lights of her Metro Flat beckoned in the distance.

She stepped into her bedroom, greeted by the reflection of Michelle Pensive in the mirror—a symbol of courage, acceptance, and unity. With delicate fingers, she began to remove the layers of makeup, each swipe revealing a bit more of Mike, yet somehow more Michelle than ever before.

The silvery-blue gown was carefully placed on the bed, a silent witness to the transformative night. Michelle—now a harmonious blend of Mike and the diva persona—Collapsing onto her bed, the emotions of the evening caught up with her. The applause, the cheers, the silent judgments, and the overwhelming support - it was a cacophony of emotions that threatened to overwhelm her. Tears, a mix of exhaustion, relief, and joy, streamed down her face, staining her pristine pillow.

These weren't tears of sadness, nor were they purely of joy. They were a culmination of a lifetime of suppression, a final exhale of all the fear and uncertainty. They were the tears of a Phoenix, having risen from the ashes of doubt, now radiant and ready to face the world.

The city lights outside her window began to dim, making way for the soft hues of dawn. Dawn's light began to seep through the gaps in her curtains, Michelle Pensive, the beautiful phoenix, drifted into a deep, well-deserved sleep, the world outside still echoing with the impressions of her unforgettable debut. Birds began to chirp, ushering in a new day—a day of promises, of acceptance, of unity.

In the heart of the city, where differences were often amplified, Michelle Pensive had, even if for a fleeting moment, unified a fragmented world. And as she drifted into a deep, peaceful slumber, she carried with her the dreams and hopes of countless souls she'd touched that night.

And somewhere in the distance, as the first rays of the sun painted the sky, a billboard showcased the face of Michelle Pensive with the caption, "Dare to Be You. #MichelleRising."

Chapter 16: Old Rivals, New Perspectives

The dim lights of Heartfelt Haven Theater gave an air of mystery and intimacy to its wooden walls and cozy stage. Laughter bubbled up in pockets as attendees, sipping from their flutes of sparkling wine, chatted in eager anticipation. Among them, Alexandria, resplendent in a fitted pantsuit, her presence a perfect blend of political finesse and genuine interest.

She adjusted her dangling earring, taking in the ambiance. This wasn't just any show; this was a liberal charity gala, meant to support community initiatives and promote inclusivity. It was her turf, her domain. And yet, despite the comforting surroundings, she felt a flutter of nerves. Maybe it was because of the previous heated debate she had at Primetime Politics Studio or perhaps it was because these social settings always had the potential for the unexpected.

Alexandria's musings were interrupted by a sudden dimming of the lights. The stage was bathed in deep purple, and a hauntingly slow melody began to play. From the shadows emerged Dark Brandie, the legendary drag queen known for his mesmerizing performances. In full glory, wearing a shimmering sequined gown that hugged his curves and a cascading wig, Dark Brandie began to captivate the audience with his sultry moves and powerful vocals.

There were moments during the performance when Alexandria felt like she was the only one in the room, so intense and direct was Dark Brandie's gaze. It was as if he was trying to convey a message, and she felt an inexplicable pull towards him.

As the performance reached its crescendo, Dark Brandie, with a flurry of fabric and sequins, finished with a dramatic pose, eliciting a rapturous applause from the captivated audience. Alexandria, like everyone else, was on her feet, her heart racing for reasons she wasn't quite sure of.

As the attendees began mingling, Alexandria decided to freshen up. As she approached the restroom, a figure stepped out, startling her. It was Dark Brandie, now in a plush robe, makeup still impeccable.

"Alexandria," he said, his voice dripping with honey, "fancy seeing you here."

"Dark Brandie," Alexandria replied, a smile tugging at the corner of her lips. "I should have known you'd be the star tonight. You were magnificent."

He gave a soft chuckle, leaning against the wall, eyes appraising her. "Why, thank you. I had a feeling you'd be here tonight. Our worlds, as different as they seem, do have a tendency to collide."

There was a pause, a charged moment where the air seemed thick with unsaid words. Alexandria broke the silence. "I admire your talent, Brandie. It's not just about the performance, it's the passion, the message."

Dark Brandie looked genuinely taken aback. "Coming from you, that means a lot." He glanced around, ensuring they were still somewhat private. "You know, Alexandria, beneath the makeup, the outfits, and the politics, we aren't all that different."

She met his gaze, curiosity evident in her eyes. "How so?"

"We both want change, in our own ways," he whispered, leaning closer. "We both know the power of presentation and the influence it holds."

Before Alexandria could respond, a loud burst of laughter from a nearby group echoed through the hallway. The moment was broken, but the connection had been made.

"We should talk, properly," Dark Brandie said, his voice taking on a serious tone. "Not here, not now. But soon."

Alexandria nodded, her heart still racing. "I'd like that."

With the Heartfelt Haven Theater's post-performance party in full swing. A vivacious tune played softly in the background, providing just the right mood for light-hearted banter and deeper, whispered conversations.

In a quiet corner, surrounded by elegantly dressed individuals, sat Alexandria and Dark Brandie. Their respective poises screamed 'old friends,' a camaraderie easy on the eyes but complex to the intuitive mind. They shared a cozy two-seater, with Alexandria occasionally fidgeting with her statement necklace and Dark Brandie running his fingers along the rim of his wine glass.

"I must say, Alexandria," began Dark Brandie with a playful smirk, "your drag persona, Alex the Conqueror, is a force to be reckoned with."

Alexandria chuckled. "Thank you, Brandie. But next to Dark Brandie's intensity, Alex is just a newbie trying to make his mark."

The room filled with an electrifying tension, with only the subtlest hints of their past adventures in drag and politics weaving through the air. Yet, amid the glitz and glamor, there was a palpable strain of something more profound, an undercurrent of unspoken words, political ambitions, and a shared history.

Dark Brandie sighed, leaning back, "You know, Alexandria, I've always admired your tenacity, both on stage and in politics. Your commitment to your ideals, even when it made you unpopular in some circles, is commendable."

His comment struck a chord. Alexandria, moved by the genuine tone, replied, "Thank you. You always had a way of seeing the bigger picture, blending your drag artistry with political acumen. It's amazing how you manage to balance both."

An amused smile curved up Dark Brandie's lips. "Speaking of politics, have you considered the proposition by the center-left democrats for a collaborative effort? It's essential, given the current political landscape."

Alexandria's eyes widened slightly, taken aback by how in-the-loop Dark Brandie seemed to be, "I didn't expect you to be so well-versed with current political ongoings."

Dark Brandie winked, "Darling, I've been in this game long enough to know that politics, like drag, is all about the presentation and understanding your audience. And... let's just say, I've had my fair share of political liaisons."

The intriguing mix of Dark Brandie's playful teasing and his political insights kept Alexandria on her toes. They laughed, exchanged casual banter, but the intensity of their conversation, masked in layers of humor, was palpable.

As the evening continued, Dark Brandie seemed a tad more pensive, as if he was holding back something. "You know," he began, pausing for a dramatic effect and sipping his drink, "politics isn't just about policies and campaigns. It's about understanding people, their desires, fears, and dreams."

Alexandria leaned in, curious, "Is that another one of Dark Brandie's pearls of wisdom?"

He chuckled, "Maybe, or maybe it's Joe's." The casual drop of his government name caught Alexandria off guard. She eyed him with a new-found curiosity.

A coy grin danced on Dark Brandie's lips as he leaned in, almost as if sharing a juicy secret. "You see, Alex, the world of politics is much like drag. It's a performance, a show, where one plays different roles. But, sometimes, the roles are not what they seem."

Alexandria, intrigued by his cryptic tone, responded, "So, is there something you're not telling me, Brandie? Another hidden layer to the mysterious persona of Dark Brandie?"

He took a deep breath, clearly hesitating. "Do you remember the president who disappeared? The one everyone speculated had run off to some exotic island, living his best life as a recluse?"

She furrowed her brows. "Of course, everyone knows about Joe. It was all over the news! There were conspiracy theories, stories… It was a sensation."

His voice grew soft, "Well, darling, you've been sitting across from him all night. Joe... is me."

She choked on her drink, spraying a mist of her fruity cocktail across the table. Coughing and sputtering, she gaped at him, eyes wide in disbelief. "You're... You're *Joe*? But... how? Why? I mean, you're... *you're Dark Brandie*!"

Brandie laughed, the sound rich and carefree. "After my term ended, I felt an overwhelming desire to be free, to discover who I truly was. Politics had consumed me, but drag gave me life, so I chose life."

Alexandria shook her head in astonishment. "But why hide it? Why the secrecy?"

His eyes looked distant, reflecting a tapestry of emotions. "I needed a break from the spotlight, from the pressure, the judgment. As Dark Brandie, I found acceptance, love, and most importantly, myself."

She leaned in, captivated by his story, a blend of intimacy, politics, and personal discovery. "But now, here you are, back in the limelight, attending political events, and I must say, looking fabulous while doing so."

A smirk appeared on Brandie's face. "Old habits die hard, my dear. But this time, I'm navigating the world of politics with the wisdom of Joe and the flair of Dark Brandie."

The revelation had her reeling, but she was keen to glean insights from him. "Given your unique perspective, Brandie, any advice for a presidential hopeful?"

He considered her for a moment, before leaning in closer, their faces inches apart, his eyes intense. "Unity, Alexandria. It's crucial. The political world is fragmented, and there's a desperate need for someone to bring it together."

She nodded slowly, hanging on his every word. "I believe in inclusivity, in love, but how do I navigate the challenges, the opposition?"

His fingers lightly traced a path on the back of her hand, sending a shiver up her spine. The intimacy of the touch combined with the weight of the conversation created a heady mix. "Stay true to yourself and your message. Make alliances, but never at the cost of your integrity. And remember, the world needs both Alexandria and Alex the Conqueror."

His words resonated deeply with her. Here was a man, once the leader of the nation, now a drag queen, imparting wisdom that was both political and profoundly personal.

"I appreciate this, Brandie," she whispered, her eyes glistening with unshed tears. "You've given me a lot to think about."

He squeezed her hand reassuringly. "Remember, behind the glitz and glamor, behind the policies and campaigns, it's all about understanding people, their hopes, dreams, and fears. Embrace that, and you'll win not just votes, but hearts."

The two shared a moment, an understanding that transcended politics and drag. As the evening's remnants began to wind down, and the theater's lights dimmed, they left with a promise of a renewed friendship, and perhaps, a budding alliance in the world of politics.

Alexandria stumbled out of the Heartfelt Haven Theater, her mind a whirlwind of emotions. Her heels clicked rhythmically on the sidewalk as she tried to digest the night's revelations. The man she'd spent the evening with wasn't just Dark Brandie, the drag sensation, but Joe, the former president who had supposedly vanished from the face of the Earth.

She hailed a cab, collapsing into the backseat and resting her head against the cool glass window. The neon lights of the city passed in a blur, but all Alexandria could see was Brandie's intense gaze and the conviction in his voice as he spoke about unity.

Reaching Cortez Cozy Corner, Alexandria's safe haven, she unlocked the door, slowly opening it to her nest, the familiar scent of her apartment greeted her. A mix of vanilla candles and the faint musky scent of old books. The slight disarray of the living room spoke of many nights spent brainstorming political strategies. Yet, as she walked past her work desk, littered with campaign brochures and statistics, she couldn't help but smile.

She strolled into her bedroom, giving a slight laugh as she saw her reflection in the large vanity mirror. "Well, Alex," she mused, "What a night!"

Carefully, she began unzipping her red sequined dress, letting it fall in a shimmering heap around her feet. It was then that she truly took a moment to look at herself. Gone was the unsure political rookie from a few months back. Here stood a woman with newfound perspectives, battling tan lines, and confidence that was slowly but surely building.

With one hand on her hip, she smirked. "Alex the Conqueror, indeed." Running her fingers through her tousled hair, she decided that maybe, just maybe, the world did need both versions of her. If Joe could be Dark Brandie and vice versa, Alexandria could be the politician and the drag king, all rolled into one fabulous package.

Her phone buzzed, breaking her introspection. Grabbing it, she saw a message from Ronnie. "I'm dropping out of the race, I love Donnie, I don't know who I can trust besides you."

Her heart skipped a beat. The political world seemed to be full of surprises lately. Typing quickly, she replied, "I know you do. Don't worry, I'm not telling anyone, it's not my place." After a moment's pause, she added, "What about the Debate tomorrow? It's the last one."

A few tense minutes passed before Ronnie's response came through. "I don't know. I just need to put on a good show."

Alexandria sighed deeply. The world of politics was a convoluted maze of public images, secret loves, and shifting alliances. But she was in it, for better or worse.

Terry, her trusted assistant, would probably have a field day when she briefed them tomorrow. She could already hear their voice, full of excitement and slight exasperation. "Alex, darling, you do manage to find yourself in the most unexpected situations!"

She climbed into bed, snuggling into her soft sheets. The events of the evening played in her mind like a movie reel. Every smirk, every touch, every whispered piece of advice. And as she slowly drifted into sleep, one thought became crystal clear. Tomorrow was another day, another opportunity. And she would face it with the passion of Alexandria and the fearlessness of Alex the Conqueror.

She didn't know if she'd win the presidency. But she did know that she would give it her all. And with allies like Dark Brandie by her side, perhaps, just perhaps, she'd make history.

Chapter 17: The Debate

The Primetime Politics Studio buzzed with energy. Banners of red, white, and blue draped from the ceiling and a sizeable in-house audience was in a fervor of anticipation. Camera crews prepped their equipment while reporters practiced their lines. Everyone knew that tonight's debate was the final face-off before the all-important vote.

Backstage, Ronnie was in a state of turmoil. Their dressing room, usually a place of calm preparation, felt like the epicenter of an internal storm. Last night's text to Alexandria lay heavy on their heart. Should they really drop out? How could they face Donnie after such a revelation?

Ronnie's fingers trembled as they adjusted the sharp line of their suit. In the mirror, Ronnie Rebel, the epitome of poise and elegance, stared back. But beneath the refined exterior, lay a torrent of emotions.

Every corner of the room seemed to scream memories. To the left, a bouquet of roses – a gesture from an anonymous admirer. On the dresser, the latest conservative strategy dossier lay next to a glitzy, sequined mask – their secret symbol of a double life in drag.

The jarring juxtaposition of the political and personal summed up their entire campaign. A chime from the phone snapped Ronnie from their thoughts. Another text from Alexandria: "You got this. Whatever you choose, you have my respect."

Ronnie took a deep breath. Alexandria was a true ally, despite their political differences. But it was the next text that made their heart skip a beat.

It was Donnie. "See you on stage, Rebel. Remember, it's all just a show."

A show. That's all it was. A performance for the masses. Ronnie chuckled, the irony wasn't lost on them. Every political rally, every campaign speech, wasn't it all just a different kind of drag show?

A knock on the door startled them. It was Terry, Alexandria's trusted assistant. With a playful roll of their eyes, they handed over a tiny box. "A peace offering from your opponent," Terry winked.

Inside was a sparkling drag brooch, shaped like the liberty torch, but with a twist – it was decked out in rainbow colors. Ronnie grinned. Alexandria's sense of humor seems to be both infuriating and endearing.

The murmurs from the audience grew louder, the debate was about to begin. Ronnie took one last look in the mirror, a mix of nerves and resolve. Tonight, they would face their biggest challenge yet: not the debate, but confronting their feelings for Donnie and deciding the future of their campaign.

As they stepped out, the blinding lights of the stage met them, and the weight of the evening pressed down. But beneath it all, an ember of hope flickered. Tonight would be a game-changer, in more ways than one.

Ronnie took center stage, the Primetime Politics Studio became a simmering pot of palpable excitement. The two opponents, Donnie and Ronnie, found themselves separated by a podium, but a magnetic force of attraction seemed to pull them together. Their dynamic was something straight out of a rom-com, with the added glitz of politics.

The moderator, an impeccably dressed man with more gel in his hair than was probably advisable, began, "Ladies, gentlemen, and esteemed guests, welcome to the final conservative presidential primary debate!"

Ronnie locked eyes with Donnie, feeling the gravitational pull. Donnie's charismatic charm practically oozed from their pores. It wasn't just about the debate; it was about what was unspoken between them.

The first question was launched, and the political jousting began. But between the lines of healthcare reform and tax strategies, were cheeky jokes and flirtatious jabs.

"Frankly," Donnie began, voice dripping with faux superiority, "I think if Ronnie focused as much on their policies as they did on their eyeshadow, we might be getting somewhere."

Ronnie smirked, "Ah, Divine Donnie, always with the zingers! But remember, it's my policies that got me here, the eyeshadow is just a bonus."

The audience roared with laughter, thoroughly enjoying the refreshing candor of the two candidates.

As they progressed, their faux-spats became more pronounced. "You know, Ronnie," Donnie drawled, "If you put as much passion into foreign policies as you do when picking out your stilettos, I might actually be worried about this race."

Ronnie leaned in, eyes glittering with mischief, "Oh, Donnie, always so concerned about my footwear. Is it because you're just a tad envious of how I rock those heels?"

The room was filled with a mix of gasps and chuckles. The sexual tension was palpable. Every retort, every shared glance, every laugh hinted at a deeper connection. Their playful bickering made the debate not just informative but downright entertaining.

During a particularly heated discussion about economic growth, Donnie said, "Ronnie, while I appreciate your point of view, I must ask—did you borrow that perspective from one of your drag shows? Because it's quite... theatrical."

Ronnie, undeterred and with a sly grin, responded, "Donnie, you should know. You were front row at my last show, remember? Or were you too busy sending me those heart-eye emojis?"

The audience burst into applause. Whistles and cheers echoed in the studio.

However, despite the banter, both candidates handled serious questions with the grace and poise of seasoned politicians. Their genuine passion for creating a more inclusive and accepting America shone through, even amidst their playful exchanges.

At one point, the topic shifted to LGBTQ rights. With a softened demeanor, Donnie stated, "No matter our differences, our debates, our playful jabs, I think Ronnie and I can firmly agree that every individual deserves respect, acceptance, and love. Politics aside, it's a matter of basic human decency." Adding while looking deeply at Ronnie "We have experienced a different side the past year, and friends dear to us deserve our support."

Ronnie nodded, eyes misty. "Absolutely. Tonight, while we share laughs and jabs, let's not forget the importance of unity and acceptance. It's the core of our nation, and it should be the core of our hearts."

Ronnie's words on unity and acceptance echoed in the Primetime Politics Studio. The initial cheekiness of the debate, rife with innuendos and light-hearted banter, had now transitioned into a space of genuine advocacy.

"It's not just about the rights of a few," Ronnie began, their voice firm yet compassionate. "It's about the acceptance of all. Every individual has the right to live, love, and express themselves without fear."

Donnie nodded, taking a moment before speaking, "While Ronnie and I may have our differences, on this we are united. MAGA – Make Acceptance Genuine Again. That's the future we envision."

A murmur of agreement rippled through the audience. Some nodded their heads, while others exchanged glances, surprised at this unexpected turn of events. The tone of the debate had shifted, taking on a depth that was both poignant and empowering.

Ronnie continued, "It's time we redefine what it means to be American. It's not just about borders or political affiliations. It's about recognizing the rich tapestry of cultures, identities, and experiences that make this country great."

Donnie picked up the thread, "We have a unique opportunity to shape the future of this nation. The America we envision is one where everyone, regardless of their background, can walk hand in hand, proud of who they are."

The audience was rapt, hanging onto every word. What started as a political showdown had transformed into a heartwarming advocacy for acceptance and unity.

Ronnie took a deep breath, their eyes glistening with emotion. "During this campaign, I've met countless individuals who have faced discrimination, prejudice, and hate. But their stories are also filled with hope, resilience, and the indomitable spirit of the American dream."

Donnie, always one for theatrics, reached into their pocket and pulled out a rainbow-colored badge. Holding it up, they said, "This is a symbol of the America we're fighting for – one where the rainbow, in all its vibrant hues, is celebrated."

The Primetime Politics Studio resonated with applause. Every clap was a testament to the power of genuine acceptance. Audience members from all walks of life – conservatives, liberals, young, old, LGBTQ+ allies – all united in this moment of hope.

The moderator, Gabriella Gold, clearly moved, wiped a tear from his eye and managed to find her voice, "Ladies and gentlemen, what we're witnessing tonight is not just a debate. It's a call to action, a plea for understanding, and a vision for a brighter, more inclusive future."

When the applause finally dwindled, Ronnie, their face flushed with a mix of emotion and studio lighting, took a step forward. "This journey," they began, voice laden with sincerity, "has not just been a political campaign. It's a journey of self-discovery, acceptance, and hope. My campaign's core is about a country that believes in the power of unity amidst diversity, where every individual, irrespective of their beliefs, gender, or color, gets the respect they deserve."

Donnie, never one to be outdone, stepped up with their signature flamboyance. "I've always believed that politics needs more glitter. More fun. More acceptance." They brandished the rainbow badge again. "And as we stand at the cusp of a new America, let's bring all our vibrant colors together. Because baby, when we come together, we shine the brightest!"

The studio erupted into applause once more. Audience members exchanged glances, some with tears, others with nods of agreement. Whispers filled the room, "This isn't just about politics anymore..."

The Primetime Politics Studio lights dimmed, indicating the end of the debate. The candidates exchanged brief, almost knowing glances, acknowledging the unspoken between them before making their exits, leaving behind an audience still grappling with the magic of the evening.

As the broadcast concluded, Alexandria sat frozen in her Advocacy Hub, the blue light from her screens painting her face. She had seen something tonight that few had noticed – the quiet transformation of two conservative candidates. A realization dawned on her, one that felt like both a punch in the gut and a rush of wind on a hot day: Donnie and Ronnie had abandoned the conservative agenda and didn't even know it yet. Her phone buzzed with a message from Brock, "Did we just witness the birth of a love story and the end of a political one?" She smirked, typing back, "In heels, no less."

Meanwhile, Ronnie, their emotions still a whirlwind from the debate, found themself standing outside Donnie's penthouse. Before they could think twice, they pressed the buzzer. Moments later, the door swung open, revealing Donnie, their hair tousled, eyes a mix of surprise and warmth. Without a word, Ronnie stepped inside, tears already brimming, and collapsed into Donnie's arms.

Being in Donnie's protective and caring embrace, the practiced words fled from Ronnie's mind. Without a word, they stepped forward, collapsing into Donnie's embrace, their body shaking with sobs. "I can't do this anymore," they whispered, voice choked with emotion. "I'm quitting… I just want you."

Donnie tightened their grip around Ronnie, burying their face into Ronnie's hair. "Shhh... We'll figure it out. Together." They led Ronnie inside, closing the door to the world outside, to the politics, the pressures, and the expectations.

The penthouse was dimly lit, casting soft shadows around the room. Donnie guided Ronnie to the sofa, and the two sat, holding onto each other as if they were lifelines.

"You mean more to me than any campaign, any election," Ronnie admitted, their voice barely above a whisper.

Donnie pulled back slightly, looking deep into Ronnie's eyes, "Same here. But what now?"

"We'll figure it out," Ronnie repeated Donnie's earlier words, a small smile playing on their lips.

Donnie grinned, "You know, for two people running for the highest office, we're terribly unprepared for our personal lives."

Ronnie chuckled, "Maybe we should stick to politics?"

Donnie smirked, "Or perhaps mix a little of both? The White House has never seen two Presidents. Imagine the headlines. Imagine the power of our combined drag shows!"

The two laughed, the tension easing. "Whatever we decide, I'm glad we're in this together," Ronnie said, leaning in for a gentle kiss.

The passion between them was evident, and as their lips met, the weight of the world seemed to lift. They were two souls, lost in the chaos of politics, who had found solace in each other.

As the night deepened, the city lights twinkled below, oblivious to the whirlwind romance unfolding above. The election would come, challenges would arise, but for now, in the heart of the city, two hearts had found their home.

Chapter 18: Truth and Transparency

The morning light filtered through the heavy drapes, casting soft glows across the room. It had been a long, passionate night for Donnie and Ronnie, where vulnerabilities were laid bare, and a future was meticulously charted out. Between stolen kisses and tangled sheets, they had hatched a plan that was bound to create ripples in the political universe.

Donnie, feeling a bit adventurous (and perhaps slightly reckless), suggested WebWonders Online Space as the platform to drop their bombshell. "It's unconventional, darling, just like us," they had said with a wink.

So, as the digital world was abuzz with the latest cat meme and conspiracy theories, Ronnie's face filled the screens. Beside them stood Donnie, their usual flamboyant self now replaced by a stoic facade, meant to support Ronnie.

Donnie squeezed Ronnie's hand, offering silent encouragement. "Dear citizens," Ronnie began, their voice heavy with emotion, "After a night of introspection and understanding, I have decided to withdraw from the presidential race." A collective gasp echoed throughout the digital space. Comments began pouring in:

SassySandra: *Wait, what?! Didn't see that coming!*
PolitiPaul: *Are they for real? Is this a new strategy?*
LoveIsLoveLina: *OMG! So bold and brave!* 🩶

Taking a deep breath, Ronnie continued, "But fear not, I am not leaving the arena. Instead, I've decided to join forces with Donnie, standing beside them, not as a competitor, but as a running mate." Donnie, beaming with pride, gently rested their head on Ronnie's shoulder.

The digital realm exploded into chaos. Speculations, memes, debates—it was the perfect recipe for a viral sensation.

Meanwhile, in a dimly lit room adorned with campaign posters and makeup kits, Alexandria stared at her screen, wide-eyed. A tub of vegan ice-cream in hand, she muttered, "Well, that's one way to shake things up." She appreciated boldness, but this? This was next level. She felt a heady mix of admiration and anxiety, wondering how this would tilt the scales of the election.

At Michelle's metro flat, she was doing her nails when the notification blared. "Oh, honey!" she exclaimed, nearly smudging her fresh coat of glittery blue. "Ronnie, Ronnie, Ronnie... always full of surprises." She leaned back on her couch, a thoughtful expression playing on her face. If there was one thing Michelle knew about politics, it was that love made for compelling narratives. And this? This was going to be one for the books.

Back on WebWonders, Donnie took their turn to address the viewers, their voice filled with conviction. "Together, Ronnie and I will create a platform that champions love, acceptance, and progress. And remember, in politics, as in life, it's always better to be united." With a flamboyant flourish, Donnie ended the stream with a playful wink and a blown kiss.

Screens went dark, but the chatter continued. Reactions poured in from every corner. Journalists scrambled to cover the story, influencers shared their hot takes, and meme creators, of course, had a field day.

The large digital clock at the entrance of NewsWave Media Outlets ticked, the second hand sweeping forward, as if trying to keep up with the pace of the newsroom below. The vast open-plan space was a veritable tempest of activity. The unmistakable aroma of freshly brewed coffee blended with the cacophony of ringing phones and incessant keyboard clatter.

"All right, people! We've got an unexpected twist in the political saga of the century!" shouted Tina, the Deputy Editor, waving a paper script dramatically. She was a woman who always wore two things: a power blazer and a determined expression. "We need a full scoop on this by EOD!"

Gary, the intern who looked perpetually flustered, dashed over, nearly tripping over a cable. "Uh, do you think this means they'll be singing duets at their rallies now?"

Tina rolled her eyes, her crimson lipstick contrasting sharply against her pale complexion. "That's *your* hot take? Go fetch me a latte."

Across the room, the TV screens featured talking heads from every spectrum of politics. Chloe, a sharp, ambitious reporter, adjusted her earpiece as she prepped to go live. She practiced her lines, emphasizing each word, "The country watches, goggle-eyed, as two presidential competitors suddenly turn co-candidates. But is there more beneath this surprise merger than meets the eye?"

Carlos, her techie, fidgeted with the backdrop. "Imagine if they do a dance number together, or, better yet, a karaoke duel!"

"Carlos!" Chloe chided, giggling. "You're terrible! We're a news outlet, not 'America's Got Talent'."

He grinned. "Well, it'd sure boost their ratings. Or ours."

The live stream from WebWonders was playing on loop, with Donnie and Ronnie's announcement going viral. Comments were pouring in by the thousands. Some were humorous, with many suggesting they should form a new party called "RonDon's Party Fiesta!" Others speculated deeper political strategies.

Tess, NewsWave's social media guru, gleefully monitored the online frenzy. "We're trending, people! RonDon2028 is officially a sensation! Let's keep this hype train moving!" She was busy crafting witty posts, interlaced with memes of the pair. An image of Donnie with heart-shaped eyes, looking at Ronnie, was particularly popular.

At the coffee station, two journalists, Dave and Mira, discussed the announcement in hushed tones. Mira, always armed with fresh gossip, whispered, "You know, my cousin went to college with Ronnie. Says they always had a thing for drama."

Dave smirked, "You think this is all for show? Some... grand strategy?"

She shrugged, taking a sip of her caramel macchiato. "In politics? It's always a possibility. But they looked genuine to me. Let's not forget, the world sees them as two straight, masculine men making a surprising alliance. If they're acting, they deserve an Oscar."

A sudden buzz caught everyone's attention as Tina yelled, "We've got a tip! Possible juicy angle coming in!" She was holding her phone like it was a piece of precious gold. "Meetings at the Unity Square Transparency Terrace — something big is happening there tonight!"

Gary's eyes widened, "Another announcement? Or maybe... the karaoke duel Carlos was dreaming of?"

A collective groan filled the newsroom.

Tina shook her head, "Whatever it is, we'll be the first to cover it! Chloe, assemble a team. We're going live from Unity Square in T-minus two hours!"

Carlos gave a thumbs up, his excitement palpable. "Karaoke or not, we're on it!"

In the heart of the city, Unity Square's Transparency Terrace was a-buzz with energy. There were more reporters than could be counted, throngs of onlookers, both ardent supporters and perplexed spectators, all drawn by the siren call of the impending revelation.

Donnie, clad in a sharp suit with an audacious flash of color at the cuffs, indicative of their flamboyant persona, adjusted their tie. Beside them, Ronnie, traditionally conservative in appearance, was a study in controlled apprehension. Their fingers brushed, a gentle show of solidarity.

Ronnie swallowed, their voice soft, "Ready for this?"

Donnie smirked, winking. "Always."

They took the stage to a hush, the crowd anticipating the next seismic shift in this political drama. The wind picked up, rustling flags and causing shadows to dance on the podium. They stood side by side, hands clasped so tightly that their knuckles whitened. The stillness was palpable, and it seemed the entire world had paused to watch.

"We stand before you," Ronnie began, "Not as mere political allies but as two hearts, united."

Donnie chimed in, their voice rich with emotion. "Life in the limelight, politics, and the need to conform often forced us to wear masks. Today, we shed them."

With that, they turned to face each other, the tension palpable. The two non-binary powerhouses, seemingly so different in their personas, now united in their vulnerability.

"For too long," Ronnie whispered, eyes locked onto Donnie's, "I've hidden who I am, behind policies and podiums."

Donnie smiled tenderly, "And I, behind wealth and bravado. But no more."

The onlookers held their breath, sensing the gravity of what was about to be unveiled. The love, which had been budding behind closed doors and political strategies, was about to be put on full display.

"I love you," Ronnie confessed, voice quaking. Their declaration was met with stunned silence from the crowd.

Donnie leaned in, pulling Ronnie into a deep, passionate kiss, which was both their answer and a proclamation to the world. It was an intimate moment, unapologetically shared in the very public arena of politics. It spoke of passion, of battles fought behind the scenes, of a love that had been simmering beneath the veneer of political alliances and agendas.

The reactions from the crowd varied widely. There were cheers, some enthusiastic claps, gasps of shock, and a smattering of confused murmurs. One could almost hear the whirlwind of social media posts, the WebWonders status updates, and the VidVerse stories being crafted on the fly.

Breaking their embrace, Donnie and Ronnie faced the crowd, still hand in hand. They raised their clasped hands high, the gesture both victorious and unifying.

"Make Acceptance Genuine Again," they started chanting, their voices low. The words seemed to roll off the terrace, gathering momentum as they went. "Make Acceptance Genuine Again!"

The crowd, slowly at first, began to join in. What started as a whisper grew into a crescendo, the words echoing off the surrounding government buildings, becoming a roar of unity and acceptance.

As if on cue, a spontaneous party erupted in the square. Music blasted from nowhere, and people began to dance and celebrate. The atmosphere transformed from tense anticipation to that of a festival.

In the midst of the revelry, figures from the political world started making appearances. Alexandria, her aura commanding and her demeanor exuding support, hugged both Donnie and Ronnie, whispering words of encouragement. Michelle, in a shimmering gown, joined the dancing, her movements graceful and filled with joy. Dark Brandie, initially appearing stoic and reserved, soon broke into a genuine smile, clapping along with the beat. Brock, always the life of the party, rallied the crowd with witty quips and shouts of encouragement.

It was a celebration unlike any other – where politics met passion, where agendas gave way to authenticity, and where love truly did conquer all.

Later, as the evening shadows deepened and the party showed no signs of slowing, it became evident that this was not just a turning point in a campaign. It was a turning point in history, a statement to the world that love and acceptance could bridge any divide.

The night was still young, and the "MAGA Couple," as they would soon be dubbed, had only just begun their dance in the limelight. But one thing was certain: the world of politics would never be the same again.

Late the next morning, Donnie and Ronnie, collectively known as the "MAGA Couple," sat in the plush red seats of the *Primetime Politics Studio*. The studio buzzed with anticipation, the in-house audience whispering and pointing excitedly. The duo's revelation had taken the internet by storm. Everywhere you looked, there were #RonDon2028 banners, memes, and even a few TikTok dance challenges.

As they prepared to go live, Donnie leaned over to Ronnie. "Are you ready, Rebel?" he whispered with a wink, his voice trembling with a mix of excitement and nerves.

Ronnie responded with a cheeky grin, "Always, Divine."

The stage director signaled for silence, the large ON AIR sign illuminated, and Gabriella Gold, with her signature silver hair reflecting the studio lights, began, "Ladies, gentlemen, and everyone beyond and in between, today we have a political game-changer, a seismic shift in the conservative universe. Please welcome Donnie and Ronnie, the 'MAGA Couple'!"

The applause was deafening.

Gabriella continued, "Now, gentlemen, the world is calling you the 'MAGA Couple.' How does that feel?"

Donnie, ever the showman, leaned into the microphone. "Well, Gabriella, I've always been about branding. And if 'MAGA Couple' is what people are calling us, then we'll embrace it. Especially if it pushes our message of acceptance."

Ronnie nodded, "It's ironic that we're uniting people under that banner, but love works in mysterious ways."

Before the duo could elaborate further, a video montage played on the large screen behind them. Clips from ultra-right-wing commentators played, each more hysterical than the last.

Alec Jons, face red, yelled, "I always KNEW they were part of a secret cabal! And this love...it's part of their strategy for global domination!"

Carl Tuckerson, in a more measured tone, tried to spin the narrative. "While I personally find this revelation... unexpected, I believe in the conservative vision of Donnie and Ronnie. Perhaps... perhaps this is what we need to unite the party and the nation."

And then, in a dimly lit room, Bill remarked, "Now, I've always been a voice of reason, right? The LGBTQ+ community has always been... around. Maybe it's time we truly see them for who they are."

The studio audience laughed at the absurdity, but the underlying message was clear. This revelation was changing minds, one pundit at a time.

Gabriella, ever the poised journalist, turned back to her guests. "Your relationship has not only impacted the political world but also the daily lives of many. How do you plan on using this newfound fame?"

Ronnie took the lead, "It's more than just fame, Gabriella. It's a responsibility. We want to promote a message of acceptance and inclusivity. If two conservative candidates can find love in the most unexpected of places, why can't the nation?"

Donnie chimed in, "Exactly! And we plan on touring the country, hosting rallies, and yes, even a few drag shows. We want to unite everyone, regardless of political beliefs, under the banner of love."

As the interview continued, there was a palpable shift in the room. The humor of the situation, combined with the genuine passion and commitment of the "MAGA Couple," was winning hearts. Even the most cynical of journalists found themselves rooting for this unlikely duo.

As the hour neared its end, Gabriella made one final inquiry, "Before we go, the nation wants to know... what's next for the 'MAGA Couple'?"

Donnie looked at Ronnie, their eyes sparkling with mischief. "Well, there's talk of a reality show, a book deal, and... well, let's just say, the White House might have its first ever Drag Ball."

Ronnie laughed, "And you know, Gabriella, maybe we'll even introduce a new line of 'MAGA Couple' merch. After all, love is always in fashion."

As the show concluded, the duo walked hand in hand, ready to face the next chapter of their unexpected love story. Their message of acceptance, combined with a healthy dose of humor, was setting the nation alight. And in the midst of the political chaos, love had found a way to unite.

With the world watching, the "MAGA Couple" was on a mission. They were proving that love wasn't bound by political parties or ideologies. It was universal, unpredictable, and utterly transformative.

And as they stepped out of the studio, hand in hand, the world cheered them on. For in the end, love always wins.

Chapter 19: Escapade

The *Countryside Caress Inn* stood like a relic from a forgotten era, a world away from the blinding city lights and relentless cacophony. Ivy had taken over the exterior, making the vintage building seem one with nature. Set on the city's outskirts, the inn breathed in serenity and exhaled nostalgia.

Donnie, the first to step out of the car, shaded their eyes from the gentle afternoon sun, observing the sprawling gardens. "You know, Rebel, it reminds me of those old Hollywood films," they remarked, relishing the scent of blooming flowers and freshly mowed grass.

Ronnie chuckled, "I half expect to see Cary Grant wandering around with a martini in hand."

The old wooden doors of the inn creaked as they opened. The couple was greeted by Mrs. Pippin, the inn's longtime owner, a petite woman with a head full of silver curls and an infectious warmth about her.

"Ah! Welcome, gentlemen!" Mrs. Pippin exclaimed. "We've prepared the rose suite for you, the one with the view of the gardens. And of course, the fireplace. Perfect for cozying up, especially with the cold front coming in."

Ronnie smiled, taking a moment to soak in the charm of the place. "It's perfect, Mrs. Pippin. Just what we needed."

The inside of the inn was just as enchanting. Antique furniture dotted the rooms, each piece with its own history, a silent witness to countless secrets whispered and dreams dreamt. There was a comforting continuity in the air, as though time had chosen to slow its pace within these walls.

As they walked down the corridor to their suite, Donnie muttered, "You know, the polls have been quite stressful, but this... this feels right." Their fingers entwined with Ronnie's, their touch reassuring.

"Yes, Divine, a little break from the whirlwind. Just us. No politics," Ronnie replied, a twinkle in their eyes.

Their suite was indeed cozy. Light from the setting sun streamed in through sheer curtains, casting a soft glow on the vintage wallpaper. An inviting bed with floral sheets took center stage, and there was an undeniable romance in the air – amplified by the soft strains of a piano drifting in from somewhere.

As Ronnie unpacked, they found a surprise in their suitcase. A navy-blue robe with "Ronnie Rebel" embroidered in gold. A matching robe in crimson, labeled "Divine Donnie", lay atop Donnie's suitcase.

Donnie smirked. "Look at that. Even our clothes are getting serious."

Ronnie playfully swatted them. "Oh hush! It was Tina's idea. She thought we'd need them for our little escape."

Evening settled in, and the duo found themselves in the inn's private dining area. Candlelight flickered, the subtle scent of lavender wafting from centerpieces. A bottle of wine sat chilling, the label hinting at its vintage quality.

Ronnie leaned in, whispering, "You know, this setting is quite... intoxicating."

Donnie's smirk grew wider, "Wait till you see what I've planned for dessert."

Mrs. Pippin soon arrived, serving a meal that was a delightful fusion of traditional and contemporary flavors. As the night progressed, the pair found themselves talking, laughing, and reminiscing – the weight of their public personas momentarily forgotten.

The sounds of clinking silverware and soft laughter resonated in the private dining area. As the night deepened, the conversation shifted from playful banter to something more intimate.

"To tell you the truth, Divine, once all this election hullabaloo is over, I've always dreamt of retiring in South Florida," Ronnie admitted, swirling the wine in their glass. "A little place by the beach, where the waves would be my alarm clock."

Donnie raised an eyebrow in mock surprise, "You, Rebel? Wanting to retire in the land of endless sun and fun?"

Ronnie smirked, "Yes, I know it's hard to believe, but beneath this tough exterior lies a heart that longs for peaceful mornings and slow, lazy afternoons."

"Sounds dreamy," Donnie mused, "I've had the same thought, you know. A beachfront property, maybe even starting a little drag club by the sea, where 'Divine Donnie' and 'Ronnie Rebel' would be the star performers every Saturday night."

Their laughter echoed in the room, and the moment felt surreal. Two presidential candidates, both fierce competitors, sharing dreams and aspirations over candlelight and wine.

"You know," Ronnie began, "I never thought I'd be in this position. I mean, running for president. It's a far cry from my days in the military and lawyering around. But there's this fire, this drive to make a change, to be the voice for those who often go unheard."

Donnie nodded, "I feel you. For me, it's always been about proving myself. Born with a silver spoon, people often underestimate what I can achieve. But politics, this race, it's more than just an ego trip. It's about legacy. It's about creating a world we're proud to leave behind."

As the evening wore on, their conversation flowed seamlessly — from childhood dreams and regrets to their hopes for the future. It was as if the universe had conspired to bring them together, two souls on a similar journey, yet each with their own story to tell.

Ronnie sighed, their fingers tracing patterns on the tablecloth. "I've been many things in life. Soldier, lawyer, politician, drag queen. But at my core, I'm just Ronnie. A person with dreams, aspirations, and a heart that seeks love and connection."

Donnie's hand inched closer, their fingers gently intertwining with Ronnie's. "You know, Rebel, beneath all our roles, at the end of the day, we're all just humans. And right now, I'm just a person enjoying a beautiful evening with someone they deeply care for."

Ronnie's cheeks flushed, the wine and the intimate conversation making them feel heady. They looked deep into Donnie's eyes. "I feel the same way. Being here, right now, with you, has been one of the most genuine moments I've had in a long time."

It was then that Ronnie noticed the subtle change in Donnie's demeanor. The way their eyes darkened a shade, the way their gaze lingered just a bit longer. Sensual undertones began to lace their words, and Ronnie could feel a warmth rising within them.

While they were engrossed in conversation, Donnie's hand slid under the table, finding Ronnie's. The touch was electric, sending jolts of excitement up their spine. Hidden from view by the pristine white linen tablecloth, their fingers entwined, the sensation both thrilling and forbidden.

Donnie's voice dropped to a whisper, "There's something about you, Rebel. It's intoxicating. I've met many people in my life, but none quite like you. Your passion, your resilience, it's... alluring."

Ronnie felt a shiver run down their spine. "And you, Divine, are an enigma. Every time I think I have you figured out, you surprise me. You're a force of nature, unapologetic and fierce, and yet, there's this vulnerability, this softness that you rarely show."

Their conversation, filled with raw emotion and honesty, brought them closer than ever. The physical distance between them seemed to vanish as they leaned into each other, lost in a world of their own.

Their feet touched under the table, a spark of electricity passing between them. The touch lingered, evolved, turned into a gentle play of feet. Soon, wandering hands joined the mix, hidden beneath the draping white linen, communicating words that their mouths didn't speak.

Mrs. Pippin, sensing the change in atmosphere, discreetly left the room, leaving behind a plate of decadent chocolate mousse – Donnie's promised dessert.

Mrs. Pippin's discreet departure and the allure of the abandoned chocolate mousse left behind seemed to blur into the background as Donnie's and Ronnie's eyes locked. The lingering touches, the teasing words, all culminated into a moment that held them both, electrifying the air around them.

Ronnie rose, fingers brushing lightly against Donnie's wrist. "Shall we?" The invitation was unmistakable, its promise a siren's call neither wanted to resist.

The journey to their suite seemed to be over in a flash, both keenly aware of the simmering tension between them. No sooner had the door clicked shut than Donnie pressed Ronnie against it, capturing their lips in a heated, intense kiss that spoke of pent-up desires and unsaid confessions.

Ronnie responded eagerly, their mouths moving with a fevered desperation, as hands roamed over clothes, seeking the warmth of the skin beneath. Their combined heat radiated into the coolness of the room, filling it with the intoxicating blend of arousal and longing.

They pulled apart for a breathless moment, eyes wide and filled with a burning intensity. As each layer was shed, they found themselves in a vulnerable state of mutual exposure, both emotionally and physically. Donnie's hands went to the hem of Ronnie's shirt, slowly lifting it, while Ronnie's fingers worked deftly on Donnie's buttons, revealing the delicate lace lingerie beneath. The soft fabric of their lingerie was a mere barrier to the heat emanating from their bodies.

"It's not just Divine Donnie that has a flair for the dramatic, huh?" Ronnie whispered with a smirk, tracing a finger over the edge of the lace, making Donnie shiver with anticipation.

"You have no idea," Donnie murmured, leading Ronnie to the bed.

Ronnie's fingers traced the contours of Donnie's collarbone, traveling downwards, exploring the expanse of their chest. Slowly finding Donnie's erection, Ronnie wrapping their fingers around the pulsating mass of excitement slowly begins to stroke it while biting Donnie's neck. Donnie moaned softly, their head tilted back, allowing Ronnie to place soft, teasing bites and kisses along their neck.

Clothes discarded, the two stood, taking a moment to truly drink in the sight of one another. The dim room light cast a gentle glow on their forms, revealing the robust bodies honed by years of public appearances, the occasional dance number, and of course, the demands of the campaign trail.

"Ronnie," Donnie whispered, their voice hoarse with need, "I've never felt this way before."

Their lips met in a searing kiss, full of longing and pent-up passion. Their tongues tangled in a dance of dominance and submission, each trying to convey feelings too deep for words.

With a surge of assertiveness, Donnie used a hand to push Ronnie onto the bed, displaying a strength and authority that took Ronnie by surprise. Ronnie felt the soft fabric of the sheets against their back and the heat of Donnie's body pressing against them. Donnie's silhouette, dominant and powerful, hovered above Ronnie's, creating a scene that was both seductive and commanding.

Their engorged members were trapped between them, the intimate pressure causing both to leak in anticipation. Donnie's hands made quick work of securing Ronnie's wrists above their head, the motion firm yet gentle. The action was as symbolic as it was physical—Donnie was taking charge, asserting their dominance, but always with a deep respect for Ronnie's boundaries.

Ronnie's heart raced. The intensity of the moment, combined with the unexpected vulnerability of being pinned beneath Donnie, was overwhelming. Their breaths came fast and erratic, the sensation of being so exposed and yet so desired sending them into a whirlwind of emotions. With a sensual arch of their back, Ronnie wordlessly begged for more intimacy, more connection.

Each rhythmic grind of their hips sent waves of pleasure radiating through their bodies. The friction between their members was electric, both exquisite and torturous. Every movement was accentuated by their entwined legs, the soft caresses of their thighs amplifying the sensation.

But Ronnie was not entirely submissive. Wrestling one hand free with a sly twist, they reached for Donnie, their fingers finding the heat and firmness they sought. Ronnie started to stroke Donnie deliberately, each glide of their hand bringing forth a groan of pleasure from Donnie's lips. This small act of defiance, a reversal in their dynamic, seemed to ignite something even deeper within Donnie.

Donnie's reaction was swift. Their face turned a shade darker, eyes reflecting the storm of desire brewing within. With a swift motion, they pinned Ronnie's renegade hand back above their head, their fingers intertwining in a firm yet gentle grip. The renewed assertion of control was a stark reminder of the delicious power play at hand.

Drawn together as if by a magnetic force, their lips met in a passionate collision. It was a dance of dominance and submission, a melding of mouths that was both fierce and tender. Donnie's tongue sought entrance, and Ronnie willingly obliged, the sensation sending tremors of delight down their spines.

Their kiss was a mirror of their emotional journey—initially hesitant, then growing in confidence and fervor. As their mouths moved in harmony, their bodies followed suit. The rhythm they established was primal, driven by instinct and need. The sensation of their members sliding against one another, lubricated by their shared excitement, was intoxicating.

Ronnie's breathing hitched, their chest heaving with the cocktail of excitement, anxiety, and pure desire. The intimacy of the moment, combined with the raw physical need, was almost too much.

The rhythm between them grew frenzied, fueled by their desire and the forbidden nature of their relationship. Ronnie's legs wrapped around Donnie's waist, pulling them even closer. The world ceased to exist outside of that room and the sensations that coursed through them.

The taste of their shared wine, the heady scent of arousal, and the music of their mingled moans filled the room. Donnie's lips trailed down Ronnie's throat, nipping and teasing as they went, leaving behind a trail of fire.

Donnie's hands roamed freely, every touch lighting Ronnie's skin on fire. The exploration soon shifted, as Donnie flipped Ronnie onto their stomach, their position now more dominant than before. The anticipation built as Donnie positioned themselves, their intent clear.

With Ronnie rolling over, Donnie took a moment to appreciate the beauty of Ronnie's exposed back, tracing a finger down the spine, eliciting a delightful shiver. Gripping Ronnie's hips, they pulled them up, their intentions clear.

Donnie, ever the dominant presence, seemed in tune with Ronnie's every thought and whim. Their fingers, skilled and determined, found Ronnie's arousal with unerring accuracy. Starting at the base, they firmly yet gently grasped and began a rhythmic stroking, pulling it back and forth between Ronnie's thighs. The sensation was heightened by the clandestine nature of their union, making every touch, every tug, feel electric.

The evidence of Ronnie's desire was palpable, their arousal leaking onto Donnie's expert hand. But Donnie wasn't content with just that. They wanted—no, needed— to taste the essence of the person who had so thoroughly captured their interest. Lowering themselves, Donnie's tongue delicately traced a path from the sensitive tip of Ronnie's manhood, savoring the slightly salty taste. The slow ascent up the shaft was meticulous, every inch explored, worshipped, and adored.

When Donnie's mouth reached the apex, they paused for a split second, as if savoring the moment. Then, with a devilish glint in their eyes and a boldness that was uniquely Donnie, they dove deeper, their tongue seeking out the most intimate part of Ronnie. The unexpected sensation of Donnie's warm tongue against Ronnie's sensitive entrance had Ronnie arching their back towards the ceiling, a sound that was half-gasp, half-moan escaping their lips.

This was uncharted territory for them, a realm of pleasure they'd never ventured into before. And yet, with Donnie, it felt right. Safe. Every flick, every teasing prod of Donnie's tongue seemed attuned to Ronnie's reactions. It was as if Donnie was playing a symphony on Ronnie's body, each note eliciting a response more profound than the last.

The rhythm they found was instinctual, raw, and untamed. Ronnie's hips began to move of their own accord, seeking more of that intoxicating sensation, pushing back against Donnie's insistent tongue. Their movements mirrored the urgency, the sheer need that had been building between them since their first encounter. Every lap, every groan, every caress was steering them towards an apex of pleasure that threatened to shatter them both.

Ronnie's fingers clutched at the sheets, their knuckles white from the intensity of their grip. The coil of tension in the pit of their stomach tightened with each passing second, the anticipation of release becoming almost unbearable. Donnie, sensing Ronnie's impending climax, redoubled their efforts, their tongue moving with a ferocity that had Ronnie teetering on the brink.

The room, dimly lit by the soft glow of a bedside lamp, echoed with the soft rustle of sheets as Ronnie, overwhelmed by the intensity of the moment, rolled onto their back. Their skin, flushed with a rosy hue, glistened with a light sheen of sweat. Each breath Ronnie took was heavy with longing, their chest rising and falling in a rhythm that spoke of a desire not yet quenched.

Donnie, reading the unspoken words in Ronnie's gaze, leaned down, their lips hovering just above Ronnie's, their breaths mingling. With a teasing slowness, they let their hand wander downwards, fingertips skimming over Ronnie's sensitized skin. Donnie's fingers gently traced the path from Ronnie's hips, feather-light touches tickling their skin and causing goosebumps to erupt. The room was thick with tension, with every inhale and exhale echoing a symphony of anticipation. The ambient lighting from the bedside lamp cast a golden hue on Ronnie's skin, emphasizing the drops of sweat that glistened from the evening's activities.

Drawing closer to Ronnie's thighs, Donnie's fingers found the sensitive inner portions, causing Ronnie's breathing to hitch. With a mischievous twinkle in their eyes, Donnie slowly explored further, their touch delicate, almost reverent. Their fingers danced across Ronnie's skin, sending shockwaves of pleasure coursing through them.

When Donnie's fingers reached their intended destination, the teasing touch caused Ronnie's back to arch off the bed. The sensation was electric, a buildup of raw emotion and need. With every circle and press, Ronnie's breaths became more ragged, their hands clenching the sheets tightly.

Their connection was palpable, a tether of raw, unfiltered emotion. Donnie paused, looking deep into Ronnie's eyes, searching for any hesitance. But what they saw was a burning desire, mixed with a hint of vulnerability. Ronnie's eyes, normally so guarded and reserved, were now wide open, bearing their soul. The slight nod they gave, combined with the biting of their lower lip, was all the confirmation Donnie needed.

With painstaking slowness, Donnie pressed forward, the initial barrier offering a slight resistance. The world seemed to stand still, the only sound being the syncopated rhythm of their heartbeats and the ragged breathing that filled the room. As Donnie pushed further inside, the sensation was overwhelming. The tight embrace was both restricting and comforting, a blend of two contrasting feelings that only amplified the intensity of the moment.

Ronnie let out a sharp intake of breath, a sound that was part gasp and part moan. The blend of pleasure and slight pain was evident in their expression, but their eyes held a fervor that spoke of deeper emotions. Their hands reached up, fingers tangling in Donnie's hair, pulling them down for a searing kiss.

They began to move in tandem, a dance as old as time, yet so uniquely theirs. Each thrust was a testament to their burgeoning feelings, a physical manifestation of the emotions that had been building throughout the evening. The depth of their connection was evident in the way their bodies responded to each other, every touch and movement amplifying the pleasure they were both experiencing.

Donnie's pace quickened, their thrusts becoming more deliberate, each one seeking to push both of them to the edge. Ronnie's moans grew louder, their legs wrapping tighter around Donnie's waist, urging them on. The room was filled with the symphony of their passion, the creaking of the bed frame, and the rustling of the sheets, creating a backdrop to their shared ecstasy.

With a final, desperate thrust of their hips, Ronnie surrendered to the overwhelming sensations, their entire body going rigid as waves of pleasure washed over them. Their climax, when it hit, was cataclysmic—a release of all the pent-up emotions, desires, and tensions of the past weeks.

As the tremors of ecstasy began to subside, Donnie slowly made their way up Ronnie's body, leaving a trail of feather-light kisses in their wake. When their eyes met, the connection was palpable, a shared understanding passing between them. This wasn't just a physical act; it was an emotional bond that had been forged in the crucible of passion.

As the aftershocks subsided, they lay entwined in each other's arms, their breathing gradually returning to normal. The room was filled with a sense of contentment, a shared moment that went beyond the physical. In that intimate embrace, two souls had connected on a level that transcended words, forging a bond that was both profound and unbreakable.

Finally, as the adrenaline subsided and exhaustion took over, they lay side by side, their fingers interlaced, eyes locked in a gaze full of understanding and affection.

"Donnie," Ronnie whispered, tracing circles on the back of their hand, "this was... unexpected, yet incredibly beautiful."

Donnie smiled, pulling Ronnie closer for a soft, lingering kiss. "Life is full of surprises, Rebel. But this? This feels right."

They lay there, side by side, the weight of the moment settling around them. Words seemed superfluous, for their actions had spoken volumes. In the quiet aftermath, the two rivals-turned-lovers found solace in each other's embrace, their breathing slowly synchronizing as they drifted into a contented slumber.

As dawn approached, and the first light began to seep through the curtains, they found solace in the warmth of their shared embrace, knowing that the world outside would soon demand their attention. But for this stolen night, all that mattered was them. The future could wait.

Donnie and Ronnie woke to the soft chirping of birds outside, with the sun peeking through the drapes of the vintage room of the Countryside Caress Inn. The aftermath of last night's intensity still etched on the rumpled sheets and in their shy morning smiles.

Stretching languidly, Donnie playfully commented, "Who knew a debate stage could lead here?"

Ronnie smirked, "From podiums to pillows. That should be our tagline."

They shared a chuckle, then a contemplative silence settled, a certain seriousness in their eyes. Both knew the weight of the previous night's revelations.

"Ronnie, have you ever thought about being Vice President?" Donnie asked suddenly.

Ronnie sat up, "What are you getting at?"

"We've both seen the poles. With the two of us together as running mates, we'd be unbeatable," Donnie replied. "Can you imagine? Donnie as President and Ronnie as VP? It's like a TV sitcom waiting to happen!"

Ronnie smirked, "And what would our show be called? 'The White House Romantics'?"

"Don't tempt me," Donnie laughed. "But seriously, think about it. Together, we could redefine politics. We've already got the charisma, the experience, and now," Donnie winked, "we've got undeniable chemistry."

Ronnie chuckled, considering it. "We'd be an unstoppable duo. Plus, think of the lavish state dinners and the behind-the-scenes gossip."

Donnie raised an eyebrow, "And here I thought you were the serious one."

They looked into each other's eyes. "All jokes aside, we could truly make a difference. Show the world that love and understanding can conquer all," Ronnie added.

Donnie squeezed their hand, "It's ambitious, it's a little crazy, but so are we."

"Are we really going to do this?" Ronnie asked.

Donnie nodded, "Why not? We're already breaking norms and setting new standards."

Just then, Donnie's phone buzzed with a notification. "It's the election committee," they said, opening the message. Their face lit up as they read, "We won the primary! We're officially the conservative candidates!"

The realization was overwhelming. Ronnie pulled Donnie into a warm embrace, their minds already racing towards the future. The upcoming battle against Alexandria would be tough, but together, they felt invincible.

The weight of the moment settled around them once again. A world outside awaited their emergence, rife with challenges and expectations. But for now, nestled in the Countryside Caress Inn, all that mattered was the solace they found in each other's arms and the hope for a brighter, more inclusive future.

Donnie kissed Ronnie's forehead, "Ready to take on the world, Rebel?"

Ronnie's eyes twinkled, "As long as you're by my side, Divine."

They looked out of the window, the morning sun now fully shining, heralding a new day, a new beginning. The path ahead was uncertain, filled with both challenges and opportunities. But one thing was for sure: together, Donnie and Ronnie were ready to face it all.

As the first light began to seep through the curtains, the world outside started to stir, signaling the beginning of a new day and new challenges. But for Donnie and Ronnie, wrapped in each other's arms in the quiet sanctity of the room, the world outside could wait. The future was uncertain, filled with potential pitfalls and challenges. Yet, in that moment, all that mattered was the here and now and the promise of a shared journey ahead.

Chapter 20:
The Rally

Unity Square was buzzing with energy, the crowd's palpable excitement lending the air an almost electric quality. Everywhere you looked, there were signs, flags, and eager faces—people from all walks of life who'd converged at the Transparency Terrace to show their support for Alexandria.

In one corner, a group of enthusiastic college students chanted slogans for LGBTQ+ rights, while in another, an elderly couple proudly waved a flag that celebrated love in all its forms. Street vendors weaved their way through the throngs, selling badges, ribbons, and even quirky hats, all adorned with Alexandria's campaign symbols.

Donnie and Ronnie's recent public declaration of love was the talk of the town. Their story, one of unexpected romance amidst the gritty world of politics, had sparked debates, inspired countless memes, and was now even influencing other politicians like Alexandria.

Backstage, Alexandria nervously adjusted her blazer, its hue reflecting the colors of the Pride flag. Every now and then, she'd peek through the curtains to gauge the crowd. "I can't believe I'm doing this," she muttered, recalling Donnie and Ronnie's passionate kiss that had broken the internet. If they could be brave, so could she. Today wasn't just about politics; it was about revealing a part of herself that she'd kept hidden for far too long. Today, the world would meet 'Alex the Conqueror'.

Beside her, Brock gave an encouraging smile. "You got this, Alexandria. You've got a message to share, and there's no better time than now."

She took a deep breath, her nerves gradually replaced by determination. This rally wasn't just about her campaign promises or policies; it was personal. She was about to share with the world a side of herself that very few knew about, a side that would no doubt raise eyebrows in the political realm but one she was immensely proud of.

As the master of ceremonies took the stage, announcing the series of speakers and performers lined up, Alexandria's heart rate increased. But as Brock gently squeezed her shoulder, a gesture of support and camaraderie, she felt a rush of courage.

By the time her name was announced, the crowd's cheers were deafening. The applause seemed to ripple, echoing off the tall buildings surrounding the square. Stepping out onto the stage, she took a moment to absorb the scene, letting the love and energy of the crowd envelop her.

Amidst the sea of people gathered at Unity Square Transparency Terrace, Alexandria's posture conveyed a fusion of regality and vulnerability. An electric energy hovered in the air, a moment pregnant with the promise of revelations.

"I stand here before you, not just as Alexandria, the politician, the grassroots advocate, the woman fighting for a better tomorrow," she began, voice full of emotion...

Now, miles away in the sumptuous, romantically-lit confines of the 'rose suite' at Mrs. Pippin's Countryside Caress Inn, Donnie and Ronnie, wrapped in plush bathrobes (but otherwise quite bare), sat on the king-sized bed. A tray of strawberries and champagne lay forgotten as they stared at the television screen, the blush from their recent... escapades still evident on their faces.

"Wait, do we have to wear clothes to watch this?" Donnie mumbled, fingers playing with Ronnie's hair.

Ronnie elbowed Donnie gently, "Focus! This is pivotal. Plus, if Alex can bare her truth, we can watch it while baring... well, all of this," Ronnie gestured with a playful smirk.

Back at the rally, Alexandria began. "From a humble neighborhood, serving patrons at a bar, to standing here today, it has been a journey of discovery, of fighting odds, of picking battles, and more importantly, picking outfits," she quipped, evoking chuckles.

"I've strived to bridge the chasm between policies and heartbeats. To ensure that each voice, each beat, each moment, is recognized and represented," her voice held a fervor, a spark. "But today is not just about policy; it's about passion. The passion with which I've lived dual lives: as Alexandria, the advocate, and Alex the Conqueror, the symbol of what it means to truly embrace oneself."

Back at the inn, Donnie reached for a strawberry, dipping it in whipped cream. They offered it to Ronnie, "You know, there's something incredibly empowering and sexy about embracing your dualities."

Ronnie arched an eyebrow, "Are we still talking about Alexandria?"

Donnie smirked, "Maybe. Or maybe I'm just plotting the encore to our earlier activities."

On stage, Alexandria's voice wavered with emotion, "Politics has always been a realm of masks. But why wear one when you can wear makeup?" She paused, allowing the laughter to ebb. "But beneath the foundation, the contouring, and the dramatics, what I've truly learned from my time as Alex is that true power lies in authenticity. In the courage to unapologetically be oneself."

Michelle, unable to contain herself, yelled, "Preach, Queen! Or should I say, King!"

"Remember, when we vote, when we voice, when we rally," Alexandria continued, fervor building, "it's not just policies we champion. It's people. It's love. It's the raw, vulnerable beats of our hearts, desperate to be acknowledged, to belong."

Her voice dropped to an intimate whisper, "Like many of you, I've felt the suffocating weight of closets. The confined spaces where our truths, our identities, our desires are hidden away. But today, in the spirit of love, acceptance, and in honor of Donnie and Ronnie's MAGA - 'Making Acceptance Genuine Always' - I urge you all to break free."

The cheers that erupted were deafening. The energy at Unity Square Transparency Terrace was nothing short of magnetic. Alexandria's vulnerability, coupled with her fervent aspirations for a unified future, had captivated hearts.

At the 'rose suite', Donnie and Ronnie sat, a hushed silence between them, absorbing Alexandria's words. The weight of their own truths, their own journey to acceptance, mirrored in her sentiments.

Ronnie turned to Donnie, their face serious yet tender, "We made a ripple, but she's creating a wave."

Donnie, eyes glistening, squeezed Ronnie's hand, "Together, we're changing the tides."

The scene at the rally was pure euphoria. As Alexandria stepped off stage, Brock enveloped her in a hug. "You did it," he whispered, pride evident in his voice.

Alexandria looked out at the sea of faces, eyes bright with tears, "We all did. This is just the beginning."

And miles away, wrapped in layers of satin sheets and lingering passions, Donnie and Ronnie realized the same. Their journey, their love, their acceptance, was a beacon for many. The world was shifting, and they, along with Alexandria, were at the forefront of this beautiful revolution.

Unity Square Transparency Terrace was alive with emotion. It was as if every individual's heartbeat synchronized in an anthem of hope, acceptance, and unity.

Brenda, a single mother of two who had worked tirelessly on Alexandria's campaign, found herself clenching her daughter's hand tighter. She whispered, "Baby, this is the world I want you to grow up in. One where you can be anything, *anyone*, and still be loved."

Her daughter, eyes wide with understanding, nodded. At the tender age of ten, the significance of the day wasn't lost on her.

Luis, a university student, had his arms draped over his boyfriend's shoulders, tears streaking down his face. They had experienced their fair share of prejudice, especially from those who wore their bigotry like a badge of honor. But here, in the embrace of the crowd, they felt seen, heard, and valid.

In the VIP section, Dark Brandie found himself surprised by his own emotions. Known for his stoicism, he was taken aback by the warmth bubbling up inside him. He had started as an antagonist, wary of Alexandria's rise. But watching her today, he realized that perhaps they were fighting for the same cause after all, just from different sides.

Brandie leaned over to Brock, remarking wistfully, "Your friend is something special."

Brock smirked, replying, "Took you long enough to notice."

At that moment, Michelle, in all her drag glory as Michelle Pensive, stood atop a makeshift platform, leading a crowd in a chant. "LOVE NOT HATE, MAKES AMERICA GREAT!"

A group of young volunteers from Alexandria's Advocacy Hub had spontaneously begun distributing heart-shaped stickers. These little tokens, simple yet profound, became badges of honor for those who wore them. They symbolized a commitment to a more inclusive America.

Near the stage, an elderly couple, married for over fifty years, swayed gently, their love story a testament to endurance. They had seen the ebb and flow of politics, the good, bad, and the ugly. But today, they witnessed something different: a movement grounded in genuine love.

Back at the Countryside Caress Inn, Donnie and Ronnie were glued to the screen, entranced by the raw energy emanating from the rally. They looked at each other, a silent acknowledgment passing between them. They were part of this tapestry, this intricate web of change.

The afternoon sun bathed the Transparency Terrace in a golden hue. Everywhere you looked, there was an embrace, a tear, a dance. The barriers that had once seemed insurmountable - age, race, gender, and sexuality - melted away.

From a nearby cafe, the barista, a transgender man who had experienced more than his fair share of discrimination, stepped out, handing out free coffees. His tip jar, instead of coins, filled up with heart stickers. A simple yet powerful symbol of the day.

NewsWave Media Outlets, always on the hunt for the next big story, had their cameras rolling. But for once, their usually cynical reporters were moved, discarding their scripts to speak from the heart.

And as the sun began its descent, casting long shadows on Unity Square, a group of children took center stage, releasing a flurry of balloons, each inscribed with a message of hope. They rose, higher and higher, much like the aspirations of those present.

Unity Square Transparency Terrace wasn't just a political event. It was a testament to the resilience of the human spirit, to the power of love, and to the belief that change, while daunting, was always within reach.

Alexandria, watching from the sidelines, felt a weight lifting. She had sown the seeds of change, and now, they were taking root. Today was not just her victory; it was a victory for everyone who had ever felt marginalized, unloved, or unseen.

Amidst the splendor of the Unity Square Transparency Terrace, a group of conservative bloggers, who ironically called themselves 'The Ultra-Righteous', had found a spot near NewsWave Media Outlets. Marissa, their self-proclaimed leader, adjusted her horn-rimmed glasses and remarked, "Y'know, Alexandria might be onto something. A message of love? That might be the game-changer conservatives need."

Her companion, Jake, who had recently discovered his penchant for high heels (much to his own surprise), arched a brow. "Are you suggesting we embrace her message? She's not one of ours."

Marissa smirked, twirling her fiery red hair. "Oh, darling. It's not about embracing. It's about adapting. If love can unify, then maybe it can give conservatives complete control. Think about it. Alexandria's touchy-feely approach with a sprinkle of our strategy? Unbeatable."

Meanwhile, at NewsWave Media Outlets, veteran reporter Daniel Silver, known for his biting sarcasm and stoic demeanor, was visibly moved. Clearing his throat, he began, "Ladies and gentlemen, I've covered countless rallies. From the flamboyant to the furious. But today? Today is different. It's not just about the left or right; it's about heart. It's about... love." He paused, blinking rapidly, clearly fighting back tears.

At the Primetime Politics Studio, the green room was abuzz. The talk was all about Alexandria and her unifying message. "She's bridging the gap," said one producer. "It's like she's taken Donnie and Ronnie's MAGA and turned it into a universal anthem."

There was something else, though. A humorous undercurrent. Helen, a liberal commentator with a penchant for sly wit, leaned in, whispering to her colleagues, "Just imagine, the ultra-right embracing a liberal message. What next? Cats and dogs living together?"

On WebWonders Online Space, hashtags were born by the second. #LoveIsTheNewRight trended alongside #MAGAforALL. Memes of Alexandria, Donnie, and Ronnie flooded timelines, some humorously merging their faces, others showcasing their drag personas side by side.

At Alexandria's Advocacy Hub, a live stream of the rally played. Young volunteers, inspired by the day's events, brainstormed new campaigns. Among them was the idea to host regular community dialogues where individuals from opposing political beliefs could find common ground. It would be named: "MAGA Mingles: Making Acceptance Genuine Always, For Everyone."

However, it wasn't all sunshine. At Tradition Towers Party Office, there was an emergency gathering. Traditional conservatives, furrowing brows, discussed the 'threat' of the liberal love epidemic. "We can't let them hijack the narrative," declared one elder. "If love is the new weapon, we need to arm ourselves!"

As evening settled, the Victory Vanguard Press Hall had invited Alexandria for a special interview. Taking a seat, the once-bartender turned presidential candidate, and now the face of a revolution, smiled at her interviewer.

"Alexandria, you've started something today," began the interviewer, her voice a mix of curiosity and admiration. "The lines between left and right seem blurrier than ever. How do you feel?"

With poise, Alexandria replied, "I feel hopeful. Politics, for too long, has been a realm of division. But today? We saw possibility. We witnessed the strength in unity. Whether you lean left, right, or somewhere in between, love is something we all understand."

"But what do you say to those who think this is just a political tactic?"

She grinned, a hint of mischief in her eyes. "Love isn't a tactic. It's the solution."

Back at the Countryside Caress Inn, Donnie and Ronnie, cuddling under the duvet, scrolled through social media on their tablets. The outpouring of support, the discussions, the memes, all painted a picture of a world ready for change.

Ronnie turned to Donnie, their voice laced with humor, "You think we should trademark our MAGA? Seems everyone's using it now."

Donnie chuckled, pressing a soft kiss on Ronnie's forehead. "It's not about trademarks, darling. It's about transformation. And together," they said, intertwining their fingers with Ronnie's, "we've started a revolution."

In a world where political games were the norm, where rhetoric often trumped reality, Alexandria, Donnie, and Ronnie had brought forth a message that transcended boundaries. It was a message that whispered of hope, shouted of change, and sang of love.

And as the night draped its velvety cloak over the city, Unity Square Transparency Terrace, which had witnessed countless events in its time, had never seen anything quite like this. For it wasn't just a political movement; it was a dance of hearts, a chorus of souls, all echoing the same sentiment: love not hate, makes America great.

Chapter 21: E-Day Approaches

The hustle and bustle inside Victory Vanguard Press Hall was electric. As one of the most significant events leading up to the elections, the final press conference promised to be a doozy. Cameras flashed, reporters scribbled, and journalists whispered, all trying to predict the next headline.

Betsy, a journalist for NewsWave Media Outlets, was scanning the room. Her stiletto heels clicked against the floor, her notebook was poised, and her thoughts teemed with possibilities. If gossip and speculation were to be believed, there was much more to this election than policy points and campaign promises.

The campaign year had been, for lack of a better term, *wild*. After the primaries, the entire nation watched, entranced, as the dynamic of the election shifted. Alexandria, the passionate liberal advocate, was pitted against a unique pairing: Donnie and Ronnie, or as they'd been humorously dubbed by late-night comedians, RonDon2028.

There were, of course, the usual barbs and jibes thrown in every direction. But what made this election year standout were the personal revelations. Donnie and Ronnie, under an unexpected turn of events, had publicized their romantic relationship. Moreover, they'd also come out about their shared passion: drag.

In a café across town, three women chatted animatedly.

"Donnie in drag?" Helen smirked. "I'd pay to see that. I mean, Divine Donnie? Brilliant!"

Sophie interjected, "Imagine the situational comedy! Getting ready for a debate and a drag show on the same day?"

Tessa, sipping her latte, purred, "And don't get me started on the spicy moments between Donnie and Ronnie backstage. The intimacy, the shared eyeliner…"

But back in the press hall, things were heating up. As more attendees poured in, the atmosphere became thick with anticipation.

Michelle, having recently embraced her transgender identity, walked in, holding her head high, but with a hint of nervousness. After all, she was a central figure in the RonDon camp. Given her history with conservative politics, her presence was a symbol of the changing times.

Brock, ever the advocate for equity, was present, ensuring that the media portrayed all candidates fairly and respectfully. Alexandria's advocacy team had prepped her for every possible question, focusing on policy over personal history. Alexandria, with her fiery spirit, was eager to address both.

Dark Brandie, once an antagonist, had softened over the campaign trail. He had his reservations about the RonDon duo but was secretly rooting for them. After all, in the world of drag, competition was fierce, but camaraderie was fiercer.

As the clock ticked closer to the start time, Betsy, along with other journalists, took their positions, eager to witness political history. This was not just another election. It was a testament to progress, continuity, and the power of authenticity. Whether it was Alexandria advocating for rights and inclusivity, Donnie and Ronnie embracing their true selves or Michelle coming into her own, this election season was a game-changer.

And as the curtains rose, the room held its collective breath, ready for the spectacle that was about to unfold.

As the lights dimmed, the attendees watched intently as the presidential candidates took their respective places on stage. A palpable excitement pervaded the hall, with some feeling as if they were witnessing a live episode of a hit reality show, complete with theatrics and melodrama.

A hush fell as Donnie stepped up, their heels echoing loudly in the vast hall. Beside them, Ronnie stood poised, their classic pinstripe suit immaculately pressed, a sharp contrast to Donnie's sparkly blazer. Alexandria, as always, looked the part of a fierce advocate in her sleek pantsuit, a glint of determination evident in her eyes.

Gabriella Gold began with a mild question about policy reform, which Alexandria handled eloquently. Then, as if taking a deep breath before a plunge, Ms. Gold turned to

Donnie and Ronnie, with her silver hair cascading around her shoulders.

"We've had reports about your public LGBTQ relationship reveal, as well as your recent revelations about drag. How do you think this will impact your election chances?"

Donnie cleared their throat, mischief sparkling in their eyes. "Well, didn't the public adore 'Divine Donnie'? As for our relationship, love is love. And if love can make Ronnie and me even more committed to this country, then that's a plus, isn't it?"

Before Gabriella Gold could ask another question, a voice interrupted, "How can you focus on running the country when you're too busy running backstage changing outfits?"

The audience gasped. It was Carl Tuckerson, looking smug. "Furthermore," he added snidely, "If you do win, who will be the first lady?"

There was a collective gasp from the audience. A low murmur of disapproval swept through the hall, like a cold gust of wind.

Donnie, drawing themselves up to their full height, replied with a tone of barely concealed disdain, "Firstly, Mr. Tuckerson, neither Ronnie nor I would don that title, for we are non-binary. We proudly go by they/them pronouns. As for your question about the 'First Lady', it is not only reductive but dripping with homophobia. Instead of sticking to outdated norms, let's focus on creating a world where everyone is treated with respect, irrespective of their gender or who they love." Chiming in with a witty retort, Ronnie replies "I've always been found of the idea of First Theys."

A smattering of applause broke out, gradually growing louder. Alexandria chimed in, "While Donnie and Ronnie are my political opponents, I won't tolerate disrespect towards their personal choices. Let's keep the focus on policies and the betterment of our nation."

Feeling outmatched, Carl Tuckerson shrunk back in his seat, but not before casting a glowering look at Donnie.

Ronnie took a moment to catch their breath and then added, "It's imperative to remember that our relationship is based on mutual respect and understanding. It's this foundation that will help us work effectively for the country if we are elected."

As the press conference proceeded, other journalists posed questions of varying sensitivity. Betsy, with her renowned professionalism, steered the narrative back to political matters. The candidates handled everything with grace and poise, deftly deflecting any negativity.

In a corner, Dark Brandie watched the proceedings, a slow smile curving his lips. His earlier reservations about the RonDon duo seemed to melt away. He made a mental note to design a fabulous costume for the upcoming drag parade, perhaps something as theatrical as the political stage.

At the back of the room, Michelle, eyes glistening, whispered to Brock, "Who would have thought? From hiding behind curtains to confronting their truth on such a massive stage!"

Brock nodded, replying softly, "It's all about embracing oneself. It's a revolution of acceptance, and today, we're all part of it."

It was the next journalist's turn, a rather sheepish looking man, possibly in his early thirties. "Considering your romantic relationship," he began, looking at Donnie and Ronnie, "How do you plan on handling potential disagreements in office?"

Ronnie, ever the thinker, was quick to respond. "Just like any other administration, with consideration, discussion, and compromise. Our relationship has taught us the value of effective communication." Donnie, not one to be outdone, winked, "And besides, making up after is always the fun part." The room erupted in laughter.

A woman from the back, with fiery red hair and freckles, raised her hand. "Ms. Alexandria, given your advocacy for the LGBTQ+ community, how do you view the conservative standpoints of Donnie and Ronnie, especially when it comes to rights?"

Alexandria's poised demeanor and passion shone through as she answered. "I believe in fighting for rights for all, irrespective of one's political affiliation. While we might have disagreements on certain issues, I'm hopeful that understanding and compassion can drive our nation's progress. Plus, I've got to say, Donnie and Ronnie have some excellent taste in heels."

Donnie and Ronnie exchanged a surprised yet amused glance. This kind of camaraderie was unexpected but pleasantly refreshing.

Dark Brandie, observing everything from his seat, leaned over to Brock. "I must admit, they're handling things better than I anticipated. Perhaps there's more to them than just sequins and sashays."

Brock, sipping on a drink, remarked, "It's the heart beneath the sequins that matters, Brandie. And they've got plenty of it."

Another reporter stood up, clearing his throat. "Donnie, Ronnie, how can the public trust you when your whole relationship and drag personas were hidden for so long?"

Ronnie leaned into the microphone, "We were navigating our truths in a world that often can be unkind. The fact that we're standing here now, transparent and genuine, should be testament enough to our commitment to authenticity."

Donnie chimed in, "Life is a journey, and sometimes, it involves a little drag. As for trust, judge us by our actions and policies. I assure you, our stilettos are firmly on the ground." Another wave of laughter filled the room.

A tall journalist, with a bowtie, asked Alexandria, "You've always been a strong advocate for transparency. What's your take on this?"

Alexandria took a deep breath. "I believe everyone has their own journey of self-realization. It's not for us to judge when or how they choose to share. What's important is that they have. Our personal stories, struggles, and choices shape us but do not define our capability to lead or serve."

Dark Brandie leaned over to Michelle, "I've got to hand it to them; they're putting on quite a show."

Michelle nodded, wiping a tear. "It's not a show, Brandie. It's their life, and I couldn't be prouder."

Throughout the conference, the questions kept coming, but the trio remained unyielding, addressing every curveball with humor, grace, and profound insight.

In a softer moment, Ronnie took the mic. "I want every person out there, regardless of who they love, how they identify, to know that they are seen, valid, and loved. It's time for us to come together as a nation and embrace acceptance and unity. After all, a country that loves together, thrives together."

Alexandria, overcome with emotion, stood and applauded, soon joined by others, culminating in a standing ovation. Donnie took Ronnie's hand, and the two shared a heartfelt, intimate moment amidst the applause.

As the press conference at Victory Vanguard Press Hall came to a heartwarming conclusion, the journalists didn't waste a second. Cameras flashed, recorders were clicked off, and fingers flew over keyboards and touchscreens. The room buzzed with an amalgamation of appreciation, shock, and skepticism.

In the sprawling newsroom of *NewsWave Media Outlets*, Tess, the in-house social media guru, energetically tapped at her screens, curating tweets, Instagram posts, and quick-fire articles. Her monitors streamed various channels, but one particular clip of Donnie and Ronnie holding hands while Alexandria applauded replayed across screens worldwide. It was a visual treat and a testament to the unyielding spirit of acceptance.

Dave and Mira, two senior journalists, huddled together, reviewing their notes and discussing the most impactful quotes. "Did you catch Donnie's bit about the stilettos? Pure gold!" Dave remarked, chuckling. Mira nodded, her gaze fixed on her screen as she shaped the story of unity amidst the diversity of political competition.

In the adjacent studio, Tina, the anchor with sharp cat-eye glasses and a penchant for sassy retorts, began her live segment. "It was a day of revelations, powerful statements, and some darn good humor, folks. The RonDon2028 team, along with Alexandria, have truly transformed this political season into a romantic comedy, sprinkled with some spicy drama!"

Just as the positive reviews started flowing, the darker side of media reared its head. Carl Tuckerson, still reeling from his public lesson in sensitivity, took to his show to lambaste the trio. "The audacity!" he exclaimed. "Hiding behind a charade of humor and glitz, hoping we forget their deceptions and focus on their... performances!"

Alec Jons, ever the conspiracy theorist, went on a bizarre rant. "I always knew there was something fishy about RonDon! But this drag revelation... it's all a ploy! A liberal strategy! They're trying to distract us!" However, halfway through, in an unexpected twist, he seemed to reconsider. "Or maybe, just maybe, they're genuinely showing their authentic selves. And if they are... well, I might need to recalibrate my opinions."

Bill, who traditionally took a staunch anti-LGBTQ+ stance, surprised his audience. "Look, in my decades of reporting, I've been wrong on many counts, particularly on LGBTQ+ rights. But after today, seeing the courage and unity displayed by RonDon and Alexandria, I've realized it's time for change. We might not see eye to eye on policies, but personal choices deserve respect. I still have reservations, but today marked a step forward."

The digital world of *WebWonders Online Space* went into overdrive. #RonDon2028 and #AlexTheConqueror trended, while memes, gifs, and fan-art flooded timelines. Opinions ranged from loving admiration to scathing criticism. Among the mix, a touching post from a non-binary teenager garnered attention: "Watching Ronnie and Donnie stand tall, with Alexandria supporting them, gave me hope. Today, I feel seen."

The mainstream media provided a mix of opinions. While some outlets played up the 'affair' angle, digging into the duo's past for any hint of scandal, others focused on the unification of the nation through the embodiment of acceptance.

The public, initially skeptical, began to warm up to the RonDon duo. They witnessed a couple who, despite facing personal challenges, stood firm, their charisma shining through. Their joint vision for the country remained undeterred by their personal revelations, reinforcing that their romantic relationship wouldn't impede their political objectives.

The crescendo of media reactions finally settled into a consensus. While it was undeniable that the journey of Donnie, Ronnie, and even Alexandria had been unusual and filled with unexpected twists, their dedication to the country and its citizens was unwavering. Their tales of self-discovery, intertwined with their political aspirations, signaled a future where personal narratives would no longer be barriers but rather bridges to understanding and acceptance.

As the media circus wound down and the stories were printed, broadcasted, and shared, the nation took a collective breath. The upcoming elections would not just be a choice of policies or parties. It would be a testament to how far society had come and how much further it intended to go.

In the quiet of the night, at *Cortez Cozy Corner*, Alexandria sat on her balcony, looking out at the city. Her phone buzzed with a message. It was from Ronnie: "Today was intense, but we made it through. Thanks for standing by us. Let the best candidate win."

She smiled, typing back, "Indeed. Here's to a brighter future, no matter who leads the way."

And as the city lights twinkled below, the weight of the day's events sank in, promising a new dawn of hope, acceptance, and unity.

In Unity Square, a flash mob formed, dancing to a remixed version of a popular song, with lyrics praising

Donnie and Ronnie's resilience. Videos of the performance went viral, with even celebrities chiming in their support.

Back in Primetime Politics Studio, as the analysts wrapped up their coverage, a consensus was emerging. The press conference was a turning point. While there were still detractors and cynics, the public narrative was veering towards positivity and acceptance.

In the Starlit Drag Lounge, as drag performances celebrated the day's events, some queens, now in their drag personas, dressed as famous presidents and famous women of America's past, took the stage. As they belted out a different ballad on love and acceptance, and danced to patriotic remixes, the crowd swayed in unison, united in their support for a changing world.

The night faded, but the events of the day continued to resonate. The media had played its part, for better or worse, but one thing was evident - the political landscape had shifted, perhaps irreversibly.

As the sun rose the next day, a large banner hung outside the Victory Vanguard Press Hall. It read, "In a world where you can be anything, be yourself." The message was clear; the world was evolving, and the dawn of acceptance had arrived.

Chapter 22: Election Night

The Destiny Dome Election Center, a colossal, architecturally futuristic arena, glowed vibrantly against the night sky. This beacon of democracy bustled with unparalleled energy as its doors swung open for spectators, journalists, and a dash of the city's elite. The aroma of anticipation was heavy, making the air almost chewy.

Inside, every inch of the place seemed covered with screens—massive LEDs flashing, smaller monitors humming, and even the odd retro television set flickering—each competing for attention. The floor plan was a delicate dance between the chaos of democracy and the order of broadcast production.

Amidst this whirlwind, Nina, a fierce journalist with a penchant for slightly too-high heels, sporting a sleek blazer and killer heels, primped her hair before going live adjusted her microphone, her lashes fluttering faster than her heartbeat. " Okay, breathe, Nina," she whispered to herself, "You've covered royal weddings and Oscar meltdowns, but this... this is the granddaddy of all spectacles!" she mumbled to herself.

As the clock ticked, the venue began to fill. On the left, a sea of conservative blue balloons floated above supporters wearing t-shirts emblazoned with Donnie and Ronnie's unmistakably glam faces. On the right, a wave of liberal green banners shouted Alexandria's promises of change. And, unsurprisingly, scattered throughout were vendors, seizing the moment—selling everything from "Vote for Me" foam fingers to politically charged churros.

At the Gilded Gala Grand Hotel, Donnie and Ronnie readied themselves for the evening's rollercoaster. Stepping into their suite felt like entering a world of lavish fantasy, with gold leaf detailing on the ceilings and plush crimson carpets underfoot. The aroma of exotic flowers from vases strategically placed around the room filled the air. From the window, a view of the twinkling city skyline promised a night of dreams and drama.

And where was the epicenter of this high-stakes preparation? In the suite's opulent bathroom, naturally—a room boasting marble counters, gilded mirrors, and a bathtub you could comfortably do laps in. It was, without a doubt, large enough to host a small campaign rally, complete with a podium, though the echoing acoustics might prove a challenge.

Ronnie, always the more meticulous of the duo, was engrossed in the task of adjusting their tie—a deep blue with subtle silver threads. Each movement was precise, ensuring the knot's perfection. The process, which had taken an impressive thirty minutes and counting, was almost meditative. "It has to be just right," Ronnie murmured, seemingly to the tie, their reflection, or perhaps to the universe.

A few feet away, Donnie lounged, draped in a plush robe that, in certain lights, seemed like it might have been woven from the threads of actual clouds. The air around them was filled with a scented mist from the nearby diffuser—'Eau de Victory,' the bottle proclaimed.

In front of the ornate mirror, Donnie practiced various expressions, trying to capture the right balance of surprise, humility, and a smidge of "I totally saw this coming." Each face was held for a few seconds, evaluated, and then adjusted.

"Donnie, darling," Ronnie called out, a playful edge to their voice, interrupting Donnie's reflection rendezvous. "You know your face will freeze that way if you keep it up, right?" They winked, a twinkle in their eye, clearly enjoying the tease.

Donnie mock-gasped, turning to face Ronnie. "And what's wrong with wanting to be eternally fabulous?" Without warning, they grabbed the nearest sponge—a luxurious, soft piece that had probably never touched soap—and lobbed it in Ronnie's direction.

The sponge landed with a soft thud on Ronnie's shoulder, and for a moment, there was a dramatic pause in the room.

Then, both erupted into gales of laughter, the stress of the evening momentarily forgotten.

In the midst of their mirth, Donnie sidled up to Ronnie, looking at their reflection together. "You know, if tonight goes sideways, we could always start a career as a comedy duo."

Ronnie raised an eyebrow, smiling. "And give up politics? I don't know, Donnie. Do you think we have enough material?"

Donnie grinned, striking a pose. "Darling, with our life? We have at least five seasons worth!"

The humor shared between them acted as a balm, a private joke in the middle of what could be the most important night of their lives. They shared a moment, eyes meeting, understanding passing between them. Tonight wasn't just about winning or losing; it was about standing together, side by side.

Feeling a bit mischievous, Ronnie plucked the sponge from where it had landed, squeezing it slightly. "You might be on to something," they mused, eyeing Donnie. "But first, let's win this thing!"

Donnie nodded, determination refueling their spirit. "To the stage!" They exclaimed dramatically, extending a hand to Ronnie.

Arm in arm, they left the bathroom sanctuary, ready to face the rollercoaster ahead. But whatever the night had in store, one thing was for sure—Donnie and Ronnie were taking it on together, with a dose of humor, a splash of style, and a heart full of hope.

The neon sign at the entrance to Alexandria's Advocacy Hub blinked rhythmically, casting a soft glow on the excited supporters and volunteers spilling onto the sidewalk. The place was abuzz with optimism, the kind that makes you believe, really believe, in the magic of possibility.

Inside the hub, banners in every hue of the rainbow hung from the ceilings, while pamphlets, badges, and—surprisingly—a plethora of glitter pots were strewn about. Some of the younger volunteers took delight in painting each other's faces with messages of hope, unity, and the occasional cheeky doodle, while others debated policy nuances and the latest poll numbers.

Then there was Alexandria. Towering not just in stature but in presence, she seemed to both absorb and radiate the energy around her. A sanctuary in the storm, she multitasked like a pro, whispering directives into her phone while simultaneously being drawn into strategy discussions. But her crowning glory at the moment was her drink—a towering concoction of froth and whimsy. Each sip she took seemed to be a silent pledge, a reminder that amidst the gravity of the occasion, one must never forget to relish life's sweet moments.

Nearby, Brock, looking debonair in his signature blazer, watched Alexandria with a mix of admiration and mischief. Sliding next to her with a plate piled high with nachos, he raised an eyebrow and teased, "Expecting a whipped cream shortage or just prepping for our victory toast?"

Alexandria took a playful swipe of whipped cream from her drink, dabbing it on Brock's nose. "Oh, Brock," she giggled. "Always finding ways to add spice to the mix."

And as they shared that light-hearted moment, the underlying tension was palpable. Volunteers huddled in groups, watching the incoming results, their faces a canvas of hope, nerves, and sheer anticipation.

Meanwhile, Michelle, on a quest of her own, strutted through the marbled corridors of the Gilded Gala Grand Hotel. Each step was a testament to her confidence and every sequin on her dress seemed to shimmer with intent. Distracted by her own dazzling reflection in a giant ornate mirror, she couldn't resist breaking into a spontaneous performance. The makeshift stage saw Michelle mouthing words of encouragement to herself, her every move exuding grace and a touch of comedic flair. It was as if she were telling the world: "Yes, I understand the gravitas of tonight, but let's not forget to dance a little."

Outside, as the stars began to pierce the twilight, screens erected in every corner of the city broadcasted live updates. From cafes to town squares, everyone seemed glued to the numbers ticking up. Whispers, gasps, cheers, and the occasional groan punctuated the electric atmosphere.

Back at the hub, as Alexandria took a moment to scan the room, she felt an overwhelming wave of gratitude. To be at the heart of such monumental change, to witness firsthand the fervor and passion of her supporters, was humbling. Their hopes and dreams were etched on their faces, and she felt the weight of their trust pressing gently on her shoulders.

Drawing a deep breath, she stepped onto the makeshift podium, signaling for attention. The room quietened instantly. "Whether tonight ends in victory or not," she began, her voice brimming with emotion, "know that we've already won. We've shown that we're a force, a movement, a dance of democracy where every voice counts."

As her words filled the room, Brock, feeling the infectious spirit of the moment, began a slow clap, which quickly spread like wildfire. The hub, once again, was a cacophony of cheers, jubilation, and the rustling of nacho bags.

As the early results began to trickle in, all eyes turned to the screens, hearts drumming a rhythm of hope and anxiety. This was it—the start of an election night that promised to be unforgettable.

And as the cameras panned, capturing the sea of eager faces, it was evident. This wasn't just an election night—it was a celebration, a party of democracy in action, where every voice, every vote, and every sequin mattered.

As the mammoth LED screens lit up with the first numbers, a collective gasp rippled through the Destiny Dome Election Center. NewsWave Media Outlets' charismatic anchor, Tyrell Tempest, with his impeccable hair and tailored suit, began the update.

"And the early figures are in!" Tyrell's voice boomed. "Alexandria's pulled a stunning initial lead!"

The liberal side of the dome erupted in a mix of cheers, gasps, and clapping. The green banners waved even more vigorously, but the sea of blue balloons seemed momentarily deflated.

On the screens, the numbers rolled like a slot machine, each update heightening the drama. The suspense was almost theatrical—fitting for an election night where the candidates had such strong ties to the world of drag.

Nina, that fierce journalist, now teetered on her too-high heels, trying to snag spontaneous reactions from the crowd. She approached a flamboyantly dressed supporter from Donnie and Ronnie's camp. "What do you make of these early figures?"

"Well, darling," the supporter replied, lashes batting dramatically, "The night is young. Just like my latest Botox!"

Laughter rippled through the vicinity.

Meanwhile, at the Gilded Gala Grand Hotel, Donnie and Ronnie's suite was thick with tension. Ronnie, eyes glued to the screen, whispered, "It's just the early votes."

Donnie, sipping a bubbly drink, responded with an attempted air of nonchalance, "Of course, darling. The night has barely started."

Back at Alexandria's Advocacy Hub, Brock's eyes twinkled with mischief as he sidled up to Alexandria. "How's it feel to be the early frontrunner?"

Alexandria, trying to contain her excitement, retorted with a smirk, "I've always enjoyed a good head start, especially in heels." She wobbled playfully on her stilettos, causing Brock to laugh heartily.

Michelle, in her conservative, yet fabulous attire, stood beside Donnie and Ronnie, offering silent support. Her presence was comforting to the duo, a constant reminder that friends were the true anchors on such rollercoaster nights.

But as the hours crept on, the tension grew palpable. Each update on the LED screens was met with cheers or groans. Drinks flowed, nachos crunched, and politically charged churros, of all things, became the snack du jour.

Amidst the sea of people, there were whispered strategy sessions, occasional comforting hugs, and bursts of spirited conversation. Somewhere amidst the crowd, two young volunteers—one from each camp—found themselves engrossed in a heated discussion. But as the minutes passed, their debate transitioned into flirtatious teasing. The magical tension of the evening seemed to create unexpected connections.

By early-mid evening, another significant update came through. Tyrell Tempest's voice rang out, "In a surprising twist, with the latest batch of votes counted, Alexandria has skyrocketed forward, maintaining her lead!"

The Alexandria section was a cacophony of celebration. But across the aisle, Donnie's camp rallied. Encouraging words, rallying cries, and Michelle's constant support kept their spirits up. If the night had taught them anything, it was that in politics, as in life, the story was far from over.

The Gilded Gala Grand Hotel's small conference hall echoed with the clink of glasses and the low hum of anxious conversations. Everywhere you looked, sequins glittered and banners swayed. Ronnie, face carefully neutral, sipped a crystal-clear drink at the mini bar. Beside them, Donnie was busy straightening their tie for the umpteenth time.

Michelle sidled up to them, adjusting her amazing hair. "You two ready for the final push?" Her voice was a blend of warmth and anticipation.

Donnie cleared their throat, their usually unshakeable confidence wavering. "This night... it's more unpredictable than my wardrobe."

Ronnie smirked, "And that's saying something."

The trio shared a knowing look, the bond between them palpable.

Before they could continue, a booming voice echoed through the hall, "Ladies and gentlemen, our esteemed candidates, Donnie and Ronnie!"

A wave of applause erupted as the pair stepped up to the makeshift stage. Donnie cleared their throat, "Tonight, we stand here united. Not just as a party, but as a nation, waiting to see what the future holds."

Ronnie chimed in, "We've had our fair share of highs and lows, but isn't that what makes our journey worthwhile?"

Somewhere in the crowd, a supporter shouted, "We love you, Ronnie Rebel!"

Ronnie winked, causing a ripple of laughter, "Thank you! We promise to dance through every challenge with grace!"

Back at the Advocacy Hub, Alexandria's base was equally buzzing. Streamers in green and white hung from every corner, volunteers buzzed around, and the scent of fresh pizza permeated the air.

Brock leaned against a counter, eyes scanning the room, taking in the electric atmosphere. Dark Brandie approached, glass in hand, "You think she's got this?"

Brock's lips curled into a confident smile, "Alexandria? She's got the heart and spirit. People see that."

In the backdrop, a stage had been set up. Alexandria, exuding calm amidst the storm, took the microphone. Her voice, steady and sure, resonated through the room. "This journey, it's been about every single one of you. About hope, about change, and about believing that we can do better."

The crowd cheered, clapping rhythmically. Dark Brandie, swaying to the beat, couldn't help but nod in agreement.

Then, as if on cue, Brock turned to the giant screen displaying a live feed from the Destiny Dome Election Center. The early numbers had Alexandria leading, but not by a margin wide enough to secure an easy victory. The night was still young.

Suddenly, a hush fell over the crowd. Alexandria's voice, softer now, held a hint of vulnerability, "Whatever happens tonight, we've started something beautiful. Remember, it's not about the finish line, but the journey, the dance, and the many steps along the way."

And in that moment, as every eye in the room remained glued to the screen, it was clear that this wasn't just about politics or performances. This was about unity, love, and embracing the uniqueness of every individual.

Across the city, living rooms, bars, and every nook and corner with a screen became a mini-election center. The rhythmic beat of hope, anticipation, and a dash of fear echoed everywhere.

Back at the Gilded Gala, Michelle took center stage, her voice surprisingly steady, "No matter the outcome, we celebrate tonight. For love, for freedom, and for the right to be ourselves unapologetically."

Donnie and Ronnie nodded in agreement, their faces a mix of pride and apprehension.

The camera feeds from NewsWave Media panned between the two central hubs, capturing the essence of the evening— a cocktail of intense emotions. As journalists hopped between the Gilded Gala and the Advocacy Hub, the world watched with bated breath.

Would the evening end in exuberant celebrations or muted acceptance? Would it be the crowning of a new era or the continuation of the old? One thing was for sure, in the world of politics, like the world of drag, only the most authentic souls would leave a lasting impression.

As the minutes turned to hours, and the night deepened, the true essence of the election became evident. It wasn't just about who won or lost, but about celebrating diversity, unity, and the sheer power of democracy.

And as the Destiny Dome Election Center continued to pulsate with energy, one thing was clear: this election was one for the books, one that would be remembered for its fierce competitors, unwavering supporters, and above all, for the sequins that shimmered brighter than ever.

The hands of the clock inched ever closer to midnight, an almost eerie silence fell across the Destiny Dome Election Center. You could practically hear the collective heartbeat of the crowd, each person desperately waiting, hoping, and praying for the outcome they wanted.

At the Gilded Gala Grand Hotel, Michelle, dressed in her captivating black sequin dress, the shimmer catching every flicker of light, began to pace. Her hair, which had begun the evening in a towering testament to gravity-defying glam, was starting to show its exhaustion, with a few curls drooping ever so slightly. But let's be honest, she still looked fabulous.

She glanced at Donnie and Ronnie, who sat close, hands intertwined. There was a tension in their shoulders, an anxiety that even their seasoned political personas couldn't hide. The weight of the evening, of their careers, of the love they shared - it all hung in the balance. Their faces were a canvas of hope and apprehension, of love and dread, of everything that made them uniquely human beneath the political facades.

Across town, Alexandria's Advocacy Hub buzzed with a different energy. There was a certain youthful optimism in the air. Maybe it was the copious amounts of pizza and carbonated drinks or perhaps the unyielding belief in their candidate. Regardless, the vibe was electric. Every time a new set of numbers flashed on the screen, a wave of gasps, cheers, or groans would ripple through the crowd.

Dark Brandie, usually so poised and controlled, was biting his nails, a habit he hadn't succumbed to since his early days in politics. Brock, noticing, gently nudged him, "Easy there, you won't have any fingers left if you continue at this rate."

They shared a chuckle, a small moment of levity in an otherwise stress-filled evening.

Back at the Gilded Gala, Michelle, always one to find a distraction in moments of distress, began to pull out her phone. The ever-so-familiar icon of WebWonders Online Space beckoned her. "Maybe I should go live," she pondered aloud, "Share some of this anxiety with my followers."

Donnie, overhearing, smirked, "Might as well make it a show, right?"

Michelle, tossing her hair dramatically, replied, "Isn't everything?"

She tapped the "Live" option, and almost immediately, numbers began to climb as viewers tuned in. The global nature of the platform meant that people from all over were witnessing this intimate snapshot of a pivotal moment in history.

"Hey, everyone," Michelle began, her voice surprisingly clear given the emotional rollercoaster she was on, "here we are, waiting for the big announcement. I'm with Donnie and Ronnie." She panned her camera to the duo, who waved, trying to muster up as much confidence as possible.

Across the city, Alexandria spotted the live stream. With a smirk, she mused, "Always the entertainer, isn't she?" And yet, she couldn't resist watching.

The comments began pouring in, an amalgamation of well-wishes, political debates, and of course, compliments on Michelle's ever-dazzling appearance. "Thanks, honey," Michelle responded to a comment about her 'on point' eyeliner. "Took me ages!"

The minutes felt like hours. Every glance at the clock, every fluttering heartbeat, and every held breath made the wait more torturous. The anxiety, anticipation, and sheer hope that lingered in the air was palpable.

In the midst of it all, Michelle's live stream served as a strange bridge between the two camps. It was a reminder that beyond the politics, the campaigns, and the glitter, they were all human. And in these defining moments, they were united in their vulnerability, hope, and anticipation.

The clock continued its relentless march, and as the world waited with bated breath, Michelle's voice was the anchor, providing real-time reactions, candid emotions, and above all, reminding everyone that no matter the outcome, life, much like a drag show, must go on.

And just as the clock was about to signal the end of the day, the screen froze. The live stream cut out, leaving everyone in suspense. The Destiny Dome Election Center went dark, only to be illuminated seconds later by the singular spotlight on the stage.

And as Michelle's words echoed, "Remember, my darlings, win or lose, always leave them wanting more," the world waited for the dawn of a new day, the final results, and the beginning of a new chapter. Michelle made it back to her flat as the clean up started at the Hotel and the connected Destiny Dome.

Chapter 23: The Wild Card

It was well past midnight, and the neon blue hue of WebWonders Online Space cast a surreal glow across Michelle's Metro Flat. The room, typically an elegant blend of political keepsakes and vibrant drag paraphernalia, was now littered with wrappers, tissues (some from tears, some from makeup touch-ups), and a few leftover pizza crusts. Despite the earlier tension of the election countdown, Michelle felt oddly at ease now, perhaps a tad tired, but mostly just grateful for the unexpected sense of community WebWonders had provided.

Michelle reclined on her plush velvet chaise lounge, her sequined gown catching every glint of light from the computer screen. As she scrolled, the juxtaposition of her glam appearance against the familiar comfort of her apartment made her chuckle. Who could have predicted that an online platform, originally designed for sharing funny cat videos and delectable recipes, would play such a pivotal role in an election?

Ping! A notification sound rang out, pulling Michelle from her reverie. It was a message from a user named "Starstruck_90sKid". *Probably another millennial,* Michelle mused.

"Hey, Michelle! Watching your live stream tonight made me realize how politics is so much more than just old men in suits making decisions for all of us. Thank you for adding a splash of color (and sequins!) to this whole affair!"

With a smile playing on her lips, Michelle typed a witty response, "Why thank you! And always remember, beneath every politician's suit, there's a diva just waiting to break free!" She punctuated her message with a wink emoji.

Just as she was about to log off, another notification popped up. This one was from an unexpected user – Alexandria herself.

"Hey, M. I've got to say, watching your livestream tonight was both hilarious and heartwarming. No matter the outcome tomorrow, you've already made history. Kudos to you, and may the best... diva win?"

Michelle's heart swelled. This message wasn't about politics. It was about respect and camaraderie. She swiftly replied, "Thank you, Alex. Tomorrow's a new day, and regardless of the outcome, let's promise to always keep things fabulous!"

Exhaustion finally catching up with her, Michelle decided to call it a night. Shutting down her laptop, she sighed, taking in the remnants of the night's rollercoaster of emotions. But before she could drift into sleep, her mind wandered to the events at the Gilded Gala, the anticipation of the election results, and the surprising bond she'd forged with thousands through a virtual platform.

As she nestled into her bed, memories of the evening danced in her mind, much like the twinkling lights of the city skyline outside her window. The digital realm of WebWonders had, in a very real way, changed the course of her journey, making her feel both vulnerable and empowered.

Her last conscious thought before drifting into a dream was a whispered promise to herself, "Tomorrow, come what may, I'll face it with sequins, sass, and an unwavering spirit."

Michelle's soft snores were interrupted by the relentless buzzing of her phone. Rubbing her eyes and adjusting her bed hair - a tangle of dark waves sprinkled with a rogue sequin or two - she reached for the device. The time flashed 2:00 am, and yet her notifications seemed to have exploded.

Viral. Everything was going viral.

Clips of her livestream had been turned into hilarious memes. One particular gif of her dramatically tossing her hair while lamenting the election anxiety had over 2 million shares. Another video of her singing a parody about politics to the tune of a famous pop song had comments like "Michelle Pensive for President!" and "Who knew politics could be this glittery?"

She clicked on the trending tab of WebWonders. To her surprise, at the top was #MichelleMoments. The content ranged from fans recreating her makeup looks to comical renditions of her livestream's funniest moments. Some even sported wigs, attempting to imitate her iconic tresses. And just as she scrolled further, a video of a toddler mimicking her signature pout and wink made her burst into fits of laughter.

But amidst the hilarity, a deeper sentiment emerged. Young adults shared how Michelle's openness about her transition gave them courage. Parents talked about conversations on acceptance and love that her livestream had sparked at home. It seemed Michelle had become an unlikely hero in the most unconventional election the world had ever seen.

And the revelation that hit her hardest was a series of tweets from LGBTQ+ youths:

"Wearing my Michelle-inspired sequin top to school today! #Proud #MichelleMoments"

"If Michelle can be herself on a global platform, so can I. Coming out to my family today. #ThankYouMichelle"

"Political views aside, seeing someone so fabulously themselves gives me hope. #MichelleForChange"

As heartwarming as the posts were, the unintended consequence of her new-found fame was evident. Screenshots of various news outlets showed her face plastered everywhere, from morning talk shows discussing the "Michelle Phenomenon" to political analysts debating her sway on conservative voters.

Her phone rang, interrupting her dive into the digital universe. The caller ID displayed "Ronnie."

"Michelle!" Ronnie's voice was a mix of excitement and urgency. "Have you seen the news? They're calling you the 'Election's Wild Card'! Your popularity might just tilt the scales for us!"

Michelle's mind raced. "Ronnie, it wasn't intentional. I just wanted to connect, to be real amidst the chaos."

Ronnie chuckled, "And that's exactly why it worked. You were genuine. The people loved it!"

"But what about the election?" she hesitated.

There was a pause. "Honestly, Michelle, while we want to win, what you've done is bigger than this election. You've sparked conversations, broken barriers, and made politics... well, glamorous!"

Michelle grinned, "Always the goal!"

They shared a lighthearted moment, but Michelle could sense an underlying tension. As candid as her stream was, it was inadvertently political. Her relationship with Ronnie and Donnie wasn't just personal anymore; it had political implications. And with Alexandria's kind message still fresh in her mind, Michelle realized that this election, regardless of the outcome, was changing them all in profound ways.

Ronnie's voice softened, "Regardless of tomorrow, Michelle, remember you've touched lives. You've become an inspiration. And for many, you're the glittering hope they needed in these trying times."

Michelle blinked back tears, "Thank you, Ronnie. Tomorrow is a new day. But tonight, let's cherish this unexpected twist in our journey."

Their conversation continued, filled with shared memories, laughter, and anticipation of what lay ahead.

As Michelle finally drifted off to sleep, her heart was light. She may have become an internet sensation, a political influencer, and the unexpected queen of an election, but more than anything, she had found herself.

At 2:30 AM, the *NewsWave Media Outlets* was buzzing with unprecedented excitement. The spacious, brightly lit newsroom resembled a beehive with reporters buzzing around in organized chaos. Screens lined one wall, flashing snippets of Michelle's livestream alongside speculative graphics, pie charts, and that wildly popular GIF of her flipping her hair.

Kayla, a vibrant reporter in her mid-30s, shouted across the newsroom, "Get me the latest polling numbers from the West Coast! If this Michelle Phenomenon is real, I need to know!"

Daryl, the stats guy with spectacles that were perpetually sliding down his nose, hollered back, "On it! And by the way, it's looking like they're extending voting hours due to the crowds. Michelle's effect is real!"

Kayla smiled knowingly. She'd been covering politics for over a decade, and just when she thought she had seen it all, Michelle Pensive sashayed into the scene.

In the *Council Chambers of Campaigning*, the atmosphere was palpable. Team Ronnie and Donnie were busy strategizing, pouring over Michelle's livestream analytics and voter sentiments.

Jasper, their youthful digital strategist with a penchant for wearing too-tight suits, declared, "Our conservative base is still intact, but Michelle's appeal is bridging gaps. We're seeing a surge in younger voters!"

Ronnie paced the room, glancing occasionally at a screen displaying Michelle's face. Their usually calculated demeanor was ruffled, a mix of apprehension and exhilaration. "We need to adjust tomorrow's schedule. We ride this wave without drowning in it."

Meanwhile, Alexandria was in her *Advocacy Hub*, surrounded by a flurry of supporters. A young volunteer timidly approached, "Alex, should we address the Michelle situation in tomorrow's speech?"

Alexandria, ever the strategist, responded, "Absolutely. Let's focus on unity, acceptance, and celebrating diversity. It's not about one person but the movement she's inadvertently energized."

In the shadows, Dark Brandie watched the drama unfold from the luxury of his *Penthouse Palace*. As one of the top drag queens and a secret political influencer, Brandie always had a flair for spotting a good story. But even he hadn't anticipated Michelle's rise to stardom.

Taking a sip of his sparkling rosé, Brandie remarked to Brock, "Never in my wildest dreams did I think Michelle would be the one to shake up this election."

Brock leaned in, a mischievous glint in his eyes. "Want to bet on the outcome?"

Brandie chuckled, "Tempting, but I'm not placing any bets until the final count."

Back at Michelle's metro flat, her phone was on fire. Notifications, messages, even a cheeky voicemail from Divine Donnie that had her blushing and laughing. "Michelle, darling! Your performance! So... unintentional, so raw. You've got them all talking, dear. We'll need to do brunch!"

But it wasn't just the political world reacting. The drag community was ablaze with chatter. Starlit Drag Lounge had announced a "Michelle Night," where every performance was inspired by her. The grand prize? A sequin top and a chance to be the next viral sensation.

Michelle awakes again, unaware of the broader implications of her newfound fame, decided to take a breather. She stepped onto her balcony, feeling the cool night air, and gazed at the city lights. The weight of the situation started to sink in. She had become a beacon of hope for many and a subject of debate for others.

Lost in her thoughts, a sudden vibration brought her back to reality. A message notification from an unknown number flashed across her screen. Tentatively, she opened it.

"Hey, Michelle. It's Alex the Conqueror. Just wanted to say, you're fabulous. Let's change the world together."

The neon-tinted streets of the city basked in the artificial glow of storefronts and billboards. But as the early hours of dawn approached, an eerie quiet settled in. Only the rhythmic hum of the NewsWave Media Outlets interrupted the stillness of the night.

Inside the Unity Square Transparency Terrace, large screens showed rolling news coverage, with Michelle's face becoming a familiar presence. The image of her, laughing, confident, and utterly herself, was juxtaposed with pundits fervently debating her potential impact on the election.

In the corner of the Transparency Terrace, a group of young voters huddled together. They whispered animatedly, smartphones in hand, sharing the latest posts about Michelle. Many of them wore glitter, rainbow pins, and Michelle-inspired outfits. "Did you see her response to Divine Donnie's brunch invite?" one of them gushed, showing off a tweet. "Absolute gold!"

Yet, for every excited supporter, there was a skeptic. At the Tradition Towers Party Office, a group of older, conservative members expressed their reservations. One particularly stern-faced gentleman muttered, "This is all a distraction. People should focus on the real issues."

Meanwhile, at the Alexandria's Advocacy Hub, Alexandria and Dark Brandie found themselves in an unlikely tête-à-tête. Their morning coffee drinks untouched, the two locked eyes.

"Michelle's turned the tables, hasn't she?" Alexandria began, her voice laced with intrigue.

Brandie raised an eyebrow. "You sound almost admiring."

Alexandria smirked. "I respect anyone who can shake things up as she has. But I can't help but wonder about the ripple effects."

They both knew that Michelle's newfound influence was like a double-edged sword. It could propel them towards an era of acceptance, or it could just as easily backfire, especially in the unpredictable realm of politics.

In the dim confines of the Starlit Drag Lounge, Michelle's effect was palpable. The DJ played a remixed version of her livestream comments, making her words sound even more profound. The crowd cheered, danced, and toasted to their newfound icon.

Yet, as the world celebrated or critiqued Michelle, the woman herself found solace on the balcony of her Metro Flat. The city stretched out before her, its twinkling lights reflecting her own starry ascent. But Michelle wasn't pondering her meteoric rise. Instead, she reflected on her journey, from the shadows of conservatism to the glaring limelight of acceptance.

A soft ding from her phone brought her back from her reverie. It was a message from Ronnie Rebel, Ronnie's drag persona:

> *"Hey, glitter queen. Donnie and I are doing a surprise performance at the Theater of Dreams. Thought we'd give the world a taste of the real wild cards. You in?"*

Michelle's heart raced. The idea was deliciously rebellious and completely in tune with the night's unexpected turns. She quickly typed back,

> *"Only if we can do a trio act. And maybe add Alex the Conqueror to the mix?"*

As the first rays of dawn began to pierce the night, Michelle's phone buzzed with messages of excitement, anticipation, and camaraderie. The world might have branded her the wild card, but in that moment, she was just Michelle — ready to take on the world with her friends, sequins, and a heart full of hope.

The sun slowly climbed, casting a golden hue over the city. The stillness of the night gave way to the bustling sounds of morning. But this wasn't just any morning. This was the day after the world had witnessed an unexpected sensation, the day it would come to terms with the unpredictability of politics in the digital age. And as the characters and readers alike embraced the dawn, they were left to ponder the profound impact of one woman's journey on an entire nation's fate.

Chapter 24:
Unveiling the Winner

Jasmine sauntered into the Primetime Politics Studio, clutching her much-needed vanilla latte. The aftermath of last night's election coverage left the studio resembling the aftermath of a hurricane – cups of cold coffee abandoned on every surface, papers strewn everywhere, and a mood of exhausted anticipation in the air.

Lenny, the director, shouted, "Jasmine! Finally, you're here. We need to get started with the morning recap."

Rolling her eyes, Jasmine shot back, "Some of us had to get our beauty sleep, Lenny. Last night was bonkers."

As she found her way to the makeup chair, a flurry of texts pinged on her phone. Sally, her BFF, had clearly been up all night, sending running commentaries. The latest message read, "*Girrrrl, did you see the WebWonders meme about Michelle's hat? It's hilarious! But also, kinda endearing?*"

Despite her fatigue, Jasmine chuckled. The unpredictable world of politics in the age of social media never failed to amuse her.

Settled in her chair, Jasmine caught her reflection and sighed. The circles under her eyes told tales of relentless election nights past. Manny, the ever-flamboyant makeup artist, clicked his tongue disapprovingly. "Darling, you look like you fought the election yourself. Relax, and let me work my magic."

While Manny painted and contoured her face to perfection, Jasmine listened to the muted arguments around the Strategy Nook. The heartthrob pundit, Ricardo, was passionately defending Alexandria's campaign strategy, while Dianne, ever the skeptic, predicted a surprise swing for Donnie.

Jasmine's mind drifted to the heated debates she'd had with Sally about the candidates. Despite their differences, there was one thing they agreed on – the unexpected sexiness of politics. Who knew watching candidates argue about tax reforms could be... tantalizing? They had even started a drinking game where they took a shot every time Donnie flirted with the camera or Alexandria shot a sultry glance at the audience.

Manny interrupted her thoughts, brandishing a mascara wand. "Eyes up, darling! Do you want to tell me why you're blushing?"

Jasmine shrugged, avoiding Manny's probing gaze. The truth was, she had a *thing* for Ricardo. Their little backstage banter last night had been the highlight of her evening. And by banter, she meant the sizzling, almost-kiss they'd shared in the shadowy corner behind the Teleprompters.

A commotion from the Strategy Nook snapped her back to reality. The final results were in. Alexandria had won, but by the slimmest of margins.

Jasmine quickly checked her reflection, bolstered by Manny's artistry and her own natural charisma. "Alright, folks," she declared, standing in her full five-foot-nine glory, heels included. "Let's get this post-election party started!"

As she made her way to her desk, her co-anchor, Harry, whispered, "Word on the street is that Donnie is planning a surprise announcement at his campaign headquarters. Might be worth sending someone over."

She nodded, distracted. Ricardo was making his way towards her, his eyes intent on her face.

"Jasmine," he murmured, his voice low and seductive, "about last night..."

She felt a shiver of anticipation. "Yes?"

He leaned in, so close she could feel his breath on her ear. "I think we should... discuss our exit polls."

With a sultry laugh, she replied, "Only if it's over a spicy margarita."

The charged atmosphere of the studio, combined with the thrill of the election results and the budding romantic tension, was intoxicating. As Jasmine prepared to go live on air, she couldn't help but think that this was going to be one election recap she'd never forget.

Amid the din of the Primetime Politics Studio, scattered whispers from campaign representatives carried tales of uncertainty. Jasmine, freshly done up by Manny, was trying to keep her personal and professional feelings apart. But with Ricardo's suggestive comments still echoing in her ears, the task seemed harder than presenting election results.

A split-screen displayed the respective campaign headquarters. On the left, Donnie and Ronnie, draped in luxurious fabrics, looked tense yet hopeful in their office at Tradition Towers Party Office. Donnie's fingers fidgeted with the ornate detailing of his tie, while Ronnie constantly refreshed a tablet, perhaps trying to read early numbers or find more of Michelle's viral memes. In contrast, on the right, Alexandria's Advocacy Hub was filled with eager volunteers, waving banners and wearing shirts with "Alex the Conqueror" emblazoned on them. Alexandria, flanked by Dark Brandie and Brock, was the epitome of calmness, her eyes focused and confident.

As the camera zoomed into Donnie and Ronnie, a moment of unexpected intimacy was captured. Ronnie placed a reassuring hand on Donnie's, their fingers intertwining, a symbol of unity amidst chaos. They exchanged a look that screamed a thousand emotions, conveying reassurance, hope, and undying support. Their bond was palpable even through the screen.

Jasmine's voiceover echoed, "As the world waits with bated breath, the final numbers are just moments away. In these decisive moments, the candidates, too, are humans filled with hopes, aspirations, and nerves."

Back in Alexandria's camp, Dark Brandie, looking dashing in a well-tailored suit, whispered something in Alexandria's ear, causing her to chuckle. The tension was palpable, but moments like these highlighted the camaraderie that often blossomed in high-stakes environments.

The screen at the Destiny Dome Election Center flickered. Numbers began to flow. Percentage bars colored in real-time. Every eye in the studio and across the country was fixated on these numbers, knowing they would shape the country's future.

As the results started to tilt in Alexandria's favor, her Advocacy Hub erupted in cheers. But Alexandria's face was a canvas of humility and gratitude. Raising her hand, she gestured for silence. She exchanged a few whispered words with Brock, whose eyes shimmered with unshed tears, probably reflecting on their shared journey.

Over at Donnie and Ronnie's, the atmosphere grew somber. Yet, in an unexpected twist, Divine Donnie came alive, comforting a visibly emotional Ronnie Rebel. As a satirical rendition of conservative ideals, their true strength lay in their unity, and it was never more evident than now.

Jasmine cleared her throat, her voice echoing the collective consciousness of a nation. "And there we have it, folks. While final results are still trickling in, it appears we're looking at a narrow win for Alexandria. The political landscape is set to change, but what remains unchanged is the passion and dedication of all candidates."

Ricardo slid into the seat next to Jasmine, his face betraying a hint of sadness. "It's been a roller-coaster, hasn't it?" he murmured.

She nodded, momentarily lost for words, the weight of the day finally sinking in. "Every time. Every election. But this one? This one feels different."

He leaned in, whispering in that sultry voice, "Every moment with you feels different, Jasmine."

Caught off guard, she met his gaze, seeing sincerity and a hint of mischief. "Well, Mr. Heartthrob Pundit, perhaps we should... analyze our feelings over that spicy margarita?"

He chuckled, "Lead the way, Ms. News Anchor."

As cameras panned out and the studio buzz began to die down, the narrative shifted. Political fervor gave way to personal tales, and amidst the high-stakes world of politics, love and relationships blossomed. And as Jasmine and Ricardo headed out, hand in hand, they embodied a nation's hope for unity, understanding, and above all, love.

The Victory Vanguard Press Hall was bustling with reporters, all desperate to capture Alexandria's first reaction. The dim hum of chattering voices and flashing cameras provided a melodious backdrop to a scene that would be etched in history. Alexandria, Brock, and Dark Brandie stood at the center, a beacon of hope and change.

Alexandria took a deep breath, her hand resting on her heart. "Tonight, we celebrate not just a victory for me, but for every single person who has ever felt marginalized or left out of the political conversation."

Dark Brandie nodded in approval, his earlier animosity nowhere in sight. He whispered to Brock, "She really is something, isn't she?" Brock just smiled, his eyes misty.

Just then, Michelle, now in full Michelle Pensive glory, made a dramatic entrance. With her feathered boa trailing behind her, she approached Alexandria. "On behalf of Donnie and Ronnie, I want to congratulate you." She said, striking a pose that would make any diva proud. "Also, if you need a fabulous Secretary of Fashion, you know where to find me!"

Alexandria chuckled, "Thank you, Michelle. Your grace and sense of humor always light up the room."

The evening took a surprising turn when Donnie and Ronnie decided to grace the Victory Vanguard Press Hall. They approached Alexandria, their heads held high. Donnie, ever the character, gave a small twirl before saying, "You may have won the election, darling, but remember, Divine Donnie is still the queen of the stage."

Ronnie added, "Congratulations, Alexandria. It was a fierce race, and you proved to be a formidable opponent."

The room grew silent, everyone waiting for Alexandria's response. She stepped forward, her gaze unwavering. "Thank you, both of you. While we may not always agree on policy, I hope we can always find common ground in our shared love for drag and our desire to make this country better for everyone."

As the night wore on, Alexandria and her team celebrated at the Gilded Gala Grand Hotel. The ballroom was filled with supporters dancing, laughing, and savoring the sweet taste of victory. The DJ played a mix of political anthems and drag classics, creating an atmosphere of jubilation.

The glimmering lights of the Gilded Gala Grand Hotel's ballroom dimmed, replaced by a seductive, smoky ambiance. A tension of titillating anticipation hung thick in the air, charged with excitement. Tonight's Hamilton tribute was rumored to be sultry, and the crowd, dressed in provocative period attire, were already restless with heated expectation.

Alexandria's presence was magnetic, embodying Hamilton with a rebellious glint in her eye. She wore a tight-fitting colonial coat that accentuated her curves, and those knee-high leather boots screamed dominance. With every lyric she lip-synced, there was a seductive undercurrent, her voice dripping with an invitation to more than just a dance.

As the music transitioned, Dark Brandie, epitomizing Eliza, flowed onto the stage. Her dress, although reminiscent of the period, had a dangerously high slit, revealing just enough to entice. As she moved closer to Alexandria, their chemistry was palpable, their interactions filled with stolen caresses and lingering touches, each one sending a jolt of electricity through the audience.

Enter Brock, exuding Thomas Jefferson's arrogant charm but with an added layer of raw sensuality. His magenta coat hugged him just right, revealing the contours of a well-sculpted body. His entrance was marked by a particularly suggestive hip gyration, causing a few gasps and giggles in the crowd.

The trio's dance became a seductive tango of power, desire, and betrayal. At one point, Alexandria, embodying Hamilton's hunger for power, pressed Brandie against her with possessive intent, their faces inches apart, lips almost brushing, the tension between them thick enough to cut with a knife.

Brock, not to be outdone, approached Alexandria from behind, their dance an evocative representation of the political battles of the era, with every movement dripping with double entendre. Their back-and-forth was a tantalizing game of push and pull, leaving the audience breathless and yearning for more.

As they segued into "Burn," Brandie, center stage, gave a performance that was heartbreakingly sensual. With each lyric, she teased, letting her dress slide down her shoulder, then pulling it back just in time, her every move oozing vulnerability and allure.

The night's climax was a masterfully choreographed number where the trio's movements became more frenetic and impassioned, their interactions charged with an undeniable erotic energy. The air was thick with lust, love, and power struggles, a potent cocktail that left the audience intoxicated.

Finally, as the last notes faded, they stood in a tantalizing tableau: Alexandria and Brock with their hands on either side of Brandie's waist, their faces close, leaving the audience guessing, wanting, and imagining.

When they exited, the ballroom was charged with an erotic energy, couples exchanging heated glances, the night promising so much more. The line between history and sensuality had been artfully blurred, leaving an impression that would not be forgotten anytime soon.

In a quiet corner, Jasmine and Ricardo watched the celebration unfold. Ricardo leaned in, his voice husky, "Who would've thought politics could be this...enticing?"

Jasmine laughed, "I always knew there was a story behind every politician, but this? This was beyond my wildest dreams." She took a sip of her spicy margarita, her eyes lingering on Ricardo. "Speaking of wild dreams, care for a dance?"

Ricardo grinned, "After you, Ms. News Anchor."

The two danced, their bodies moving in sync with the beat, the electric chemistry between them palpable. As the night deepened, the newly elected President Alexandria Ocasio-Cortez's message of love, acceptance, and unity resonated with everyone present, painting a hopeful picture for the future.

The close victory emphasized that every vote mattered, that every voice counted. But more than anything, it showcased the importance of inclusivity and acceptance, not just in politics but in everyday life. The journey was long, the battle hard-fought, but at the end of the night, love and understanding prevailed.

The Gilded Gala Grand Hotel ballroom was a tantalizing melting pot of celebration and reflection. The large, ornate chandeliers reflected muted, dimmed golden hues across the room, which now bustled with whispers, laughter, and hints of sultry chemistry.

Near the bar, Michelle, draped in a dazzling ensemble, her hair flawlessly cascading down her back, was visibly contemplative. Brock, always the mediator, sidled up next to her, placing a comforting hand on her shoulder. "Quite the night, huh?"

Michelle sighed, her gaze distant. "It's all changing, Brock. The lines between our personal lives and our political affiliations have blurred. I never imagined this."

Brock chuckled, "Isn't that the beauty of it, though? A world where we can be our true selves, regardless of politics."

Dark Brandie, having overheard, sauntered over with a contemplative look. "You know, I've seen many elections in my time, but nothing like this," he admitted, his voice carrying the weight of years and experiences. "Your friend, Alexandria, she's onto something."

Brock nodded, "It's a new era, Brandie. An era where we all come together."

The lights had dimmed, and the echo of laughter from earlier was replaced by a heavy, palpable anticipation. The playful tension between Jasmine and Ricardo reached an exhilarating high. Ricardo, with his confident demeanor slightly faltering, pulled Jasmine close, their breaths mingling and bodies aligning just so, like two jigsaw pieces that were made for each other. "How about we leave this place and find a quiet corner?" Ricardo's voice, usually so assertive, had a raspy edge now. "I've got more... analysis to do."

Jasmine, always ready with a witty retort, smirked, her lips tingling with the anticipation of what might come next. "Mr.

Heartthrob Pundit," she teased, "are you suggesting we... fact-check in private?"

His laugh was deep, a sound that reverberated through the air and somehow made it warmer. "You're incorrigible," he whispered, his lips inches from hers. "Let's get out of here before you corrupt me completely."

The two of them, lost in their bubble, navigated the crowd and found a dimly lit corridor that led to a secluded alcove. The shadows seemed to dance in tandem with their racing heartbeats. With a sultry glint in her eyes, Jasmine swiftly closed the gap between them the sultry atmosphere in the dimly lit corner of the upscale lounge was palpable. Low, soulful music playing in the background, creating a bubble around Jasmine and Ricardo, shielding them from the outside world.

Jasmine's eyes locked onto Ricardo's, a playful challenge evident in her gaze. She moved closer, diminishing the space between them, the charged air surrounding them growing heavier by the second. Her hand slid stealthily, delving into the confines of his pants. Her fingers met with his warm, throbbing bulge, the sensation magnified by the intimacy of their position. His arousal was undeniable, and Jasmine could feel the steady heartbeat pulsing beneath her fingertips, the tactile proof of his desire for her.

Ricardo's eyes widened a fraction as he felt the wetness seep through his underwear, further evidence of his excitement. Jasmine withdrew her hand slowly, taking with her a glistening evidence of his anticipation. To his shock and surprise, she brought her finger up and placed it teasingly by Ricardo's mouth. Taking her silent cue, he hesitated only momentarily before wrapping his lips around her finger, tasting himself. The intimate gesture added yet another layer to their burgeoning chemistry.

With a confident smirk, Jasmine spoke, her voice dripping with allure. "I always thought you'd be the kind who'd appreciate a woman taking the lead." Her fingers began to play with the hem of Ricardo's shirt, her touch feather-light yet charged with intent.

Caught off guard, Ricardo found his voice betraying a hint of vulnerability. "Ye-yes," he responded, his words more of a breathless exhale, a testament to Jasmine's power over him.

Without breaking eye contact, Jasmine began to undress slowly. Each button she undid revealed more of her tantalizing leather and PVC ensemble. The glossy material clung to her body, accentuating her curves and leaving little to Ricardo's imagination. He could see her womanhood outlined beneath the tight fabric, beckoning him.

Realizing it was his turn to respond, Ricardo moved closer, his intent clear. But Jasmine, ever the assertive one, beat him to it. In a swift motion, she lay back and peeled her lingerie aside, revealing herself fully to him.

Ricardo, intoxicated by the sight before him, dropped to his knees. But before he could act, Jasmine, ever the assertive one, reached out, gripping a handful of his hair, guiding his head to her waiting center. He didn't resist, letting her lead, understanding the unspoken dynamics at play.

Jasmine's strong thighs wrapped around Ricardo's head, her heels digging into his back, urging him closer. The intimate dance had begun in earnest, their breaths mingling, their bodies speaking a language only the two of them understood.

Every flick of Ricardo's tongue, every gentle caress, sent shivers of pleasure rippling through Jasmine. Each touch, every move was perfectly synchronized with her breath, her moans, her very heartbeat. It felt like an eternity of bliss, an intricate dance of give and take. The sensation left her reeling, momentarily breathless, and drowning in waves of ecstasy. The luxurious fabric beneath her provided scant comfort as she clung to it, trying to anchor herself in the midst of the storm of pleasure Ricardo was stirring within her.

When the waves finally ebbed, leaving her awash with a pleasant afterglow, Jasmine slowly regained her composure. There was a fierce determination in her gaze as she got to her feet, the mischievous glint in her eyes unmistakably evident. Reaching into her purse, she retrieved a few toys she had thoughtfully packed earlier, clearly prepared for every possibility.

Ricardo watched in anticipation, his eyes widening in surprise and intrigue as Jasmine unveiled each item. The highlight of her collection was a harness, accompanied by a realistic faux appendage. His gaze alternated between the new toy and Jasmine's eyes, trying to gauge her intentions, a mix of nervousness and excitement evident on his face.

Once she was securely fastened, Jasmine approached Ricardo, the power dynamics clearly defined. Her confident stride and unwavering gaze communicated her intentions. Guiding him gently yet firmly against the wall, his hands instinctively splayed out in a gesture of surrender, as if entrusting himself fully to her whims.

Jasmine's touch was deliberate as she began her exploration. With the utmost care, she started by using her fingers, generously lubricated, to familiarize herself with his most intimate parts, ensuring he was comfortable and relaxed. The initial touch made Ricardo gasp, his body tensing momentarily, but he quickly relaxed into her touch, trusting Jasmine implicitly.

There was a silent understanding between them; both knew they were stepping into uncharted territory, a journey of discovery. Jasmine, always the dominant force, took things slowly, ensuring every push, every pull was perfectly calculated to enhance Ricardo's pleasure. He could feel every sensation amplified, every touch sending shockwaves throughout his body. The blend of slight discomfort and pure pleasure was unlike anything he had experienced before.

With Jasmine taking control, each move was perfectly choreographed, an intricate dance of trust and intimacy. Ricardo, lost in the sensations, let himself be carried away, allowing Jasmine to guide him through this new experience. Every thrust, every motion, was an electrifying blend of sensations, creating a symphony of pleasure his manhood soon erect and throbbing, a steady flow of excitement dripped from the head with each thrust.

Jasmine becoming rougher and rougher with each thrust. She grabs his hair pulling his head back "You are a good little girl, aren't you?" All Ricardo could do is whimper.

For Ricardo, it was an overwhelming experience, one that blurred the lines between pain and pleasure. The sensations were intense, and he felt himself teetering on the edge, every move bringing him closer to the precipice.

Time seemed to stretch, the only sounds being their mingled breaths and soft moans. Eventually, overwhelmed by the intensity of it all, Ricardo succumbed to the rising tide of pleasure, a new sensation pleasure he's never experienced before, a touchless climax, exploding with ropes of excitement splattering the wall he was splayed against, letting out a soft cry of release.

Ricardo's manhood still engorged he collapsed to the floor rolling onto his back to find Jasmine removing her harness, but even in his post-orgasmic haze, the lingering feeling of arousal was undeniable. The familiar weight of his arousal pressed against his abdomen, throbbing in time with his heartbeat. Then, in the soft glow, he saw her silhouette. Jasmine, the embodiment of sensuality, approached with feline grace. Her eyes, dark and inscrutable, locked onto his as she positioned herself above him. The world seemed to blur, the only focus being the magnetic pull between them.

Taking her time, Jasmine lowered herself, aligning with Ricardo. Their shared breaths heavy with anticipation, creating a rhythm in the stillness of the room. The sensation of Ricardo's warmth was electrifying. As she descended, she felt the fullness of him, every pulse, every heartbeat echoing through her. The initial melding made Jasmine gasp, her eyes fluttering closed as she adjusted to the sensation.

For a moment, she just sat there, taking him in, absorbing the feel of him inside her. Then, placing her hands firmly behind her, she began her dance. The motion was slow at first, a gentle rocking that allowed them both to savor the moment. Each rise and fall were accompanied by a soft sigh, a whispered moan, as they rediscovered each other in this new context.

As the rhythm picked up, so did the intensity of their connection. Ricardo's eyes never left Jasmine's, the profound connection between them evident in their gazes. They were in perfect sync, two bodies moving as one, chasing the ultimate pinnacle of pleasure.

Jasmine's movements became more erratic, more impassioned. Her breaths came faster, the rise and fall of her chest quickening with each thrust. The sensation of being so completely connected, of feeling every heartbeat and tremor from Ricardo, was overwhelming. She could sense her climax building, a familiar tension coiling deep within her.

With one particularly deep thrust, Jasmine lost control. Her movements became less rhythmic, more frenzied, as she sought the relief, she so desperately craved. Ricardo watched in awe, the sight of her so utterly lost in passion pushing him closer to the edge as well.

Finally, with a cry that echoed through the room, Jasmine's climax washed over her. Tremors of pleasure wracked her body as she fell forward onto Ricardo, the two of them a tangled mess of limbs and shared ecstasy.

The two of them, breathless and sated, slumped against the wall, the reality of their surroundings slowly filtering back. They shared a glance, a blend of mischief and satisfaction, both knowing that this was just the beginning of many more adventures to come.

As the evening transitioned into the early hours, the ballroom painted a picture of unity and promise. Political opponents were now seen exchanging friendly conversations, conservatives and liberals sharing drinks, and a renewed sense of hope seemed to be in the air.

Outside, the night had given way to the first hints of dawn, casting a soft glow on the city. The political landscape was changing, and with it, personal perceptions and relationships were evolving. The significance of Alexandria's victory was clear – it wasn't just a political win, but a win for inclusivity, acceptance, and the promise of a united future.

In the now almost empty ballroom, a solitary figure remained. Alexandria stood on the balcony overlooking the city, her thoughts introspective. Her victory was just the beginning. The real challenge lay ahead – to bring about real change and to ensure that the messages of love, unity, and acceptance became the norm and not just election slogans.

As the golden hues of dawn streamed into the room, they painted a world that was inching closer to understanding, acceptance, and boundless love.

The ballroom, now almost empty, was filled with the echoes of laughter, conversations, and the sweet notes of romance. The politics of the past had given way to the promise of a new dawn, one where acceptance and love reigned supreme. And as the golden hues of the chandeliers faded, they left behind a world that was just a little bit better, a little more hopeful, and a lot more united.

Chapter 25: New Beginnings

The late evening news played in the background, showcasing Alexandria's recent political win. But in the plush quarters of Donnie's suite, another kind of tension was brewing. Donnie, sprawled luxuriously across satin sheets, felt every ounce of their usual commanding presence melt away under Ronnie's expert ministrations. The room was lit by the soft glow of bedside lamps, casting a sultry ambiance that accentuated the curves and valleys of their bodies.

Ronnie leaned in, their lips a breath away from Donnie's inner thigh, the soft puffs of air causing the hairs on Donnie's skin to stand on end. The delicate kisses they pressed against Donnie's soft skin were in stark contrast to the fiery looks exchanged between them. Each gentle nip and lick were deliberate, the slow pace maddening and exhilarating all at once. Donnie's fingers curled into the sheets, their other hand reaching out to grip a fistful of Ronnie's hair, urging them on, deeper into uncharted territories.

"That... Ronnie... God!" Donnie gasped, their voice laden with a heady mix of surprise and pleasure. They could feel Ronnie's smirk against their skin, the playful arrogance that always made their debates so heated. It wasn't just the physical sensations—though those were undoubtedly electric—it was the playful, teasing banter between them that made everything feel heightened.

Ronnie drew back momentarily, their gaze locking with Donnie's. The mischievous glint in their eyes was unmistakable. "Who knew debating skills could translate so well into... other areas?" Ronnie quipped, their voice dripping with innuendo.

Donnie chuckled breathlessly, trying to muster their usual composure. "Maybe we should've shifted our campaigns to the bedroom. We'd have had the entire nation voting in our favor."

Ronnie laughed at the remark, their head dipping once more. They dragged their tongue torturously slowly, from the base to the tip, making Donnie's entire body quiver in anticipation. Their methodical exploration was both a tease and a promise, drawing moans and sighs from Donnie that resonated through the room.

Pausing, Ronnie lifted their head, lips glistening and eyes darkened with lust. "Debates might be timed, Donnie, but this? I'm going to take my sweet time."

Donnie groaned at the insinuation, their back arching off the bed. The sensation of being utterly exposed, of being known inside-out, was both vulnerable and exhilarating. The slow burn of Ronnie's teasing had them on the edge, the climax within grasp but always just out of reach.

It felt like hours and mere seconds all at once. The boundaries of time blurred as sensations took over—Ronnie's hot breath against their skin, the teasing licks, the playful bites, the weight of Ronnie's gaze holding them captive.

The mounting pressure, the tantalizing build-up, reached its peak, and Donnie felt a rush of warmth spread through their entire body. Their grip on Ronnie's hair tightened as waves of pleasure coursed through them. Their voice, usually so composed and commanding, broke in a series of gasps and moans.

As the aftershocks subsided, Ronnie, ever the playful provocateur, placed one last lingering kiss on Donnie's thigh before moving up to cradle them in their arms. Their lips met in a passionate, languid kiss, tasting and savoring the evidence of their intimate rendezvous.

Drawing back, Ronnie smirked, brushing a stray hair away from Donnie's flushed face. "Now, wasn't that more fun than any political debate?"

Donnie, still catching their breath, chuckled. "Oh, without a doubt. But remember, every debate has a rebuttal round."

Brushing a stray hair out of Ronnie's face, Donnie sighed deeply, their expression turning contemplative. "You know, amidst all this...fun, I can't help but think about our political ambitions."

Ronnie, tracing lazy patterns on Donnie's chest, nodded. "It's taken a toll, hasn't it?"

"It has," Donnie admitted, biting their lip. "I sometimes wonder, Ronnie, if the world of politics is worth it when it keeps pulling us apart."

Ronnie propped themselves up, looking intently at Donnie. "Are you suggesting we leave it all behind?"

Donnie hesitated before replying, "I'm suggesting we prioritize. You and I, our love—that's what truly matters. Not the headlines, not the power plays."

Their conversation flowed from the political scandals to the secrets they'd kept, from the strain on their relationship to the weight of public expectations. Together, they reminisced about the times they'd laughed so hard they'd cried and the moments they'd held each other through the storms. As the early morning rays crept into the room, they reached a consensus. Their love was too precious to be eclipsed by political ambitions. The decision was clear. They would walk away from the world of politics.

To seal the agreement, Ronnie reached into the nightstand, pulling out a sleek, silver anal plug. They winked at Donnie, who chuckled in surprise. Ronnie's fingers played over the cool, sleek silver of the anal plug. Holding it up with a teasing flourish, they winked at Donnie. "For us, and our new chapter."

Donnie, ever the charismatic, couldn't suppress a chuckle. "You never fail to surprise me," they murmured, a glint of anticipation shining in their eyes.

The world beyond the suite faded away as Ronnie focused on the task at hand. The smooth metal felt heavy, promising in its weight. With a sultry look, Ronnie slowly began to insert the plug, taking their time, letting the cold metal contrast with the warmth of their body. A sharp intake of breath betrayed the intense sensation, their eyes never leaving Donnie's.

With the plug securely in place, Ronnie gracefully moved to straddle Donnie. The proximity, the shared heat, and the sensation of the plug made everything more heightened. Their lips met in a fervent kiss that spoke of a love matured through trials and intimate nights. Donnie's hands wandered up Ronnie's spine, fingers dancing over the warm skin, feeling the shivers and twitches they caused.

Ronnie's mouth left Donnie's only to trace a path of fire down their neck, pausing to suckle and nip at the pulse point, drawing a heady moan. As they continued their descent, they took a moment to tease Donnie's nipples with their tongue, circling and flicking in a rhythm that had Donnie arching into the touch. Each bite, each nip, pulled a deeper moan from Donnie's lips.

The dance of lips and tongues continued, as Ronnie explored every inch of Donnie's torso. They paused to revel in the taste and texture of every dip and curve, marking Donnie as theirs with every kiss and lick. The spicy scent of their arousal mingled in the air, making the atmosphere even more electric.

The dimmed lights of the room, casting sultry shadows, played beautifully on the contrasting canvas of their bodies, melding together in a passionate embrace. Ronnie, with a wicked grin, locked eyes with Donnie, capturing all their attention with the smoldering look of desire and mischief.

Inching closer to Donnie's most intimate area, Ronnie paused just millimeters away. The heat between them was palpable, the magnetic pull undeniable. Instead of diving right in, Ronnie trailed their fingers along the sensitive inner flesh of Donnie's thighs, reveling in the soft tremors their touch elicited.

Donnie tried to squirm, seeking more contact, but Ronnie held them in place with a firm hand on their hip. "Patience," Ronnie murmured, their voice dripping with promise.

Letting their fingertips dance back up, they began to pepper the path they had traced with soft, lingering kisses. Each touch was deliberate, an exploration, a promise of what was to come. Ronnie's lips felt like fire, lighting up every nerve ending they came into contact with. The sensation was maddening, leaving Donnie aching for more.

With each teasing gesture, Ronnie was drinking in Donnie's reactions—every hitched breath, every soft moan, every pleading gaze. It was a heady feeling, having such control, knowing that they held the power to bring such pleasure.

Moving subtly, Ronnie shifted their position, tilting their hips to offer a teasing view of their own arousal. The strategic move was a silent invitation, a challenge for Donnie to take control. And it was a sight Donnie couldn't resist. Ronnie shuffled forward, positioning their hips so that their arousal brushed against Donnie's lips. Donnie's eyes darkened, and without hesitation, they captured Ronnie, tasting and savoring them, letting out a groan of satisfaction.

Reaching out, Donnie slid their hand along Ronnie's thigh, pulling them closer. Their mouths met in a heated clash of lips and tongues, tasting and teasing each other with a fervor that spoke of unsaid promises and shared pasts.

But Ronnie, never one to let things get too comfortable, drew back just enough to hover over Donnie. Suddenly, Donnie felt a shift in the room's energy. Ronnie pulled back slightly, their eyes dark with desire. "Do you trust me?" they murmured, their voice husky.

Donnie nodded; their voice breathy with anticipation. "Always."

With that affirmation, Ronnie with a mischievous smile, they dipped a finger into the nearby lubricant, coating their fingers generously. They continued their intimate exploration, adding a third finger, ensuring Donnie was well-prepared for the next step. And then, when Donnie was writhing and moaning, desperate for release, Ronnie positioned themselves at Donnie's entrance, pushing forward slowly, giving Donnie time to adjust. Ronnie letting the finger glisten seductively in the soft glow of the rooms light their's digit approached Donnie's entrance.

The sensation of that wet fingertip, gently circling the sensitive area, was maddening. The teasing touch had Donnie's back arching, their hips pushing up in a silent plea for more. Ronnie took their time, enjoying every second of their dominance, watching Donnie's eyes darken with anticipation and desire.

Then, with a soft, reassuring smile, Ronnie slowly slid their finger inside. They watched Donnie intently, looking for any signs of discomfort. But all they were met with was a deep, intense gaze, filled with pure want.

As their finger ventured deeper, seeking, searching, the room was filled with tension. And then, with a slight shift, Ronnie hit that sweet spot, making Donnie gasp and clutch the sheets beneath them. The sound was raw, unfiltered—pure pleasure—and Ronnie reveled in it, moving their finger in a rhythm designed to drive Donnie wild.

Donnie whimpered, their hips bucking up involuntarily. "Please, Ronnie," they gasped, their voice laced with need.

Ronnie grinned wickedly, "As you wish." With a slow, deliberate motion, they pushed in, their finger slick and searching. Every inch, every motion was observed closely, looking for signs of discomfort or pleasure. But what Ronnie saw in Donnie's eyes was pure ecstasy. They crooked their finger just right, hitting that sweet spot that had Donnie seeing stars.

Donnie's voice, thick with arousal, broke the silence. "Ronnie," they moaned, their fingers threading through Ronnie's hair, pulling them closer. "Every time with you is like discovering a whole new world. I can't...I can't get enough."

Ronnie leaned in, pressing their lips to Donnie's in a soft, lingering kiss. "That's the plan," they whispered, their voice rough with emotion.

"God, Ronnie," Donnie moaned, their voice deep and raspy. The sensation was intense, overwhelming in its pleasure. Ronnie began a slow rhythm, their finger sliding in and out, each thrust met with a gasp or a moan from Donnie.

Ronnie leaned down, their lips brushing against Donnie's ear. "You feel so good," they whispered, their voice thick with desire. "I could touch you like this forever."

Feeling bold, Ronnie introduced a second finger, stretching and prepping Donnie, their thumb rubbing gentle circles around the sensitive area. The combined sensations had Donnie writhing, their fingers gripping Ronnie's shoulders, nails digging in.

Pulling their fingers out, Ronnie replaced it with their mouth, tasting and teasing Donnie to the brink of madness. The combination of sensations—the soft flicks of Ronnie's tongue, the gentle press of their lips, the roaming hands that seemed to be everywhere all at once before the settled wrapping around Donnie's manhood, slowly stroking it, Donnie's arousal so full and hard it started to hurt—had Donnie teetering on the edge.

With a final, wicked grin, Ronnie intensified their actions, drawing Donnie closer and closer to the precipice until, with a shattering cry, Donnie was lost to the waves of pleasure that rolled over them, their very self, quaking with each eruption of excitement from their rod.

As the tremors subsided, Ronnie crawled up to cradle Donnie in their arms, the two of them breathing heavily, their limbs entangled, the sweat on their brows glistening in the dim light.

Donnie, still reeling from the intensity of their climax, turned to Ronnie, their eyes shining with love and adoration. "You," they murmured, pressing a soft kiss to Ronnie's lips, "are truly incredible."

And there, in the silent aftermath of their passionate encounter, the two of them lay, wrapped up in each other, the world outside forgotten as they basked in the warmth of their shared intimacy.

The morning sun cast a golden hue across the opulent penthouse. Donnie stretched their limbs, letting out a contented sigh as they snuggled deeper into the silken sheets of their bed. They could feel the warmth of Ronnie's body next to theirs, the rhythmic breathing of their partner filling the room with a sense of calm.

Opening their eyes, Donnie looked out of the massive window panes, taking in the metropolis below. The city had seen them rise, falter, love, and now, take one of the biggest decisions of their lives. They turned their gaze to Ronnie, who was now stirring, a slight smile playing on their lips.

"Good morning," Donnie whispered, brushing a loose strand of hair off Ronnie's forehead.

Ronnie blinked their eyes open, meeting Donnie's gaze. "Mm, morning. What time is it?"

"Does it matter?" Donnie replied with a chuckle, "Today, we are escaping all this chaos." They gestured at the sprawling city beneath them.

Ronnie smirked, pulling Donnie closer. "You're right. Today is about us. No politics, no drama."

Their laughter filled the room, a sound so genuine, so refreshing amidst the constant storm of the political arena.

Hours later, the two found themselves on a private jet, heading to the serene Miami Mermaid Beachfront. Away from the constant scrutiny, away from the politics that had consumed their lives, they hoped to find a moment of respite and clarity.

Ronnie, gazing out of the plane window, turned to Donnie, their hand resting gently on Donnie's. "Are we doing the right thing?"

Donnie squeezed Ronnie's hand, "We are doing what feels right for us, Ronnie. I've spent enough of my life chasing dreams that weren't truly mine. Now, I want to chase happiness, with you."

Their eyes locked, and in that moment, every uncertainty vanished.

The Miami Mermaid Beachfront was every bit as captivating as they had imagined. The white sands sparkled under the sun, the waves crashing melodically on the shores. But today, it wasn't just another idyllic day at the beach; an aura of anticipation hung in the air. Media vans, supporters holding placards, and a makeshift stage had been set up for their public concession.

Stepping onto the dais, Donnie took a deep breath, their voice strong, yet laden with emotion. "Thank you all for being here today. This journey, our journey, has been filled with challenges, learning, and immense growth."

Ronnie continued, "But through it all, we've realized that sometimes, life throws you a curveball, and you need to reassess your priorities. Our love for one another, our understanding of self, has made us reevaluate our path."

Donnie nodded, their eyes misty, "And so, today, we have decided to concede the election gracefully."

A hushed murmur ran through the crowd. Camera flashes went off. Reporters scribbled furiously.

"But this isn't a retreat," Ronnie clarified. "It's merely a redirection of our energies. We've chosen love over ambition. Authenticity over appearances."

Taking a moment to compose themselves, Donnie addressed their supporters. "To all those who believed in us, supported us, cheered for us, we are eternally grateful. We may be stepping away from the political limelight, but our commitment to love, acceptance, and unity remains unwavering."

As the duo wrapped up their speech, the crowd erupted in applause, a mix of respect, admiration, and perhaps, a bit of surprise. Cameras zoomed in on them, capturing every raw emotion, every tear shed, every embrace shared.

Stepping down from the stage, Donnie and Ronnie were swarmed by supporters. But amid the chaos, they found solace in each other's arms. They had publicly embraced their true selves, a significant turning point not just in the story but in their lives.

The Miami Mermaid Beachfront, with its sprawling white sands and gently crashing waves, took on an entirely new persona. It was as if the beach itself had thrown on a feather boa, donned a pair of glittering stilettos, and was ready to party.

Cacophonous beats echoed from one end of the beach to the other as vibrant floats began their journey down the sandy stretch. Spectators, decked out in colorful attire, cheered, whistled, and danced to the rhythms. The air was charged with an infectious energy.

Donnie and Ronnie, having exchanged their formal suits for flamboyant beach drag outfits, led the parade. Donnie, as Divine Donnie, looked utterly magnificent in a shimmering silver bikini paired with a cascading turquoise wrap that flowed behind them like a sparkling ocean wave. Their makeup was a blend of beachy blues and purples, with oversized sunglasses that sparkled with embedded crystals. Ronnie, as Ronnie Rebel, had opted for an elegant white one-piece, adorned with pearl embellishments. Their dramatic wide-brimmed hat, with a hint of irony, shielded them from the sun's rays.

The duo waved MAGA flags, which in this story had come to symbolize **M**ake **A**cceptance **G**enuine **A**gain. Their faces beamed with pride, not for the political ambitions they once held, but for the love, acceptance, and unity they now championed.

As the parade progressed, it was a sight to behold. Floats showcasing drag kings and queens in beach attire — some in high-waisted retro swimsuits, others in revealing bikinis, and yet others in gender-fluid designs that transcended typical beachwear. Sequins shimmered, feathers fluttered, and the mood was ebullient.

However, the highlight was yet to come. As the parade neared its peak, a float approached that left the crowd in awe.

It was Michelle Pensive, looking every bit the diva. She wore a jaw-dropping gold bikini that gleamed against her skin, and she proudly did not tuck, showcasing her bulge with confidence. With her long flowing hair and sun-kissed makeup, she epitomized beach glamour. She twirled, danced, and blew kisses to the audience, leaving a trail of admirers in her wake.

A group of spectators, fanning themselves, exchanged shocked whispers. "Is that Michelle?!" "She looks incredible!" "I can't believe she's here!" One even faintly exclaimed, "I need a glass of water!"

Ronnie leaned towards Donnie, their voice barely audible above the beats. "Did you know Michelle would be here?"

Donnie, equally surprised, shook their head, "No idea, but she's stealing the show!"

Meanwhile, Michelle, riding the crest of the audience's admiration, spread her arms wide, taking in the cheers, the applause, and the countless camera flashes. It was her moment, and she embraced it wholeheartedly.

A moment arose when a rather enthusiastic spectator, overwhelmed by Michelle's beauty, tried to climb onto the float to get a closer look. Their attempt was met with playful chiding from Michelle, "Easy there, darling! There's enough of Michelle to go around!"

Ronnie elbowed Donnie playfully, "Looks like Michelle's giving you a run for your money."

Donnie laughed, feigning indignation, "Well, we can't let her have all the fun, can we?" And with that, Donnie struck a pose, giving Michelle a playful challenge. Michelle responded with a wink and blew a kiss their way.

The entire beachfront echoed with laughter, cheer, and the harmonious beats of celebration. Everyone, irrespective of their backgrounds, joined in the festivities, dancing, and cheering. The energy was infectious, the vibes, electric.

Somewhere between the dancing, the waving of flags, and the playful challenges, Donnie and Ronnie found themselves in a quiet moment. The world faded as they gazed into each other's eyes. Donnie whispered, "We did it," his voice filled with wonder.

Ronnie nodded, pulling Donnie closer, "We did. And it's just the beginning."

The parade culminated in a central area where a massive stage had been set up. Donnie and Ronnie climbed onto it, holding hands, their faces radiant with happiness. "Thank you, Miami!" Donnie exclaimed; their voice full of gratitude. "Today, we celebrate love, acceptance, and unity! It doesn't matter who you are or where you come from. All that matters is who you choose to be!"

Ronnie chimed in, "And remember, it's never too late to redefine yourself, to chase happiness, and to choose love!"

The crowd erupted into cheers, the air filled with love and acceptance. Donnie and Ronnie's choice to step away from the political race had been a shock to many, but in this moment, on this beach, surrounded by supporters and well-wishers, their decision seemed perfect.

The lingering energy from the parade still hung in the air as the sun started its golden descent over Miami Mermaid Beachfront. Its radiance bathed the onlookers, floats, and even the sand beneath their feet in a warm, amber glow.

Donnie, holding a MAGA flag in one hand and Ronnie's hand in the other, felt an overwhelming surge of happiness. It wasn't about the crowd or the cameras anymore; it was about them, about acceptance, about love. Donnie began to lead a chant, their voice, though strong, carried a subtle undertone of emotion, "Love over hate! Love over hate!"

Ronnie, ever the supportive partner, jumped right in, their voice joining Donnie's in a harmonic symphony of hope. The crowd, electrified by the couple's spirit, echoed back in unison, the words resonating across the vast stretch of the beach.

As the chant grew louder and more rhythmic, Donnie and Ronnie turned to face each other. The world faded away, and in that fleeting moment, it was as if they were the only two souls on that beach. They pulled each other close, sealing their commitment with a deep, passionate kiss that spoke of promises, dreams, and endless possibilities.

As they broke apart, the surrounding crowd cheered, clapped, and some even shed tears of joy. The very atmosphere seemed to vibrate with love, acceptance, and unity. They had achieved more than they had ever hoped for – not a political victory, but a victory of the heart.

And then, as if on cue, the surroundings began to morph. Torches were lit around the beach, casting a gentle, flickering light. Music systems sprung to life, churning out peppy, groovy tunes. The Miami Mermaid Beachfront, renowned for its daytime beauty, was now transforming into a nighttime paradise. Beach balls were tossed into the air, fire dancers showcased their breathtaking moves, and tables laden with delicious treats and refreshing drinks were set up.

As night took hold, a makeshift dance floor was illuminated. Donnie, always the life of the party, pulled Ronnie onto the floor, their moves perfectly synchronizing to the rhythm of the waves crashing nearby. They swayed, twirled, and lost themselves in the music and in each other.

Off to the side, Michelle, looking every bit the glowing diva from the parade, joined the dance floor, her graceful moves and infectious enthusiasm drawing a crowd around her. She embodied the spirit of the night – free, confident, and unapologetically herself.

Ronnie, pulling away slightly from their dance, gazed deeply into Donnie's eyes. "Today marks the beginning of our new journey, Donnie. A journey where we put love first."

Donnie's eyes sparkled in the torchlight. "And I can't wait to embark on this journey with you, every step of the way."

As they continued dancing under the canopy of stars, surrounded by the sounds of laughter, music, and the gentle lapping of waves, they knew that they had found their place in the world. They were exactly where they were meant to be, with the people they were meant to be with, doing what they were meant to do.

And as the hours rolled on, Miami Mermaid Beachfront bore witness to a celebration of love, acceptance, and new beginnings. The night was magical, filled with memories that would last a lifetime.

The sun might have set on Donnie and Ronnie's political ambitions, but a new dawn arose in their lives—one filled with the promise of love, understanding, and endless adventures.

Their political chapter, and their story, might have ended, but for Donnie and Ronnie, this was just the beginning. A beginning of a life where they chose love over everything else, where they embraced their true selves, and where every day promised a new adventure.

Chapter 26: The Last Word

The soft hum of the air conditioning and the faint ticking of the clock were the only sounds in Alexandria's Advocacy Hub. Alexandria sat there, lost in her thoughts, surrounded by mementos of her campaign journey. Photographs of rallies, meetings, debates, and late-night strategy sessions were scattered around, each telling a story of challenges faced and victories achieved.

From a young grassroots organizer who championed the rights of the marginalized, to her journey of becoming President-Elect, Alexandria's trajectory had been nothing short of meteoric. As she traced the rim of her coffee mug with a finger, she remembered the countless nights spent planning, the heated debates, and the sacrifices made along the way. The weight of her achievement was not lost on her.

As she was lost in her reverie, the soft creak of the door announced a visitor. Before she could turn around, she felt strong hands gently massaging her shoulders. A warmth flooded her body, and she instinctively reached back, intertwining her fingers with those of her partner, Riley.

"You looked miles away," Riley whispered, leaning forward to plant a gentle kiss on her temple.

She turned her chair around to face him, offering a smile. "Just reflecting on this whirlwind of a journey."

Riley smirked, his dark eyes twinkling with mischief. "Reflecting? Or plotting to turn the White House into a drag stage?"

Alexandria laughed, a sound that filled the room. "Well, every President has to leave their mark, don't they?"

Their playful banter was a reminder of how Riley had been her rock, grounding her when the going got tough, reminding her to laugh even when the stakes were high.

"Oh, speaking of marks," she said with a wry smile, pulling him closer, "I think I've earned a more personal... reward, don't you think?"

He raised an eyebrow, intrigued. "Oh, really?"

She nodded and inched closer, her breath mingling with his. "How about a token of appreciation for my, let's say, tireless dedication?"

Riley's teasing smile, mingling with the glint in his eyes, was enough to make Alexandria's heart race. "Well, Madam President-Elect," he began, voice low and dripping with mischief, "consider this your reward." He took a deliberate step towards her, closing the gap, and Alexandria felt that familiar pull—an irresistible gravity that always drew them together.

Their lips met, and it was as if a dormant volcano had erupted. The passion that had been simmering under the surface burst forth, and their kiss deepened, fervent and demanding. It wasn't just the culmination of the day's events or the culmination of their journey together; it was the pure, undiluted essence of their connection. The kind of connection that made you forget where you ended and the other began.

Pulling away was a feat in itself. Both were left breathless, their chests heaving in sync, as the aftermath of their fiery kiss lingered in the air. Riley leaned his forehead against Alexandria's, the intimacy of the gesture contrasting starkly with the passion that had just unfurled. Their eyes locked, raw emotions passing between them—a silent conversation that spoke louder than words ever could.

The surroundings of the Advocacy Hub, filled with reminders of Alexandria's journey, suddenly felt both overwhelmingly large and comfortably intimate. In this moment, the room served as a testament to her determination and strength, and yet, it also became their private sanctuary, protecting the fragile cocoon of their intimacy.

Without breaking their gaze, Riley, in one swift motion, scooped Alexandria into his arms, her thighs encircling his waist. Her fingers instinctively found the nape of his neck, curling into the soft hair there. With a bold move, he placed her atop her desk, which was momentarily cleared of its usual clutter. The world outside, with its expectations and responsibilities, faded further into oblivion.

The intensity between them grew palpable, a tangible force that threatened to consume them. Alexandria, cheeks flushed, and pupils dilated, shimmied out of her underwear. Riley, always attuned to her desires, took the hint immediately, sinking to his knees before her. The gesture, so vulnerable yet powerful, made Alexandria's heart skip a beat.

Riley's tongue began its tantalizing journey, sending jolts of pleasure up Alexandria's spine. The expertise of his movements, coupled with the sheer intimacy of the act, had her gripping the edges of the desk, her other hand tangled in his hair, guiding him deeper. Every touch, every flick was deliberate, designed to bring her closer to the edge. The outside world was long forgotten as waves of pleasure washed over her, leaving her trembling in its wake.

With a final, lingering touch, Riley rose, his face flushed, lips glistening. The sight was almost too much for Alexandria. She reached for him, fingers deftly unfastening his pants, freeing the desire that had been building. The urgency in her voice was unmistakable as she whispered, "I want to feel you in me."

The dim light from the outside street lamps filtered through the blinds, casting an almost ethereal glow on Alexandria's figure as she lay atop the heavy wooden desk. The ambient buzz of the city outside felt light years away in the intimacy of the moment. Every piece of paper, every pen, every official document scattered in the haste of passion.

A haze of desire clouded Alexandria's vision as her fingers moved purposefully, skillfully undoing Riley's belt and zipper. The urgency in her touch echoed the intensity of her whisper. "I want to feel you in me."

The very air between them seemed to crackle as Riley freed himself from the confines of his clothing. The tension was palpable, thick enough to slice through. As his eyes bore into hers, the message was clear; they were about to cross a line, one that would further solidify the depth of their connection.

He positioned himself between her legs, the tips of their noses brushing against each other, their breaths mingling. Time seemed to slow down, every heartbeat echoing like the tolling of a bell. And then, with a measured restraint, he entered her.

The sensation was electric. Alexandria gasped, the feeling of fullness, of connection, overwhelming her. Each slow, deliberate thrust was calculated, a dance of intimacy and passion. The bulging head of Riley's arousal pressed and rubbed against sensitive spots she didn't even know she had. The pleasure was exquisite, toe-curling, soul-searing. She clung to him, fingers gripping the fabric of his shirt, nails digging into his back, a silent plea for more, deeper, faster.

Riley obliged, adjusting his angle, deepening the penetration. With each thrust, Riley hit all the right spots, sending shockwaves of ecstasy throughout Alexandria's body. The desk beneath her creaked and groaned under their combined weight, but they hardly noticed, lost as they were in the intensity of their connection. Alexandria's fingers clutched at his collar, pulling him closer. She needed him, all of him.

Feeling a primal urge, she wrapped her legs tightly around his waist, deepening their connection. Her body seemed to have a mind of its own, gyrating and moving in sync with his, creating a rhythm that was both raw and beautiful. As they moved together, the world outside ceased to exist. The stresses of the campaign, the weight of the presidency, all of it faded away, leaving just the two of them, lost in each other.

The world seemed to shrink to just the two of them—the heavy wooden desk, the moonlight peeking through the blinds, and the unbridled passion that threatened to consume them both. Alexandria's hips rolled in rhythm with Riley's thrusts, amplifying the sensation. The room was filled with the sounds of their pleasure—the slap of skin on skin, ragged breaths, whispered encouragements.

As the pleasure intensified, Alexandria released his collar. Her back arched gracefully, pushing her closer to him, craving every inch, every sensation. The room was filled with the sounds of their heavy breathing, the occasional moan, and the rhythmic creaking of the desk.

Their eyes locked, the raw intensity of their connection on full display. There was something profoundly beautiful about the vulnerability they shared in that moment—two souls laid bare, physically and emotionally.

The coil of pleasure that had been building within Alexandria tightened, her body trembling on the brink of release. She felt the telltale signs in Riley too—the increased pace, the depth of his thrusts, the way his eyes darkened with need.

With one final, deep thrust, they both let go. The sensation of him pulsating inside her, combined with her own climax, was overwhelming. It was a release like no other, a culmination of their shared history, their love, their desire. Alexandria's vision whited out as waves of pleasure crashed over her, her body convulsing in ecstasy. She felt every pulse, every throb of Riley's release, the warmth of him filling her.

Finally, as the last shudders of pleasure subsided, they collapsed into each other's arms, breathless and spent. The room, which had been filled with such intensity just moments before, was now filled with a comfortable silence, broken only by their ragged breathing.

For a few moments, they stayed locked in that position, lost in the afterglow of their passion. Riley's forehead rested against hers, their panting breaths mingling, their hearts racing.

As they slowly disentangled themselves, Riley helped Alexandria sit up, his fingers brushing stray strands of hair from her face. Their eyes met, and without words, they shared a moment of understanding. In the heart of the city, amidst the chaos of their lives, they had found solace in each other's arms.

They lay there for what felt like an eternity, wrapped in each other's arms, basking in the afterglow of their passion. The desk, which had borne witness to their love, was now a mess, papers scattered everywhere. But neither of them cared. In that moment, all that mattered was the bond they shared, a bond that had only grown stronger with each passing day.

As they finally disentangled themselves, Riley reached out, helping Alexandria to her feet. They shared a knowing smile, the kind that comes from sharing something special, something profound.

As they began to straighten up the room, Riley paused, looking at Alexandria with a mix of admiration and love. "You truly are an incredible woman, Alexandria," he said, his voice filled with emotion. "And I'm lucky to have you in my life."

She blushed, the weight of his words hitting her. "And I'm lucky to have you," she replied, leaning in for another soft, lingering kiss.

In that intimate Advocacy Hub, surrounded by remnants of her incredible journey, Alexandria was reminded of the unbreakable bond she shared with Riley. A bond that had only grown stronger with the trials they faced together.

With Riley by her side, she felt invincible. Ready to take on the world and make a real difference. She might have been reflecting on the past, but her gaze was firmly set on the future. A future where love, acceptance, and inclusivity would take center stage.

Alexandria lay there for a moment longer, the coolness of the wood pressing against her back, the warmth of Riley's body a comforting counterpoint. Slowly, she sat up, her mind shifting from the passion of the present to the immense responsibilities of the future.

She stood, her fingers brushing over the scattered papers, a reminder of the path she'd walked, the battles she'd fought. From the energetic days of grassroots campaigns to fierce debates on the Primetime Politics Studio stage, each step had been a crucial one.

The night outside the window of Alexandria's Advocacy Hub was serene, the glimmer of the city lights hinting at the vast number of souls depending on her. This was the precipice of real change.

"I want to make a difference, Riley," Alexandria whispered, more to herself than to him. "I want to make sure that every individual, no matter who they are or where they come from, feels seen, valued, and heard."

Riley stood up beside her, his hand finding hers, fingers interlocking. "I know you will," he said softly, his voice full of confidence.

Drawing a deep breath, Alexandria began outlining her vision for the upcoming term. "Firstly, we need to address the rights of the LGBTQ+ community, ensure that they are given the same privileges and opportunities as everyone else. I mean, if Donnie and Ronnie can embrace their drag personas, there's hope for everyone."

Riley chuckled, "I'll never forget the day Divine Donnie and Ronnie Rebel set the stage on fire at the Starlit Drag Lounge. Talk about unexpected turns."

"I still think Michelle Pensive's drag was the best comedic relief," Alexandria quipped. The thought of Michelle, in her innocent yet extravagant drag, always brought a smile to her face.

The pair continued talking, discussing Alexandria's goals for a more inclusive education system, one that would teach the youth about acceptance and diversity from an early age. The importance of environmental sustainability, a subject close to Alexandria's heart, was also on the agenda. She was determined to push for policies that would curb emissions and promote green initiatives.

As the hours ticked by, the room was filled with ambitious ideas and plans. From enhancing healthcare access for all to addressing housing inequality and job opportunities, every topic was discussed with passion and depth.

"I want to create a platform, perhaps on WebWonders Online Space, where every citizen can voice their concerns, share their stories. A place where every voice matters," she mused, imagining a digital space of unity and understanding.

"I'm with you, every step of the way," Riley affirmed, squeezing her hand. "With your vision and determination, the nation is in good hands."

As dawn approached, a pinkish hue painting the sky, Alexandria looked out of the window once more. There was hope on the horizon. A hope that was reinforced by her strong bond with Riley, her own inner strength, and her commitment to a brighter, more inclusive future.

"We have a lot of work ahead of us," she whispered, more determined than ever.

Riley wrapped his arms around her, pulling her close. "And we'll face it together."

The sky had been washed with the pale pinks and golds of dawn, promising a new day as Alexandria prepared to address the nation. After the passionate interlude in her Advocacy Hub, the real world was beckoning. She was about to be in the spotlight at the Victory Vanguard Press Hall, one of the most pivotal moments in her career.

Adjusting her blazer in the Luminous Lights Dressing Suite mirror, she glanced at the reflection of Riley behind her. "Do you think this is too formal?" she asked, tugging at the collar.

Riley grinned. "I think you could wear a potato sack, and the nation would still hang on to every word you say. But for what it's worth, you look stunning."

Giggling, she playfully swatted his arm. "Always the charmer. But seriously, this speech... it's more than just politics. It's personal. It's about every individual who ever felt marginalized. It's for Michelle and for Donnie and Ronnie. It's for every drag artist out there. It's for love and acceptance."

He held her gaze. "And you're the perfect voice for it."

Taking a deep breath, she exited the suite. The atmosphere at the Press Hall was electric. Every reporter was ready, every camera poised. The murmurs subsided as she took her position at the podium. Behind her, a massive screen flashed the logo of NewsWave Media Outlets, ready to broadcast her words far and wide.

"Good morning," she began, the nerves clear in her voice but overshadowed by her conviction. "Today, I address you not just as your future president but as a fellow citizen, who, like many of you, has been on an extraordinary journey."

Mentioning her grassroots origins, she segued into her dual life as Alex the Conqueror, a Drag King that commanded attention and respect. She spoke about the lessons from that world, the value of acceptance, the sheer joy of being one's true self, and the importance of love.

She cited the unexpected journey of Donnie and Ronnie, using their transformation as a beacon of hope for all. The nods and murmurs of agreement from the reporters gave her a surge of confidence. "If the conservative duo can dazzle in heels and own their truth, then why can't our nation, known for its diversity, create a space where everyone belongs?"

She moved on to the meatier parts of her speech — her plans for the country, her dream for an inclusive nation, and her hope to empower every citizen. "We're launching a new platform on WebWonders Online Space," she announced, "where every voice, no matter how marginalized, will be heard."

She also highlighted her team's unwavering support, thanking them for their dedication. Pausing for a moment, her voice softened, "And Riley, your faith in me, in us, has been my rock. Our love story is a testament to the fact that when hearts connect, differences fade away."

She finished with an impassioned plea to the nation. "Let's move forward, not as separate parties but as a united front. Let's make our country a haven of acceptance, love, and understanding."

The hall erupted in applause. She stepped down, heart pounding, feeling both drained and exhilarated.

Riley met her as she exited, wrapping her in a tight embrace. "You were phenomenal. I'm so proud of you," he murmured, planting a soft kiss on her temple.

"The hard part is only beginning," she replied, smiling wryly.

He chuckled. "Good thing you have the nation's most dashing guy by your side."

She laughed, linking her arm with his. "Always."

As Alexandria and Riley stepped out of the Victory Vanguard Press Hall, they were bombarded by reporters, their mics thrust forward, camera flashes lighting up the evening like a swarm of fireflies.

"Alexandria! A word about your first action in office?"

"Miss Ocasio-Cortez! Will you be attending the Miami Mermaid Beachfront pride parade with Donnie and Ronnie?"

A brisk wind tousled Alexandria's hair as she shielded her eyes from the glare. "One step at a time!" she called out, waving and offering a radiant smile.

Riley, ever the protector, guided her to the awaiting car. As they settled in the backseat, Alexandria let out a sigh of relief. "That was... overwhelming."

Riley chuckled, his eyes dancing with mischief. "I did warn you about the hard parts, didn't I? Welcome to the world of top-tier politics and paparazzi!"

She playfully nudged him. "And to think you're a part of this package deal!"

He pretended to ponder. "Hmm, dashing, supportive boyfriend or the chaos of politics? Tough choice."

She leaned in, her lips inches from his. "Definitely the boyfriend," she whispered before sealing the deal with a soft kiss.

Moments later, they arrived at Alexandria's Advocacy Hub. The atmosphere inside was charged, a reflection of the whirlwind day. Volunteers were bustling around, discussing strategies, answering phone calls, and checking screens displaying the latest news updates.

As Alexandria entered, a round of applause erupted. The young volunteers, looking at her with a mix of admiration and hope, were the future she was fighting for. She was their beacon of change.

A loud cheer went up as Michelle Pensive entered, her makeup flawless and her wig perfectly styled. "Congratulations, darling!" she gushed, enveloping Alexandria in a hug. "Your speech was everything!"

Alexandria laughed, "Thanks, Michelle. You're always such a breath of fresh air."

"I do try," Michelle replied with a theatrical flip of her wig.

Brock approached next, holding a large tray of celebratory cocktails. "To new beginnings!" he toasted, handing Alexandria a sparkling glass.

"To hope and change!" she responded, clinking her glass with his.

Hours passed in a blur of congratulations, laughter, and anecdotes from the campaign trail. Alexandria, ever the gracious host, ensured everyone felt acknowledged and appreciated.

As the clock struck midnight, the crowd began to disperse. Alexandria found herself alone in her office, looking out over the cityscape. The twinkling lights below mirrored the stars above, symbolizing dreams, aspirations, and the vast universe of possibilities.

Riley entered quietly; his silhouette framed by the door. "It's been a long day. How do you feel?"

She took a deep breath. "I feel... ready. Ready to bring acceptance and equality to the forefront. Ready to make the world a better place."

He walked over, encircling her waist with his arms. "And you will. With every ounce of passion, intelligence, and love you possess."

She leaned her head back onto his shoulder. "We have a tough road ahead. But knowing you're with me makes everything seem possible."

Riley gently turned her around, their eyes locked in an intense gaze. "You know what? Today, right now, let's just be Riley and Alexandria. Not the president and her first gentleman. Not the faces of a campaign. Just two people in love."

She smiled; the weight of the world momentarily lifted. "Just us."

He brushed a stray strand of hair behind her ear, leaning in to capture her lips. The world outside faded away as they lost themselves in the warmth and intimacy of the moment.

The city continued its vibrant hum, but in that Advocacy Hub, time seemed to stand still. And as dawn approached, heralding a new day, Alexandria Ocasio-Cortez, the voice of change, stood with the man she loved, ready to shape the future.

Epilogue

Alexandria:

A multi-hued tapestry painted the Miami Mermaid Beachfront. The brilliant colors of the sky, peppered with jubilant kites and fluttering banners, met the glittering sands below. As families, couples, and individuals congregated, three figures took the center stage: President Alexandria, the irresistibly flamboyant Donnie, and the graceful Ronnie. They were a vision, grand marshals of the pride parade, representing not just their individual stories but a testament to a transformed nation.

Walking ahead of the parade, Alexandria, adorned in a dress that reflected her vibrant spirit, beamed. The trio's vibrant energy flowed into the procession. Donnie, true to Divine Donnie's style, glimmered in a radiant costume, while Ronnie, showcasing Ronnie Rebel's elegance, greeted the crowd with poised waves.

The early months of Alexandria's presidency were a medley of change and dynamism. From the famed White House, she took bold strides in policy-making. She worked relentlessly, shaping legislation that emphasized inclusivity and equity. The country responded with optimism, as progressive policies were implemented, and issues, long-ignored, were addressed.

Amidst the rigorous demands of presidency, Alexandria's personal life flourished. The nation paused and celebrated as Alexandria and Riley exchanged vows on the sprawling South Lawn of the White House. Under a canopy of twinkling fairy lights and amidst rows of blooming roses, their union symbolized hope and unity.

And as if the universe joined in their celebration, the couple soon welcomed twins. The echoes of laughter and innocent babble added warmth to the historic corridors of the White House. Alexandria, despite her responsibilities, was a hands-on mother, embracing every challenge, from midnight lullabies to morning briefings, with equal enthusiasm.

However, merging motherhood with presidential duties made for amusing anecdotes. Like the time she inadvertently carried a pacifier to an official meeting, or when a policy document had suspicious crayon marks.

Her term progressed with achievements and challenges, navigated with grace and tenacity. Allies like Brandie and

Brock were her pillars. Brandie's presence in strategy meetings, always accompanied by witty remarks and vibrant attire, was refreshing. Brock, with his extensive connections, facilitated groundbreaking campaigns and reforms.

Amusing moments peppered the term; Donnie and Ronnie's costume trials, which they insisted on showcasing at the White House, led to many a laughter-filled evening. There was the unforgettable moment when Donnie's dramatic cape got entangled with a historic statue, much to Ronnie's amusement.

The turning point came with Dark Brandie's transformation. Once a critic, a poignant conversation with Alexandria at a White House gala made him a supporter, advocating for the progressive causes she championed.

As the end of her first term neared and election fervor gripped the nation, the support for Alexandria was palpable. Massive rallies echoed her achievements, chants demanding a second term filled the air.

On election night, the tension was palpable. The vast halls of the White House were abuzz with whispers, hopes, and speculations. And then, the announcement came, sealing Alexandria's second term. Victory!

Standing at the famed balcony of the White House, looking over the expansive grounds teeming with supporters, Alexandria felt a rush of emotions. The weight of her responsibilities was profound, but her commitment unwavering.

"As we stand at the cusp of another chapter," she addressed the gathered masses, "I promise to serve, to uphold our shared ideals, and to lead with love and determination. Together, we'll march towards a brighter, more inclusive future."

Amidst roaring applause, the night sky lit up with fireworks. A dazzling display, signifying hope, love, and a renewed mandate for President Alexandria.

Donnie and Ronnie:

Donnie, adorned in a tropical shirt with colors that rivaled the Miami sunset, took a sip from their pineapple-infused cocktail at the Miami Mermaid Beachfront Lounge. They gazed at the dancing crowd, a blend of drag queens, activists, and everyday people who came to enjoy a sun-soaked afternoon of love and acceptance.

Next to them, Ronnie, ever the image of elegance even in beachwear, remarked, "It's surreal, isn't it? From the political grandeur to being the kings – or should I say queens – of this beachside lounge."

Donnie winked. "Why choose? We're a bit of both. And who would've thought? The MAGA movement, redefined as 'Make Acceptance Great Always.' It has a certain ring to it."

In the time since they'd stepped back from the political arena, Donnie and Ronnie found a new calling. From staunch conservatives, they had transitioned into champions of love, acceptance, and unity. And while their methods might be unconventional – involving sequins, feather boas, and the most dazzling of high heels – they made a genuine impact.

The Miami drag scene had flourished under their guidance. They used their wealth and influence to set up scholarships for LGBTQ+ students, funded counseling for those in need, and most controversially, pushed for inclusive literature in schools across Florida.

Their beachside lounge became a beacon for everyone who sought a place where they could be unapologetically themselves. The lounge wasn't just about drag; it was about family.

One evening, as Ronnie Rebel graced the stage with a rendition of an old love ballad, a young man approached Donnie, eyes glistening with tears. "Thank you," he whispered. "In this place, I found acceptance from my family, who learned to see beyond my sexuality."

Moved, Donnie squeezed his hand. "This is just the beginning," they promised.

In the midst of this transformation was their joint venture – a proposal to include diverse literature in Florida schools. Their aim was to represent all shades of love, breaking stereotypes, and fostering a new generation that thrived on acceptance.

While Donnie was the charm, Ronnie was the strategy. They attended meetings, engaged with school boards, and faced a mix of applause and criticism. There were those who questioned their sincerity, given their political past. Others called it a publicity stunt.

Yet, one evening at their Mermaid beachside lounge, as Donnie, in their Divine Donnie persona, was about to take the stage, a teacher approached them. She handed over a letter written by a student, which read, "For the first time, I saw myself in a story. I felt normal. Thank you."

Tears streamed down Donnie's face as they read the note aloud. It was moments like this that solidified their purpose.

Ronnie, typically more reserved, took to the beaches and streets, often handing out literature and engaging in one-on-one conversations with parents, educators, and students. They faced resistance, of course, but with every challenge, Ronnie's conviction only grew stronger.

The duo also started "Read with Rebel & Divine," a monthly event where they read stories to children, answering questions and nurturing young minds to be accepting and kind.

Word of their efforts reached President Alexandria, who invited them to the White House. On a balmy evening, as the trio sat in the East Room, surrounded by portraits of past presidents, Alexandria confessed, "You know, I never thought I'd say this, but I'm proud of what you both have achieved. Your transformation, the work you're doing—it's commendable."

Donnie, ever the flamboyant, flirted, "Why, Madam President, are you trying to charm me?" They batted their eyelashes comically.

Ronnie, rolling their eyes but with a smile playing on their lips, chimed in, "No, Donnie. But I think she might have a point."

As days turned into weeks and weeks into months, Donnie and Ronnie's beachside lounge saw faces from all walks of life—transgender teens finding their voice, parents learning to accept their queer children, and even conservatives reevaluating their stances.

While they had their fair share of challenges, Donnie and Ronnie never wavered from their path. They became symbols of change, proving that transformation was possible regardless of one's past.

One sun-soaked Miami day, as the two stood hand in hand, overlooking the vibrant parade that danced on the Miami Mermaid Beachfront, Donnie turned to Ronnie, "From politics to this... do you have any regrets?"

Ronnie, their eyes reflecting the colors of the parade, replied, "None. We found our truth, our purpose. And in this journey of acceptance and love, we found ourselves."

And as the music played, the crowd cheered, and the waves kissed the shore, the two former political rivals danced, not as

Michelle:

The air inside Starlit Drag Lounge was electric. Dim lights bathed the room in a sultry glow as a mix of seasoned drag enthusiasts and first-timers chattered excitedly. Tonight, Michelle Pensive was making her appearance after months of being out of the limelight.

In the dressing suite backstage, Michelle adjusted her wig and examined herself in the mirror. The reflection showed a queen of unparalleled poise, but behind her stunning façade, Michelle held memories of a challenging journey.

A knock interrupted her introspection. It was Dark Brandie, looking as captivating as ever with his signature mesmerizing aura.

"Michelle, you're glowing," Brandie greeted, offering a bottle of sparkling water.

Michelle chuckled, "Honey, it's the makeup. But thank you."

As Brandie sat down, the two shared a warm moment. "Remember our first drag showdown together? We were fierce competitors. And now, look at you."

Michelle's eyes gleamed, "It's been quite a ride. From hiding in Mike's Metro Flat, scared of my own shadow, to now... it's surreal."

Brandie took her hand, squeezing it, "You've become an icon, Michelle. A beacon of hope. Not just for the LGBTQ+ community, but for anyone who's ever felt trapped in the wrong identity."

They were interrupted by the stage manager. "Five minutes, Michelle."

Michelle took a deep breath, preparing to immerse herself into the character that had given so many people strength.

The crowd erupted in cheers as Michelle Pensive glided onto the stage, embodying both extravagance and innocence. Her performances were a mix of humor, drama, and, most importantly, a raw honesty that resonated with everyone who watched. Through her art, Michelle told tales of self-acceptance, love, and transformation.

Post-performance, Michelle's fan base at the lounge was a testament to her impact. Young trans individuals approached her, their eyes filled with admiration. Parents of LGBTQ+ children sought advice. Even a few senior citizens, who initially seemed out of place, shared stories of their late-life realizations and thanked her for being a guiding light.

Everywhere she went, Michelle became the emblem of courage and change. WebWonders Online Space was filled with #MichelleMagic, where stories of her influence were shared far and wide. Michelle began holding workshops at Alexandria's Advocacy Hub, teaching younger drag enthusiasts the art and, more importantly, the heart of drag.

One particular evening, after a heart-wrenching performance at the Heartfelt Haven Theater, a young girl approached Michelle with teary eyes. "I came out to my parents last week. They didn't understand. But tonight, I brought them here. They saw your performance, and it changed everything. Thank you."

Moments like these made every struggle worth it for Michelle. Her transformation from a conservative traditionalist to a gay icon wasn't just personal; it was revolutionary.

At Diva's Den Costume Boutique, where Michelle often sourced her outfits, she started a line of clothing that celebrated every body type and gender identity. The line promoted self-love and body positivity, further cementing Michelle's iconic status.

But not everything was glitz and glitter. Michelle had her share of critics. People who couldn't understand her journey or chose not to. But, with the support of friends like Donnie,

Ronnie, and even once-rival Brandie, she navigated through the negativity, often with humor.

One day, while browsing through Unity Square Transparency Terrace, a group of hecklers began to mock her. Without missing a beat, Michelle sashayed over in her stilettos and began an impromptu drag performance right there, using the hecklers as backup dancers. The crowd, amused, cheered her on. By the end, even the hecklers couldn't resist Michelle's charm, and what started as a mockery turned into a celebration.

In a quiet moment at Countryside Caress Inn, Michelle reflected on her recent journey into to activism with Brandie, who'd been her rock throughout. "You know, Brandie, when I first started, I thought drag was just about the costumes and makeup. But it's so much more. It's about showing the world that it's okay to be different. It's okay to be you."

Brandie smiled, "Michelle, you've not just dressed up in drag. You've draped yourself in courage, acceptance, and love. You're an inspiration."

And as the sun set, casting a golden hue over the world, Michelle Pensive, the Trans-Fem Gay Icon, looked ahead, ready to continue her journey of inspiring and being inspired. Every sequin, every wig, every heel, and every performance were a testament to her iconic status—a symbol of transformation and triumph in a world that often needed a reminder of the beauty of self acceptance.

Brandie:

When Dark Brandie made his grand exit from the stage, the world believed it was the end of an era. But the Crimson Moon Tavern, a cozy venue tucked away on a quaint street, begged to differ. Brandie, no longer performing under the blinding stage lights, now offered his wisdom and experience to budding drag artists. His transition from the fierce competitor and antagonist to a mentor was something no one saw coming.

On one such night, the tavern was abuzz with the whispers of a surprise appearance. The young performers, painted in glitter and sequins, exchanged nervous glances. But as Brandie entered the dimly lit room, the atmosphere shifted from nervous anticipation to sheer reverence.

"Alright, kiddos, let's see what you've got!" Brandie announced, clapping his hands with enthusiasm. A young performer named Luminous Lila, known for her brilliant, fiery outfits, took a deep breath before stepping onto the small stage.

Her performance, a mix of dance, song, and dramatic pauses, drew cheers and applause from the crowd. Yet, through the entire act, she kept stealing anxious glances at Brandie. As she finished, taking a bow with a flourish, Brandie's thunderous applause was the validation she sought.

"You've got something, Lila," he said, pointing a finger at her, "but remember, it's not just about the dazzle. It's about the story. What's *your* story?"

The question caught her off guard. "I- I just want to be famous," she stuttered.

Brandie's chuckle filled the room. "Darling, we all do! But the ones who last, the ones who truly shine, are those who perform with a purpose, with a message. Find yours."

Throughout the evening, Brandie continued to offer pearls of wisdom, correcting postures, suggesting makeup tweaks, and even demonstrating a dance move or two. The Crimson Moon Tavern, under his watchful gaze, was fast becoming a breeding ground for the next generation of drag superstars.

Away from the limelight, Brandie found a different kind of intimacy. The nights were often filled with laughter and heartfelt conversations at his penthouse. Brock, a long-time friend and promoter, often joined these gatherings. The two would reminisce about their early days, their struggles, and the transformation of the drag scene over the years.

"I must admit," Brock began one evening, swirling a glass of red wine, "I never imagined this side of you, Brandie."

Brandie smirked, "Neither did I. But there's a certain joy in nurturing talent, in seeing them succeed. It's... addictive."

Their eyes met, a shared understanding passing between them. The two had seen each other at their best and worst, been rivals, allies, and everything in between.

"You ever think about... settling down?" Brock asked hesitantly.

Brandie arched an eyebrow, "Are you proposing, Brock?"

Brock snorted, "In your dreams! I meant, you know, finding someone. Companionship."

The question hung in the air for a moment. Brandie took a deep breath, "I had my moments, fleeting romances. But right now, this... this mentoring, it's fulfilling in a way I never imagined. Maybe, someday, I'll find someone who understands this new chapter of my life."

Time flew, and the Crimson Moon Tavern gained a reputation not just as a performance venue but as an institution. An annual event, 'Brandie's Stars,' became the most sought-after platform for aspiring drag artists.

And as the years rolled by, the one-time antagonist, the fierce competitor, found his true calling - not in the spotlight, but in the shadows, creating stars, fostering talent, and leaving an indelible mark on the world of drag.

The final act of this chapter unfolded in the Crimson Moon Tavern, reminiscent of the Starlit Drag Lounge. As the curtain rose, the stage revealed an ensemble of Brandie's protégés, each a testament to his mentorship. And as the final notes of their performance echoed through the hall, Brandie stepped onto the stage, no longer the fierce performer but a proud mentor.

The applause was deafening. The audience, many of whom had followed his journey from the beginning, rose in a standing ovation. And as Brandie took a bow, the spotlight, once his fiercest competitor, now bathed him in a warm glow, marking the end of an era and the beginning of a legacy.

And so, in the cozy, neon lit, corners of the Crimson Moon Tavern, amidst laughter, music, and dance, the story of Dark Brandie continued. Not as the star of the show, but as the guiding star for many. A story of transformation, acceptance, and above all, love.

Afterword

"From Podium to Pillows" is more than just a narrative about politics and drag; it's a heartfelt testament to the power of authenticity, resilience, and love. In the vibrant tapestry of its plotlines, the story not only confronts societal norms but also unabashedly celebrates the spectrum of identities that form the LGBTQ+ community.

The intersections of politics and the drag world, each with its own code of conduct and value system, present an intriguing arena of conflict, collaboration, and camaraderie. As readers traverse through the various political stages and drag venues, they are invited to confront their own prejudices, rethink rigid societal constructs, and cheer for characters who defy convention in favor of self-truth.

By interweaving the complexities of both worlds, the novel prompts readers to reevaluate the divisive nature of our contemporary society. Each chapter is a testament to the fact that, even in seemingly polarized environments, it is possible to find common ground. More than that, it is in our differences, in our authentic selves, that we discover the beauty of humanity.

In the ever-evolving political arena of the story, candidates grapple with the intersection of their public personas and private desires. They challenge and reimagine the narrative around what it means to be a leader in a world that is increasingly diverse and demanding of representation. It's an unspoken reminder that behind every politician is a human being, with dreams, desires, and secrets that shape their every move.

While it is evident that "Podium to Pillows" celebrates the resilience and indomitable spirit of those marginalized by a society rooted in conservative ideals, it also subtly extends an olive branch to the very same society. By presenting characters that are undeniably relatable in their vulnerabilities, the narrative seeks to bridge the gulf that often exists between the LGBTQ+ community and conservatives. The story doesn't just shine a spotlight on the darkness—it also showcases the transformative power of understanding, acceptance, and unity.

In the heart of the story, there lies a plea for compassion. It beckons readers to look beyond the superficial divides of politics and societal expectations, urging them to embrace the shared humanity that binds us all. Each character's journey is a testament to the enduring spirit of hope—the belief that love and acceptance can pave the way for a brighter, more inclusive future.

It is my hope that "Podium to Pillows" serves as both a mirror and a beacon. A mirror reflecting our collective societal biases and a beacon guiding us towards a future where love transcends boundaries, where identities are celebrated without reservations, and where every individual, regardless of their background, is given the chance to shine.

In a world that often prioritizes division over unity, may this novel inspire us all to find common ground, to champion acceptance, and to celebrate the diverse tapestry of identities that make our society beautifully vibrant.

With heartfelt admiration for the resilient souls this novel represents,

Nicholas Wells

Made in the USA
Monee, IL
06 February 2024